Children
of the Alley

The following titles by Naguib Mahfouz
are also published by Doubleday
and Anchor Books:

Anchor Books

A DIVISION OF RANDOM HOUSE, INC.

NEW YORK

Children of the Alley

Naguib Mahfouz
translated by Peter Theroux

FIRST ANCHOR BOOKS EDITION, NOVEMBER 1996

Copyright © 1959 by Naguib Mahfouz
English translation copyright © 1959 by Peter Theroux

*All rights reserved under International and Pan-American Copyright
Conventions. Published in the United States by Anchor Books, a
division of Random House, Inc., New York, and simultaneously in
Canada by Random House of Canada Limited, Toronto.*
Children of the Alley *was first published in Arabic in 1959,
under the title* Awlad haratina.
*Protected under the Berne Convention.
This translation is published by arrangement with
The American University in Cairo Press.
Originally published in hardcover in the United States by Doubleday
in 1996. The Anchor Books edition is published by
arrangement with Doubleday.*

Anchor Books and colophon are registered trademarks of Random House, Inc.

The Library of Congress has cataloged the Doubleday hardcover edition of this work as follows:
Mahfūz, Najīb, 1912–   [Awlād al-hāratinā. English]
*Children of the alley / by Naguib Mahfouz;
translated by Peter Theroux. —1st ed.*
p.   cm.
I. Theroux, Peter.   II. Title.
PJ7846.A46A913   1996
892'.736—dc20
95-15510   CIP

BOOK DESIGN BY TERRY KARYDES
ILLUSTRATION BY MIKE REJTO

ISBN 0-385-26473-9

WWW.ANCHORBOOKS.COM

PRINTED IN THE UNITED STATES OF AMERICA

TRANSLATOR'S ACKNOWLEDGMENTS

My thanks are due to Naguib Mahfouz
and to Sasson Somekh,
whose generous guidance never failed.

—*Peter Theroux*

Contents

Children
of the Alley

Preface

This is the story of our alley—its stories, rather. I have witnessed only the most recent events, those of my own time, but I have recorded all of them the way our storytellers told them. Everyone in our alley tells these stories, just as they heard them in coffeehouses or as they were handed down for generations—these sources are my only basis for what I'm writing. Most of our social occasions call for storytelling. Whenever someone is depressed, suffering or humiliated, he points to the mansion at the top of the alley at the end opening out to the desert, and says sadly, "That is our ancestor's house, we are all his children, and we have a right to his property. Why are we starving? What have we done?" Then he will tell the stories and cite the lives of Adham and Gabal, of Rifaa and Qassem—some of our alley's great men.

But this ancestor of ours is a puzzle! He has lived longer than any man dreams of living—his long life is the stuff of proverbs. He has dwelled aloof in his house for long ages, and no one has seen him since he isolated himself up there. The stories of his old age and isolation are bewildering, and perhaps fantasy and rumor have helped to make them so. Anyway, he was called Gabalawi, and our alley was named for him. He owns everything and everyone in it, and everything in the desert around it. Once I heard a man say about him, "He created our alley and from our alley grew Egypt, the most important place in the world. He lived here alone when the place was empty and desolate, and became master of it by force and his standing with the ruler. There will never again be anyone like him. He was tough; the wild beasts dreaded his very name." And I heard someone else say, "He was truly noble. He was unlike other leaders. He didn't collect protection money or behave

arrogantly; he was kind to humble people." Then came a time when
some people talked about him in a way unsuited to his rank and dignity
—you know how people can be. I always found talk about him fascinat-
ing, never boring. How often that moved me to stroll around his tall
mansion trying to catch a glimpse of him—always in vain. How often I
stood before his massive gate, gazing at the stuffed crocodile mounted
above it. How often I sat in the Muqattam Desert, not far from his high
walls, able to see no more than the tops of the mulberry, sycamore and
palm trees enclosing the house, and the closed windows that disclosed
no sign of life. Is it not sad to have a grandfather that we never see,
and who never sees us? Is it not strange of him to disappear inside that
locked mansion, while we live in the dirt? If you are curious about
what brought us to this, here are the stories; you will hear all about
Adham, Gabal, Rifaa and Qassem—though none of it will soothe or
comfort you.

I said that no one had seen him since he secluded himself. That did
not bother most people, as all they ever cared about was his estate, and
his much-talked-about Ten Conditions. This was how the dispute
started before I was born, whose ferocity has only grown with the
passing of generations, up until today—and tomorrow. So I do not want
any bitter ridicule when I speak of the close family ties that bind the
people in our alley. We were and still are one family, which no stranger
has penetrated. Everyone in our alley knows everyone else, men and
women alike; and yet no alley has ever known the terrible quarrels ours
has, nor have any people even been as divided by controversy as we, and
for every decent man you will find ten gangsters brandishing clubs and
ready to pick a fight. The people are even used to buying their safety
with bribes, and their security with obedience and abasement, and were
severely punished for the smallest thing they said or did wrong—or even
for thinking something wrong. The strangest thing is that the people in
nearby alleys, in Atuf, Kafr al-Zaghari, in al-Darasa and al-Husseiniya,
envy us because of our alley's property and our tough men. They say
property and a well-protected alley mean wealth and invincible protectors. All that is true, but they don't know that we are crushed by misery,
that we live in squalor, with flies and lice, that we are content with

crumbs, that we are half naked. They see our protectors strut around on top of us and are struck with admiration, and our only comfort is to look up at the mansion, and say, in sorrow and pain, "There is Gabalawi, the owner. He is our ancestor and we are his grandchildren."

I have witnessed the recent period in the life of our alley, and lived through the events that came about through the coming of Arafa, a dutiful son of our alley. It is thanks to one of Arafa's friends that I am able to record some of the stories of our alley. One day he said to me, "You're one of the few who know how to write, so why don't you write down the stories of our alley? They've never been told in the right order, and even then always at the mercy of the storytellers' whims and prejudices; it would be wonderful if you wrote them carefully, all together so that people could benefit from them, and I'll help you out with what you don't know, with inside information." I acted on his advice, both because it struck me as a good idea and because I loved the person who suggested it. I was the first in our alley to make a career out of writing, though it has brought me much contempt and mockery. It was my job to write the petitions and complaints of the oppressed and needy. Although many wretched people seek me out, I am barely better off than our alley's beggars, though I am privy to so many of the people's secrets and sorrows that I have become a sad and brokenhearted man.

But, but—I am not writing about myself or my troubles, which amount to nothing compared with those of our alley—our strange alley with its strange stories! How did it happen? What was it all about? And who were the children of our alley?

Adham

1

The site of our alley was a wasteland. It was part of the Muqattam
Desert that stretched to the horizon. There was nothing in the void but
the mansion Gabalawi had built almost as if to challenge all the fear and
savagery and lawlessness. Its huge, high wall encircled a roomy expanse,
the western part of which was a garden, and the eastern part a three-
story residence. One day the benefactor summoned his children to his
lower reception chamber adjoining the garden. All his sons came: Idris,
Abbas, Ridwan, Galil and Adham, in silk galabiyas, and stood before
him, so awestruck that they glanced up at him only furtively. He ordered
them to sit down and they sat on the chairs around him. He gazed at
them a little while with his eyes, as piercing as a falcon's, then rose and
moved toward the chamber door, and stood in front of the great door,
gazing out at the vast garden crammed with mulberry, sycamore and
palm trees flanked by bowers of henna and jasmine, above whose
branches the twittering of birds could be heard. The garden rang with
life and song, while the chamber was shrouded in silence. The brothers
thought that the ruler of the wasteland had forgotten about them. His
height and bulk made him seem superhuman, like an alien from another
planet. They exchanged glances; this was the way he was when he had
something weighty on his mind. What worried them was that he was as
powerful in this house as he was out in the open land, and they were
powerless against him.

The man turned to them without leaving his place and spoke in a
deep, grating voice which echoed powerfully through the chamber,
whose high walls were covered with curtains and carpets.

"I think it right that someone else should take over managing the
property."

He gazed at them closely once more, but their faces gave away nothing. Managing the property was not a thing to tempt anyone who loved leisure and calm and youthful pursuits, besides which Idris, the eldest son, was the natural candidate for the job; none of the others there questioned that. "What a pain—no end of problems, and those miserable tenants!" said Idris to himself.

"I have chosen your brother Adham to look after the property under my supervision," continued Gabalawi.

Their faces reflected the impact of this surprise, and they quickly exchanged looks of astonishment—all except for Adham, who timidly lowered his gaze in confusion. Gabalawi turned away from them. "That is why I summoned you here," he said casually.

Idris felt a surge of rage so strong that it felt like drunkenness. His embarrassed brothers looked at him, each of them—except for Adham, of course—hiding his anger at this insult to Idris and to all of them in silent protest. Then Idris spoke so calmly that the voice might have come from some other body.

"But, Father—"

"But?" Gabalawi cut him off coldly and turned toward them.

They cast their eyes down lest he read their minds, except for Idris, who said insistently, "But I am the eldest brother—"

"I think I knew that," said Gabalawi crossly. "I am your father."

Idris answered in a steadily escalating fury, "The eldest has rights which cannot be put aside except in cases of—"

The old man held him in a long gaze, as if giving him time to compose himself, then said, "I assure you that in making my decision I took everyone's good into account."

Idris absorbed this blow with waning patience. He knew how backtalk irritated his father, and knew that he must expect harder blows if he kept this up, but his anger left him no chance to consider the consequences. He took a few steps until he was almost touching Adham, puffed up like a haughty rooster to show everyone the differences in brawn, complexion and beauty between him and his brother, and spoke up with the randomness of a shower of spittle drops from a thirsting mouth. "My full brothers and I are the sons of a respectable lady—*he's* the son of a black slave woman!"

Adham's tawny face paled but he did not flinch. Gabalawi shook his fist. "Watch out, Idris," he warned.

But Idris was overcome by a mad tempest of rage, and shouted, "And he's the youngest of us all—why should he be preferred to me, unless the times we live in belong to servants and slaves!"

"Be quiet for your own good, you fool!"

"I'd rather lose my head than live with this disgrace!"

Ridwan raised his head to face his father and smiled gently. "We are all your sons, and it is our right to grieve if we have lost your favor. It will be just as you say. We only want to know why."

Gabalawi turned from Idris to Ridwan, containing his anger for reasons of his own.

"Adham knows what kind of people the tenants are, and he knows most of them by name. And he can read and do sums."

Idris and his brothers were astonished to hear this. Since when was familiarity with the common people anything to set a man apart? Or knowing how to write? Would Adham's mother have sent him to school for any reason other than her doubt that he could make it in a man's world?

"Is all this excuse enough to humiliate me?" asked Idris derisively.

Gabalawi made a gesture of irritation in Idris' direction. "These are my wishes, and all you need to do is hear and obey." He turned abruptly to Idris' brothers. "What do you say?"

Abbas could not bear his father's glare, and said dejectedly, "I hear and obey."

Galil was quick to lower his eyes and say, "Yes, Father."

"I will obey," said Ridwan, his mouth dry.

Idris let fly an enraged yelp of laughter that so changed his features he actually became ugly. "You cowards!" he shouted. "I expected nothing but sickly failure from any of you. Thanks to your cowardice, this black slave's boy will rule over you."

"Idris!" Gabalawi bellowed, his glowering eyes shining with danger.

But fury had destroyed Idris' reason, and he too shouted. "What kind of a rotten father are you! You were always a boss and a bully and that's all you'll ever be! We're your own sons and you treat us the same way you treat all your other victims!"

Gabalawi took two slow but purposeful steps toward him, his features distorted ominously, but his voice low. "Be quiet."

"You won't frighten me, you know I can't be frightened. If you want to raise the son of a slave above me, I won't serenade you with any of this hearing and obeying."

"Don't you know the punishment for defying me, you fiend?"

"The real fiend is that son of a slave."

Gabalawi's voice suddenly rose to a hoarse shout. "She is my wife, you troublemaker, watch out or I'll flatten the ground with you."

The brothers were terrified, none more than Adham, for they all knew their father's almighty temper, but Idris' rage had reached such a pitch that he no longer recognized danger. He was like a madman attacking a crackling inferno.

"You hate me. I never knew it before, but that's it—you hate me. Maybe it was that slave woman that made you hate us. You are the lord of the desert, owner of the estate property, and the biggest gangster of all, but a slave was able to manipulate you, and tomorrow the people will have all kinds of things to say about it, lord of the desert!"

"I told you to be silent, fiend!"

"Don't curse me to please Adham, even the stones of the earth will rise up. Your grotesque decision will make us the talk of every neighborhood and alley!"

Gabalawi's shout could be heard even in the garden and the harems: "Get out of here!"

"This is my house, my mother is here, and she is its rightful mistress, no one can deny it!"

"You are banished from here forever!"

His great face darkened until it was the color of the Nile at full flood, and he moved forward with that river's inexorable majesty, his granite fists clenched. Everyone knew Idris was a dead man. This would be only the latest of the tragedies this house had endured silently. How many pampered women had a single word transformed into wretched beggars? How many men had limped out of this house, after long service, their backs showing welts from lead-tipped whips, their mouths and noses running with blood? The consideration everyone enjoyed in good times was of no help to anyone, no matter how exalted, in times of wrath. So everyone knew Idris was a dead man. Even Idris, the first-born, his father's rival in strength and beauty! Gabalawi took two steps closer to him.

"You are not my son and I am not your father. This is not your house, and you have no mother, brother or friend here. The world is before you—go forth with my anger and my curse. Time passing will teach you your true worth as you wander forlornly, having lost my love and protection!"

Idris stamped his foot on the Persian carpet. "This is my house—I will never leave!"

His father grabbed him even before Idris saw him coming, and holding him by the shoulder in a grip tight as a vise, pushed him along in front of him, backward, through the door to the terrace. Idris fell staggering down the stairs, then Gabalawi pushed him down the path enclosed with rosebushes and henna planted over with jasmine, down to the great gate, where he threw him out and bolted the gate. Everyone in the big house heard Gabalawi's shout. "Damnation to anyone who lets him back in or helps him!"

He raised his head to the shuttered windows of the harem and shouted again. "And divorce to anyone who dares to try!"

2

From that black day onward, Adham went to work in the estate office in the reception hall to the right of the mansion's main gate. He worked zealously, collecting rents, paying out money to creditors and submitting the accounts to his father. He dealt with the tenants with honesty and decorum, and they liked him although they had a reputation for being surly and crude. The rules of the estate were secret, known only to Gabalawi, whose decision to have Adham run things awakened fears that this might be a prelude to his making Adham his heir. In truth, the father had never betrayed any sign of partiality among his sons until that day, and the brothers had lived harmoniously together thanks to the reverence their father inspired, and his justice, and even Idris—despite his strength, beauty and occasional excess of high spirits—had never offended any of his brothers until that day. He had been a generous and sociable boy who attracted friendship and admiration. Perhaps the four full brothers harbored a feeling of apartness from Adham, though none of them showed him any discourtesy, in word, deed or behavior; and perhaps Adham was most conscious of all of this apartness. He may have been too aware of the difference between their radiant color and his dark color, their strength and his slenderness, their mother's high status and his mother's humble origin. And though this may have caused him inner suffering, some pain he repressed, the fragrant air of the house, laden with aromatic herbs, and obedience to his father's power and wisdom, did not allow any resentment to settle in his soul, and he grew up with a pure heart and mind.

"Give me your blessing, Mother," Adham said before reporting to the estate office for the first time, "for what is the work he has entrusted to me but a test for you and me both?"

"May success be your shadow, my boy," she answered humbly. "You are a good boy, and good people always prevail."

Adham left for the reception hall under the eyes of watchers in the terrace and garden, and those peering from windows. He sat in the official estate trustee's chair, and began his work. His work was the most important being pursued in the whole desert region between Muqattam on the east and ancient Cairo to the west. Adham's watchword was honesty, and for the first time in the history of the estate even the tiniest payments were recorded in the ledger. He paid his brothers their salaries with such tact that they forgot the bitterness of their feud with him, and he was prompt in turning all revenues over to his father.

"How do you like the work, Adham?" his father asked him one day.

"Because *you* entrusted it to me, it is the greatest thing in my life," said Adham humbly.

The man's great face beamed, for despite his omnipotence he was charmed by the sound of praise. Adham loved sitting with Gabalawi. When he did, he stole admiring and loving glances at him. And how he loved to listen, with his brothers, to the stories of long ago, the exploits of the adventurers and youths, how Gabalawi had strutted around this area brandishing his fearsome club and conquering every place where he set foot. After Idris was expelled, Abbas, Ridwan and Galil met on the rooftop just as they had before, eating, drinking and gambling; Adham could only relax sitting in the garden. He had loved the garden and loved playing the flute, and he still played it even after he had taken over managing the estate, though he no longer gave it most of his time. If he finished up his work early, he spread out a carpet by the edge of a stream and leaned his back against the trunk of a palm or sycamore tree, or lay flat in a bower of jasmine to rest, gazing at the sparrows and doves. He played his pipe to imitate the chirping, cooing and warbling—what lovely mimicry it was!—or watched the most beautiful of skies through the tree branches. Once his brother Ridwan came by when he was like this and looked at him jeeringly.

"What a waste of your time, looking after this property!"

"If I weren't worried about making our father angry, I'd complain," Adham said, smiling.

"Let us praise the Creator of leisure!"

"May it do you good too," said Adham innocently.

Ridwan spoke, masking his provocation with a smile: "Don't you want to be like us again?"

"What could be better than spending my time in the garden, with my flute?"

"Idris was dying to work," said Ridwan bitterly.

Adham lowered his gaze. "Idris had no time to work—he got mad for other reasons. This garden is where true happiness is."

When Ridwan had gone, Adham said to himself, "The garden and its singing inhabitants, and water, and sky, and my delighted self—this is life. And it's as if I'm looking for something. But what is it? Sometimes the flute almost tells me what, but the question goes unanswered. If this sparrow could talk, she would tell me so that my heart might rest secure. Even the shining stars know something. As for collecting rents—it's a false note in my melodies."

One day, as Adham stood gazing at the shadow he cast on the path between the roses, a second shadow detached itself from his, signaling the arrival of someone from the lane behind him. The new shadow seemed to drift out of his rib cage. He turned around to see a black girl about to flee after noticing his presence. He gestured for her to stay, and she did.

Adham looked at her for a long time. "Who are you?" he asked softly.

"Umaima," she stammered.

He remembered the name. She was a slave, a relative of his mother's, and much as his mother would have been before his father married her. He felt like talking to her.

"What brings you to the garden?"

"I didn't think anyone was here," she answered, her eyes cast down and nearly closed.

"But you are not allowed here."

"I'm sorry," she said almost inaudibly.

She backed away until she disappeared in the lane and then his ears caught the sound of her running footsteps. Suddenly he was murmuring feelingly, "You are adorable!" He had never felt more like one of the creatures in the garden than at this moment, and it seemed to him that the roses, jasmine and carnations, the sparrows, doves and he were all part of the same melody. "Umaima is beautiful—even her thick lips are beautiful. All of my brothers except proud Idris are married, and isn't my color like hers? And how bewitching it was to see her shadow mingled with mine, as if it were a part of my longing-racked body! My father won't mock my choice—after all, didn't he marry my mother?"

3

Adham went back to the estate office, his heart overflowing with a beauty as subtle as perfume. He did his best to review the day's accounts, but the only picture in his mind was of the black girl. It was not strange that he should have seen Umaima for the first time only today, for the women in the mansion were like the internal organs which a man knows of, and thanks to which he lives, but which he never sees. Adham sank into his rosy daydreams until he was torn out of them by an enraged bellow so near that it seemed to be exploding from somewhere in his own office.

"I am here in the desert, Gabalawi! I curse all of you! A curse on all your heads, men and women, and I challenge anyone who doesn't like what I have to say! Are you listening, Gabalawi?"

"Idris!" Adham called, and came into the garden from the foyer. He saw his brother Ridwan coming toward him, looking visibly upset.

"Idris is drunk," was Ridwan's hurried greeting. "I saw him from the window, falling-down drunk. What new scandals are in store for our family?"

Adham closed his eyes in pain. "My heart is breaking with sorrow, Ridwan."

"What should we do? This is a catastrophe threatening us."

"Don't you see that we must talk to our father about this?"

Ridwan frowned. "Father never changes his mind, and this will only make him twice as mad at Idris."

"Can nothing spare us from these troubles?" Adham murmured sadly.

"Yes, the women are crying in the harem, Abbas and Galil are busy with recriminations, and our father is alone in his chamber and no one dares go near him."

Adham was lost in worried thought, sensing that this conversation was leading him into a predicament. "Don't you see that we must do something?"

"Of course, all of us want to be safe, and nothing threatens safety more than seeking it at any cost. Besides, I'm not going to do anything rash—not even if the sky falls. As far as family honor goes, it is being soiled this very minute, in the form of Idris."

So why did you come to me? Overnight Adham himself had become as inauspicious as a cawing crow. He sighed. "I have nothing to do with all this, but I won't be able to live with myself if I do nothing."

"You have enough reasons that obligate you to do something," Ridwan told him as he left.

Adham was left alone, with the words *You have enough reasons* ringing in his ears. Yes. He was on the spot though he had done nothing. Like a jug crashing onto a man's head, pushed by the wind. Every time someone felt sorry for Idris, he cursed Adham. Adham headed for the gate, opened it gently and passed through it. Idris was not far off, staggering around in circles and rolling his eyes. His hair was disheveled, and the front of his shirt was open, exposing his chest hair. When his eyes lit on Adham, he bounded up and pounced at him, like a cat diving at a mouse, but he was too drunk and fell down. He gathered dirt in his fist and threw it at Adham. It hit him in the chest and scattered down his cloak.

"My brother," Adham said to him gently.

Idris continued to rage and stumble around. "Shut up, you dog! You son of a bitch! You are not my brother and your father is not my father. I will bring this house down on your heads!"

"You were the pride of this family," Adham pleaded. "And one of its noblest sons!"

Idris cackled humorlessly. "Why did you come here, slave boy? Go to your mother and put her back in the servants' quarters where she belongs."

"Don't give in to your anger," said Adham in the same kind tone. "Don't slam the door on people who want to help you."

Idris raised his fist. "It's a rotten house where only cowards can feel at home, who dunk their food in servility and worship their degradation. I will never come back to any house where you are in charge. Tell your father I am living in the wasteland that produced him, that I've become a thief as he was, and an evil troublemaker as he is. Everywhere I spread corruption people will point to me and say, 'He's a child of Gabalawi!' This way I can drag you all through the mud, all of you who think you're gentlemen, when you're just thieves."

"Wake up, Idris," Adham begged, "Don't say things you'll regret. The way back isn't closed to you unless you close it yourself. Everything can still be as it was, I promise you."

Idris took a halting step toward him, as if walking against the wind.

"By what power do you make promises, slave boy?"

Adham gazed at him warily. "The power of brotherhood."

"Brotherhood! I shoved that down the first toilet I found."

"I've never heard you use this kind of language before," said Adham, sounding pained.

"Your father's injustice helped me speak the truth."

"I don't like people seeing you this way."

Idris let out a screech of angry laughter. "They'll see me worse than this every day—I'll cover you all with shame and scandal and sin. Your father expelled me without a second thought and now he can just take what he gets."

He pounced at Adham, who swiftly stepped aside. Idris nearly fell on the ground, but righted himself against the wall, panting with fury as his eyes scanned the ground for a stone. Adham retreated softly to the gate and slipped in, his eyes brimming with tears. Idris was still yelling. Adham turned to the terrace and saw his father through the door as he crossed the hall, then started toward him almost without realizing, his sorrow momentarily stronger than his fear. Gabalawi looked at him, his eyes revealing nothing. His commanding height and broad shoulders loomed against a portrait painted in a wall niche behind him.

Adham lowered his head somewhat. "Peace be upon you."

Gabalawi gave him a searching look, and spoke in a voice that cut to the depths of his heart: "Say what you have come to say."

"Father, it's about my brother Idris—" Adham whispered.

His father stopped him with a voice like steel on stone: "Don't mention his name in my presence ever again." Then, as he went back in: "Get back to work!"

4

Still the sun rose and set on the desolate land as Idris deteriorated into ever more terrible mischief, adding some new folly to his credit every day. He loitered outside the mansion, shouting the filthiest curses, or sat near the gate, as naked as the day he was born, basking in the sun and singing the most indecent songs. He roamed the nearby neighborhoods, domain of the bullies and gangsters, menacing pedestrians with rude stares and starting fights with anyone who got in his way. People avoided him and did not speak to him, but whispered to one another, "He's Gabalawi's son!" He never worried about food—he simply reached out for whatever food attracted him, whether in a restaurant or on a cart, and ate until he was stuffed, then went on his way without a word of thanks from him or payment for the others. When he felt like fun he reeled into the first bar he found and drank barley beer until he was drunk, at which point he became a veritable fountain of his family's secrets and all their gossip, their ridiculous traditions and loathsome cowardliness. He particularly emphasized his rebellion against his father, the biggest bastard in the whole city. Then he started rhyming, only to collapse laughing, or singing and dancing, and his happiness was complete if the night ended with a brawl—then he left with a greeting for everyone. He was known everywhere for this behavior. People stayed away from him as much as they could, but were resigned to him as they were to any other natural disaster; his family, of course, suffered terrible pain and sadness. Idris' mother was defeated by grief, and she became paralyzed and then died. When Gabalawi had come to bid her farewell, she pointed her good hand at him accusingly and fell back dead in sorrow and anger. Grief settled over the family like a cobweb; the brothers' long talks on the rooftop stopped, and Adham's flute was no longer heard in the garden.

One day Gabalawi exploded again; this time the victim was a woman. His bellowing voice resounded as he cursed Nargis, a servant girl, and threw her out of the house. He had found out that day that she was pregnant, and questioned her until she confessed that Idris had raped her before his expulsion. Nargis left the mansion wailing and smiting her cheeks, and wandered all day long until Idris found her and took her in without welcome but without mistreatment, as the time might come when she would make herself useful.

But every tragedy, however great, eventually becomes a mere fact of life, and life at the mansion returned to its normal course, just as a populace returns to the homes an earthquake has forced them to leave. Ridwan, Abbas and Galil resumed their evening conversations on the roof, and Adham his evenings communing with his flute. Umaima, he noticed, shed light in his mind and warmed his senses; the image of her shadow mingled with his was sharply etched in his memory, and he went to see his mother in her room, where she sat embroidering a shawl, to tell her everything.

"She is Umaima, Mother—your relative," he concluded.

His mother smiled a rather pallid smile which showed that her pleasure at the news could not erase the pain of her illness, and said, "Yes, Adham, she is a good girl, as right for you as you are for her. She will make you happy, God willing."

When she saw a blush of delight appear in his cheeks, she went on. "Don't show her any attention yet, my boy, or all will be lost. I'll talk to your father about it, and perhaps I'll be blessed with the sight of your children before death claims me."

Gabalawi did summon him, and when Adham saw his father's kind smile, he said to himself, "There's nothing like his severity except his kindness."

"Now you're looking for a wife, Adham. How time goes by! This house scorns the poor, but in choosing Umaima you honor your mother, and you will have fine children. Idris is lost to us, Abbas and Galil have no children, and so far none of Ridwan's children have lived. None of them have inherited anything but my arrogance. So fill this house with your children, or I will have lived for nothing."

No one in the neighborhood had ever seen anything to match Adham's wedding procession, and to this very day the memory of it is the stuff of proverbs in our alley. Lamps were suspended from tree branches that night, and over the walls, so that the mansion seemed to be a lake of light in the midst of the dark plain. A large tent for the singers, both men and women, was set up on the roof. Tables holding food and drink filled the hall, the garden and the open desert outside the mansion gate. The wedding procession started at the edge of Gamaliya after midnight and included everyone who loved Gabalawi or feared him, until everyone had joined. Adham walked proudly between Abbas and Galil in a silk galabiya and an embroidered cloth around his skullcap. Ridwan walked in front, flanked on the right and left by people bearing candles and roses, led by a vast crowd of singers and dancers. The singing resounded with the moaning of the instruments and the applause of Gabalawi's and Adham's well-wishers until the whole neighborhood woke up and trilled with joy. The procession moved from Gamaliya to Atuf and Kafr al-Zaghari and al-Mubaida, to the cheers of the gangsters themselves. People danced and bars gave out free beer, so that even young boys got drunk. Water pipes were passed around in all the tea shops along the procession street as a gift to the partygoers, and the air became fragrant with hemp and Indian hashish.

Suddenly, in the light of the processional lamps, Idris loomed like a demon radiating darkness at the end of the street—at the curve where the street led into the desert. The lamp bearers stopped marching, and mumbles of "Idris" flitted through their number. The singers noticed him and stopped singing, their throats blocked by fear. The dancers saw him and froze where they stood. Then the flutes and drums fell silent, and the laughter died away. Most wondered what to do now—if they let him have his way they would not be safe from his harm, but if they opposed him they would be opposing a son of Gabalawi.

Idris brandished his club and shouted, "Whose procession is this, you cowardly trash?"

No one spoke up. They craned their necks toward Adham and his brothers.

"When were you ever friends of the slave boy or his father?" Idris asked.

Ridwan stepped forward and called out, "Brother, the wisest thing is for you to let this procession through."

"You should be the last one to talk, Ridwan!" Idris glowered. "You are the brother of a traitor and the son of a coward, a worthless fool who sold out his honor and brotherhood for a comfortable life!"

"These people have no part in our differences," said Ridwan gently.

Idris screeched with laughter. "These people *know* what scum you all are, and if it weren't for their fine old tradition of cowardice you wouldn't see one of them piping or singing in this procession."

"Your father entrusted your brother to us, and we must protect him," Ridwan replied firmly.

Idris emitted another screech of laughter and said, "Can you defend yourself, let alone the slave boy?"

"Where is your sense, Idris? Using your head is the only thing that will bring you back home."

"You're lying. You know you're lying."

"As far as I'm concerned, I don't blame you, but let the procession through in peace."

Idris' response was to tear into the procession like a raging bull. His club swung up and down, smashing lamps, splitting drums and scattering roses, as the terrified people fled like sand before a gale. Ridwan, Abbas and Galil stood together to shield Adham, redoubling Idris' rage.

"You cowards, defending someone you hate, afraid you won't be fed!"

He lunged at them, and they let their own clubs absorb his blows as they withdrew, without hitting back. Suddenly he threw himself between them, struggling toward Adham; there were screams from the windows above, and Adham prepared to defend himself.

"Idris," he called, "I am not your enemy. Come to your senses."

Idris raised his club.

"Gabalawi!" someone yelled.

"Your father is coming," Ridwan said to Idris.

Idris jumped to the side of the road and looked back. He saw Gabalawi approaching amidst a halo of servants bearing torches, clenched his teeth and shouted in mockery.

"Soon I'll delight your eyes with a bastard grandson!"

He rushed away in the direction of Gamaliya, as the crowd divided to make a path for him, until he was swallowed by the darkness. His father went to where the brothers stood, pretending to be calm before the thousands of watchful eyes, and spoke in a tone of command: "Let things be as they were before."

The lamp bearers took their places again, the drums and pipes sounded, the singers sang, the dancers danced, and once again the procession moved along its route.

All night long the mansion was alive with music, drinking and singing. When Adham went into his room, which overlooked the Muqattam Desert, he found Umaima standing by the mirror, her white veil still over her face. He was drunk and befuddled, barely able to stand on his feet, but came near her, doing his utmost to control himself. He lifted the veil from her face, which shone with the most breathtaking beauty, and bowed his head to kiss her on her full lips, and said drunkenly, "What matters besides happy endings?"

He made for the bed, alternating firm steps with stumbles, and threw himself across its width still in his turban and turned-up shoes, as Umaima gazed at his reflection in the mirror, smiling tenderly.

5

Adham discovered in Umaima a happiness he had never known before. Being naive, he expressed it in everything he said and did until his brothers made fun of him. At the close of each prayer he extended his hands, palms upward, and rejoiced, "Praise the Lord of Grace; praise Him for my father's contentment; praise Him for my wife's love; praise Him for the station I enjoy, in place of those more deserving; praise Him for my garden, song, flute and companion." All the women in the mansion said that Umaima was a good wife. She looked after her husband as if he were her son, loved and served her mother-in-law and the rest of her in-laws too, and kept her home as spotlessly clean as though it were a part of her own body. Adham was a husband whose heart overflowed with love and companionship. Running the estate had always detracted from his innocent fun in the garden, and now love consumed the rest of his day, and overwhelmed him so that he did not even think of himself. The blissful days passed, lasting longer than the cynical Ridwan, Abbas and Galil might have wished, eventually giving way to a profound serenity, as a raging downhill stream ends in a placid river. Wonderment returned to Adham's heart; he felt that time did not pass in a flash, that night followed day, that intimate conversation lost all its meaning if it lasted forever, that the garden was a true delight too good to leave, and yet that none of this meant that his heart was straying from Umaima. His heart was still all hers, but life has phases one recognizes only day by day. He went back to his favorite spot by the brook, and gazed kindly and almost pleadingly around at the flowers and birds. Umaima had followed him, radiantly lovely, and sat beside him.

"I was watching from the window to see what was holding you up. Why didn't you ask me to come down too?"

"I didn't want to bother you." He smiled.

"Bother me? I love this garden. Do you remember how we first met here?"

He took her hand in his, resting his head against a palm trunk, and lifted his gaze to the branches and the sky between them. Umaima was again telling him how much she loved the garden. The more intent he was upon silence, the more she talked, for she hated silence as much as she loved the garden, and her sweetest words were reserved for praising their life within it. Then she went on at length about recent goings-on in the mansion, especially as concerned her three sisters-in-law. Then she lowered her voice almost reprovingly. "Are you there, Adham?"

He smiled. "Aren't you always in my heart?"

"But you aren't listening to me."

That was true. He had not welcomed her appearance but it did not bother him. If she had tried to leave, he would have earnestly persuaded her not to. He truly felt her to be a part of him.

"I love this garden," he said apologetically. "Before I met you, sitting here was the sweetest thing I knew. Its lofty trees and rushing brooks and twittering birds all know me as much as I know them, and I want you to love them as much as I do. Have you seen what the sky looks like through the branches?"

She raised her eyes for a moment and then smiled at him. "It really is beautiful, and deserves to be the thing you love most in life."

Adham saw the implicit reproof in her words and hastily replied, "That was before I knew you."

"And now?"

He squeezed her hand tenderly. "You make its beauty complete."

She looked at him. "It's a good thing it doesn't get jealous when you spend time with me."

Adham laughed and pulled her toward him until her cheek was against his lips. "Aren't these flowers more interesting than my brothers' wives?"

"The flowers are more beautiful," said Umaima seriously, "but your brothers' wives talk about nothing but you, your running of the estate—always the estate!—your father's confidence in you, and so on and on and on."

Adham frowned, suddenly far from the garden. "They're into everything!"

"I really worry about the evil eye on you."

"God damn the estate!" said Adham. "It weighs me down, turns people against me and makes me lose sleep! Who wants it!"

She put a finger to his lips. "Don't be ungrateful for good things, Adham. Running the estate is an important responsibility, and might open new doors to us we haven't even dreamed of."

"All it's brought so far is trouble. And look at Idris."

She smiled, but her smile did not express delight as much as it underlined the deep worry so conspicuous in her eyes.

"Look at our future the same way you look at the branches and the sky and the birds," she said.

Umaima diligently kept by his side in the garden, only rarely falling silent; he had grown accustomed to her, and listened with only half his attention, or less. Whenever he liked he picked up his flute and played whatever music came to him. He could say, in perfect contentment, that everything was good; he had even gotten used to Idris' mischief. But his mother's sickness grew more serious, and she suffered pains she had never known before, to his intense grief. She often called him to her side to pray lavishly over him, and once begged him to "pray to the Lord to deliver you from evil and guide you to the right path." She did not let him leave, but wailed and lectured him and reminded him of her last wishes until she died in his arms. Adham wept for her and so did Umaima. Gabalawi came and looked at her wearily, then solemnly shrouded her up, his hard eyes shining with desperate sorrow.

No sooner had Adham gone back to his old familiar ways than an abrupt change came over Umaima. He did not understand it. It started when she stopped spending time with him in the garden, which did not please him as he had sometimes imagined it might. When he asked her why she stayed away, she gave him any excuse—work, or weariness. He noticed that she no longer greeted him with her former excitement;

when he greeted her, she responded without any real joy, as if she were only showing courtesy—a bothersome courtesy. What was wrong? He had already experienced something similar himself, but his love had held, and he got past it. He might have become stern with her, and was sometimes tempted to, but was held back by her fragility and pallor, and her own incredible gentleness toward him. Sometimes she seemed sad, sometimes confused, and once he caught such a fugitive look in her eye that he felt a wave of fear and exasperation at the same time. He told himself, "Be patient with her—either she'll improve, or she can go to Hell!"

He went to see Gabalawi in his office, to show him the month's final accounts. His father gave them a cursory glance and asked him, "What's the matter?"

Adham raised his head in surprise. "Nothing, Father."

The man narrowed his eyes to slits and murmured, "Tell me about Umaima."

His glance fell under his father's penetrating stare. "She's fine. Everything's fine."

"Tell me what is on your mind," said Gabalawi with a hint of irritation.

Adham was silent for a long moment, fully believing that his father would find out everything, so he admitted: "She's very changed. She seems afraid of me."

A strange glint appeared in Gabalawi's eyes. "Are you two having trouble?"

"Nothing."

Gabalawi looked at him delightedly. "Stupid! Treat her gently, and don't go near her until she asks you. You are going to be a father."

6

Adham sat in the estate office receiving new tenants one after the other. They stood in line, the first before him and the last at the rear of the large reception hall. When the last tenant's turn came, Adham asked him rather brusquely, without raising his head from his ledger, "What's your name?"

He was taken aback by the voice that said, "Idris Gabalawi."

Adham looked up in fright and saw his brother standing before him, then bounded to his feet to defend himself, watching Idris warily. But Idris seemed different, even unrecognizable: shabby, quiet and humble, dejected and pliant, like a starched shirt soaked in water. Although this appearance disarmed Adham of all his old resentment, he was still not completely reassured.

"Idris!" he said in a tone of mingled caution and hope.

Idris hung his head and said, with unfamiliar gentleness, "Don't worry. I'm only your guest in this house, if you can find it in your heart to let me."

Were these sweet words really coming from Idris? Had his suffering refined him? Truly, this humility was just as uncanny as his depravity had been. And wasn't receiving him as a guest an insult to Gabalawi? Still, he had not invited Idris, though he now found himself motioning him to sit by him. They sat together and exchanged curious gazes until Idris spoke.

"I hid in the crowd of tenants so that I could get to you alone."

"Did anyone see you?" asked Adham uneasily.

"No one from the house, don't worry about that. I haven't come to cause you any trouble, but I need your sweet nature!"

Adham lowered his eyes from shame as blood rushed to his face.

"Maybe you're shocked by the change in me. Maybe you're wondering what's happened to my arrogance and boasting. You must know that I have endured suffering few people could survive, but in spite of all that I'm not telling anyone but you. People like me can only forget their pride with kind people."

"God bless you, and us—how your fate has ruined my life!"

"I should have known that all along, but anger had blinded me, and alcohol took away my dignity. Then the life of a vagrant and a thug finished off everything that was human in me—would you ever have thought this of your older brother?"

"Never—you were always a good brother and the best of men!"

"Those days are gone," lamented Idris. "Now I'm worthless. I hang around the desert hauling this pregnant woman around with me, wrecking every place I go, making a living doing terrible things and being hateful."

"You are tearing at my heart, Idris."

"Forgive me, Adham. I've always known you to be like this. Didn't I carry you around in my arms? Didn't I watch you grow up from boyhood, and wasn't I always aware of your nobility and wonderful qualities? What a terrible thing anger is!"

"Nothing is more terrible, Idris."

Idris sighed and spoke as if to himself. "With all I have done to you, there is no punishment too harsh for me."

"God give you rest, Idris. Do you know, I always knew you'd come home? Even when our father was angriest at you, I spoke up for you."

Idris smiled, showing rotten yellow teeth. "That's what I always knew in my heart. I knew that if there was any hope of my father changing his mind, it would be on your account."

"I can see God at work guiding your good soul—don't you think the time has come for us to talk to Father?"

Idris shook his disheveled head in despair. " 'Older by a day, wiser by a year'—and I'm ten years older than you are, not just one. I know that our father can forgive anything except an insult from anyone. Father will never forgive me after what's happened. I have no hope of ever going home to the mansion."

This was perfectly true; this is what bothered Adham and depressed him. He murmured gloomily, "Is there anything I can do for you?"

Idris smiled again. "Don't even think of giving me money, because I know how honestly you must run the estate—if you gave me a helping hand it would be your own money, and that I cannot accept. Today you're a husband and tomorrow you'll be a father. I haven't come to you here driven by my poverty—I've come to tell you I'm sorry for the things I've done to hurt you, and to return your friendship. And I have something to ask."

Adham looked at him attentively. "Tell me what you want, Idris."

Idris moved his head closer to his brother as if he were afraid the walls would hear him. "I want to feel secure about my future—I've lost the present. I'm going to be a father, like you—what kind of a life will my children have?"

"I am at your command for anything I can do."

Idris clapped Adham gratefully on the shoulder and said, "I want to know if our father is going to deprive me of my share of the inheritance."

"How would I know that? But if you want to know what I think—"

"I'm not asking what you think." Idris interrupted him restlessly. "I want to know what your father thinks."

"You know that he never tells anyone what he's thinking."

"But he must have a record of his will with the estate deed."

Adham shook his head but said nothing.

"Everything is in those documents," urged Idris.

"I don't know anything about them, and you know no one in our house knows anything about them. The work I do is completely under our father's supervision."

Idris transfixed him with a sad stare. "The estate documents are in a big book. I saw it once when I was small and asked what was in it. That was when he loved me the best. He said it was all about us, and wouldn't talk about it or answer my questions about it. Now there is no question but my fate is decided in it."

Adham felt cornered. "God knows," he said.

"It's in a secret room off of our father's bedroom. You must have seen the little door at the end of the wall, on the left. It's always locked, but the key is kept in a little silver box in the drawer of his bedside table. The big book is on the table in that narrow room."

Adham raised his thin eyebrows in alarm. "What do you want?"

"Any peace of mind left for me in this world," sighted Idris, "depends on finding out what is written about me in that book."

Adham seemed alarmed. "It would be easier for me just to ask him what's in the Ten Conditions!"

"He wouldn't say—he'd get angry, and might think badly of you for asking, or get thinking about why you were asking in the first place, and he'll get angry. I would hate for you to lose your father's trust as punishment for acting charitably toward me. He certainly doesn't want to broadcast his Ten Conditions—if he wanted us to know that, we would all know. The only sure way to the book is the one I've described to you. It will be very easy to do at dawn, when he goes out for his walk in the garden."

Adham paled. "What a horrible thing to ask of me, Idris."

Idris hid his frustration with a weak smile. "It's not a crime for a son to read what concerns him in his father's papers."

"But you're asking me to steal a secret that our father guards with his honor."

Idris sighed audibly and said, "I said to myself when I decided to come to you, 'There's nothing harder than convincing Adham of something he considers contrary to his father's will,' but I was deluded by hope and thought, 'Maybe he'll do it if he sees how badly I need his help,' and after all it's no crime. It will go smoothly, and you'll see that you can lift a soul from Hell at no cost to yourself."

"May God keep us from evil!"

"Amen—but I'm begging you to save me from torment!"

Adham rose anxiously and was followed by Idris, who showed him a smile signaling his hopeless surrender.

"I have really troubled you, Adham; one of the things about my wretchedness is that I bring trouble to everyone I meet, one way or another. Idris is still a cruel curse."

"How much it pains me, not being able to help you—it is the worst pain I know."

Idris came near him and placed his hand tenderly on Adham's shoulder, then kissed him affectionately on the forehead. "I'm the only one responsible for my hard life—why should I ask more of you than you're capable of? Let me leave you in peace—what will be, will be."

And with that, Idris left.

7

Excitement crept into Umaima's face, after a long absence, as she asked Adham earnestly, "Hasn't your father ever told you about the book before?"

Adham was sitting cross-legged on their sofa, gazing out the window at the shadow-shrouded desert. "He has never told anyone about it."

"But you—"

"I'm only one of his many sons."

"But he chose you to run the estate," said Umaima with a light smile.

Adham turned to her and spoke sharply. "I just said he never told anyone about it."

She smiled again to soften his irritation. "Don't trouble yourself about it—Idris doesn't deserve that much," she said slyly. "All the terrible things he's done to you can never be forgotten."

Adham turned to the window and said sadly, "The Idris who visited me today is not the same Idris who did terrible things to me. He was so sad and repentant—I can't get the sight of him out of my mind."

"That's what I thought, from what you were saying," Umaima said in plain delight. "And that's why I'm concerned, but you seem so depressed, and that's not like you."

He gazed at the impenetrable blackness, his busy head unable to think. "There's no use worrying."

"But your repentant brother is asking you to take pity."

" 'My eye sees far but my arm is short.' What can I do?"

"You should make up with him and your other brothers, or some-day you'll find yourself all alone before them."

"You're thinking of yourself, not Idris."

She shook her head as if to banish any thought of cunning. "It's my right to think of myself—in doing that I'm thinking of you too, and of my baby."

What did this woman want? And this blackness—it obliterated even the massive Muqattam. He relaxed in silence until she spoke again.

"Don't you remember ever entering the little room?"

He broke his short silence. "Never. I wanted to go in there when I was a boy, but my father didn't let me, and my mother wouldn't let me near it."

"You must have really wanted to go in."

He was discussing the matter with her because he expected her to help him resist Idris, but she was pushing him toward him. He needed someone to support the correctness of his stand against his brother; this he needed badly, yet he was like a man calling in the dark for a watch-man and having a robber emerge instead.

Umaima was asking him another question. "Do you know the drawer with the silver box in it?"

"Anyone who's been inside the room knows it—why do you ask?"

She slid seductively down the sofa nearer to him. "Can you swear that you don't really want to see the room?"

"No," he said crossly. "Why would I?"

"Who wouldn't want to see the future?"

"Your future, you mean."

"Mine and yours, and that of Idris, whom you feel so sorry for in spite of all he's done to you!"

The woman was expressing his own thoughts; that was what made him mad. He stretched his head toward the window as if wishing to escape from it.

"I don't want anything my father doesn't want."

Umaima's penciled eyebrows rose. "Why should he hide it?"

"That's his business—you're asking so many questions tonight!"

"The future!" said Umaima, almost to herself. "To know our future —to do something for poor Idris—and all it would cost us would be reading a sheet of paper, with no one the wiser. I dare any friend *or* enemy to prove any bad intentions if we did that, or to show that it hurt your dear father in the least!"

Adham was watching a star brighter than all the others and paid no attention to her words. "How beautiful the heavens are! If it weren't for the night mists I'd be sitting in the garden, watching it through the branches."

"Those conditions of his must benefit somebody."

"I don't care about benefits that only cause problems."

"If only I knew how to read," sighed Umaima, "I would go look in the silver box myself."

He wished she could; this made him twice as angry at her and at himself too. He felt as though he had already succumbed to the forbidden deed—as though it were already a foregone conclusion. He turned to her, frowning; by the light of the suspended lamp which danced in the breeze from the window, his face looked gloomy and weak despite his scowl.

"I was lost as soon as I told you about it!"

"I don't want anything bad to happen to you, and I love your father as much as you do."

"That's enough of this talk—don't you prefer to rest at this time of day?"

"I guess my heart won't rest until you've done this simple thing."

"O God, give her back her sense!" groaned Adham.

She looked at him calmly. "Didn't you disobey your father when you met with Idris in the reception hall?"

His eyes widened in surprise. "He was standing there in front of me! I had no choice!"

"Did you tell your father that he visited?"

"What's with you tonight, Umaima?"

"If you can disobey him in something that can hurt you," she said in a triumphant tone, "why can't you disobey him in something that can help you and your brother and hurts nobody?"

He could have ended the conversation there if he wished, but this was a steep slope. And the truth was that he had let her go on like this because part of him needed her support.

"What do you mean?" he asked irritably.

"I mean stay up until dawn, or until the coast is clear."

"I thought pregnancy had only taken away your sex drive—now I see it's taken away your sense too," said Adham angrily.

"You are convinced by what I say—I swear by this new life inside me. But you're afraid, and fear does not become you."

His face darkened with a look very different from the profound resignation inside him. "This is a night we'll remember as our first fight."

"Adham," she said with special tenderness, "let's really think about this."

"It won't do any good."

"That's what you say now, but you'll see."

He felt the heat of the fire he was moving into. "If you burn," he said to himself, "your tears will never put it out." He looked toward the window and imagined that the dwellers of that twinkling star were lucky to be so far from this house.

"No one has ever loved his father as I love mine," he muttered weakly.

"You would never be capable of hurting him."

"Umaima, go to bed."

"You're the one who won't let me sleep."

"I was hoping you'd talk sense to me."

"I did."

He said to himself in a near-whisper: "I wonder—am I headed for my ruin?"

She stroked the hand that rested on the arm of the sofa and chided him. "Our fate is one—you cold thing!"

He answered with a resignation that indicated his decision: "Not even that star knows my fate!"

"You will read your fate in that book," she said impetuously.

He looked out at the wakeful stars and the skeins of cloud illuminated by their serene light, and imagined that they had heard his conversation. "What a beautiful sky!" he mumbled.

"You taught me to love the garden," he heard Umaima say flirtatiously. "Let me return the favor."

8

At dawn, the father left his room and headed for the garden. Adham was watching at the end of the hall, and Umaima was behind him, her hand on his shoulder in the dark. They followed the heavy, even sound of his footfalls but could not make out their direction in the dark; it was Gabalawi's habit to take a walk at this hour without a light or any company. When the footsteps died away, Adham turned to his wife.

"Maybe we should go back," he whispered.

She pushed him and whispered back in his ear, "Look, you're not doing anything wrong."

He moved forward with cautious steps with excruciating ambivalence, one hand closed over the small candle in his pocket while he felt along the wall with the other, until he felt the doorjamb.

"I'll stay here and keep a lookout. Go in, and be careful!"

She reached out and pushed the door open, then withdrew. Adham edged warily toward the room and caught the penetrating odor of musk. He closed the door behind him and stood staring into the darkness until he made out the row of windows looking out onto the wasteland and beginning to show the light of daybreak. Adham felt as though the crime—if it was a crime—had taken place with his entering the room, and that he must complete the deed. He moved along the left wall, occasionally bumping into chairs, and passed by the door of the little room, until he reached the end. He followed the middle wall, and almost immediately came upon the table. He pulled open the drawer and felt inside it until he found the box. He paused to compose himself. He then went back to the door, found the keyhole, slipped the key inside and turned it. The door opened, and now he was slinking into the little room no one except his father had ever entered before. He closed the door, took out his candle and lit it: he was in a square, high-ceilinged room with no opening but the door. A small carpet was laid on the floor, and against the right wall was an elegant table with the huge book on it, chained to the wall. Adham's throat was dry and he swallowed painfully, as if his tonsils were inflamed. He grit his teeth as if to squeeze the fear out of his quaking limbs. With the candle in his hand, he approached the table and studied the volume's cover, ornamented with gold-leafed script, then put his hand out and opened it. Only with difficulty could he control himself and concentrate his mind. He read, in slanted Persian-style script, the formula "In the name of God."

He heard the door open suddenly. He jerked his head toward the sound involuntarily, almost as if the opening door had controlled his head. He saw Gabalawi in the light of the candle, his large body filling the doorframe, aiming a cold, harsh stare at him. Frozen into silence, Adham gazed into his father's eyes. He could not speak, move or even think.

"Get out," Gabalawi ordered him.

But Adham could not budge. He stood like a mere object, though no object can feel despair.

"Get out!" screeched Gabalawi.

His terror spurred him awake and he moved. Gabalawi moved out of the doorway, and Adham left the room, the candle still burning in his hand. He saw Umaima standing silently in the middle of the room, tears streaming from her eyes. His father motioned him to stand beside his wife, and he did; then he spoke sternly: "I want you to give me truthful answers."

Adham's features expressed his obedience wordlessly.

"Who told you about the book?" asked the man.

"Idris," said Adham, like a broken vessel that instantly spills its contents.

"When?"

"Yesterday morning."

"How did you meet?"

"He sneaked in with the new tenants and waited until he could be alone with me."

"Why didn't you kick him out?"

"It would have hurt me to, Father."

"Don't call me Father," snapped Gabalawi.

"You are my father," replied Adham, gathering all his courage, "in spite of your anger and my foolishness."

"Did he tempt you to that deed?"

"Yes, sir," answered Umaima, although the question had not been directed to her.

"Be quiet, vermin." Gabalawi turned back to Adham. "Answer me!"

"He was desperate and depressed and remorseful, and was only concerned for the future of his children!"

"So you did this for him!"

"No—I told him I couldn't."

"What made you change your mind?"

Adham sighed despairingly. "Satan!" he muttered.

"Did you tell your wife what went on between you and him?" asked Gabalawi suggestively.

Now Umaima began sobbing. Gabalawi told her to be quiet, and directed Adham, with a movement of his finger, to answer.

"Yes."

"What did she say to you?"

Adham was silent. He swallowed.

"Answer me, you scum!"

"I saw that she was eager to know what was in the will, and didn't think that would hurt anybody."

Gabalawi glared at him contemptuously. "So you admit betraying someone who favored you above others better than you."

"I'm not trying to excuse what I did," Adham virtually wailed, "but your forgiveness is greater than any sin or excuse."

"You conspired against me with Idris after I kicked him out of here as a favor to you?"

"I have not conspired with Idris, I made a mistake, and my only hope is in your forgiveness."

"Sir—" cried Umaima plaintively.

"Quiet, vermin," Gabalawi interrupted. He frowned at each of them in turn, and spoke in a terrible voice: "Get out of this house."

"Father!" begged Adham.

"Get out," said the man harshly, "before you are thrown out."

9

This time the immense mansion gate swung open to witness the expulsion of Adham and Umaima. Adham walked out carrying a bundle of clothes, followed by Umaima with another bundle and some food. They cowered as they walked mournfully away, both crying from hopelessness. When they heard the gate snap shut behind them they wailed loudly, and Umaima sobbed, "Death is too good for me!"

"You're right, for once," quavered Adham, "but death is too good for me too."

They had not gotten far from the house when they heard a mocking, drunken laugh. Looking around for its source, they saw Idris in front of the hut he had built of discarded planks and tin sheets, and his wife, Nargis, sitting, silently spinning. Idris laughed in gloating mockery until the astonished Adham and Umaima stopped to gape at him. Then he began to dance and snap his fingers, and Nargis looked annoyed and went into the hut; Adham looked on with eyes reddened from tears and rage. At once he realized how he had been tricked, and saw the vile and criminal truth. He saw his own folly and stupidity, which even now animated this criminal's gloating, joyous dance. This was Idris, who had become the embodiment of evil. Adham's blood boiled and rose until it filled his brain. He grabbed a handful of dirt and threw it, screaming in a voice choked with rage. "You trash! You abominable thing! Even the scorpions are more human than you!"

Idris answered him with even wilder dancing; he rocked his head right and left, raised his eyebrows playfully and kept snapping his fingers.

Adham's anger rose again. "Depraved—rotten—worthless—that's what liars are—and those are your good points!"

Idris' middle now undulated with the same grace as his head and he mouthed obscene soundless laughter.

Ignoring Umaima, who was trying to urge him to keep walking, Adham shouted, "Go on, keep acting like a whore—you're the lowest of the low!"

Idris shook his buttocks as he spun slowly and amorously around. Blind with rage, Adham threw his bundle to the ground and pushed away Umaima, who was trying to hold him back, and leaped at Idris. He got him around the neck and tried with all his strength to crush it. Idris gave no sign of feeling the stranglehold, and continued to dance gracefully. Maddened, Adham punched him again and again, but Idris went on teasing and even sang, in his most grating voice, a babyish rhyme:

Duckie, duckie, duckie, spin!
Where'd you get your kitty's chin?

Then he stopped, cursed violently and hit Adham so hard in the chest that he was thrown back and staggered, then lost his balance and fell on his back.

Screaming, Umaima ran to him and helped him up, dusting him off. "What do you want with this beast?" she said. "Let's get out of here!"

He picked up his bundle without a word, and his wife took hers, and they resumed walking until the end of the property, when exhaustion overtook him. He dropped the bundle and sat on it, saying, "Let's rest a little." The woman sat opposite him and began to cry again.

Then Idris' voice reached them, as strong as thunder; he stood before the mansion, looking menacingly up at it as he bellowed, "You kicked me out to please the lowest of your children—and do you see how he has treated you? Now you yourself are throwing him out into the dirt, just as you did to me, and you're worst off of all. Take notice that Idris cannot be beaten! Stay up there with your stupid, sterile sons —the only grandchildren you'll ever have will creep in the dirt and roll around in filth, and someday they'll live by peddling potatoes and melon seeds. The gangsters in Atuf and Kafr al-Zaghari will slap them around. Your blood will be mixed with the commonest blood. You'll squat alone in your room, changing your will in rage and failure—you'll suffer from loneliness and old age in the dark, and when you die not one eye will weep!"

Idris turned to Adham and continued to shout frenziedly. "You weakling, how will you live by yourself? You have no strength, and no one strong to depend upon! What good will your reading and arithmetic do you in the desert? Ha, ha, ha!"

Umaima was still crying, until Adham grew annoyed and told her dully, "That's enough crying."

"I'll have a lot more crying to do," she replied, drying her eyes. "I'm the guilty one, Adham."

"You're not the only one. If I hadn't been so weak and cowardly none of this would have happened."

"The sin is mine alone."

"You're just taking all the blame to keep me from yelling at you," yelled Adham.

Her appetite for self-criticism blunted, Umaima kept her head bowed and said softly, "I didn't think he'd be that cruel with us."

"I know him better. I have no excuse."

She hesitated before asking, "How am I supposed to live here when I'm pregnant?"

"We have to live in this wasteland after having lived in the mansion! I wish tears could help us, but all we can do is build a hut."

"Where?"

He looked around, and his gaze rested in the direction of Idris' hut.

"We shouldn't go too far from the mansion," he said uneasily, "even if we have to end up near Idris' hut. Otherwise we'd be all alone at the mercy of this desert."

Umaima thought a little, and seemed convinced. "Yes, and so we can be within his sight, in case he takes pity on us."

Adham groaned. "Grief is killing me—if it weren't for you, I'd think all this was a nightmare. Will he never forgive us? I won't be insolent to him like Idris—no way! I'm nothing like Idris—will he treat me the same way?"

"This place has never known a father like yours," said Umaima bitterly.

"When will your tongue learn?" He glared at her.

"I haven't committed a crime or a sin, for God's sake!" said Umaima irritably. "Tell anyone what I did, and how I'm being punished, and I bet you he won't even believe it. I swear to God, in the history of fatherhood there has never been a father like yours."

"And the world has never known a man like him. This mountain, this desert and this sky testify to that—any other man would have avoided the challenge."

"The way he acts, none of his children will be left in the mansion."

"We were the first to leave, and we were the worst ones in it."

"I am not," said Umaima hotly. "We are not."

"The true judgment comes only through a test."

They fell silent. There was not a living thing to be seen in the desert except for stragglers far off, at the foot of the mountain. The sun cast its fierce rays from the clear sky, and baked the vast sands, which glittered with scattered stones or fragments of glass. The mountain stood alone on the horizon except for a tall boulder in the east that looked like the head of a body buried in the sands, and Idris' hut at the eastern end of the mansion, planted defiantly but pathetically in the ground. The very air warned of hardship, trouble and fear.

Umaima sighed audibly. "We are going to have to work very hard to make life bearable."

Adham gazed up at the mansion. "We are going to have to work even harder to make that gate open for us again."

10

Adham and Umaima started building their hut at the western end of the mansion. They brought stones from Muqattam and gathered boards from the foot of the mountain and from the outskirts of Atuf, Gamaliya and Bab al-Nasr. It became clear to them that building their home would take much more time than they had supposed, and by this time they had run out of the stores of cheese, eggs and molasses Umaima had taken from the house. Adham decided to go out and look for a job; he would sell some of his more expensive clothes to buy a hand cart, from which he would peddle potatoes, chickpeas, cucumbers and other produce, depending on the season. Umaima became so emotional watching him collect his clothes that she burst into tears, but he did not respond. Then he said, with mingled irony and irritation, "These clothes aren't right for me anymore. Wouldn't it be silly to hawk potatoes in an embroidered camel-hair cloak?"

With the desert as a backdrop, he pushed his cart toward Gamaliya, Gamaliya which had not yet forgotten his wedding; his heart sank and his voice died—he stopped calling out for buyers, and he almost sobbed aloud. He quickly switched to the more remote neighborhoods, and doggedly pushed his cart and cried his wares from morning till night, until his hands were hard, his sandals were worn out and his feet and limbs were racked with pain. How hateful it was—haggling with the women, being forced by exhaustion to nap on the ground by a wall, stopping in a corner to relieve himself. This life seemed unreal, and the days in the garden, running the property, the little room that overlooked

Muqattam were like fairy tales. He said to himself, "Nothing is real in this world—the mansion, that unfinished hut, that garden, this handcart, yesterday, today and tomorrow. I probably did the right thing to build the hut in front of the mansion, so that I don't lose my past the way I've lost my present and future. Would it be inconceivable for me to lose my memory as I've lost my father and myself?" He went home in the evening to Umaima, not to relax, but to work on building the hut. One noon he sat in Watawit Alley to rest, and fell asleep. A movement woke him, and he saw boys stealing his cart. He got up and threatened them, and one boy who saw him warned his friends with a whistle; they overturned the cart to distract him from going after them. The cucumbers tumbled all over the ground while the boys dispersed like locusts. Adham was so enraged that he forgot his decent upbringing and screamed obscenities at them, then bent down to retrieve his cucumbers from the mud. His anger redoubled with no outlet, so he asked emotionally, *Why was your anger like fire, burning without mercy? Why was your pride dearer to you than your own flesh and blood? How can you enjoy an easy life when you know we are being stepped on like insects? Forgiveness, gentleness, tolerance have no place in your mansion, you oppressor!* He seized the handles of the cart and set out to push it as far as he could get from this accursed alley, when he heard a taunting voice.

"How much are the cucumbers, uncle?"

Idris stood there with a mocking grin, wearing a brilliantly striped long shirt, a white turban on his head. When Adham saw him smiling and scornful, not wrought up or angry, his world turned black. He pushed the cart to leave, but Idris blocked his way and spoke in surprise: "Doesn't a customer like me deserve good service?"

Adham tensely raised his head and said, "Just leave me alone."

Idris did a sarcastic double take. "You don't like having your brother talk to you this way?"

"Idris," said Adham patiently, "haven't you done enough to me as it is? I don't want you to know me—I don't want to know you."

"What kind of talk is this? We're practically neighbors!"

"I didn't want to be your neighbor, but I wanted to be near the house I was—"

"—evicted from," snickered Idris.

Adham fell silent, but his bloodless face showed his anger.

"The soul yearns for the place it has been thrown out of, isn't that right?"

Adham said nothing.

"You want to go back to that house, you shrewd thing—you really are weak, but full of cunning. But let me tell you that I'll never let you go back and leave me here—not if the sky falls to the earth."

"Haven't you done enough to me?" asked Adham, his nostrils flaring with anger.

"Haven't *you* done enough to *me?* I was kicked out because of you, and I was the brilliant star of the mansion!"

"You were kicked out because of your own pride."

Idris shrieked with laughter. "And you were kicked out because of your own weakness—there's no room in the mansion for strength or weakness! Look what a dictator your father is! He allows no one but himself to show strength or weakness. He is so strong that he ruins the people closest to him, and so weak that he marries a woman like your mother!"

"Let me go," stammered Adham, frowning angrily. "If you want trouble, find someone your own size."

"Your father starts trouble with the strong and the weak."

Adham kept silent and glowered even more darkly.

"You don't want to be lured into disparaging him! How clever of you! It proves that you dream of going back there." He took a cucumber from the cart and made a face. "How did you let yourself get sucked into peddling these dirty cucumbers? Is this the best you could do?"

"I'm happy with this work."

"You mean poverty has left you no choice—while your father lives like a king. Think about that. Wouldn't you do better to team up with me?"

"That's not what I was cut out for," said Adham sullenly.

"Look at my clothes! The owner was parading around in this yesterday, as if he had any right to!"

Adham looked shocked. "How did you get it?"

"The way strong people get anything they want."

He had committed robbery or even murder!

"I can't believe that you are my brother Idris," said Adham sadly.

"Why should anyone be surprised," laughed Idris, "who knows that I'm a child of Gabalawi?"

"Now will you get out of my way!" exclaimed Adham, his patience gone.

"Whatever you say, moron."

Idris filled his pockets with cucumbers, threw Adham a look of contempt, spat on the cart and walked away.

Umaima rose to greet him when he arrived at the hut. Shadow was enveloping the desert, and a candle guttered inside the hut. The stars flashed in the sky, and in their light the mansion loomed like a giant apparition. Umaima saw from his silence that she was better off avoiding him in this mood. She gave him a jug of water to wash in and brought him clean clothes. He washed his face and feet, changed his clothes, then sat on the ground and stretched his legs out. She approached him cautiously and said, to placate him, "I wish I could bear some of your burden for you."

As if she had picked at a scab, he shouted, "Shut up! You're the source of all this trouble and hardship!"

She slid away from him, so far that she became almost invisible in the darkness, but he shouted at her again.

"You're the best reminder of my stupidity. I curse the day I first saw you."

He heard her sobbing in the dark, but it only made him angrier. "God damn your crying! Your tears are just leaks from the wickedness that fills your whole body."

"Nothing you say is worse than what I'm going through!" she bawled.

"I don't want to hear another word! Get away from me!"

He wadded up his discarded clothes and threw them at her.

"My belly!" she moaned.

His anger began to cool and he began to worry about what might happen. She inferred from his silence that he was sorry and said in a pained voice, "I'll get away from you, since that's what you want." She got up and started off.

"Do you think this is a good time to act like a spoiled brat?" he shouted. He started to get up, and called, "Come back. Forget it."

He squinted into the darkness until he saw her shape coming his way. He rested his back against the wall of the hut and looked up at the sky, wishing he could be sure that her belly was unhurt, but he was too proud. He would ask her very soon; and he eased into it by telling her, "Wash some of the cucumbers for our supper."

11

A PEACEABLE ENOUGH PLACE TO SIT. *No greenery or water, no birds* singing on branches, just the bleak, hostile desert ground, which at night wore such mysterious blackness that a dreamer could imagine it to be whatever he wished. The dome of the heavens, studded with stars, the woman inside the hut, and solitude that speaks. Sorrow like coals buried in ashes. The high wall of the mansion repelling the sad exile. *This tyrant father, how can I make him hear my cry? It is wisest to forget the past, but the past is all we have; that is why I hate my weakness and curse my depravity. I can stomach misery as a mate and beget children for him. A sparrow, which no power can bar from the garden, is more fortunate than I am in my dreams. My eyes yearn for the water that gushed between the rosebushes. Where is the fragrance of the henna plants and jasmine, where the peace of mind, my flute, you cruel man? Half a year has gone by—when will your icy cruelty thaw?*

From a distance Idris' raucous singing could be heard: "A strange world, God, a strange world!" And here he was, lighting a fire in front of his hut, a flame that shot high and then sank into the ground. His hugely pregnant wife came and went, bringing food and drink. Overcome by a wave of drunken resentment, Idris broke the silence with a bellow directed at the mansion: "Time for your roast chicken and greens, people! I hope it poisons you!" Then he resumed singing.

"Every time I manage to be alone in the dark," Adham said sadly to himself, "that devil stokes up his fire and makes noise and ruins my peace." When Umaima appeared at the door of the hut, he realized that she had not slept, as he had thought; her pregnancy had exhausted her, and hard work and poverty had worn her down.

"Why aren't you sleeping?" she asked tenderly.

"Just let me enjoy the only hour I have to enjoy life," he snarled.

"You'll be out pushing your cart first thing in the morning—you need to rest."

"When I'm alone I'm a respectable man again, or I can pretend to be. I contemplate the sky and remember days gone by."

She sighed audibly. "I wish I could see your father leaving the house or going in—I'd throw myself at his feet and beg him to forgive me."

"How many times have I told you to forget that idea?" asked Adham impatiently. "That way will do nothing to get us back in his good graces."

Umaima was silent for a long time, then said, "I'm thinking of the fate of this thing in my belly."

"That's all I think of too, even though I've become one of the lower beasts."

"You are the best man in the world," she murmured sadly.

Adham laughed derisively. "I'm no longer a man at all. No one but animals think only about food."

"Don't be sad. How many men have started out like you, and then got rich and ended up owning stores and houses."

"Are you having labor pains in your brain?"

"You'll be an important man someday," Umaima persisted. "Our child will grow up rich."

Adham slapped his hands together in sarcastic despair. "Will I make us rich selling beer, maybe? Or hashish?"

"By working, Adham."

"Working to eat is the worst curse in the world!" he snapped. "In the garden I used to live, and do no work except for looking at the sky or playing my flute, but now I'm just an animal. I push that cart in front of me day and night to earn some garbage to eat in the evening, and to shit in the morning. Working to eat is the worst curse of all. The only life is in the mansion, where no one works so they can eat—everything there is fun and beauty and singing."

Idris' voice split the air. "That's the truth, Adham, work is a curse—it's a humiliation I haven't learned yet. Didn't I invite you to team up with me?"

Adham turned toward the voice and saw Idris standing nearby. He often sneaked over unnoticed in the dark and eavesdropped for as long as he pleased, and joined the conversation when he felt like it.

"Go home," said Adham irritably.

"I was just *saying,*" Idris pronounced with mock seriousness, "as you were, that work is a curse which impairs the dignity of man."

"You're inviting me to be a thug, which is more disgusting than a curse."

"If work is a curse and crime is disgusting, how is a man supposed to live?"

Adham said nothing; he hated this conversation. Idris waited for him to speak, and when he didn't, he spoke again.

"Maybe you want to get along without working. That would have to be at the expense of others."

Adham persevered in his silence.

"Or maybe you want to get along without working and without hurting anybody!" He cackled. "It's a puzzle, slave boy!"

"Spite the devil and go home," shouted Umaima angrily.

Idris' shrill wife called him home, and he left as he had come, singing, "Strange world, O God, strange world!"

Umaima turned pleadingly to her husband. "Please avoid arguing with him at any cost."

"He just appears. I have no idea where he comes from."

Silence fell and soothed their irritation. Again Umaima spoke up tenderly. "I know in my heart that I'll make this hut into a mansion like the one we left, right down to the garden and nightingales, and our child will be happy and secure there."

Adham got up with a smile she could not make out in the dark and brushed the dirt from his clothes. " 'Sweet pickles! Get your cucumbers here!' And the sweat pours off me, the children harass me, the ground burns my feet—all for a few coins."

She followed him into the hut. "But someday we'll be rich and happy."

"If you had to work, you wouldn't have time to dream."

As they lay down on their straw pallet, Umaima said, "Isn't God mighty enough to turn our hut into a mansion like the one we left?"

"All I want is to go back to the mansion," Adham said, yawning. Then he yawned more deeply. "Work is a curse!"

"Maybe so," whispered Umaima, "but it is a curse that can only be defeated by more work!"

12

One night Adham was awakened by low cries. He floated a moment between sleep and waking before he recognized Umaima's agonized moans of "Oh, my back! Oh, my belly!" He sat up and looked toward her.

"You're always doing this now, and it turns out to be nothing. Light the candle."

"Light it yourself," she groaned. "This is really it."

He got up and groped among the kitchen utensils for the candle, found and lit it and stuck it on their low table. In the feeble light, Umaima lay half propped on her elbows, groaning and raising her head to breathe with obvious difficulty.

"That's what you think whenever you're in pain," the man said.

Her face fell. "No, this time I'm sure this is it."

He helped her support her back against the wall of the hut.

"It will be this month, anyway. Can you hold on until I go to Gamaliya and get the midwife?"

"Be careful. What time is it now?"

Adham went outside to look at the sky, then said, "It's almost daybreak. I'll be quick."

He set out walking briskly toward Gamaliya, and before long was threading his way through the blackness holding the hand of the elderly midwife to guide her. Umaima's screams were shredding the silence as he neared the hut. His heart pounded and he lengthened his strides until the midwife protested.

They entered the hut together, and the midwife took off her cloak and spoke cheerfully to Umaima. "This is your happy ending—be patient and you'll be fine."

"How are you?" Adham asked.

"I'm almost dead from the pain," she moaned. "My body is being broken apart—my bones are breaking—don't leave me."

"He'll be fine waiting outside," said the midwife.

Adham left the hut for the open air, and discerned a figure standing nearby, someone he recognized before he saw him clearly. His chest constricted, but Idris affected politeness.

"Is she in labor? The poor thing—my wife went through it not that long ago, but the pain doesn't last. Then you take your luck, whatever fate has in store—that's how I got Hind. She's a sweet thing, but all she does is wet herself and cry. Take it easy."

"It's in God's hands," said Adham through clenched teeth.

Idris laughed harshly. "Did you get her the Gamaliya midwife?"

"Yes."

"She's a filthy, grasping old thing. We used her, and she cost too much, for what she did, so I kicked her out. She still curses me out every time I go past her house."

"You shouldn't treat people that way," said Adham a little hesitantly.

"Little man, your father taught me to treat people badly."

Umaima's voice rose in a ragged scream, like an echo of the tearing going on inside her; Adham pressed his lips together to keep in what he wanted to say, then went worriedly over to the hut and called out in a gentle voice, "Be brave."

"Be brave, Umaima," Idris repeated very loudly.

Adham was concerned that his wife would hear Idris, but he swallowed his anger and said only, "I think we should stand farther away from the house."

"Come home with me. I'll give you tea, and we can watch Hind snore."

But Adham moved away from his hut without heading toward Idris', silently cursing his brother. Idris followed him.

"You'll be a father before sunup," said Idris. "It's a big change, but one of the good things is that you can enjoy the kind of bond your father broke with such ease and empty-headedness."

Adham gave voice to his exasperation: "You're bothering me with that kind of talk."

"What else do we have to talk about?"

Adham kept reluctantly silent for a few moments, then said almost pityingly, "Idris, why do you always follow me around when you know we're not even friends?"

Idris burst into laughter. "You impudent boy! I was woken up from a deep sleep by your wife's screaming, but I didn't get mad. On the contrary, I came over to help you. Your father heard the screaming just as well as I did, but he just went back to sleep, like some heartless stranger."

"We both know the fate he had in store for us," said Adham crossly. "Can't you ignore me the way I ignore you?"

"You hate me, Adham, not because I was the cause of your being kicked out—you hate me because I remind you of your weakness. What you hate in me is the reflection of your own sinfulness. I no longer have any excuse for hating you; in fact, now you are my comfort—you help me to forget. And remember, we're neighbors, and the first living things in this desert. Our children will learn to walk here side by side."

"You love to torment me."

Idris did not reply for such a long time that Adham hoped the conversation was over, but then he asked, "Why can't we get along?"

"Because I'm a peddler earning a living, and you're a man whose hobbies are fighting and trouble."

Umaima's screams intensified and rose in pitch, and Adham raised his head imploringly, seeing suddenly that the darkness was lifting—that dawn was ascending over the mountain.

"How terrible pain is!" cried Adham.

"And how wonderful leisure is!" laughed Idris. "You were born to run the estate and play your flute."

"Go ahead and laugh. I'm in pain."

"Why? I thought your wife was the one in pain."

"Just leave me alone!" yelled Adham, touchy with anxiety.

"Do you think you can become a father without paying a price?" asked Idris with maddening calm.

Adham exhaled but said nothing.

"You are wise," said Idris sympathetically. "I came to offer you some work that could help make your descendants happy. What we hear happening in there is a beginning, not an end—our yearnings can only be satisfied by building a hill of noisy children over our heads—what do you think?"

"It's nearly light—go and get some sleep."

Sustained screams rose again, until Adham felt useless where he was and went back to the hut, now emerging from the dark. As he got there Umaima was letting out a deep sigh, like the end of a sad song.

"How are you?" he asked as he came to the door.

"Wait," said the midwife. His heart was eager for relief, as the voice had a triumphant ring. Before long the woman appeared at the door.

"Two boys!"

"Twins?"

"God bless them both!"

Idris' laughter rang out behind his back, and he heard him say, "Idris is now the proud father of a girl and uncle to two boys!"

He headed back to his hut, singing, "Where have luck and fortune gone? Tell me, Time, tell me."

"Their mother would like to name them Qadri and Humam," said the midwife.

Transported by joy, Adham murmured, "Qadri and Humam—Qadri and Humam."

13

"Let's sit down and eat our food," said Qadri, *wiping his face on his* shirttail.

Humam looked at the sinking sun and said, "Yes—it's late."

They sat cross-legged on the sand at the foot of Muqattam, and Humam untied the knot of the red-striped handkerchief and took out ·their bread, falafel and leeks. They began to eat, glancing up now and then at their sheep, some of which roamed while others ruminated peacefully. There was nothing in the twins' features or physiques to help tell them apart, though the hunter's look so striking in Qadri's eyes lent his appearance a certain distinctive sharpness.

"If this desert were ours, and we didn't have to share it," said Qadri with his mouth full, "we could let the sheep graze all over the place and we wouldn't have to worry."

"But this desert is for shepherds from Atuf, Kafr al-Zaghari and al-Husseiniya, and we can avoid trouble by being friends with them."

Qadri laughed mockingly, spraying bits of food from his mouth.

"In these dead-end neighborhoods, they have only one way of handling people who look for their friendship: they slap you around."

"But—"

"No buts, Humam, there's only one way. You grab a man by his shirt and hit him on the head and let him fall on his face. Or his back."

"That's why we have more enemies than we can count!"

"What, is someone paying you to count them?"

Humam was deep in thought, at a profound distance, whistling softly for a moment before reverting to wise silence. He selected a single leek, hefted it and stuffed it into his mouth with gusto, then smacked his lips.

"That's why we're alone and spend so much time not talking."

"What do you need to talk for? You sing all the time anyway."

Humam looked at him confidingly and said, "I get the impression that being alone depresses you sometimes."

"I can always find something to be depressed about, being alone or whatever else."

Silence fell, interrupted only by eating sounds. They saw from this distance a group coming down from the mountain toward Atuf, chanting. One called out and the rest sang responses.

"This part of the desert is part of our own area. If we were to head north or south, we probably would never make it back," said Humam.

Qadri yelped with laughter. "You'd find people in the north and south both who'd love to kill me, but not one who'd dare fight me."

Humam was gazing at the sheep. "I'm not saying you have courage, but don't forget that we live thanks to our grandfather's name and our uncle's fearsome reputation, regardless of whatever feud we have with him."

Qadri knit his eyebrows in disagreement, but did not speak his protest. He looked over at the mansion, which loomed even at a distance, far off to the west, like a colossal temple of obliterated features, and said, "That place! I've never seen anything like it. Surrounded on all sides by the desert, near streets and alleys known for their fights and nastiness, owned by the worst tyrant around, and that's our grandfather, the one his grandchildren have never seen, even though they live under his nose!"

Humam looked toward the mansion and said, "Father talks about him with nothing but respect and admiration."

"All Uncle Idris does is curse him!"

"Anyway, he's our grandfather," said Humam mildly.

"So what good is that, boy? Our father slaves behind his cart and our mother wears herself out all day and half the night, we go around with these sheep, barefoot and practically naked, while he sits up there behind his walls, heartless, enjoying an easy life we can't even imagine."

They finished eating. Humam shook out the handkerchief, folded it, thrust it into his pocket and threw himself on his back, his arms behind his head, to stare up at the crystalline sky that radiated invisible peace. The horizon was filled with flapping kites. Qadri got up and faced away to piss.

"Father says that he used to go out a lot in the past and pass them as he went out and came back, but today no one sees him, as if he's afraid."

"How I would love to see him," said Humam dreamily.

"Don't think you'd be seeing anything too incredible. You'd find that he looks like Father or Uncle Idris, or like both of them. I'm amazed how Father talks about him with nothing but respect after what he did to him."

"Well, either he loves him very much or he accepted that the punishment was justified."

"Or he still has hopes of a pardon!"

"You don't understand our father. He's a kind and friendly person."

Qadri sat down again. "I don't much like him, and I don't like you. I swear, there is something wrong with our grandfather. He doesn't deserve anyone's respect—if he had one particle of decency in him, he wouldn't have treated his own flesh and blood so insanely. I think of him the same way our uncle does—as one of the curses of the age."

"Maybe the worst things about him," Idris said, smiling, "are things you're so proud of—I mean, strength and bravery."

"He was given this land for nothing—he didn't work for it, but he's cruel and tyrannical."

"Don't deny what I came to admit not that long ago—the ruler himself couldn't stand to live alone in this wasteland."

"Do you really think that story they tell us justifies his being so mad at the world?"

"You find lesser reasons to push people around!"

Qadri took a drink from the jug until he was full, then burped. "And what sin have his grandchildren committed? Does he know anything about shepherding, the bastard? I wish I knew what he's leaving us in his will!"

Humam sighed. "A fortune," he said dreamily, "that will spare us hardship. We'll be free to do what we want, and spend our lives having fun and singing."

"You sound like Father—we work in the dirt and the mud and dream of playing the flute in the shade of the garden. You want the truth? I like Uncle Idris better than our father."

Humam sat up and yawned, then stood and stretched. "Anyway, we amount to something. We have a home that's big enough for us, and a living that feeds us, and goats to tend—we sell their milk, and fatten them up to sell them too, and Mother makes us clothes from their wool."

"What about the flute and the garden?"

Humam did not answer. He picked up the staff laid at his feet and headed off in the direction of the sheep.

Qadri stood up and shouted mockingly at the mansion, "Is it all right with you that we're your heirs, or will you punish us in your death as you did in life? Answer, Gabalawi!"

"Answer, Gabalawi!" rang the echo.

14

From a distance they saw someone coming toward them, though they could not make out its features. The figure approached slowly until at last they recognized her, and when they did, Qadri straightened up instinctively and his beautiful eyes shone. Humam watched his brother with a smile, then looked nonchalantly at the sheep and reminded him in a low voice, "It will be dark soon."

"Let dawn come—who cares?" Qadri said disdainfully. He took two steps forward, waving his arms to welcome the young woman. She had to struggle to get close to where they stood, partly because of the distance she had come and partly because it was hard for her to walk in the sand in her slippers, fixing them both with a glittering gaze from her tempting yet insolent green eyes. She was wrapped in her cape up to her shoulders, leaving her bare head and neck free, and the wind played with her braids.

Qadri called out with charm that swept all sign of harshness from his face.

"Greetings, Hind!"

"Greetings," she said to him, adding, to Humam, "Good afternoon, cousin."

"Good afternoon, cousin, how are you?" said Humam with a smile.

Qadri took her hand and guided her to the great boulder that stood a few yards from where they stood, and they went around the boulder until they were on the side facing the mountain, apart from the desert and its inhabitants. He pulled her toward him, put his arms around her and gave her a long kiss on the mouth until their front teeth met, and the young woman was lost for a moment in a stuporous surrender. She managed to free herself from his embrace, and stood breathing heavily, adjusting her cape. She met his intense gaze with a smile, but her smile vanished as if something flitted through her mind, made a face and said with a bored air, "I only got away after a battle! Some kind of life this is!"

Qadri frowned to show that he knew what she meant. "Don't think about it," he said sharply. "Our parents are idiots. My kind father is stupid, and if anything your cruel father is even stupider. They want to bequeath us nothing but their hatred! Idiots! Tell me how you were able to get away."

She exhaled noisily. "It was just like any other day—my parents fighting all day long. He slapped her a couple of times, and she screamed at him and swore, and took out her anger on a jug—she smashed it. But that's all she did today. Sometimes she grabs him and tries to strangle him, even while he's smacking her, and curses him when he beats her. But when he's drunk, the only safe thing is to get out of there. I've wanted to run away so many times. I hate my life so much. But I calm myself down by crying until my eyes hurt. Never mind. I waited until he got dressed and went out, then I took my cape—as usual, my mother tried to stop me, but I got her out of my way and left."

Qadri held her hand in his and asked, "Didn't she guess where you were going?"

"I don't think so. I don't care. Anyway, she wouldn't dare tell my father."

Qadri gave a brief bark of laughter and asked, "What do you think he'd do if he knew?"

She echoed his laugh, a little bewildered, but said, "I'm not afraid of him, even though he's tough—I can even tell you I love him, and he loves me, in a naive way—in spite of his cruelty. It doesn't occur to him to tell me I'm the dearest thing he has in the world. Maybe that's why I'm so miserable."

Qadri sat on the ground by the rock, inviting her to join him by patting the spot beside him; she sat down, shedding her confining cape. He leaned toward her and kissed her cheek.

"So it seems it might be easier to try my father than to try yours; even so, he gets furious at the mention of your father's name—he denies that there's any good in him at all."

She laughed, remembering what she had heard him called. " 'You human!' That's how my father curses him."

He stared at her contemptuously.

"Well, your father criticizes mine for being uncouth, and mine criticizes yours for being too nice. Anyway, they've never agreed on anything."

Qadri thrust his head up as if butting the air, and said warningly, "But we will do whatever we want."

Hind looked at him tenderly. "My father can do whatever he wants, too."

"There are plenty of things I can do. What does my drunken uncle want for you?"

She laughed in spite of herself, and spoke in a tone of mingled protest and pleasantry. "Talk about my father with more respect." She pinched his ear. "I always ask myself what he wants for me. Sometimes I think he doesn't ever want me to get married."

He stared at her in surprise until she resumed.

"One time I saw him look up angrily at our grandfather's house, and say, 'If he wanted his children and grandchildren to live in disgrace, does he want the same for his granddaughter? The only proper place for Hind is in that locked mansion.' And one time he told my mother that a man from Kafr al-Zaghari wanted to marry me. My mother was really happy, and he got furious and yelled at her, 'You slut, you stupid thing, who do you think this person from Kafr al-Zaghari might be? The lowest servant in the mansion is better than he is, and probably cleaner.' My mother sighed and asked him, 'So who is good enough for her?' and he shouted, 'The dictator hiding behind the walls of his house knows who. She's his granddaughter, and there is no one on earth who's good enough for her! I want her to have a husband like me.' My mother couldn't help herself, and said, 'Do you want her to be miserable like her mother?' He pounced on her like an animal and kicked her hard until she ran out of the hut."

"He's out of his mind."

"He hates our grandfather, and curses him every time he mentions him, but deep inside he's proud to be his son."

Qadri made a fist and pounded his thigh. "We would probably have been better off if that man were not our grandfather."

"Probably," said Hind bitterly.

He gathered her to his chest with ardor that matched his words, and hugged her tightly. He held her in his arms until thoughts of their weary trouble gave way to the deep passion they felt.

"Give me your mouth," he said.

At this point Humam left his post by the boulder and headed quietly toward the sheep with a sad and timid smile. He imagined that the very air was drunk with the breath of love, and that love heralded trouble. But he said to himself, "His face was so serene and tender. He only looks that way when he's behind the boulder. There's nothing like the magic of love to wipe away our cares." The sky was growing pale as it surrendered to dusk, and soft breezes blew by from the west. Enchantment overtook the scene like a faint melody of farewell. A billy goat leaped on a she-goat. Humam resumed talking to himself: "Mother will be pleased when that goat gives birth; but the birth of a human can bring terrible trouble. We are cursed before we are born; I can't believe this hatred—there is no possible reason for it, except that it is between two brothers. For how long will we suffer from such hatred? If the past could be forgotten, the present would be wonderful, but we will keep on staring at that mansion, which gives us the only glory we can claim, and causes all the misery we know." His gaze settled on the mating goats and he smiled as he rounded up the sheep, whistling and swinging his staff. He turned toward the silent boulder, which stood in its place as if indifferent to all existence.

15

Umaima woke up, as usual, when there was only one star left in the sky. She called Adham until he awoke, sighing. The man got up and left his room, still slow with sleep, for the connected outer room where Qadri and Humam were sleeping, and woke them up. The hut, which had been enlarged, now looked like a little house, and was surrounded by a wall that also enclosed a backyard as a sheepfold. The wall was covered with tendrils of ivy, which gave a graceful look to its roughness and showed that Umaima had not yet given up her old dream of improving her hut as far as possible on the model of the mansion. Father and sons met in the yard around a bucket filled with water, washed their faces and put on their work clothes. The air blown into the hut bore the scent of burning wood and the sound of the younger brothers' crying. Finally they sat down around the low table before the hut entrance, eating from a pot of stewed fava beans. The autumn air was damp and almost cold at this early hour, but blew against strong bodies capable of bearing up under its gusts. From a distance, Idris' hut, also enlarged, was visible, and the mansion stood in its silence, looking in on itself, as if nothing bound it to this outer world. Umaima came in with a jug of fresh milk, set it on the table and sat down.

"Why don't you sell the milk to our esteemed grandfather?" asked Qadri sarcastically.

Adham turned his head, now gray at the temples, to Qadri and told him, "Eat and be quiet. A little quiet is the most we can hope for from you."

"It's almost time to pickle the lemons, olives and green peppers," said Umaima, munching a mouthful of food. "You used to love pickling days, Qadri—do you remember how you used to help stuff the lemons?"

"We were always happy when we were small, even when we had no reason," said Qadri bitterly.

"What's wrong with you today, Abu Zaid al-Hilali?" asked Adham, putting the jug back in its place. This was the name of a fabulous folk hero.

Qadri laughed but said nothing.

"Market day is coming," said Humam. "We have to get the sheep ready."

Umaima nodded. Adham turned to Qadri.

"Qadri, don't be difficult. I can't meet anyone who knows you without their complaining to me about you. I'm afraid you take after your uncle!"

"Or my grandfather!"

Adham's eyes flashed with indignation. "Don't talk that way about your grandfather. Have you ever heard me do that? And he's never done anything to hurt you."

"As long as he's hurt you, he's hurt us," Qadri protested.

"Be quiet. Do us all a favor and be quiet."

"Because of him, we have to live this life, the same life as Uncle Idris' daughter."

"What does she have to do with us?" said Adham crossly. "Her father was the root of the problem."

"I mean, it isn't fair for women of ours to grow up in this desert wasteland. Tell me who will marry that girl?"

"Why not the devil himself—what business is it of ours? I'm sure she's an animal just like her father." He glanced at his wife as if to seek her support.

"Yes, just like her father," said Umaima.

"Damn her and her father," spat Adham.

"This argument is ruining our meal," said Humam.

"Don't exaggerate," said Umaima tenderly. "The happiest time is when we're together."

Suddenly Idris' voice could be heard from afar, bellowing curses and obscenities.

"Morning prayers," muttered Adham in disgust. He finished his breakfast and got up, then went out to his cart and began pushing it in front of him, calling out, "Take care." "Goodbye," they answered. He headed off toward Gamaliya. Humam got up and took a side path to the enclosure, and before long the sheep were bleating loudly and the sound of their hoofs filled the path as they streamed out. Qadri rose, took his staff and waved goodbye to his mother, then followed his brother. As they neared Idris' hut, he blocked their way.

"What are you asking, big guy?"

Qadri gazed at Idris with real curiosity while Humam avoided looking at him, but he persisted.

"When may I expect a reply from the sons of the cucumber man?"

"Go to the market if you want to buy," said Qadri sharply.

"What about if I decide to take one?" laughed Idris.

"Please, Father, no scandals," called Hind from inside the house.

"Mind your business, you," he answered her lightly. "I'm talking to the slave boys."

"We're not bothering you—don't bother us," said Humam.

"Oh, that's Adham talking. You should be among the sheep, not behind them."

"My father told us not to answer your bullying," said Humam angrily.

Idris screeched with laughter. "God reward him—if it weren't for that I'd have disgraced myself by now." He added roughly, "You two are respectable people because of my good name. God damn you all! Get out of here!"

They went on their way, occasionally waving their staffs.

Still pale with rage, Humam spoke to Qadri. "What a bastard. That man is disgusting—even at this hour of the morning his breath stinks of liquor."

They drove the sheep from behind out into the desert.

"He talks a lot," said Qadri, "but he's never harmed us."

"He's stolen sheep from us more than once," argued Humam.

"He's drunk, and unfortunately he's our uncle, there's no way around that."

Silence fell as they neared the big boulder; scattered clouds filled the sky, and sunlight saturated the vast desert.

Humam could no longer contain what he wanted to say. "You'd be making a terrible mistake if you married into his family."

Qadri's eyes shone with anger. "Save your advice. I get all I need from Father."

"Our life is bad enough," continued Humam, still stung by Idris' insults. "Don't make it worse."

"Who cares if it kills you all, these troubles you create yourselves," exclaimed Qadri. "I'll do whatever I want."

They had reached the spot where the sheep grazed. Humam turned to his brother. "Do you think you won't suffer the consequences of what you do?"

Qadri grabbed Humam's shoulder and shouted, "You're just jealous."

Humam was shocked. He had not expected this from his brother, though on the other hand he was used to his surprises and outbursts. He removed Qadri's hand from his shoulder and said only, "God help us."

Qadri folded his arms on his chest and nodded derisively.

"The best thing I can do is leave you alone until you're sorry," said

Humam. "You won't admit you're wrong. You won't admit it until it's too late."

He turned away and walked toward the shady side of the boulder. Qadri stood sullen-faced in the blazing sun.

16

Adham's family was sitting in front of the hut, eating their supper by the dim starlight, when something happened whose like the desert had not seen since the expulsion of Adham. The mansion gate swung open and a figure with a lamp stepped out. All eyes turned to the lamp in speechless surprise, and followed it as it moved in the dark like an earth-bound planet. When it was halfway between the mansion and the hut, everyone focused on the human shape, trying to make it out by the reflected lamplight. "It's old Karim, the gatekeeper of the mansion," said Adham. Their surprise doubled when they realized that he was coming toward them; they all stood, some still holding food, some still chewing, but no one moving. The man came right up to them and stopped, his arm upraised.

"Good evening, Adham, sir."

Adham trembled when he heard this voice for the first time in twenty years. It stirred in the depths of his memory the sound of his father's deep voice, the fragrance of jasmine and henna and his home-sickness and sorrows; the ground seemed unable to support him.

"Good evening, Karim," said Adham, blinking back tears.

"I hope you and your family are well?" said the man with emotion he did not hide.

"God be thanked, Karim."

"I would love to tell you what is in my heart, but I am commanded to tell you only that my master has sent for your son Humam to meet him, immediately."

There was silence and they exchanged glances in confusion until a voice asked, "Only Humam?"

They turned around resentfully to see Idris, who was listening nearby, but old Karim did not reply. He raised his hand in farewell and headed back toward the mansion, leaving them in the dark.

Furious, Idris shouted at him, "Walk away without answering me, you old bastard?"

Qadri recovered from his shock, and asked angrily, "Why only Humam?"

"Yes, why only Humam?" echoed Idris.

"Go home and leave us in peace," Adham told him, perhaps finding an escape from his crisis by speaking.

"Peace? I stand where I want."

Humam looked silently at the mansion, his heart pounding so hard that he half imagined the sound echoed off of Muqattam Mountain.

"Go to your grandfather, Humam," said Adham resignedly. "Go in peace."

"And me?" Qadri turned menacingly to his father and asked sharply, "Aren't I your son too?"

"Don't talk like Idris, Qadri. You are my son too. Don't blame me, it's not my fault—I didn't invite him."

"But you could prevent him from discriminating between brother and brother," complained Idris.

"That's none of your business." Adham turned to Humam. "You have to go. Qadri's turn will come, I'm sure of that."

"You're a rotten father, just like your own father," said Idris as he left. "Poor Qadri. Why is he being punished for nothing? Our family curse strikes the smart ones first! God damn this crazy family."

He left and was swallowed by the darkness.

"You hate me!" Qadri shouted at Adham.

"Don't copy him. Come, Qadri—go on, Humam."

"I wish my brother could come," said Humam in a wounded tone.

"He'll follow you."

"It's unfair! Why does he prefer him to me? He doesn't know either one of us, so why does he invite him?"

"Go," said Adham to Humam, giving him a push.

"Be careful," Umaima whispered, then hugged Qadri, crying, but he pushed her arms away and followed behind his brother.

"Come back, Qadri!" Adham called. "Don't risk your future."

"No power on earth will make me turn back," said Qadri angrily.

Umaima sobbed louder, and indoors the younger children cried too. Qadri took longer steps to catch up with his brother, and when he came alongside him in the dark he saw the figure of Idris, walking along holding Hind's hand. When they arrived at the gate of the mansion, Idris pushed Qadri to the left of Humam and Hind to his right, then retreated a few steps.

"Open up, Karim," he shouted, "the grandchildren have come to see their grandfather."

The gate opened. On the threshold stood old Karim with his lamp. He spoke politely. "Kindly enter, Humam, sir."

"This is Humam's brother Qadri," Idris called out, "and this is Hind, who is the very picture of my mother, who died weeping."

"You know, Idris, sir, that no one may enter here who has not been invited."

He motioned to Humam, who entered. Qadri followed, holding Hind by the hand, but a severe voice Idris recognized sounded from the garden.

"Go, in your sin, you pests!"

They froze where they stood. The gate swung shut. Idris flew at them and grabbed them by the shoulders, and asked in a voice trembling with rage, "What sin is he talking about?"

Hind squealed with pain as Qadri whirled around toward Idris and threw his hands off of his shoulder and Hind's. She turned and ran, vanishing swiftly in the darkness. Idris stepped lightly back, then threw a punch which the boy absorbed despite its sharp impact; then Qadri punched him back even harder. They exchanged savage blows and kicks under the mansion wall.

"I'll kill you!" shouted Idris. "You son of a whore!"

"I'll kill you first!" shouted Qadri.

They punched one another until blood ran from Qadri's mouth and nose, and Adham came running like a madman. "Leave my boy alone, Idris."

"I'll kill him for what he's done," screamed Idris.

"I won't let you kill him—I won't let you live if you do kill him."

Hind's mother arrived, screeching. "Hind has run away, Idris! Find her before she disappears!"

Adham pushed himself between Idris and Qadri, and shouted at his brother, "Come on—you're fighting over nothing. Your daughter is chaste, no one has touched her, but you frightened her and she ran away. Go find her before she disappears."

He clasped Qadri to him and dragged him back quickly, saying, "Hurry. Your mother had fainted when I left her."

Idris fled into the darkness, shouting as loudly as he could, "Hind! Hind!"

17

Humam followed old Karim down the path that led under the bower of jasmine toward the terrace. The night was a new thing here in the garden: sweet and pleasant, with the fragrance of flowers and herbs, whose delight filled the depths of his heart. The boy was overcome with a feeling of bliss and grandeur and a yearning love for this place; he knew that these were the most exalted moments of his life. His eyes picked up lights behind some of the windows' half-blinds, and a powerful light from the door of the reception hall that threw a geometrical shape on the garden below. His heart pounded as he imagined life in the drawing rooms behind these windows—what it must be like, and who lived it— and pounded even harder when a strange truth occurred to him: that he was one of the family of this mansion, a product of this life, and now was meeting it face to face, as he stood barefoot in his simple blue galabiya and faded skullcap. They went up the steps and turned right at the terrace level toward a small door, which opened onto a stairway, and ascended in a silence like that of the tomb, until they came to a long gallery lit by a lamp suspended from the ornamented ceiling. They went to the great closed door in the middle of the gallery. "In some spot like this," thought Humam, deeply touched, "perhaps in this very spot at the top of the stairs, my mother kept a lookout twenty years ago. What a depressing thought!" Old Karim rapped at the great door to request entry for Humam, pushed him along and stepped aside, motioning him to enter. The boy entered slowly, gracefully, and a little fearfully. He did not hear the door close behind him, and had only a strange feeling at the light that flickered in the ceiling and the corners. All his attention was drawn to the central spot where the man sat cross-legged on a cushioned seat. He had never seen his grandfather before, but had no doubt of the identity of the seated figure before him: who could this imposing being be if not his grandfather, of whom he had heard such marvels? He approached him, transfixed by the large-eyed gaze which overpowered the whole contents of his memory, yet filled his heart with safety and peace. He bowed so low that his forehead nearly touched the edge of the cushion, and extended his hand; the other gave his, which Humam kissed reverentially, then spoke with unexpected courage.

"Good evening, Grandfather."

He was taken aback by the strong voice that replied—in which the music of mercy could be heard. "You are welcome, my son. Sit down."

The boy went to a chair to the right of the cushioned seat and perched on the edge.

"Make yourself comfortable," said Gabalawi.

Humam shifted back into the chair, his heart overflowing with happiness; his lips moved in whispered thanks, then silence fell. He studied the designs in the carpet beneath his feet, feeling the impact of the gaze trained on him, just as we feel the sun upon us without looking at it. His attention was suddenly drawn to the little room located to his right; he looked at its door with a twinge of fright and melancholy.

"What do you know about that door?" the man asked.

His limbs trembled and he marveled at how the man saw everything. "I know that all our troubles came out of it," he said humbly.

"What did you think of your grandfather when you heard the story?"

Humam opened his mouth to answer, but Gabalawi spoke first. "Tell the truth."

Humam was so affected by his tone of voice that he did speak frankly. "My father's conduct seemed to me a terrible mistake, and it seemed to me that the punishment was extremely harsh."

Gabalawi smiled. "That is approximately what you think. I abominate lying and deception, and that is why I evict from my house anyone who shames himself."

Humam's eyes filled with tears.

"You seemed to me a good boy. That is why I sent for you."

"Thank you, sir," said Humam in a voice wet with tears.

"I have decided to give you a chance no one from outside here has ever had: to live in this house, to marry into it and to begin a new life in it."

Humam's heart beat in a rapture of joy as he awaited new words to complete this marvelous melody, as a music lover listens for song after an overture, but the man's silence was unbroken. He hesitated, then spoke. "Thank you for your kindness."

"You deserve it."

The boy's gaze alternated between his grandfather and the carpet before he asked anxiously, "My family?"

"I have clearly told you what I want," Gabalawi reproached him.

"They deserve your forgiveness and your affection," Humam pleaded.

Gabalawi's question was distinctly cool: "Did you not hear what I said?"

"Of course, but these are my mother and father and brothers and sisters, and my father is a man—"

"Did you not hear what I said?"

The voice was annoyed. Silence fell. To indicate that the conversation was at an end, the man said, "Go tell them goodbye, then come back here."

Humam rose, kissed his grandfather's hand and left. He found old

Karim waiting for him; the man got up and followed the boy in silence.
When they reached the terrace, Humam saw a girl standing in the light
at the beginning of the garden; she hurried away and vanished, though
not before he noticed her profile, neck and slim figure. His grandfather's
voice echoed in his ears: "To live in this house, to marry into it." To
marry a girl like this one; to live the life my father knew. How had this
gamble ruined him? How, and with what heart, had he borne a life
spent pushing a handcart? *This fortunate chance is like a dream, my father's
dream for the past twenty years. But I have a terrible headache.*

18

Humam went back to the hut to find his family waiting up for him.
They surrounded him and plied him with questions.

"What was it about, my boy?" asked Adham impatiently.

Humam noticed that Qadri had a bandage over one eye, and went
closer to examine his brother's face.

"There was quite a battle between your brother and that man," said
Adham despondently, indicating Idris' hut with a gesture. The place was
shrouded in darkness and silence.

"All because of the nasty, false accusation he made against her at the
mansion," said Qadri angrily.

Humam pointed to Idris' hut. "What's going on there?"

"The man and his wife have gone looking for their daughter," said
Adham sadly.

"And whose fault is it but that damned bastard's?" shouted Qadri.

"Lower your voice," Umaima implored.

"What are you worried about?" shouted Qadri. "Nothing but a
fixation on a return that will never happen—believe me, you will never
leave this hut for as long as you live."

"That's enough of that," snapped Adham. "You're out of your

mind, by our God Almighty. Didn't you want to marry that fugitive girl?"

"I will too."

"Shut up. I'm tired of your silliness."

"Living next door to Idris will be worse than ever now," said Umaima anxiously.

Adham turned to Humam. "I asked you what it was about."

"My grandfather invited me to move to the mansion," replied Humam in a voice that betrayed no pleasure.

Adham waited for the rest of the story; when Humam had nothing to add he sounded despairing. "What about us—what did he say about us?"

Humam shook his head sadly and whispered, "Nothing."

A laugh like a scorpion's sting escaped Qadri, who then asked sarcastically, "So what are you doing back here?"

What am I doing back here? I don't know except that happiness was not made to bless people like me.

"I didn't forget to remind him about all of you," Humam answered sadly.

"Thanks," said Qadri contemptuously, "but why did he choose you over us?"

"You know I had nothing to do with that."

"Well, Humam, of course you are better than any of us," Adham sighed.

"And you, Father, never so much as mention him without some blessing he doesn't deserve!" said Qadri bitterly.

"You don't understand anything," said Adham.

"That man is worse than his son Idris."

"You are tearing my heart, and depriving me of all hope," said Umaima piteously.

"There's no hope anywhere but in this desert," said Qadri scornfully. "Get used to that and forget everything else. This stinking house is no good—I'm not afraid of the desert, I'm not even afraid of Idris himself. I can repay him double for every time he hit me. Spit on this house and forget it."

Can life go on like this forever? Adham wondered. Why, Father, did you revive our hopes in you before it pleased you to forgive us? What will soften your heart, if not all the time that has passed? What good is there in hoping when all this torment has not purified us enough to earn the forgiveness of the one we love?

To Humam he spoke in a voice as dim as twilight: "Tell me what you think, my boy."

"He told me to come and say goodbye, then go back there."

Umaima vainly tried to hide her sobs in the darkness.

"What's keeping you?" Qadri asked maliciously.

"Go, Humam," said Adham resolutely. "Go with our blessing, and God be with you."

"Go, you gallant creature, and don't think about anyone else," Qadri said mock seriously.

"Don't make fun of your nice brother!" shouted Adham.

Qadri laughed. "He's worse than all of us."

"If I decide to stay, it won't be thanks to you!" yelled Humam.

"Go," pleaded Adham. "Don't hesitate."

"Yes—go in peace," said Umaima through her tears.

"No, Mother," said Humam. "I'm not going."

"Are you crazy?" exclaimed Adham.

"No, Father, I need to think about it. We need to talk about it."

"No, we don't. Don't make me sin again."

Humam pointed to Idris' hut and said decisively, "I think some things will be happening."

"You're too weak to keep trouble away from yourself, let alone from others," Qadri sneered.

"I think I'll just ignore whatever you say," Humam said disdainfully.

"Go, Humam," Adham urged him again.

"I will stay by your side," Humam said, and went into the hut.

19

Nothing was left of the sun but its aurora, and all passersby were home by now, so Qadri, Humam and the sheep had the desert to themselves. The whole day had passed, but they had exchanged only the few words demanded by their working together. And Qadri had gone away for much of the day—seeking out news of Hind, guessed Humam, who stayed alone in the shade of the boulder, not far from the flock.

"Tell me," Qadri suddenly asked Humam, with a hint of menace, "what are you going to do about the visit to your grandfather? Have you changed your mind?"

"None of your business," said Humam crossly.

Rage rose up in Qadri's heart and showed in his face like dusk falling over Muqattam.

"Why did you stay? When will you go? When will you get the nerve to admit what you're going to do?"

"I stayed to bear my share of the hardship created by your trouble-making."

Qadri laughed savagely. "That's what you say to hide your jealousy."

Humam shook his head as if in utter wonderment, and said, "You deserve pity, not jealousy."

Qadri moved closer, his limbs trembling with anger, and spoke in a voice choked with rage. "There's nothing more disgusting than you pretending to be wise."

Humam stared at him wordlessly but said nothing.

"The human race should be ashamed of having you as a member," Qadri continued.

Humam gazed unblinkingly into the burning eyes that faced him, and spoke firmly. "You should know that I'm not afraid of you."

"Has the big bully promised to protect you?"

"Hatred makes you stink—it turns you into a loathsome thing."

Qadri punched him in the face. The blow did not surprise Humam, who hit him back even harder.

"Don't be crazy," said Humam.

Qadri stooped briefly and snatched up a rock, which he then hurled at his brother with all the strength in his body. Humam started to dodge the rock, but it struck him in the forehead. A gasp escaped him and he froze where he stood, fury flashing in his eyes. Abruptly the fury disappeared from them, like a fire put out by heavy soil. A dark vacancy took its place as his eyes seemed to be gazing within him. He staggered, then fell on his face. Qadri's mood changed. His anger vanished, leaving him like melted iron turned cold, and fear seized him. He waited impatiently for the fallen man to get up or even budge, but in vain. He bent over him and reached out to shake him gently, but Humam did not move. He turned him on his back to clear his nose and mouth of the sand; the other lay still, his eyes staring. Qadri knelt beside him and shook him again, rubbed his chest and hands, staring in terror at the stream of blood gushing from the wound. He called him pleadingly but he did not respond. His silence was intense and profound, as if it were a part of his very being—like his motionlessness, so different from that of a living person or an inanimate object. There was no feeling, no activity, no concern with anything at all; as if he had fallen to the earth from some unknown height for some unknown reason. Qadri recognized death instinctively, and began to pull the hair of his head despairingly. He looked all around, frightened, but there was no living thing except for insects and the sheep, all of whom moved indifferently away from him. _Night will come and darkness will reign._ He got up decisively and found his staff, and went to a spot between the big boulder and the hill; there he dug a hole with his hands, working doggedly, bathed in sweat and shaking all over. He hurried over to his brother and called him one last time, not expecting a reply. He seized him by the feet, dragged him to the hole and placed him in it. He looked at him, sighed and after a moment's hesitation began to pile dirt on him. Then he stood and wiped the sweat from his face with the edge of his galabiya. When he saw a stain of blood soaking through the sand, he covered it with dirt; then he flung himself on the ground, exhausted. His strength deserting him, he felt an urge to cry, but the tears would not come. "Death defeated me," said Qadri. He had not invited it; he had not wanted it; it had come on its own. If only he could turn himself into a young goat— he would get lost among the sheep; or a grain of sand—he would vanish into the earth. Since I cannot bring him back to life, I will never be strong again. That sight will never, ever leave my head from now on! What I buried was neither a living thing nor a lifeless object, but something I made with my own hands.

20

Qadri went home, driving the flock before him. Adham's cart was not in its place. His mother's voice called to him from inside. "Why are you two so late?"

He answered as he drove the sheep along the path to the enclosure. "I fell asleep. Hasn't Humam came back yet?"

Umaima raised her voice above the racket of her two younger boys. "No—isn't he with you?"

Qadri swallowed hard and said, "He left me at noon without telling me where he was going. I thought he'd be back here."

Adham had come in after pushing his cart into the yard. "Did you two quarrel?"

"No!"

"I think you must have been the reason he went away—but where is he?"

Umaima went out into the yard as Qadri closed the gate of the enclosure and went to wash his face and hands in the basin by the clay jug. He had to face facts. The world had changed, but despair was powerful. He joined his parents in the dark, drying his face with the edge of his galabiya.

"Where has Humam gone?" wondered Umaima. "He's never been gone like this before."

Adham agreed with her and said, "Yes. Tell us why and how he left."

Qadri's heart flip-flopped at the picture he saw in his mind. "I was sitting in the shade of the rock, and turned around, and saw him going away, coming this way. I was going to call to him, but I didn't."

"If only you had called to him," said Umaima uneasily, "instead of giving in to your anger."

Adham looked helplessly into the surrounding darkness, and saw a dim light through a little window in Idris' hut, indicating that once again life was on the move there, but he ignored it, focusing instead on the mansion.

"Maybe he went to his grandfather's," he wondered.

"He wouldn't do that without telling us," Umaima disagreed.

"Maybe he was too ashamed to," Qadri suggested weakly.

Adham gave him a dubious look, worried by the absence of sarcasm and hostility from Qadri's voice.

"We urged him to go but he refused."

"He was ashamed to agree in front of us," said Qadri wearily.

"That's not like him. What's wrong with you? You look sick!"

"I had to do all the work myself."

Adham cried out as if calling for help, "I mean it—I am really afraid now!"

"I'll go to the mansion and ask about him," said Umaima hoarsely.

Adham shrugged despairingly. "No one will answer you, but I swear he hasn't gone there."

Umaima puffed anxiously and said, "God! I've never been this worried. Do something, man!"

Adham sighed loudly in the dark. "We'll go look for him everywhere."

"Maybe he's on his way home," said Qadri.

"We have no time to waste," cried Umaima. She paused uneasily and looked out at Idris' hut. "Could he have run into Idris on the road?"

"Idris' enemy is Qadri, not Humam," said Adham irritably.

"He wouldn't think anything of killing any one of us. I'm going to him!"

Adham held her back, saying, "Don't complicate things even more. I promise, if we don't find him I will go to Idris, and to the mansion too." He pierced Qadri with a fearful glance. What was on his mind to keep him so quiet? Did he have nothing more to say? *Where are you, Humam?*

Umaima began to rush out of the yard, but Adham moved quickly and clasped her shoulder. Suddenly the mansion gate swung open and they all turned toward it. After a moment the figure of old Karim appeared, coming nearer to them. Adham went out to him.

"Welcome, Karim!"

Karim greeted him and announced, "My master is asking what has delayed Humam."

"We don't know where he is," wept Umaima. "We thought he might be up there with you."

"My master is asking what has delayed him."

"God help me from my heart's forebodings!" cried Umaima.

Old Karim left. Umaima began to wag her head in a way that warned of an outburst. Adham guided her before him into the inner room where the toddlers were crying, and shouted at her ferociously. "Don't leave this room! I will come back with him! Just don't leave this room!"

He went out into the yard and found Qadri sitting on the ground. He leaned over him and whispered, "Tell me—what do you know about your brother?"

Qadri jerked his head up at him but something kept him from speaking.

"Tell me, Qadri, what you did to your brother."

"Nothing," said the boy almost inaudibly.

The man went back inside and came out with a lantern, which he lit and placed on his cart. It cast light on Qadri's face, which the man studied with alarm. "Something in your face tells me you're suffering."

Umaima's voice called out from within, so mingled with the children's voices that no one could make out what she was saying.

"Be quiet, woman—die, if you want, but do it quietly!"

His searching gaze resettled on his son. Suddenly he began to shake; he snatched the edge of Qadri's sleeve, panic-stricken. "Blood! What is this? Your brother's blood?!"

Qadri stared at his sleeve, flinched involuntarily and bowed his head in desperation. This despairing action was his confession, and Adham pulled him to his feet, then pushed him outside. He pushed him with a brutality of which he had not known himself capable, as a darkness blacker than the surrounding night shrouded his eyes.

21

He pushed him toward the desert, saying, "We'll go through the desert of al-Darasa so that we won't pass Idris' house."

They advanced deeper into the desert, Qadri stumbling as he was forced along by his father's iron grip on his shoulder. Adham took long steps and asked, in a voice like an old man's, "Tell me. Did you hit him? What did you hit him with? How was he when you left him?"

Qadri did not answer. His father's hand was like iron, but he did not feel it. His pain was intense but he said nothing. He wished that the sun had never risen.

"Have a heart, Qadri—say something. What do you know about heart? I condemned myself to torment the day you were born. For twenty years I've been haunted by curses, and here I am begging for mercy from someone who doesn't know what it is."

Qadri began to cry, until his shoulder began to shake under Adham's unyielding grip, and kept on crying until Adham saw how agonized he felt, but Adham said, "Is that your answer? Why, Qadri? Why? What got into you? Confess now, in the dark, before you see yourself in daylight."

"I hope day never comes," exclaimed Qadri.

"We are a family of darkness, we will never see daylight! I thought evil lived in Idris' house, but here it is in our own blood. Idris cackles and gets drunk and disgraces himself, but we kill one another. God! Did you kill your brother?"

"Never!"

"Then where is he?"

"I didn't mean to kill him!"

"But he's dead!" shouted Adham.

Qadri sobbed, and his father's grip tightened on his shoulder. So Humam had been murdered—the flower of all his work, his grandfather's pet—as if he had never been. *Without this tearing pain, I would never have believed it.*

They came to the big boulder.

"Where did you leave him, murderer?" asked Adham in a heavy voice.

Qadri headed toward the spot where he had dug his brother's grave and stood there, between the boulder and the mountain.

"Where is your brother?" Adham asked. "I don't see anything."

"I buried him here," said Qadri almost inaudibly.

"You buried him?!" screamed Adham. He drew a box of matches from his pocket, struck one and studied the grave by its light until he saw a disturbed patch of earth and the path of the corpse that ended there. Adham moaned in pain and began to scoop away dirt with his trembling hands. He worked grimly until his fingers encountered Humam's head. He dug his hands under Humam's armpits and gently pulled the corpse out of the dirt. He knelt beside it and laid his hands on Humam's head, his eyes closed, like a statue of hopelessless and defeat. He sighed deeply.

"Forty years of my life seem like feeble nonsense when I look at your corpse, my son."

Suddenly he stood and stared at Qadri, standing on the other side of the corpse, and felt a blind rage for several moments before speaking. "Humam will go back home carried on your back," he said heavily.

Qadri started in terror and drew back, but the man swiftly stepped around the corpse and grabbed him by the shoulder, screaming, "Carry your brother!"

"I can't," wailed Qadri.

"You were able to kill him."

"Father, I can't."

"Don't call me Father! Anyone who kills his own brother has no father, no mother and no brother!"

"I can't."

Adham's grip closed more tightly on him. "It's the killer's job to carry his victim."

Qadri tried to squirm out of his grasp but Adham would not let him, and in his shocked condition could not stop hitting Qadri in the face, though the boy did not flinch or cry out from the pain. Then the man stopped hitting him and said, "Don't waste time—your mother is waiting."

Qadri trembled when he remembered his mother, and pleaded, "Just let me disappear."

Adham pushed him toward the body. "Get going. We'll carry him together."

Adham turned to the corpse and put his hands under Humam's armpits, and Qadri bent and put his hands under the ankles. They lifted the body together and moved slowly toward the desert of al-Darasa. Adham was so sunk in pain and shock that he had no sense of physical pain, or of any other feeling. Qadri still suffered from the throbbing of his heart and the shaking of his limbs. His nostrils were filled with a piercing, earthy smell, while the touch of the corpse spread from his hands to every part of his own body. The darkness was opaque, though the horizon twinkled with the lights of companionable neighborhoods. Qadri felt his despair cutting off what breath he had left, and he stopped.

"I'll carry the body alone," he told his father. He placed one arm under the back and the other under the knees, and walked in front of Adham.

22

When they got near the hut they were greeted by Umaima's fearful voice. "Did you find him?"

"Stay inside," Adham ordered her.

He reached the hut before Qadri to make sure she did not come out. Qadri stood at the entrance to the hut, not wanting to move. His father motioned him in, but he could not go in.

"I can't face her," Qadri whispered.

"You've done a much worse thing," his father hissed angrily.

Qadri did not budge from where he stood. "No," he said, "this is worse."

Adham pushed Qadri firmly before him to force him into the outer room, then pounced at Umaima to contain with his hand the scream that had not quite left her mouth.

"Don't scream, woman," he said harshly, "we can't attract any attention until we solve this. Let's accept our fate in silence and live patiently with our pain. The evil came out of your belly and my loins. We are all cursed."

He still forcibly blocked her mouth. She tried to free herself from his hand, but in vain. She tried to bite it but could not. Her breathing came hard, and then her strength failed and she fell over in a faint. Qadri stood holding the corpse in silence and shame, his eyes fixed on the lantern to avoid seeing her. Adham moved toward him and helped him to lay the corpse down on the bed and tenderly shrouded it in a sheet. Qadri looked at the shrouded body of his brother on the bed they had shared all their lives, and felt that he no longer had a place here. Umaima moved her head, then opened her eyes; Adham went to her and spoke firmly: "Don't scream."

She wanted to stand, and he helped her get up, still warning her against speaking. She began to throw herself on the bed, but the man prevented her, so she stood, defeated, then began to vent her agony by pulling frenziedly at her hair, tearing out wisp after wisp. The man did not care what she did, but told her roughly, "Do whatever you want, but do it quietly."

"My boy!" she cried hoarsely. "My boy!"

"This is his corpse," said Adham distractedly. "He is no longer your boy or my boy. This is who killed him. Kill him if you want."

Umaima slapped her cheeks in grief and screamed at Qadri, "The lowest animals don't do what you did!"

Qadri bowed his head silently while Adham screamed ferociously at him, "Has he died for nothing? You have no right to live—that's justice!"

"Just yesterday he was our shining hope," wailed Umaima. "We told him, 'Go,' and he wouldn't. If only he had! If only he hadn't been so kind, so noble, so compassionate, he would have gone. And his reward is murder? How could you do this? Is your heart a stone? You aren't my son and I'm not your mother!"

Qadri did not utter a syllable but said to himself, "I killed him once, but he's killing me once every second. I'm not alive. Who says I'm alive?"

"What will I do with you?" asked Adham gruffly.

"You said I have no right to live."

"How could you let yourself kill him?" cried Umaima.

"Crying won't do any good now," said Qadri despairingly. "I'm ready to be punished. Killing is the least I deserve."

"But you've made our lives worse than death too," said Adham bitterly.

Umaima began to scream and slap her cheeks again. "I will never be happy again—bury me with my boy! Why won't you let me raise my voice?"

"Not out of fear for your throat," said Adham with bitter sarcasm, "but because I'm afraid that Satan will hear you."

"Let him hear what he wants," said Umaima scornfully. "I don't want to live anymore."

Suddenly Idris' voice sounded at the entrance of the hut.

"Brother Adham! Come here! Poor man!"

A shudder ran through them all.

"Go back to your hut," called Adham. "I warn you, don't provoke me."

"Worse and worse! Your tragedy has spared you my anger. Enough of this kind of talk! We are both suffering—you lost a dear, precious son, and my only daughter is gone. Our children were our only consolation in our exile, and they're gone! Poor man, come and let's comfort one another."

The secret had got out! But how? For the first time Umaima's heart was fearful for Qadri.

"I don't care about your gloating," said Adham. "It's nothing compared to my pain."

"Gloating!" Idris sounded shocked. "Don't you know that I wept when I saw you pick up his body from the grave Qadri dug for him?"

"Goddamned spying!" shouted Adham.

"I didn't weep only for the deceased but for his killer too! I said to myself, 'Poor Adham, you have lost two boys in one night.' "

Oblivious to everyone, Umaima began to scream. Abruptly Qadri left the hut, and Adham followed behind him.

"I don't want to lose them both!" shouted Umaima.

Qadri wanted to pounce on Idris, but Adham pushed him away from him, then stood threateningly in front of the man. "I'm warning you, don't interfere with us."

"You're so stupid, Adham—you don't know the difference between a friend and an enemy. You want to fight your brother to defend your son's murderer."

"Get out of here."

"Whatever you say," laughed Idris. "My deepest condolences on your loss. Have a nice day!"

Idris disappeared into the darkness. Adham turned to Qadri, only to find Umaima standing there and asking about him. Worried, he went out to look for him in the darkness.

"Qadri!" he shouted at the top of his lungs. "Qadri! Where are you?"

He heard Idris' powerful shout: "Qadri! Qadri! Where are you?"

23

Humam was buried in the estate cemetery at Bab al-Nasr. A large crowd of Adham's friends walked in the funeral procession, most of them fellow peddlers, some of them customers who liked his good character and fair dealing. Idris forced himself on the funeral and took part in the obsequies, and even stood with the family to receive condolences, as he was the uncle of the deceased. Adham kept a grudging silence; a horde of local bullies, gangsters, thieves, hoodlums and other dissolutes joined the funeral procession. At the burial, Idris stood over the grave and offered Adham words of comfort; Adham patiently said nothing as tears rolled down his cheeks. Umaima vented her grief unabashed, slapping her cheeks, wailing and rolling in the dust.

When the mourners left, Adham turned angrily to Idris. "Is there no end to your cruelty?"

Idris affected amazement. "What are you talking about? You poor thing."

"I never thought you could be this cruel," said Adham sharply, "but death is the end of everything—what is there to gloat about?"

Idris slapped his palms together in resignation. "In your grief you have forgotten your manners, but I forgive you."

"When are you going to realize that you and I have nothing to say to one another?"

"Heaven forgive us, aren't you my brother? That's a bond that can never be broken."

"Idris! You've done enough to me."

"Sorrow stinks, but we're both bereaved. You lost Humam and Qadri and I lost Hind—now the great Gabalawi has a whore for a granddaughter and a murderer grandson! Anyway, you're better off than I am—you have other children to make up for the ones you lost."

"You still envy me?" Adham sighed sadly.

"Idris envious of Adham?" Idris was astounded.

"If the punishment you get isn't as horrible as the things you've done, I hope the world drops into Hell!"

"Hell! Hell?"

The gloomy days that followed were overloaded with pain. Umaima was overcome by grief, and her health failed; she began to look emaciated. In a few short years, Adham looked older than a long life would have made him, and they both suffered from feebleness and sickliness. One day their illness intensified and they went to bed, Umaima with the two little boys in the inner room, and Adham in the outer room—Qadri and Humam's room. The day passed, night came and they lit no lamp. Adham was content with the moonlight that shone in from the yard. He dozed and slept intermittently, in a state between sleeping and waking. He heard Idris' mocking voice from outside the hut.

"Is there anything I can do for you?"

His heart sank and he did not answer. He always dreaded the hour when his brother left home for his nights out. Now here came the voice again.

"Look, everybody! Look how kind I am, and how stubborn he is!" And he went away singing: "Three of us climbed the mountain to hunt. One was killed by passion, the second lost by love."

Adham's eyes filled with tears. *This evil never tires of its pleasure. It fights, kills and yet wins respect. It is cruel and overpowering and laughs at punishment—its laugh rocks the horizons! It delights in harassing the weak, it adores funerals and sings over tombstones. Death comes near me and it still mocks me with laughter. The victim is in the earth and the killer is lost, and in my hut we weep for them both. Childish laughter in the garden has given way to scowling age wet with tears. Within the remnant of my body there is only pain. Why all this misery? Where have my dreams gone? Where?*

Adham imagined that he heard footfalls. Slow, heavy footfalls that stirred misty memories, as a strong, sweet smell may defy perception and definition. He turned his face to the entrance of the hut and saw the door open, then saw it blocked by a huge form. He started in surprise, and peered through the dark, his hopes enclosed by fears, then a deep moan escaped him.

"Father?" he murmured.

He seemed to be hearing the old voice: "Good evening, Adham."

His eyes swam with tears. He tried to get up but could not. He felt a delight, a bliss that he had not known in twenty years.

"Let me believe," he stammered.

"You are crying, but it is you who sinned."

"The sin was great and the punishment was great," said Adham in a voice choked with tears. "But even the lowest insects don't despair of finding some shade."

"So you are teaching me wisdom!"

"I'm sorry, I'm sorry, I'm plagued by grief and illness—even my sheep are threatened with ruin."

"That is very nice, that you are concerned for the sheep."

"Have you forgiven me?" Adham asked hopefully.

There was silence, then: "Yes."

"Thank God!" said Adham, his whole body trembling. "Only a little while ago I was trapped in the lowest pit of despair!"

"And you found me there!"

"Yes—it is like waking up from a nightmare."

"That's what makes you a good son."

"I begot a murderer and a victim," sighed Adham.

"The dead don't come back. What do you ask?"

Adham sighed. "I used to yearn to be back singing in the garden, but today nothing can make me happy."

"The estate will belong to your children."

"Thank God."

"Don't excite yourself. Go back to sleep."

In more or less close succession, first Adham, then Umaima, then Idris left this life. Their children grew up. Qadri came back after a long absence, with Hind and their children. They grew up together and married among the others, and grew in number. Their neighborhood flourished, thanks to income from the estate, and thus our alley entered history; and from all these people were descended the people of our alley.

Gabal

24

The estate put up houses in two facing rows, thus creating our alley.
The two rows ran from a spot in front of the mansion and extended
straight out in the direction of Gamaliya. The mansion stood isolated on
all sides, at the head of the alley on the desert side. Our alley, Gabalawi
Alley, is the longest in the whole area. Most of its houses have courtyards, as in Hamdan Alley, though there are more huts from halfway
down the alley to Gamaliya. And the picture would not be complete
without the house of the estate overseer at the end of the right-hand row
of dwellings, and the gangster's house at the end of the left row, just
opposite.

The mansion had closed its gates on its owner and his closest servants. All Gabalawi's sons had died young and there was no offspring left
who had grown up and died in the mansion, except for Effendi, who
was then the estate overseer. Some of the people of the alley were
peddlers, though a few ran shops or coffeehouses; a great many were
beggars, and there was a business employing everyone who was able—
that was the drug business, especially hashish, opium and aphrodisiacs.
The mark of our alley then, as now, was crowding and noise. Barefoot
and nearly naked children played in every corner, filling the air with
their shouts and covering the ground with their filth. The entrances of
the houses were jammed with women—this one chopping *moloukhia,*
that one peeling onions and a third stoking a fire, all exchanging gossip
and jokes, and curses and swears as needed. There was no end to the
singing and weeping, and the insistent drumming of musical exorcisms.
Handcarts clattered by constantly, as arguments and fistfights broke out
here and there. Cats meowed and dogs whined and both species fought
over mounds of garbage, rats scampered down the walls and through the

courtyards, and it was not rare for people to band up to kill a snake or scorpion. Flies, outnumbered only by lice, joined diners in their plates and drinkers in their mugs, frolicked around their eyes and buzzed by their mouths, on intimate terms with everyone.

As soon as a young man found that he possessed daring or brawn, he started interfering with peaceable people, attacking anyone minding their own business and imposing himself as a protector on a neighborhood somewhere in the alley. He would take protection money from working people, and live with nothing to do but be a bully. So you found gangsters like Qidra, al-Laithy, Abu Sari, Barakat and Hammouda. Zaqlut was another of these; he picked fights with one gangster after another until he had beaten them all and became the boss of the whole alley, and he made all them pay him protection money. Effendi, the overseer, saw that he needed someone like this to carry out his orders and keep away any trouble that loomed, so he kept him close by and paid him a salary from the estate income. Zaqlut took up residence in a house opposite the overseer's, and helped to strengthen his authority. When this happened, fights among the gangsters dropped off, since the biggest one of all did not like these rivalries whose outcome might be the strengthening of one of the lesser gangsters, which would threaten his own position. And so they found no outlet for their pent-up mischief but poor and peaceable citizens. How did our alley reach such a pitiful state?

Gabalawi promised Adham that the property would go to benefit his children. The houses with courtyards were put up, money was given out, and for a while people enjoyed a happy life. For a while after the father closed his gate and shut out the world, the overseer followed his good example, but then ambition stirred in his heart and he began to help himself to estate funds. At first he embezzled small amounts and reduced the wages he paid out, then closed his hand over all the money, reassured by the protection of the gangster he had bought. The people had no choice but to take up the most menial and despised jobs; their numbers exploded and their poverty increased, until they were sunk in squalor and misery. The strong turned to terrorizing others, the poor turned to begging, and everyone turned to drugs. They toiled and slaved in return for morsels of food, some of which the gangsters took, not with thanks but with a slap, a curse and an insult. Only the gangsters lived in comfort and luxury; above them was their boss and above everyone was the overseer; the people were crushed beneath all of them. If any unfortunate man was unable to pay his protection money, revenge was exacted against the whole neighborhood, and if he complained to the boss, he was beaten and turned over to the local gangster to be beaten again; if he dared to take his complaint to the estate overseer, he would end up getting beaten by the overseer, the alley boss and every neighborhood gangster in turn. This was the horrid state of affairs which I myself witnessed in this, our own era, a mirror image of what the storytellers describe of the distant past. The poets of the coffeehouses in every corner of our alley tell only of heroic eras, avoiding public mention of anything that would embarrass the powerful. They sing the praises of the estate overseer and the gangs, of justice that we do not enjoy, of mercy we do not experience, of dignity we do not see, of piety that seems not to exist and honesty we have never heard of. I often wonder why our ancestors stayed—why *we* stay—in this accursed alley, but the answer is easy. In the other alleys we would only find a life worse than what we endure here—assuming their gangsters did not kill us to pay back what our gangsters have done to them! The most incredible thing is that people envy us! Our neighbors in other alleys say, "What a blessed alley! They have a matchless inheritance, and gangs whose very names curdle your blood!" Of course, we get nothing from our estate but trouble, and nothing from our protectors but insults and torment. In spite of all that we are still here, patient in our cares. We look toward a future that will come we know not when, and point toward the mansion and say, "There is our venerable father," and we point out our gangsters and say, "These are our men; and God is master of all."

25

The patience of the Al Hamdan ran out, and waves of rebellion raged
through their neighborhood.

The Al Hamdan lived at the top of the alley near Effendi's house
and Zaqlut's, around the original site of Adham's hut. Their patriarch
was Hamdan, the owner of the Hamdan Coffeehouse, which was the
most beautiful in the whole alley; it stood halfway down Hamdan Alley, surrounded by houses with courtyards. Old Hamdan sat to the
right-hand side of the coffeehouse entrance in his gray cloak, an embroidered turban on his head, keeping a close eye on Abdoun, his
constantly scurrying waiter, and exchanging gossip with the customers.
The coffeehouse was narrow but long, extending back to the poet's
bench at the end, under an idealized color picture of Adham on his
deathbed, gazing at Gabalawi, who stood at the door of the hut.
Hamdan made a sign to the poet, who reached for his rebec and tuned
it; then, to the melodies of its strings, he began to extol the overseer,
beloved of Gabalawi, and Zaqlut, the finest of men; then he chanted
a passage from Gabalawi's life, before the birth of Adham. The sounds
of sipping coffee, tea and cinnamon brew rose with twisting smoke
from the water pipes to form a diaphanous cloud around the ceiling
lamp. Every eye was on the poet, and heads wagged in admiration
at the beauty of the narration or the piety of an exhortation. The
fluent and fabulous moments passed as quickly as passion, and as the
end came the poet was showered with cries of approval. It was at this
point that the Al Hamdan were stirred to the depths by a wave of
rebellion. Bleary-eyed Itris spoke from his seat in the middle of the
coffeehouse, commenting on the Gabalawi story they had heard:
"There was good in the world then—even Adham was never hungry
for a day."

An old woman named Tamar Henna appeared standing before the coffeehouse, lowering the basket of oranges from the top of her head, and spoke to bleary-eyed Itris: "God bless your lips, Itris, your words are as sugary as sweet oranges!"

"Go away, woman," old Hamdan scolded her. "Give us a break from your nonsense."

But Tamar Henna sat down on the ground close to the coffeehouse door and said, "What could be nicer than sitting beside you here, old Hamdan!" She pointed to her basket of oranges. "All day and half the night I've been tramping around and hawking those things, sir, all for just a few coins!"

The old man nearly answered her, but he caught sight of Dulma approaching, glowering, his face stained with dirt. He stared at him until he stood in front of him in the doorway, and then Dulma shouted, "God damn that bastard! Qidra—Qidra is the biggest bastard—I told him, be patient until tomorrow, and God will provide so I can pay you. And he threw me on the ground and crushed me until I nearly suffocated."

From the farthest end of the coffeehouse they heard the voice of Daabis: "Come here, Dulma. Sit beside me. God damn the bastards, this alley is ours, but they beat us in it as if we were dogs. Dulma can't pay Qidra, and Tamar Henna roams around peddling oranges even though she can't see an arm's length in front of her. And you, Hamdan, son of Adham, where is your courage?"

Dulma went inside.

"Son of Adham, where is your courage?" asked Tamar Henna.

"Go to hell, Tamar Henna, you're fifty years too late for a husband, why do you still bother these men?"

"Men? What men?" the woman asked.

Hamdan scowled, but Tamar Henna broke in before he could speak, as if in apology. "Look, just let me listen to the poet."

"Tell her the story of how the Al Hamdan were shamed in this alley," Daabis told the poet bitterly.

"Calm down, Uncle Daabis," the poet soothed him with a smile. "Take it easy, master!"

"Master!" snapped Daabis. "Our master beats and oppresses people, and kills them. You know who our master is!"

"Qidra or some other devil might turn up among us suddenly," said the poet uneasily.

"They're all children of Idris!" declared Daabis.

The poet spoke to him very softly: "Calm down, Uncle Daabis, before you get this place demolished on top of us!"

Daabis rose from where he sat and crossed the coffeehouse with long steps, then sat on the bench to Hamdan's right. He was about to speak when his voice was drowned out by the sudden racket of boys crowding like locusts in front of the coffeehouse and exchanging insults.

"Devils' children!" Daabis shouted at them. "Don't you have dens to creep into at night?"

But they ignored his shouts until he jumped up as if stung and swooped at them. They raced down the alley shouting "Hurrah!" as a chorus of women's voices rang out from the windows of the building across the street from the coffeehouse: "For God's sake, you scared those boys!" He waved his hand irritably and took his seat again.

"What is a man supposed to do? There's no rest, with these children, and gangsters, and that overseer!"

Everyone agreed with this. The Al Hamdan had lost their claim to the estate; the Al Hamdan lived in the dust of misery and degradation; the Al Hamdan were in the power of a gangster who was not even one of them—he was from one of the most disreputable neighborhoods. Qidra swaggered among them, slapping or demanding protection money from whomever he felt like; and their exhausted patience sent the waves of rebellion raging through their neighborhood.

Daabis turned to Hamdan. "Everyone agrees, Hamdan. We are all Al Hamdan, there are many of us, our lineage is well known, and we have as much right to the estate as the overseer himself."

"O God, may this night end well," murmured the poet.

Hamdan drew his cloak around him and raised his arched, bushy eyebrows. "We have said it and said it again: something is going to happen. I can smell it now."

Ali Fawanis raised his voice in greeting as he entered the coffeehouse, holding the edge of his galabiya, his gray skullcap tilted over his eyebrows, and quickly added, "Everyone is ready, and if money is needed they'll give it—even the beggars."

He squeezed in between Daabis and Hamdan, and called out for Abdoun, the coffee waiter. "Tea, no sugar!"

The poet harrumphed loudly to catch his attention, and Ali Fawanis smiled and reached into his breast pocket for a purse, which he opened, extracting a small wrapped item, which he tossed to the poet. He tapped Hamdan's leg questioningly.

"We are going to court," was Hamdan's answer.

"It's the only thing to do," said Tamar Henna.

"Think of the consequences," said the poet, unwrapping his gift.

"No shame is worse than the way we live now, and numbers are on our side. Effendi cannot ignore where we come from, or the fact that we're related to him, and to the estate owner too."

The poet gave Hamdan a meaningful look and said, "We've never been short of solutions."

"I have a great idea," said Hamdan, as if in answer to this.

Everyone's eyes turned to him.

"Let's go to the overseer."

"What a mighty step," said Abdoun, as he offered Ali Fawanis his tea. "Then we can start digging our graves."

"Listen to your future from your children!" laughed Tamar Henna.

"We have to go," said Hamdan resolutely, "and we will go together."

26

A crowd of Al Hamdan men and women gathered in front of the overseer's house, led by Hamdan, Daabis, Itris, Dulma, Ali Fawanis and the poet, Ridwan. It had been Ridwan's idea for Hamdan to go alone, thus putting to rest suspicions of insurrection and avoiding punishment for it, but Hamdan told him frankly that "killing me would be easy, but they could not kill all of the Al Hamdan." The crowd drew stares from everyone in the alley, especially their next-door neighbors, women's heads appeared in the windows, eyes peeped from below the baskets and trays being carried on people's heads and from behind handcarts, and crowds, old and young alike, asked one another what Hamdan's people wanted. Hamdan seized the brass door knocker and rapped at the gate, which opened a few moments later to reveal the gatekeeper's sour face and breezes laden with the scent of different types of jasmine. The gatekeeper looked irritably at the crowd.

"What do you want?"

"We would like a meeting with his excellency the overseer."

"All of you?"

"We are all equally worthy of meeting him."

"Wait here until I summon you in." He tried to close the gate but Daabis swiftly squeezed in, saying, "It's more polite to have us wait inside."

The others pushed in behind him like chicks behind their mother, among them Hamdan, in spite of his resentment of Daabis' impetuosity. The demonstration moved down the covered passage between the terrace and the garden.

"You have to get out of here!" shouted the gatekeeper.

"Guests aren't thrown out. Go and tell your master we're here."

The man's lips moved in protest but nothing came out; his sullen features shifted, and he turned and headed quickly indoors. Their eyes followed him until he disappeared behind the curtain drawn across the hall entrance, and then their eyes either remained on the curtain or roamed over the garden, the fountain surrounded by palm trees, the grape arbors set against the walls of the house and the jasmine climbing up the garden walls. They gazed around, overwhelmed and yet with senses dulled by worry, and soon resumed watching the curtain drawn across the hall entrance.

The curtain was pulled aside and Effendi himself came out, scowling. He took a few decisive, angry steps to the top of the stairs, and stood there. His angry face, his camel slippers and the long loop of worry beads in his right hand were all that could be seen of his securely cloaked person. He cast a disdainful look at the demonstration, then his gaze settled on Hamdan, who now spoke very courteously.

"A very good morning to the overseer!"

Effendi returned the greeting with a mere hand gesture, then asked, "Who are they?"

"Al Hamdan, Your Excellency."

"Who let them into my house?"

"This is their overseer's house," was Hamdan's subtle reply, "and so it is their house and their sanctuary."

Effendi's features did not soften. "You're trying to justify your rude behavior!"

"We are one family," said Daabis, exasperated by Hamdan's mildness. "We are all children of Adham and Umaima."

"That is history," said Effendi crossly. "I wish to God people knew who they were."

"We live in an agony of poverty and mistreatment," said Hamdan. "We all share the opinion that we should turn to you to relieve our agony."

Here Tamar Henna spoke up. "By your life, our life disgusts even the cockroaches."

"Most of us are beggars," said Daabis in a rising voice. "Our children are starving, and our faces are swollen from being slapped by gangsters. Does that befit the dignity of children of Gabalawi, inheritors of his property?"

Effendi's grip tightened on his worry beads. "What property?"

Hamdan tried to keep Daabis from speaking, but he plunged ahead with the obliviousness of a drunk. "The estate—don't get angry, sir, the great estate owned by everyone in our alley, by every one of us, and which includes every property in the surrounding desert. Gabalawi's estate, sir."

Rays of anger darted from Effendi's eyes. He shouted, "This is my father's and my grandfather's property and you have nothing to do with it! You spread fairy tales and you believe them, but you have no proof and no justification!"

Many of them, including Daabis and Tamar Henna, said, "Everyone knows that—"

"Everyone? So? If you spread stories among yourselves that my house belongs to one of you, is that reason for you to claim my house, you scum? An alley of nothing but drug addicts! Tell me when any of you have seen one penny of the income from the property!"

There was silence, then Hamdan answered. "Our ancestors used to get it."

"What's your proof?"

"They told us," Hamdan replied, "and we believe them."

"Lies and more lies!" shouted Effendi. "Show yourselves out of here before I throw you out."

"Tell us about the Ten Conditions," said Daabis purposefully.

"Why should I?" shouted Effendi. "Who are you? What do you have to do with them?"

"They are ours!"

At this point the voice of Lady Huda, the overseer's wife, rose behind the gate.

"Leave them and come in! Don't get hoarse arguing with them!"

"Help us reason together, my lady," said Tamar Henna.

Lady Huda's voice trembled with fury: "Highway robbery in broad daylight!"

"God forgive you, my lady," Tamar Henna replied a little resentfully, "the truth is known to our ancestor, who has closed himself up behind his gates."

"Gabalawi!" bellowed Daabis in a voice like thunder, his head upraised. "Come and see what has become of us! You have left us to the mercy of ruthless people!"

His voice echoed so strongly that some of them thought their ancestor might actually hear it from his mansion.

Then Effendi spoke in a voice that shook with anger. "Get out. Get out now!"

"Let's go," said Hamdan unhappily.

He turned from where he stood and went to the gate. They all followed him in silence, even Daabis, though he raised his head once again and cried out with the same power, "Gabalawi!"

27

Effendi strode into his hall, pale with fury, to find his wife standing there glowering.

"That was something," she said. "We haven't heard the last of it either. It will be the talk of the alley, and if we ignore it we will have no peace."

"Rabble—trash—and they want the estate!" sneered Effendi. "Since when can anyone know what his origins are, in an alley like a beehive?"

"Settle it once and for all. Arrange something with Zaqlut. Zaqlut gets his share of the estate income but does nothing in return—let him earn what he takes from us!"

Effendi stared at her for a long time, then asked, "And Gabal?"

"Gabal! He's our foster son—like my very own son," she reassured him. "Our house is all he knows of the world—he doesn't know the Al

Hamdan and they don't know him. Even if they did consider him one of them, they'd plead his case to us. I'm not worried about him. He'll come back from doing his rounds among the tenants and he'll attend the meeting."

Zaqlut came at the overseer's invitation. He was of medium height, bulky but with a strong physique, a ruddy, ugly face and scabby wounds on his neck and chin. They sat close to one another.

"I've heard some bad news," said Zaqlut.

"How quickly bad news gets around," said Huda irritably.

Effendi eyed Zaqlut slyly. "It hurts your prestige just as much as it hurts ours."

"It has been a long time since I've used my club or shed any blood," said Zaqlut in his voice as deep as the bellow of a bull.

"How deluded those Al Hamdan are," said Huda, smiling. "They've never had a strong man of their own, but even the vilest one of them thinks he's the master of the alley."

"Peddlers and beggars," spat Zaqlut. "No strong man will ever come from that cowardly trash."

"So what can we do, Zaqlut?" asked Effendi.

"I'll step on them—crush them like cockroaches."

Gabal, entering the hall, heard what Zaqlut said. His face was flushed after his rounds in the desert, and the vitality of youth enlivened his strong, slender body and his face with its frank features, especially his straight nose and large, intelligent eyes. He greeted those present politely and began to speak about the properties rented that day, but Lady Huda interrupted him.

"Sit down, Gabal, we've been waiting for you. There's something very important going on."

Gabal sat down, his eyes reflecting the gravity still visible in the lady's.

"I see that you can guess what's on our minds," she said.

"Everyone is talking about it out there," he said quietly.

The lady looked over at her husband and then shrieked, "Did you hear that? Everyone's waiting to see what we're going to do!"

Zaqlut's features grew even uglier. "Just a little fire a handful of dirt can smother. I can't wait to get started!"

"What do you say?" Huda asked Gabal.

"It's none of my business, my lady." He was looking at the floor to hide his anxiety.

"I want to know what you think!"

He thought a while, feeling Effendi's stabbing gaze, and Zaqlut's angry looks, then said, "My lady, I'm blessed in being your foster son, but I don't know what to say. I'm only one of the children of Hamdan!"

"Why do you mention Hamdan when you have no father or mother or other family among them?" said Huda sharply.

Effendi made a brief sound of scorn, something like a laugh, but did not speak.

It was clear from Gabal's face that he was in real pain, but he spoke. "My father and mother were from them. That's simply the truth."

"My son is disappointing me," observed Huda.

"God forbid—even Muqattam Mountain could never budge my loyalty to you, but denying facts doesn't change them."

His patience exhausted, Effendi stood up and spoke to Zaqlut. "Don't waste your time listening to this."

Zaqlut stood, smiling, and the lady spoke to him, looking aside at Gabal. "Don't overdo it, dear Zaqlut. We want to discipline them, not destroy them."

Zaqlut left the hall.

Effendi threw Gabal a look of rebuke. "So, Gabal, you're one of the Al Hamdan?" he asked mockingly.

Gabal took refuge in silence until Huda rescued him.

"His heart is with us, but it hurt him too much to deny his family in front of Zaqlut."

"They are miserable, my lady," conceded Gabal, "even though they are the aristocrats of the alley, if you consider their origins."

"There are no origins in that alley!" screeched Effendi.

"We are the children of Adham," said Gabal seriously, "and our grandfather is still alive—may God prolong his life!"

"Who can prove that he's his father's son?" asked Effendi. "He can say that every so often if he likes, but it should not be used to steal what belongs to others."

"We don't wish them any ill, on condition that they don't covet our wealth," said Huda.

Effendi wanted to end the conversation. He said to Gabal, "Get back to your work, and don't think of anything but that."

Gabal left the hall for the estate office in the garden reception area. He needed to enter some rental deals in the ledger and review the final monthly accounts, but he was too depressed. It was strange, but the Al Hamdan did not love him. He knew it; he remembered how coolly he was welcomed in the Hamdan Coffeehouse the few times he called there. Even so, it saddened him, the harm that was in store for them. It saddened him even more, the provocative behavior that enraged him. He wanted to keep the danger away from them, but was worried about angering the household that had taken him in, adopted and raised him. How would it have been for him had Lady Huda's affection not overtaken him? Twenty years ago the lady had seen a naked boy bathing in a ditch filled with rainwater; she took pleasure in watching him, and her heart—which barrenness had kept from enjoying the blessing of motherhood—warmed toward him. She sent someone to bring him, crying and afraid, in to her. She made inquiries about him and learned that he was an orphaned child cared for by a woman who sold chickens. The lady summoned the chicken seller and asked her to give the child up to her, and she welcomed the idea excitedly. And so Gabal grew up in the overseer's house, and under its roof he was blessed with the happiest family life of anyone in the alley. They sent him to school, he learned to read and write, and when he came of age Effendi turned over the management of the estate to him. Wherever the estate had holdings the people called him "Your Excellency," and respectful and admiring looks followed him wherever he went. Life seemed good, promising every wonderful thing, until the rebellion of the Al Hamdan. Gabal found that he was not one person, as he had imagined he was all his life; he was two people. One of them believed in loyalty to his mother and the other wondered bewilderedly, "What about the Al Hamdan?"

28

The rebec sounded to accompany the tale of Humam's death at Qadri's hand. All eyes turned toward Ridwan the poet with slightly uneasy attention. This was a night different from other nights, a night following a day of insurgency, and many of the Al Hamdan were wondering whether it would pass in peace. The alley was shrouded in darkness; even the stars were invisible behind the autumn clouds. There was no light other than what shone weakly from locked windows or the lamps on handcarts scattered through the alley. Corners echoed with the racket of boys who collected there like moths around the cart lamps, while Tamar Henna spread a piece of burlap in front of one of the Hamdan houses, singing:

> At the gate of our alley
> We have the finest coffee man.

Cats howled intermittently, rapt in sexual rivalries or quarreling over food supplies. The poet's voice rose poignantly in his narration: "Adham cried in Quadri's face, 'Where is your brother Humam?' " At that moment, Zaqlut appeared in the circle of light drawn on the ground by the coffeehouse lantern. He appeared suddenly, like part of the darkness made light, glowering, menacing, and terrifying. Evil shone in his eyes as his grip tightened on his fearsome club, and a dreadful, stony stare from his eye sockets fixed on the coffeehouse and its customers as if they were mere insects. The poet's words died in his mouth. Dulma and Itris sobered up instantly. Daabis and Ali Fawanis stopped whispering, and Abdoun stood still. Hamdan's hand tensed over the hose of the water pipe. There was a silence like death.

A few hurried movements ensued: customers who were not of the

Al Hamdan left quickly, and the local gangsters Qidra, Al-Laithy, Abu Sari, Barakat and Hammouda appeared and formed a wall behind Zaqlut. Word spread through the alley quickly, as if a house had collapsed. Windows were opened, children ran around, and in the grown-ups' hearts worry warred with gloating.

Hamdan was the first to break the silence. He stood as if in welcome and spoke. "Welcome to Zaqlut, protector of our alley. Please come in, all of you."

But Zaqlut ignored him as if he did not see or hear him. His eyes shone with cruelty, and he spoke harshly. "Who's in charge in this neighborhood?"

Hamdan answered, though the question was not directed at him. "Qidra."

Zaqlut turned to Qidra and asked mockingly, "Are you the protector of the Al Hamdan?"

A few steps brought Qidra's short, compact body closer. His face was a picture of provocation. "I am their protector against everyone—except you, sir."

Zaqlut smiled with a certain antagonism and said, "Was this alley of women the only territory you could find?" Then he shouted through the coffeehouse, "Women! Bastards! Don't you know who's in charge in this alley?"

"Zaqlut, sir, we have no problem with you," said Hamdan, pale.

"Shut up, you stupid old man. Now you're going to grovel for attacking your masters—the masters of all your people!"

"We didn't attack anyone," said Hamdan, sounding deeply worried, "we only brought a complaint to his excellency the overseer."

"Do you hear what this son of a whore is saying?" shouted Zaqlut. "Hamdan, you trash, have you forgotten what your mother used to do? I swear, not one of you is going unharmed into this alley until you've said, as loudly as you can, 'I am a woman's woman.' "

Immediately he raised his club and slammed it down on the table so that cups, glasses, plates, spoons, boxes of coffee beans, tea and sugar, cinnamon, ginger and tiles flew all over. Abdoun jumped backward, bumped into a table and fell down with it. Abruptly Zaqlut aimed a blow at Hamdan's face. Hamdan lost his balance and fell over to the side, smashing his water pipe. Again Zaqlut raised his club, shouting, "No sin will go unpunished, you sons of whores."

Daabis grabbed a chair and threw it at the great lantern, smashing it. Just as blackness engulfed the place, Zaqlut hit the old woman behind the table. Tamar Henna shouted, and the women of the Al Hamdan echoed it from their windows and doorways; it was as if the whole alley had become the throat of a dog being pelted by stones. Enraged, Zaqlut landed blows in every direction, striking people, chairs and even the walls. There were confused waves of screams, cries for help and wails, and bodies flew in every direction and collided with one another.

"Everyone is confined to his house!" shouted Zaqlut in a voice like thunder.

There followed the sound of retreating steps as everyone rushed to obey the order, whether they were of the Al Hamdan or not. Al-Laithy brought a lantern, whose light revealed Zaqlut and the gangsters around him in an empty alley in which nothing could be heard but women's shouts.

"Spare yourself the trouble, teacher of misfortunes," Barakat flattered him. "We can discipline these cockroaches."

"If you like," added Abu Sari, "we will grind the Al Hamdan into dirt for you to trample on your horse."

"If you order me to punish them," said Qidra, the protector of the Hamdan, "you would be giving me my greatest wish—serving you, sir."

"Good God, what an animal!" shrieked Tamar Henna from behind the door of a house.

"Tamar Henna," Zaqlut shouted back, "I defy any man of the Al Hamdan to count the men you've fornicated with!"

Tamar Henna answered but her last words were muffled by a hand over her mouth that prevented her from going on: "God is our witness, the Al Hamdan are the true—"

Zaqlut spoke to the gansters loudly because he wanted the Al Hamdan to hear. "No man of the Al Hamdan leaves his house without a beating."

"If you think you're a man, come on out!" Qidra shouted menacingly down the alley.

"And the women, sir?" asked Hammouda.

"Zaqlut deals with men, not women," was the sharp reply.

Day came, and no man of the Al Hamdan left his house. Each gangster sat before the coffeehouse in his territory, watching the street. Zaqlut passed through the alley every few hours, and the people outdid one another greeting, flattering and praising him with "A lion among men, protector man of our alley," "Good for you—you turned those Al Hamdan men into women!" and "Praise God, who humbled the arrogant Al Hamdan with your strong arm, Zaqlut!" And no one voiced the slightest word of complaint.

29

DOES OUR MISERY PLEASE YOU, GABALAWI? *wondered Gabal as he* lay on the ground under the rock where, the stories said, Qadri and Hind sought solitude and Humam was killed. He gazed into the dusk with eyes that no longer saw anything but ruined happiness. He was not the kind of person who likes seclusion because he has a great many problems, but recently he had felt an overpowering desire to be by himself. What was happening to the people of Hamdan convulsed his soul. Perhaps in this desert the voices that abused and tormented him would be stilled. Voices called, "Traitor to the Al Hamdan! Scum!" as he passed by, and voices from deep inside him cried, "A life lived at the expense of others will never be happy." The Al Hamdan were his people; his mother and father had been born into them and were buried among them. They were oppressed—and by such obscene oppression!— and their property had been usurped. Who was their oppressor? The giver of his own happiness, the man whose wife had plucked him out of the mud and raised him up high, with the mansion family. Everything about the alley was run according to the law of terror, so it was not strange that its finest people should be imprisoned in their homes. Our alley has never known one day of justice or peace. This has been its fate ever since Adham and Umaima were expelled from the mansion—do you know that, Gabalawi? It seems that the injustice will grow darker and more painful for as long as you are silent. How long will you be silent, Gabalawi? The men are prisoners in their houses and the women are exposed to every insult in the alley. I endure the disgrace in silence. And yet, strange to say, the people of our alley laugh! How can they laugh? They celebrate winners, any winner, and cheer any strong man, no matter who he is, and bow down before bullies' clubs—all this to conceal the terrible fear deep inside them. We eat humiliation like food in this alley. No one knows when it will be his turn for the club to come down on his head. He looked up at the sky and found it silent, serene and sleepy, framed by clouds, the last kite flapping away. No people were about, and the time had come for the insects to take over. Suddenly Gabal heard a coarse voice nearby, shouting, "Stop, you son of a whore." He awoke from his reverie and stood up, trying to remember where he had heard that voice, then he headed around Hind's Rock to the south and saw a man running away in terror, and another man running after him, almost catching up. He looked more closely and saw that the runner was Daabis and the pursuer was Qidra, the Al Hamdan area gangster, and immediately he knew what was happening. He kept watching the chase, which was coming nearer, with an anxious heart. Before long Qidra caught up to Daabis and grabbed him by the shoulder, and both men stopped running, panting from exertion.

"How dare you leave your room, you snake?" shouted Qidra, laboring for breath. "You won't get back there unharmed now."

"Let me go, Qidra," cried Daabis, protecting his head with his arms. "You run our alley—you're supposed to defend us."

Qidra shook him so hard that his turban flew off. "You son of a bitch," he shouted, "you know that I defend you against any creature but not Zaqlut."

Daabis' gaze strayed over to where Gabal stood, and when he saw and recognized him, he shouted out, "Help me, Gabal, help me. You're one of us more than you're one of them!"

"No one will save you from me, you bastard," Qidra threatened him furiously.

Gabal found himself moving toward them, until he stopped right beside them. "Be gentle with this man, Qidra," he said quietly.

Qidra glared at him coldly and answered, "I know what I have to do."

"Maybe he left his house for a good reason."

"He left it because it was his predestined fate!" He tightened his grasp on his shoulder until Daabis moaned audibly.

"Be gentle with him," said Gabal sharply. "Don't you see that he's older than you are, and weaker?"

Qidra released Daabis' shoulder and hit him on the back of the head so hard that he bent over, then kicked him in the back with his knee. Daabis collapsed on his face, and in no time Qidra was kneeling on him, punching him again and again and asking hatefully, "Weren't you listening to what Zaqlut said?"

The anger in Gabal's blood ignited and he shouted, "God damn you and Zaqlut. Leave him alone, you shameless man!"

Qidra stopped beating Daabis and looked up at Gabal, amazed. "What are you saying, Gabal! Weren't you there when his excellency the overseer ordered Zaqlut to discipline the Hamdan?"

"Leave him alone, you shameless man!" shouted Gabal, his anger rising.

"Don't think that your service in the overseer's house can protect you from me, if you want what's coming to you!" said Qidra in a voice trembling with rage.

Gabal flew at him like a man who had lost his mind, and kicked him over on his side, shouting, "Go back to your mother while she still has a son alive!"

Qidra jumped to his feet and snatched his club from the ground, then raised it nimbly, but Gabal, moving more quickly, punched him in the stomach so hard that he reeled back in pain. Gabal seized this opportunity to grab the club from his hand, and he stood looking warily at him. Qidra took two steps back, then stooped quickly and picked up a stone, but before he could throw it the club came down on his head and he screamed, turning where he stood, then fell on his face, blood spurting from his forehead. Night was falling, and Gabal looked around but saw no one but Daabis, who had stood up and was dusting off his clothes and palpating the injured parts of his body. He then came over to Gabal.

"Thank you, Gabal. You're a great brother," he said softly.

Gabal did not answer, but leaned over Qidra and turned him on his back. "He's out cold," he murmured.

Daabis now leaned over him, and spat on his face. Gabal pushed him completely away and leaned over him again. He began to shake him gently, but there seemed no hope of waking him.

"What's wrong with him?" he asked.

Daabis crouched over him and put his ear to his chest, then put his face close to Qidra's. He lit a match, then stood up and whispered, "He's dead."

Gabal's body went all gooseflesh. "Liar!" he said.

"Dead, dead, by your life!"

"Oh, my God."

Daabis took it lightly. "Think how many people he's beaten—how many he's killed. Let him go to the garbage heap!"

"But I have never hit anyone or killed anyone," said Gabal sadly, as if talking to himself.

"You were only defending yourself."

"But I didn't intend to kill him, and I didn't want to."

"You are strong, Gabal," said Daabis seriously. "You have nothing to fear from them. You could become our protector if you wanted."

Gabal clutched his forehead in his hand and cried, "Oh, God, no— am I a killer from my first blow?"

"Be sensible. Let's bury him before all hell breaks loose."

"Hell is going to break loose whether we bury him or not."

"I'm not sorry. Now it's the others' turn. Help me hide this animal."

Daabis picked up the club and began to dig in the earth not far from the spot where Qadri had dug long ago. A moment later, with a heavy heart, Gabal joined him. They worked silently until Daabis spoke, to ease the melancholy in Gabal's thoughts.

"Don't be sad. In our alley, killing is as common as eating dates."

"I never wanted to be a killer," Gabal sighed. "Good Lord, I never knew I could get so angry!"

When they had finished digging, Daabis got up, wiped his brow with his sleeve and blew his nose to clear out the smell of dirt that filled his nostrils.

"This hole is big enough for that bastard and the rest of them too," he sneered.

"Respect the dead," said Gabal, sounding troubled. "We're all going to die."

"When they respect us in life, we can respect them in death."

They lifted up the corpse and carried it to the hole, and Gabal laid the club at its side, then they covered it with dirt.

When Gabal lifted his head he saw that night had hidden the world and everything in it, and he sighed deeply, and stifled the urge to weep.

30

Where is Qidra?

This is what Zaqlut and the other gangsters were asking. They all wondered where their friend was—he had vanished from sight just as the men of Al Hamdan had vanished from the alley. Qidra's house was in the next neighborhood over from the Al Hamdan's. He was a bachelor and spent his nights out, and never came back home until dawn or later. It was not uncommon for him to stay away from his house for a night or two, but he had never been away for a whole week with no one knowing where he was, especially in these days of siege when he was expected to be alert and watchful as never before. They had doubts about the Al

Hamdan, and it was decided to search their houses, which were attacked by the gangsters led by Zaqlut and carefully searched from the cellars to the roofs. They dug up the length and breadth of the courtyards, insulted the men of the Al Hamdan in every possible way—with slapping, kicking and spitting on them—but uncovered nothing suspicious. They split up to go all around the desert questioning people, but no one was able to give them any helpful guidance. Qidra was now the main topic as the hashish pipe was passed in the meeting place by the grape arbor in Zaqlut's garden. Darkness swathed the garden except for the wan light of a small standing lamp set just a few inches from the brazier to light Barakat's work as he cut the hashish and flattened out the pieces. He stoked the coals and pressed them into the top of the pipe to keep it going. The lamp shook in the current of breeze and its dancing light was reflected on the stolid faces of Zaqlut, Hammouda, al-Laithy and Abu Sari, showing heavy-lidded eyes whose distracted gazes held dark intentions. The croaking of frogs sounded like muted cries for help in the calm of the night. Barakat passed the hashish pipe to al-Laithy, who passed it to Zaqlut.

"Where has the man gone? It's as if the earth swallowed him up."

Zaqlut drew in a deep breath and dug into the hollow pipe with his index finger, then exhaled a blast of thick smoke.

"The earth did swallow up Qidra. He's been lying inside it for a week."

They looked at him worriedly, all except for Barakat, who was absorbed in what he was doing.

"No gangster disappears without a reason," Zaqlut went on, "and I know when I smell death."

After a coughing fit that bent him double as wind bends a blade of grass, Abu Sari asked, "Who killed him, sir?"

"Think! Who would it be but one of the men of Al Hamdan?"

"But they can't leave their houses, and we searched them."

Zaqlut struck the side of his cushion with his fist and asked, "What do the other people in the alley say?"

"In my neighborhood," said Hammouda, "they think that the Al Hamdan have something to do with Qidra's disappearance."

"Pay attention, you idiots, as long as the people think that Qidra's killer was one of the Al Hamdan, we have to think the same thing."

"What if the killer was from Atuf?"

"Even if he was from Kafr al-Zaghari, we aren't as concerned with punishing the killer as we are with frightening the others."

"Wonderful!" exclaimed Abu Sari.

Al-Laithy emptied the brazier and returned the pipe to Barakat and said, "God help the Al Hamdan."

Their dry chuckles mingled with the croaking of the frogs, and their heads shook threateningly from side to side. A sudden strong breeze blew, followed by the rattling of dry leaves. Hammouda slapped his hands together.

"It's no longer a question of trouble between the Al Hamdan and the overseer—it's a question of our honor."

Again Zaqlut struck his cushion with his fist.

"None of us has ever been killed by anyone in his alley." His features hardened in such fury that his companions grew afraid of him and were careful to make no sound or movement that might turn his fury on them. Silence fell, in which only the gurgle of the hashish pipe, a cough or cautious clearing of a throat could be heard.

"Suppose Qidra comes back unexpectedly?" Barakat asked.

"I'll shave myself clean, you girlish little hash-head," sneered Zaqlut.

Barakat was the first to laugh, then they all fell silent again. In their mind's eye they saw the massacre: clubs crushing heads, blood flowing until it dyed the ground, voices screaming from windows and roofs, the mounting death rattle of dozens of men. Immersed in their violent desires, they exhanged cruel looks. They cared nothing for Qidra himself; none of them had liked him. In fact, none of them liked any of the others, but they were united by the common desire to terrorize, and to put down sedition.

"What next?" asked al-Laithy.

"I have to go back to the overseer as we pledged," said Zaqlut.

31

"Your Excellency," said Zaqlut, *"the Al Hamdan have killed their* protector, Qidra." He was watching the overseer, but at the same time he could see Lady Huda to his right and Gabal to her right.

Somehow the news did not come as a surprise to Effendi.

"I have heard reports of his disappearance. Have you really given up hope of finding him?"

The morning light pouring through the door of the hall redoubled the hideousness of Zaqlut's face as he said, "He will not be found. I am an expert in these little schemes."

Huda noticed that Gabal's gaze was fixed on the wall across from him, and said nervously, "If it's true that he's been killed, that is dangerous."

The grip of Zaqlut's folded hands tightened. "And it calls for a terrible punishment, or we are finished," he said.

"He's a symbol of our dignity," said Effendi, playing with his string of prayer beads.

"He's a symbol of the whole estate!" said Zaqlut meaningfully.

"Maybe it's just a story—maybe this crime didn't take place!" Gabal said, breaking his silence.

Rage ignited in Zaqlut's breast at the sound of Gabal's voice. "We must not waste our time with talk."

"Show proof of his murder."

"No one of the people of our alley would disappear this way unless he had been killed," said Effendi in a tone of voice that affected power in order to hide the anxieties behind it.

The sweet breezes of autumn could not soften the atmosphere of bloody intentions.

"This crime cries out to us in a voice that will be heard in the other alleys—what's all this talk but a waste of time!"

"The men of the Al Hamdan are imprisoned in their houses," Gabal insisted.

Zaqlut's voice laughed, but not his face. "A nice puzzle!" he said mockingly. He relaxed in his seat and menaced Gabal with a piercing look. "All you care about is exonerating your people."

Gabal made a valiant effort to stifle his anger, but his voice had an edge to it as he said, "What I care about is the truth. You attack people for the most trivial reasons, sometimes for no reason at all, and right now all you care about is getting permission to stage a massacre of innocent people."

"Your people are criminals," said Zaqlut. Hatred shone in his eyes. "They murdered Qidra while he was defending the estate!"

"Sir overseer," said Gabal, turning to Effendi, "do not let this man quench his bloody thirst."

"If we lose our dignity, we will lose our lives," said Effendi.

"Do you want us buried alive in our alley?" Huda asked, looking at Gabal. "You are forgetting the people who have made you what you are, but you remember the criminals."

The wave of rage in Gabal's breast rose until it unsettled his restraint, and he shouted, "They are not criminals, but our alley is full of criminals!"

Huda's hand clutched the edge of her blue shawl. Effendi's nostrils flared and he turned sallow.

Zaqlut, encouraged, spoke out in hateful scorn: "You have an excuse for defending the criminals, as long as you're one of them!"

"It's incredible—you sneering about criminals, when you're the king of crime in our alley."

Zaqlut surged out of his seat, his face dark with anger. "If it weren't for your status among the people of this house, I'd tear you into pieces right now!"

"You're out of your mind, Zaqlut!" said Gabal in a tone of frightening calm, which, however, disclosed his true feeling.

"How dare you two talk like this in my presence!" shouted Effendi.

"I'm rough with him to uphold your dignity," said Zaqlut malevolently.

Effendi's fingers nearly broke the string of beads. "I forbid you to defend the Al Hamdan," he snapped at Gabal.

"This man is inventing lies about them for his own evil reasons."

"Let me judge that for myself!"

There was a silence. From the garden came the twittering of birds, and from the alley a burst of loud cheers accompanied by filthy curses. Zaqlut smiled and said, "Does his excellency the overseer give me permission to discipline the criminals?"

Gabal, convinced that the fateful moment had come, turned to the lady and said despairingly, "My lady, I will be compelled to join my people in their prison to share their fate."

"Oh, all my hopes!" cried Huda, visibly shaken.

Gabal was so upset that he bowed his head, but a sharp feeling made him look over at Zaqlut, whose lips were curled in a hateful, gloating smile. "I have no choice," he said miserably. "I will never forget your generosity as long as I live."

Effendi stared harshly at him.

"I must know—are you with us or against us?"

Feeling that his present life was finally at an end, Gabal spoke sadly: "What am I but the foster son of your kindness? I can never be against you, but I would be ashamed to leave my people to their ruin while I enjoy the grace of your protection."

Huda was fidgeting with anxiety at this crisis that threatened her motherhood. She said, "Dear Zaqlut, we will postpone this discussion to another time."

Zaqlut scowled in such pain that a mule's hoof might have struck his face. He shifted his gaze between Effendi and his wife and stammered, "I don't know what will happen in the alley tomorrow!"

"Answer me, Gabal," said Effendi, trying to avoid looking at Huda. "Are you with us or against us?" The rage within him rose and filled his head, and he screamed without waiting for an answer, "Either stay with us as one of us or you go back to your people!"

Stirred by the effect these words had on Zaqlut's face, Gabal said determinedly, "Sir, you are throwing me out, and I will go."

"Gabal!" came Huda's tormented scream.

"This is the man his mother gave birth to," said Zaqlut mockingly.

Unable to sit any longer, Gabal stood and walked firmly toward the hall door. Huda got up, but Effendi put out his arm to stop her. Gabal was gone. Outside, the wind blew, stirring the curtains and making the window shutters flap. The hall was filled with tension and gloom.

"We must act," said Zaqlut serenely.

"No," said Huda, with the nervousness and persistence that warned of her obstinacy. "For now the siege is enough. And beware of harming Gabal!"

Zaqlut kept his temper; he could not be provoked after having scored this triumph. He raised questioning eyes to the overseer.

Effendi looked as though he were sucking a lemon when he said, "We'll talk about it later."

32

Gabal cast a farewell look at the garden and reception hall and recalled the tragedy of Adham, retold every night to the accompaniment of the rebec, and walked to the gate. The gatekeeper stood up and asked, "What brings you out again, sir?"

"I am leaving and I'll never be back, Hassanain," said Gabal agitatedly.

The man's jaw dropped and he stared at him for a confused moment, then mumbled, "Because of the Al Hamdan?"

Gabal lowered his head silently.

"Who could believe that?" asked the gatekeeper. "How could Lady Huda allow it? O God in Heaven! How will you live, my boy?"

Gabal crossed the threshold of the gate, looking over at the alley jammed with people, animals and garbage. "The same way the people of our alley live," he answered.

"You were not born for that."

Gabal smiled a little distractedly, and said, "Only chance saved me from it."

He walked away from the house and the gatekeeper's voice anxiously warning him to beware the gangsters' anger.

The alley stretched before his eyes with its dust, pack animals, cats, boys and animal dens, and he realized the scale of the upheaval in his life; the troubles that awaited him; the ease he had lost. But his anger eclipsed his pain, and he seemed not to care about the flowers, birds and compassionate motherhood.

Hammouda appeared in his path and spoke with smooth insolence. "I hope you'll help us punish the Al Hamdan!"

He ignored him and headed for a certain large house in Hamdan's neighborhood and knocked. Hammouda followed him and asked in surprised disapproval, "What do you want?"

"I'm going back to my people," he answered quietly.

Astonishment narrowed Hammouda's eyes; he did not seem to believe what he had heard.

Zaqlut saw them as he was on his way home from the overseer's house. "Let him go in," he shouted at Hammouda. "If he comes out again, bury him alive."

Hammouda's astonishment left him and a stupid smirk spread across his face. Gabal kept knocking until windows opened in the house and in the neighbors' houses and heads popped out, including those of Hamdan, Itris, Dulma, Ali Fawanis, Abdoun, Ridwan the poet and Tamar Henna.

"What does the aristocrat want?" sneered Dulma.

"With us or against us?" asked Hamdan.

"They threw him out, so he's come back to his filthy roots," shouted Hammouda.

"Did they really throw you out?" asked Hamdan, moved.

"Open the door, Uncle Hamdan," said Gabal quietly.

Tamar Henna trilled her shrill joy and shouted, "Your father was a good man, and your mother was an honorable woman."

"Lucky you—recommendations from a slut," laughed Hammouda.

"Not as much as your mother, with her famous nights at the Sultan Baths!" shrieked Tamar Henna angrily. She was quick to close her window, and the stone that flew from Hammouda's hand struck the outer shutter with a report that made the boys on the street corners cheer.

The door of the house opened and Gabal entered its damp air and strange smell. His people welcomed him with hugs and a clamor of loving words, but the welcome was cut short by a loud fight at the far end of the courtyard. Gabal looked and saw Daabis arguing fiercely and struggling with a man named Kaabalha.

He went over to them and pushed himself between them and spoke sharply. "You argue with each other while they imprison us in our houses!"

"He stole a sweet potato from a pot on my windowsill," said Daabis, breathing heavily.

"Did you see me take it?" shouted Kaabalha. "Shame on you, Daabis!"

"Show mercy to one another so that Heaven will show mercy to us!" shouted Gabal angrily.

"My sweet potato is in his belly—I'll pull it out with my hand!" Daabis insisted.

"I swear to God, I have not tasted a sweet potato in a week," said Kaabalha, adjusting his cap on his head.

"You are the only thief in this building."

"Don't condemn someone without evidence the way Zaqlut did with you," said Gabal.

"I'm going to punish this son of a whore," shouted Daabis.

"Daabis, son of a radish seller!" Kaabalha shouted back.

Daabis flew at Kaabalha and punched him. Kaabalha stumbled, blood flowing from his forehead, and Daabis hit him again and again, ignoring the protestations of the bystanders, until Gabal lost his temper, intervened and seized him tightly by the neck.

Daabis tried futilely to free himself from Gabal's grip. "Do you want to kill me the way you killed Qidra?" he gasped.

Gabal pushed him violently and he fell against the wall and glared at Gabal, enraged. The men looked from Gabal to Daabis and back again, wondering if Gabal had really killed Qidra. Dulma hugged him and Itris shouted, "God bless you—you prince of the Al Hamdan!"

"I only killed him to defend you!" Gabal told Daabis bitterly.

"But you loved doing it," said Daabis softly.

"You are ungrateful, Daabis. For shame!" shouted Dulma. He pulled Gabal by the arm. "You'll be my guest in my apartment, come, leader of the Al Hamdan!"

Gabal gave in to Dulma's grasp, but felt that a bottomless abyss was opening under his feet this day.

"Is there no way to escape?" he whispered in Dulma's ear as they walked together.

"Gabal, are you afraid someone will betray you to our enemies?"

"Daabis is an imbecile."

"Yes, but he's not that low!"

"I'm afraid that their accusation against you will be strengthened because of me!"

"I'll show you the escape route if you want it, but where would you go?"

"The desert is wider than anyone knows."

33

Gabal was able to escape only as the night was nearly over. He moved from roof to roof in the peace of the night, and while sleep was still soothing sleepers' eyelids, he found his way to Gamaliya. In spite of the intense blackness he went on to al-Darasa, then turned toward the desert, headed for Hind and Qadri's rock. By the time he reached it, by the faint starlight, he could not hold off sleep any longer, after so much weariness and wakefulness. He threw himself onto the sand, wrapped up in his cloak, and slept. He opened his eyes with the first rays of sun that touched the top of the rock, and got up immediately in order to reach the mountain before anyone happened through the desert. But before he set off, his eye was drawn to the spot where he had buried Qidra. His arms and legs trembled as he looked at it. His mouth grew dry, then he fled, very upset. All he had done was kill a criminal, but he ran from the grave like a fugitive. He said to himself, "We were not born to kill, but we can no longer count our dead!" He marveled to himself at how he had found no place to sleep but the place where he had buried his victim! He felt his urge to flee mounting; he would have to bid farewell forever both to those he loved and to those he hated: his mother, Hamdan and the gangsters. He reached the foot of Muqattam, his soul overflowing with grief and homesickness, but he kept on, moving south, until he reached Muqattam Marketplace in midmorning. He took a long look at the desert behind him and said, relieved, "Now at least there is some distance between us." He looked closely at Muqattam Market-place, that small clearing surrounded on all sides by alleys, whose walls rang with an uproar in which the voices of men and the braying of donkeys intermingled. A saint's feast day seemed to be in progress, to judge from the crowds in the square, the peddlers, lunatics, dervishes and entertainers, even though the real action of the feast would not start until sundown. His eyes looked over the surging waves of people, and he saw, at the edge of the desert, a hut made of sheet metal surrounded by wooden seats. Despite its wretchedness it seemed to be the most popular coffeehouse in the marketplace: it was full of customers. He made for an empty chair and sat down, his body desperately craving rest. The proprietor came over to him, intrigued by his unusual appearance among the others: he wore a fine cloak, a high turban and expensive red leather shoes. He ordered a glass of tea and sat back to watch the people. Before long he heard a rising noise from the public pump, and saw people crowding around it to fill their vessels with water. The jam was like a violent riot complete with victims. The shouting grew louder and people were cursing, then there were sharp, high-pitched screams from the center, from two girls trapped in the heart of the struggle. They began to retreat to save themselves, and extricated themselves from the battle with empty buckets. Their bright yellow dresses draped their bodies from the neck to the heels; only their radiantly youthful faces were exposed. His eyes took in the shorter of the two but did not linger, then focused on the other, with the dark eyes, and stayed there. They walked to an empty spot near his seat, and he saw a family resemblance in their features, though the one that had caught his eye was more beautiful. Elated, Gabal said to himself, "What amazing features—I never saw anyone like this in our alley." The girls stood, rearranging their hair and putting their kerchiefs on, then set down the buckets upside down and sat on them.

"How are we going to fill the buckets in that crowd?" complained the shorter of the two.

"This feast—God help us! Father is waiting and getting mad," said the charming one.

Gabal joined the conversation without a second thought. "Why didn't he come himself to fill the buckets?"

They turned to him as if in protest, but his good appearance had a soothing effect, and his girl said only, "What is it to you? Did we complain to you?"

Delighted to hear her speak, Gabal apologized. "I just wanted to say that it would be easier for a man to deal with holiday crowds!"

"It's our job; he has a harder job."

"What does your father do?" he asked, smiling.

"None of your business."

Gabal got up, paying no attention to the staring eyes around him, and when he was standing before them he said, "I will fill the buckets for you."

"We don't need you," said the charming one, turning her face away.

"Do it, and thank you," said the short one daringly. She stood up and pulled the other girl up. Gabal took the buckets by the handles and moved his strong body through the throng, bumping into men and being pushed until he reached the pump, behind which the water seller sat at his wooden stand. He gave him two coins, filled the buckets and brought them to where the two girls stood. He was disturbed to see that they were arguing with some boys who had been harassing them, and he set down the buckets. He turned menacingly to the boys. One of them began to throw a punch at him but Gabal knocked him down with a blow in the chest, so the others came to attack him as a group, swearing at him.

Suddenly a strange voice bellowed at them, "Get out, you ugly little creeps."

Everyone looked at this short, compact middle-aged man with his bright eyes, whose galabiya was belted at the waist. "Balqiti, sir," called the boys, ashamed, and ran off, looking crossly at Gabal. The girls flocked to the man and the short one said, "Today it was hard because of the holiday, and those brats."

"When you were late, I remembered the festival," Balqiti answered her, looking Gabal over at the same time. "So I got here just in time." He turned to Gabal. "You are a good man—how rare they are these days!"

"It was nothing," said Gabal shyly, "just a little help—no thanks are in order."

Meanwhile the girls had taken the buckets and silently left the place. Gabal yearned for his eyes to feast on their beauty, but did not dare withdraw them from Balqiti's bright gaze. He imagined that this man could see into his depths, and was afraid that he could read his desires, but Balqiti said, "You chased those evil boys away. Men like you deserve respect. How dare those boys harass Balqiti's daughters? Liquor! Didn't you notice that they were drunk?"

Gabal shook his head.

"I can smell like a genie! Let it pass. Do you know me?"

"No, sir, I do not have that honor."

"Obviously you aren't from around here." This was said self-assuredly.

"That's right."

"I am Balqiti the snake charmer."

Gabal's face lit up with sudden remembrance. "This is indeed a pleasure. You are well known in our alley."

"What alley is that?"

"Gabalawi Alley."

Balqiti's narrow white eyebrows arched. "I am pleased and honored," he said melodiously. "Is there anyone who does not know of Gabalawi, owner of the estate? Or that Zaqlut! Have you come for the saint's day, sir?"

"Gabal—please." Then he added cunningly, "I've come to look for a new place to live."

"You've left your alley?"

"Yes."

Balqiti looked at him more closely. "Wherever there are gangsters there are emigrants! But tell me—did you kill a man or a woman?"

Gabal's heart almost stopped, but he said in a strong voice, "Your jokes aren't as charming as you are!"

Balqiti's ruined old mouth emitted a laugh. "You aren't one of the common mob the gangsters toy with. You aren't a thief. Someone like you leaves his alley only if it's murder."

"I told you—" Gabal began sternly but awkwardly.

"Sir," Balqiti interrupted, "I don't mind if you're a killer, especially after you've proved you decency to me. There's not a man here who hasn't stolen or plundered or killed, and just so that you can trust in the truth of what I say, I would like to invite you for a cup of coffee and a few puffs at my house!"

"I would love it. I would be honored," said Gabal, his hopes rekindled.

They walked side by side through the marketplace toward an alley up ahead, and when they had left the crowds behind them Balqiti asked him, "Did you want to see anyone special here?"

"I don't know anyone."

"Or anyplace to stay?"

"Or anyplace to stay."

"Be my guest, if you wish, until you find someplace to stay," said Balqiti expansively.

"You are so kind, Balqiti, sir," said Gabal, his heart dancing with joy.

"It's nothing to marvel at," the man laughed. "In my house I have snakes and serpents—what problem could a man be? Does this frighten you? I'm a snake charmer, and in my home you will learn how to get used to snakes."

They crossed the alley for the open desert. At the beginning of the desert Gabal saw a small stone house set far from the alley. It was unpainted but was new compared with such a tumbledown alley. Balqiti pointed to it proudly. "The house of Balqiti the snake charmer!"

34

"I chose this isolated spot for my house," Balqiti told him when they reached the house, "because people think a snake charmer is just a big snake himself!"

They entered a good-sized hall together. It led to a locked room at the end, flanked by two more closed doors. Balqiti pointed to the door facing the entrance and continued: "That's where I keep my work tools, the live ones and the other kind. Don't be afraid of anything—the door is strong and locked, and I promise you that the snakes are easier to live with than a lot of people. The ones you fled from, for example." His ruined mouth emitted a laugh. "People are frightened of snakes—even gangsters are frightened of them, but I owe them my livelihood. Thanks to them I built this house!" He pointed to the right-hand door. "That's where my two daughters sleep. Their mother died a long time ago, leaving me in old age, unfit to remarry." He pointed to the door on the left. "That's where we will sleep."

They heard the short girl's voice calling from a side stairway leading to the roof: "Shafiqa, help me with this washing. Don't stand there like a stone."

"Sayida!" called Balqiti. "Your voice will upset the snakes. And you, Shafiqa, don't stand there like a stone."

Her name was Shafiqa! What a sweet girl! Her unfriendliness hadn't hurt much. That wordless thanks in her black eyes. Who would tell her that he had accepted this perilous hospitality only for those eyes?

Balqiti pushed the left-hand door and held it open for Gabal, then followed him in and reclosed it. Leading Gabal by the arm, the man walked to a couch that ran the length of the right-hand wall of the small room, and they sat down together. With one look Gabal sized up the room. He saw a bed across the room, covered with a brown blanket, and on the floor between the bed and the couch a decorated mat and in its center a copper platter so stained that it had lost its color. In it rested a pyramidal brazier of ashes, a pipe lying beside it, and along the surface of its rim a skewer, pincers and a handful of dry honeyed tobacco. From the one open window he could see only desert, the colorless sky and a towering wall of Muqattam in the distance. Through it, amid the dead silence, the shout of a shepherdess sounded and a soft wind blew in, charged with the heat of the blazing sun. Balqiti was studying him to the point where it was irritating, and he considered diverting his attention by starting a conversation, but then the ceiling above them shook from footsteps on the roof, and his heart bounded. Instantly he imagined her feet, and his heart was filled with a yearning that this house should be happy, even should its snakes get loose. He said to himself, "This man might assassinate me and bury me in the desert, just as I buried Qidra, and my girl would never know that I was her victim."

Balqiti's voice brought him back: "Do you have work?"

"I'll find work, any work," he answered, remembering the last coins he had in his pocket.

"Perhaps you aren't in urgent need of work?"

This question made him a little uncomfortable. "Well, I'd be better off looking for work sooner rather than later!"

"You have a fighter's body!"

"But I hate violence."

Balqiti laughed and asked, "What work did you do in your alley?"

Gabal hesitated before saying, "I was managing the estate."

"Oh, how terrible—how did you lose such a good job?"

"Bad luck."

"Did you have your eye on some lady?"

"God forbid, old man."

"You are very careful, but you'll get used to me quickly and then share all your secrets."

"God willing."

"Do you have money?"

His panic returned, but he stifled it and said innocently, "I have a little, but I still have to look for work."

Balqiti winked. "You are as sharp as a devil. Do you know, you'd make a good snake charmer. Perhaps we could work together. Don't be surprised. I'm an old man in need of an assistant."

He did not take this suggestion seriously, but was moved by a profound desire to strengthen his ties to Balqiti. He was about to speak but the other man spoke first.

"We can take our time thinking about that. For right now——" He got up, leaned over and lifted the brazier, then took it outside to light it.

Before midafternoon the two men went out together. Balqiti wandered as he generally did while Gabal went to the marketplace to look around and to shop. He returned at evening to the desert and headed for the isolated house, guided by the glow from his window.

As he neared the house his ear caught angry voices arguing and he could not help eavesdropping. He heard Sayida say, "If it's true what you're saying, Father, he has committed a crime, and we can't face those alley gangsters."

"He doesn't look like a criminal," said Shafiqa.

"How well have you gotten to know him, snake girl?" said Balqiti with pronounced sarcasm.

"Why did he leave his good job?" asked Sayida.

"There's nothing unusual in a man leaving an alley so famous for its gangsters!"

"Since when do you have this gift for knowing the unknown?" asked Sayida pertly.

"Living with snakes has made me beget two serpertns," sighed Balqiti.

"You're letting him stay here, Father, without knowing anything about him?"

"I do know things about him, and I'll find out everything else. I have two eyes to depend upon in case of need. I invited him here because I was impressed with his decency, and I have no reason to change my mind."

He would not have hesitated to leave if things had been different. Hadn't he left his privileged life without a second thought? But he would give in to the power that drew him to this house. His heart bounded with intoxication at the sound of the voice defending him; a comforting voice that dispelled the lonesome night and the desert, and made the crescent moon floating over the mountain smile in the darkness like someone bringing good news. He waited in the darkness, then coughed, went up to the door and knocked. The door opened, revealing Balqiti's face, reflecting light from the lamp he held in his hand. The two men went to their room, and Gabal sat down after leaving on the copper platter a package he had brought. Balqiti looked at it questioningly.

"Dates, cheese, halva and hot falafel," said Gabal.

Balqiti smiled and pointed first at the pipe, then at the package, saying, "The best nights come from this and that." He clapped Gabal warmly on the shoulder. "Isn't that right, estate boy?"

Gabal's heart contracted in spite of himself. His imagination was overcome by images of the lady who had taken him in, the garden—its music, jasmine arbors, birds and rushing streams—the security, peace and tender dreams of that lost world of grace, until life almost seemed rotten. Then a wave swept away his despairing memories and he felt secure, thinking of this friendly, sweet girl, of the magic power that had drawn him to a house with a den of snakes. He said with an enthusiasm that surprised him, like the flicker of a lantern blown by a gust of wind, "What a nice life you have here."

35

Sleep did not come to him until shortly before dawn—he was
tormented by fear. Her specter visited him in a vision of fears as jasmine
leaves on dry grass crawling with insects. He was seized by illusions bred
by the shadows of this strange house. He told himself in the dark, "What
are you but a stranger in a house of snakes, stalked by a crime, your heart
shaken by love." If he were left alone, all he would want would be peace
and quiet. He was not afraid of the snakes as much as he was afraid of
treachery from the man whose snores rose and fell from his bed. And
how did he know that those snores were real? He did not trust anything
anymore. Even Daabis, who owed him his life, would broadcast his
secret folly; Zaqlut would be enraged; his mother would weep, and the
whole miserable alley would be in flames. The love that had drawn him
to this house, to the room of his companion, the snake tamer—how did
he know he would live long enough to give his feelings a voice? Thus
sleep did not come to him until shortly before dawn—he was tormented
by fear.

His heavy eyelids opened when morning light shone through the
window. He saw Balqiti sitting bent over on his bed, rubbing his legs
under the covers with his skinny hands. He smiled with pleasure despite
the familiar giddiness in his head from lack of sleep. He cursed the
visions that had nested in his head in the dark, and scattered in the light
like bats. Weren't they visions appropriate for a killer's dark mind? Yes,
our noble family has had murder in its blood since the very beginning.
He heard Balqiti yawn loudly in a voice as undulating as a charmed
snake, but then his chest shook with a long, hacking fit of coughing until
Gabal thought his eyes would pop out. When the coughing fit passed,
he emitted a deep moan.

"Good morning," said Gabal. He sat on the couch and Balqiti turned to him, his face still red from the coughing.

"Good morning, Gabal, sir, who barely slept last night!"

"Do I look it?"

"No, but you tossed and turned in the dark, and turned your head toward me as if you were afraid!"

You snake! Only be a nonpoisonous snake, for the sake of her dark eyes.

"The truth is, it was sleeping in an unfamiliar place that kept me up."

"You couldn't sleep for one reason," laughed Balqiti, "which is, you were afraid of me. You said, 'He'll kill me and take my money, then bury me in the desert, as I did with the man that I killed.' "

"You—"

"Listen, Gabal, fear is a terrible thing. It is the thing that makes snakes strike!"

"You read things that are not there in men's hearts."

"Look, you know I did not go beyond the truth, former estate manager."

"Sayida, come here!" called a powerful voice from inside. His heart bounded with unexpected pleasure. This dove in a snake pit who had found him innocent and led him to the shady tree of hope. Balqiti spoke as if commenting on Shafiqa's action.

"Ours is a busy house from first thing in the morning. These girls set off and come back with water and beans to feed their old father, then send him out with a bag of snakes to make a living for himself and for them."

Peace filled his heart: he felt like a member of this family. Friendly warmth flooded his soul, and he longed with irresistible spontaneity to open his heart and surrender fully.

"Sir," he said, "I am going to tell you the truth—my whole story."

Balqiti seemed preoccupied with rubbing his legs but smiled.

"I am a killer, as you said, but I have my story."

He told him what had happened.

"What a tribe of tyrants," said Balqiti when he had finished. "But you, you are a decent man, and I think no less of you." He shifted triumphantly as he sat. "You deserve that I should be equally frank with you. You should know that my origins are in Gabalawi Alley."

"You!"

"Yes, and I fled from it when I was very young because of trouble with the gangsters!"

"They are the worst thing about the alley," said Gabal, whose surprise was still evident.

"Yes, but we have not forgotten our alley, gangsters or no gangsters. That's why I liked you when I found out your background."

"What neighborhood are you from?"

"Hamdan, the same as you."

"Marvelous!"

"Don't marvel at anything in this world, but this is all long-gone history, and no one remembers me anymore except for Tamar Henna herself, who is related to me."

"I know that courageous woman! But which gangster was making trouble for you? Zaqlut?"

"Back then all he ran was one squalid little neighborhood."

"As I said, they are the worst thing about our alley."

"I spit on the past and all its works!" he added energetically. "From this very moment you should start thinking of your future. I'll tell you again, you'd make a wonderful snake charmer, and there's a good area to work in, south of here, far from our alley. In any case, your gangsters and their hoodlums can't show themselves in this alley."

Of course, he knew nothing of the art of snake charming, but he welcomed it as a means of joining this family, and spoke in a voice that gave away how pleased he was. "Do you really think I'd be good at it?"

The man jumped to the floor with acrobatic speed and set his short frame before him, thick white hair visible in his wide collar. "Yes, and I'm never wrong about these things." He extended his hand, and they shook. "I'll tell you the truth—I like you more than any of my snakes."

Gabal laughed as hard as a child and grasped the man's hand to keep him from going. Balqiti stood looking quizzical until Gabal blurted out what he could no longer keep inside. "Sir, Gabal wants to be part of your family."

Balqiti smiled with bloodshot eyes. "Really?"

"Yes, by God!"

Balqiti laughed briefly and said, "I was wondering when you would ask me that. Yes, Gabal, I'm no fool, but you are a man I can give my daughter to with an easy mind. Fortunately, Sayida is a wonderful girl, just like her late mother."

Gabal's delighted smile faltered as a wilted flower's petals droop, afraid that his dream would vanish just as he was about to seize it.

"Only—"

"Only you want Shafiqa! I know, my friend. Your eyes told me, and the girl's talk, and my experience with snakes. Forgive me—this is the way snake charmers make deals among themselves."

Gabal sighed from the bottom of his heart and felt a soothing rush of peace and relief; youth, freedom and enthusiasm filled his chest. He forgot the beautiful house and his privileged rank, and no longer feared the pain and hardship in store for him. Let an impenetrable curtain fall over the past; let oblivion swallow up all the pain of bygone days, and his heart's longing for the mother he had lost.

That morning, Sayida trilled with joy. The happy news spread quickly through the neighboring alleys. And Gabal's wedding procession wound through Muqattam Marketplace.

36

"It does a man no honor to live the life of a rabbit or a rooster!" said Balqiti in a tone of rather scornful criticism. "But here you are. You haven't learned a thing, and your money has almost run out!"

They were sitting on an animal-skin rug by the door of the house. Gabal's legs were stretched out on the sunny sand, a blissful calm shimmering in his eyes. He turned to his father-in-law and smiled. "Our father, Adham, lived and died desiring the lovely, innocent life he had singing in the garden!"

Balqiti laughed loudly. "Shafiqa!" he called. "Come get your husband before his laziness kills him."

Shafiqa appeared in the doorway, sorting lentils on a dish in her hand. She wore a purple scarf over her head that set off the purity of her face. "What is it, Father?" she asked without even lifting her eyes from the dish.

"He wants just two things: your happiness and a life without work."

"How can I be happy if he starves me to death?" she asked, laughing reproachfully.

"That's a conjurer's secret," said Gabal.

Balqiti poked him in the side with his elbow and said, "Don't make light of the hardest of professions. How do you hide an egg in a spectator's pocket and pull it out of another pocket on the other side of the show? How do you turn marbles into chicks? How do you charm a snake?"

"Teach him, Father," said Shafiqa, looking radiant with happiness. "All life has taught him is how to sit in a cozy chair in the estate office."

"Time to go to work," said Balqiti, getting up and going into the house.

Gabal contemplated his wife lovingly. "Zaqlut's wife is a thousand times less lovely than you, but she spends all day on an elegant couch, and twilight in the garden smelling the fragrance of jasmine and frolicking in the running brook."

"That's the way with people who live off other people's work," she said, sarcastic but bitter.

Gabal scratched his head, thinking, then said, "But there is a way to complete happiness."

"Stop dreaming—you weren't dreaming when you got up and came to my side in the marketplace, and you weren't dreaming when you drove that human vermin away from me. That's why I fell in love with you."

He wanted to kiss her; his conviction that he knew better than Shafiqa did not lessen the worth of what she was saying.

"I fell in love with you for no reason at all," he said.

"In these alleys around us, only crazy people dream."

"Sweetheart, what do you want from me?"

"To be like my father."

"What a sweet thing to say," he reproached her gently. "Where does your sweetness come from?"

Her lips parted to form a smile, and her fingers worked quickly through the lentils.

"When I fled the alley, I was the most miserable person in the world, but if that hadn't happened I would never have married you!"

She laughed. "We owe our happiness to the gangsters in your alley, the same way my father owes his living to snakes and serpents."

"Even so," sighed Gabal, "the finest citizen our alley ever knew believed there was a way to provide people with a living while they could stay in their gardens and sing."

"Oh, not that again! Look, here comes my father with his bag—get up, and God go with you."

Balqiti came in with his bag, Gabal got up, and the two men set off on their accustomed road.

"Learn with your eyes as much as you learn with your mind," Balqiti said. "Watch what I do. Don't ask me anything in front of people, and be patient until I explain what you miss."

Gabal found the work truly difficult, but he applied himself to it from the very start and got used to its demanding dexterity regardless of how much effort it cost him. The fact is that he had no other job open to him unless he could be happy as a wandering peddler, a gangster, thief or bandit. The alleys in his new neighborhood were no different from his own alley, except for the estate and the stories that had grown up around it. Any lingering sorrow over the dreams of his past, memories of his bygone grandeur or hopes for which the Al Hamdan had suffered, as Adham had suffered before them, had vanished somewhere in the depth of his heart. He was determined to forget by propelling himself into the vastness of his new life, to embrace it and open his heart to it. He would take refuge in his dear, beloved wife whenever he felt the danger of depression or shame in his rootlessness. He overcame his sorrows and memories and learned so brilliantly that Balqiti himself was surprised. He practiced tirelessly in the desert and worked day and night. He spent days, weeks and months, and his resolve did not weaken, nor did fatigue overtake him. He learned the lanes and alleys, and got used to the snakes and sepents. He performed in front of thousands of children, and tasted the sweetness of success and profit. He received the good news that he was going to become a father. He lay on his back to gaze at the stars when he was able to relax. He spent the nights passing the pipe to Balqiti and back again and spinning the tales told by the rebec in Hamdan's coffeehouse. Every now and then he wondered where Gabalawi was. When Shafiqa expressed her fear that his past would ruin his life, he said, "The child in your belly belongs to those people. Hamdan's people are his people. Effendi is the king of criminality and Zaqlut is the king of terrorism. How good can life be with people like that around?"

One day he was showing off his tricks in Zainhum, in the middle of a crowded circle of children. He turned around and there in front of him he saw Daabis, who had cut through to the front row and was now gaping at him in amazement. Unsettled, Gabal avoided looking at his face and could no longer go on with his act. He stopped, despite the clamor of protest from the children, took up his bag and walked away.

It was not long before Daabis came up behind him, shouting, "Gabal! Is that you, Gabal?"

He stopped walking and turned around. "Yes, what brings you here, Daabis?"

"Gabal a snake charmer!" Daabis had not recovered from his surprise. He then asked, "When did you learn this—how?"

"It isn't the strangest thing in the world," said Gabal casually.

Gabal walked along and the other followed him until they reached the foot of the mountain, then they sat in the shade of a knoll in a place where there were only grazing sheep and a naked shepherd, sitting and picking lice from his clothes. Daabis scrutinized his friend's face.

"Why did you flee, Gabal? How could you think so badly of me that you'd expect me to betray you? By God, I would never betray any of the Al Hamdan, not even Kaabalha! To whom would I betray you? Effendi? Zaqlut?! May Almighty God burn them all. They asked about you so much, and when I heard them asking I nearly drowned in my sweat."

"Tell me," Gabal asked him earnestly, "how did you risk their revenge by sneaking away from your house?"

Daabis made an insouciant gesture with his hand. "They lifted the siege a long time ago. No one asks about Qidra anymore, or his killer. They say that Lady Huda is the one who saved us from death by starvation, but we have been condemned to permanent degradation. We have no honor. We have no coffeehouse! We go to work far from the alley, and when we go home we vanish behind our walls. If any gangster finds one of us he'll have some fun slapping him or spitting on him. They think more highly of the dirt in our alley than they do of us, Gabal. How fortunate you are in your exile."

"Forget my good fortune and tell me if anyone has been mistreated," said Gabal resentfully.

Daabis picked up a brick and smacked it against the ground. "They killed ten of us during the siege!"

"God in Heaven!"

"They took them as ransom for rotten Qidra of the even rottener mother, but they weren't our friends!"

"Weren't they all of the Al Hamdan, Daabis?"

Daabis blinked shyly and moved his lips in an inaudible apology. "And the others were blessed only with slaps and spit."

Gabal felt responsible for the souls that had gone, and the pain wrung his heart. He felt bloody regret staining every moment of peace that had passed since his flight. Daabis took him by surprise when he said, "You may be the only happy member of the Al Hamdan today."

"I have never stopped thinking of all of you for a single day!" exclaimed Gabal.

"But you're far away from all the trouble."

"I have never fled from the past," said Gabal sharply.

"Don't lose your peace of mind over something hopeless. We no longer have hope."

"We no longer have hope," repeated Gabal, but in a mysterious tone of voice.

Daabis stared at him with concern and curiosity, but said nothing out of respect for the grief etched on Gabal's face. He looked at the ground and saw a beetle creeping hastily along until it disappeared under a heap of stones. The shepherd shook out his garment to cover his sunburned body with it.

"Honestly," said Gabal, "I have not been happy. I only look it."

"You deserve happiness, you really do," Daabis soothed him.

"I got married and found new work, as you can see, but I have always had a secret voice nagging me in my sleep."

"God bless you! Where are you living?"

He did not answer. He seemed to be talking to himself. "Life will never be good with thugs like that around."

"That's the truth, but how can we be rid of them?"

The shepherd raised his voice to call his sheep, and he walked toward them with his long staff under his arm. Then they heard him singing an indistinct melody.

"How can I meet you?" Daabis asked.

"Ask in Muqattam Marketplace for the house of Balqiti the snake charmer, but don't tell anyone about me yet."

Daabis rose and gripped his hand, and walked away followed by grief-stricken eyes.

37

It was nearly midnight. Gabalawi Alley was sunk in shadows except for the faint light trickling out of the coffeehouse doors, all but closed to keep out the cold. The winter night was starless, youths were confined in their rooms, and even the dogs and cats had sought shelter in the courtyards. In the overpowering silence the monotonous rebec melodies could be heard telling their stories, but the Hamdan district was swathed in mute blackness. Two shapes moved in from the direction of the desert and kept close by the mansion walls, then passed in front of Effendi's house, traversing the Hamdan district until they stopped before the middle building. One of them knocked at the door, and the knock echoed like a drumbeat in the silence. The door opened to show the face of Hamdan himself, pale in the light of the lamp in his hand. He raised the lamp to see his visitor's face and hesitated briefly before crying out in surprise, "Gabal!"

He stepped out of the doorway, and Gabal came in, carrying a large bundle and a bag, followed by his wife, who was carrying another bundle. The men embraced, and Hamdan glanced at the woman, noticing her belly. "Your wife? Welcome to you both. Follow me. Take your time."

They crossed a long covered porch until they came to a broad open courtyard, then headed for a narrow stairway and climbed it to Hamdan's apartment. Shafiqa went into the women's quarters, and Hamdan took Gabal into a spacious room with a balcony that overlooked the courtyard of the building. In no time word of Gabal's home-coming circulated, and a crowd of Al Hamdan men showed up, led by Daabis, Itris, Dulma, Ali Fawanis, Ridwan the poet and Abdoun. They shook hands with Gabal delightedly and sat on cushions in the room, watching the returning visitor with concern and curiosity. Gabal was assailed with questions, and he told them about some of his recent life. They exchanged looks of sorrow. Gabal saw their frail spirits reflected in their emaciated bodies: ruin was overtaking their limbs. They told him about the humiliation they endured, and Daabis said that he had told him everything in their meeting a month before, and that he was sur-prised at his visit now.

"Have you come to invite us to emigrate to your new place?" he asked ironically.

"This is the only place we have," said Gabal sharply.

They were intrigued by the tone of authority in his voice, and Hamdan's curiosity was clear in his eyes. "If they were snakes, you could deal with them," he said.

Tamar Henna came in with glasses of tea. She greeted Gabal warmly and extolled his wife; she notified him that they would have a son. But, she added, "there isn't any difference between our men and women anymore!"

Hamdan scolded her as she left the room, but the men's eyes re-flected abject agreement with her comment. The clouds of dejection that hung over the group grew darker. No one tasted his tea.

"Why did you come back, Gabal?" asked Ridwan the poet. "You aren't used to insults."

"I have told you repeatedly that patience in the face of what we have to bear is better than loitering around among strangers who hate us," said Hamdan with a trace of something like triumph.

"It isn't what it looks like," said Gabal sternly.

Hamdan shook his head and said nothing, and there was only silence until Daabis spoke. "Friends, let's let him rest."

Gabal motioned for them to stay. "I have not come here to rest, but to talk to you about something important, more important than you know."

Their eyes were drawn to him in surprise, and Ridwan murmured that he hoped it was good news.

Gabal surveyed them with his penetrating eyes. "I could have spent my whole life with my new family, without ever thinking of coming back to our alley," he said, and paused a while before continuing. "But a few days ago I felt like taking a walk by myself, despite the cold and the dark, and I went out into the desert, and my feet led me to the spot above our alley. It was a place I hadn't gone near since I fled."

Their eyes were bright with interest.

"I walked on in the utter blackness—even the stars had disappeared in the clouds. My mind was somewhere else until I almost collided with a huge form, and at first I thought it was a gangster, but then it seemed to me unlike anyone in our alley, or like any person at all. He was as tall and broad as a mountain. I was filled with terror and tried to back away, but then he told me in a strange voice, "Stay, Gabal." I froze where I stood, sweat trickling over my skin, and asked him, "Who—who are you?"

Gabal paused in his story, and interest drew their heads forward.

"Was he from our alley?" asked Dulma.

"He said he wasn't like anyone in our alley or like any person at all," Itris was quick to point out.

"But he was from our alley," said Gabal.

They all asked who it had been, and Gabal said, "He told me in his strange voice, 'Be not afraid, I am your grandfather—Gabalawi.' "

They all shrieked with surprise and looked around in disbelief.

"You are joking, of course," said Hamdan.

"I am telling the truth, and only the truth."

"You weren't drunk?" asked Ali Fawanis.

"I have never been drunk in my life!" shouted Gabal angrily.

"If his wineglasses could talk—only the best vintages," said Itris.

Anger filled Gabal's face like a dark cloud. "I heard him with my own ears when he told me, 'Don't be afraid, I am your grandfather—Gabalawi.' "

"But he hasn't left his house in a long time, and no one has seen him!" said Hamdan gently, to soothe his anger.

"He could go out every night without anyone seeing him."

"But no one but you has met him!" Hamdan wondered warily.

"I did meet him!"

"Don't be angry, Gabal, I didn't mean to doubt you, but the imagination can be a deceiver. By God, tell me—if the man can come out of his house, why doesn't he want people to see him? Why does he let them violate his children's rights?"

"That is his secret, and he knows what he is doing," said Gabal with a frown.

"It's more likely that people are right when they say he became reclusive because of his old age and poor health."

"We're just confusing ourselves with words," said Daabis. "Let's listen to his story, if there's more to hear."

"I told him, 'I never dreamed of meeting you in this life,'" Gabal resumed. "He said, 'You are meeting me now.' I looked hard to see his face, which was above me in the dark, and he told me, 'You will not be able to see as long as it is dark.' I was baffled that he could see me trying to look at him, and I said, 'But you can see me in the dark.' He said, 'I can see when it is dark since I got used to walking in darkness, before the alley existed.' I was amazed. I said, 'Praise be to the Lord of the Heavens that you still enjoy your health.' He told me, 'You, Gabal, are one of those in whom people trust, as a sign of which you fled from luxury out of anger for your oppressed family, and what is your family but my family too? They have a right to my estate which they must possess, they have dignity which must be upheld, and a life which should be easy.' I asked him—in an outburst of emotion that lit up the darkness!—'How?' 'By force you will all defeat injustice and achieve your rights,' he said, 'and you will have a good life.' I shouted from the depths of my heart, 'We will be strong!' and he said, 'Victory will be your ally.'"

Gabal's voice left a silence like a dream that had enthralled all of them. They were thinking and exchanging looks, and kept their eyes on Hamdan until he ventured out of his silence. "Let us ponder this story in our hearts and minds!"

"This is no drunken hallucination," said Daabis forcefully. "Everything in it is true."

"It is no delusion, unless our rights are a delusion," said Dulma, sounding convinced.

"You didn't ask him what's keeping him from establishing justice himself?" Hamdan asked a little hesitantly. "Or what made him turn the management over to people who have no feeling for our people's rights?"

"I did not ask him," snapped Gabal. "I couldn't have asked him. You didn't meet him in the desert and the darkness, and feel the terror of his presence. If you had, it wouldn't have occurred to you to argue with him, and you wouldn't have doubted him."

Hamdan nodded in apparent resignation. "That talk truly does sound like Gabalawi, but it would be even more fitting for him to do the job himself."

"Wait until you all die in your shame!" shouted Daabis.

Ridwan the poet cleared his throat and looked cautiously around at their faces. "He talks well, but think where it might lead us."

"We've gone once to beg for our rights, and we know what happened," said Hamdan wearily.

"Why are we afraid?" young Abdoun suddenly shouted. "There is nothing worse than the way we live now!"

"I'm not afraid for myself," said Hamdan in a pleading tone of excuse. "I'm afraid for all of you."

"I'll go to the overseer by myself," said Gabal contemptuously.

Daabis shifted closer to where Gabal was seated, and said, "We are with you. Don't forget that Gabalawi promised him victory!"

"I will go alone, when I decide to go," said Gabal. "But I want to be reassured that you will be with me, a firm, unwavering group ready to confront adversity and survive it!"

"With you until death!" shouted Abdoun, leaping zealously to his feet.

The lad's enthusiasm spread to Daabis, Itris, Dulma and Ali Fawanis. Ridwan the poet asked a little slyly whether Gabal's wife knew the reason he had come back, and Gabal told them how he had confided his secret to Balqiti, how that man had advised him to consider the consequences, how he had insisted on returning to his alley, and how his wife had chosen to follow him to the end.

At this point Hamdan asked, in a voice that made plain his solidarity with the others, "When are you going to the overseer?"

"When my plan is ripe."

"I'll prepare a place for you in my apartment," said Hamdan. "You are our dearest son, and this is a great night. Perhaps the rebec will tell of it someday with the story of Adham. Now let's make a covenant for better and for worse!"

At that moment the drunken, quavering voice of Hammouda rang out as the gangster came home with the dawn:

> *"Boys and wine, drink and be cleansed.*
> *Come in the alley, stagger and limp.*
> *Be generous with me*
> *And I'll let you suck down shrimp!"*

His voice kept their attention only for a moment. They then joined hands to make their pledge, with ardor and expectation.

38

The alley learned of Gabal's homecoming. They saw him strolling with his bag, and they saw his wife going to Gamaliya to do her shopping. They talked about his new trade, which no one in the alley had ever plied before. He performed his magic act, however, in every neighborhood but his own. He avoided using the snakes in his act, so no one realized that he was an expert with snakes. He passed by the overseer's house many times, as if he had never gone there in his life, enduring deep inside a terrible longing for his mother. Gangsters—Hammouda, al-Laithy, Barakat and Abu Sari—saw him, but did not slap him as they did the other Al Hamdan, but they did crowd him off the sidewalk and mocked his bag. One day he encountered Zaqlut, who stared at him coldly, then blocked his path.

"Where have you been?" Zaqlut asked.

"Somewhere in the wide world," replied Gabal in a dream.

"This is my turf," the man said, as if trying to start a fight. "It is my right to ask you whatever I want, and you have to answer me."

"I answered you."

"Why have you come back?"

"The same reason any man comes back home!"

"I wouldn't have come back if I were you," said Zaqlut menacingly.

He pounced forward suddenly, and would have ended up on top of him had Gabal not quickly stepped aside, restraining his own rage. Then came the sound of the overseer's gatekeeper calling him; Gabal, surprised, turned that way and went to him. They met in front of the house and shook hands warmly. The man asked him how he was, and informed him that the lady wanted to see him. This was an invitation Gabal had expected since his reappearance in the alley. His heart had told him it was coming, no question about it. For his part, he could not visit the house, because of the circumstances of his leaving it; even apart from that, he had decided not to request a meeting in order not to raise any suspicions before it took place—suspicions in the heart of the overseer or among the gangsters. In any case, he no sooner entered the house than the news was all over the alley. As he walked up the terrace, he shot a quick glance at the garden, at the sycamores, the high mulberry trees, the flowers and rosebushes that filled every corner. The usual fragrances had disappeared in winter's grip, and a calm light as peaceful as dusk filled the air, as if diffused from the scattered white clouds. He went up the stairs, resolutely resisting the flock of memories in his heart, and entered the hall, in the center of which the lady and her husband were sitting and waiting. He looked at his mother and their eyes met; deeply moved, she stood up to receive him, and he knelt at her hands and kissed them. She kissed his forehead lovingly, and he stood, overcome with love and happiness. He turned his head to the overseer and saw him sitting draped in his cloak, watching them with icy eyes. He extended his hand, and the overseer rose halfway to shake it, then sat down quickly. Huda's eyes searched Gabal with mixed surprise and panic: he looked handsome in a rough galabiya, drawn in at his thin waist with a thick belt, and worn-out red leather slippers on his feet. His luxuriant hair was covered by a dark skullcap. Her eyes were brilliant with sorrow, and spoke wordlessly of her sorrow at his appearance and the sort of life he had settled for, as if she were gazing at a brilliant hope that had collapsed into wreckage. She motioned for him to be seated. He sat on a chair by her, and she sat down looking almost ill. He realized what she must be going through, and spoke to her in a strong voice about his life in Muqattam Marketplace, about his trade and his wife. He spoke happily of that life in spite of its crudeness, and told her that he was content. This made her angry.

"Live whatever life you want, but how could my house not be the first house you visited when you came back to the alley?"

He almost told her that going to her house was the main purpose of his return, but he postponed that because the moment was not ripe yet and because he still had not overcome his emotions at this meeting.

"I did want to come to your house, but I couldn't find the courage to intrude after what—"

"Why did you come back if life was so sweet abroad?" Effendi asked coldly.

The lady directed a look of rebuke at her husband, which he ignored.

Gabal smiled. "Perhaps, sir, I came back in the hope of seeing you!"

"Yet you didn't visit us until we invited you, you mean thing," Huda scolded him.

"Believe me, my lady," said Gabal, bowing his head, "that whenever I remembered the circumstances that compelled me to leave this house, I cursed them from the bottom of my heart."

Effendi stared at him distrustfully, and was going to ask what he meant, but Huda spoke first.

"You have learned, of course, how we pardoned the Al Hamdan for your sake?"

Gabal knew that it was time for this pleasant family scene to end, as he had known from the outset it would have to, and that it was time for the struggle to begin.

"The truth, my lady, is that they are suffering a disgrace worse than death, and that it has killed some of them."

Effendi gripped his worry beads tightly and exclaimed, "They are criminals, and they got what they deserved."

"Let's forget all about the past," pleaded Huda with an urgent gesture.

"It would not have been right for Qidra's blood to have been spilled in vain," Effendi insisted.

"The gangsters are the real criminals," said Gabal firmly.

Effendi stood impulsively and turned rebukingly to his wife. "Do you see the result of my giving in to you and inviting him to our house?"

"Sir," said Gabal in a voice that proclaimed all of his strength, "I intended to come to you anyway. Perhaps my awareness of the favor I harbor for this house is what made me wait until I was invited here."

The overseer showed a look of apprehensive distrust. "What do you expect from this visit?"

Gabal stood bravely to face the overseer, knowing perfectly well that he was opening a door that would admit howling storms, but he had derived unshakable courage from his meeting in the desert. "I have come," he said, "to claim the Al Hamdan's rights to the estate and to a peaceful life."

Anger darkened Effendi's face, and the lady's mouth gaped in despair. The man fixed his burning gaze on Gabal. "You actually dare to revive this conversation? Have you forgotten the tragedies that befell you after that ridiculous old man of yours dared to advance these impossible demands? I swear, you must be crazy, and I have no time to waste with lunatics."

"Gabal," sobbed Huda, "I was going to invite you and your wife to live with us."

"I am only repeating in your hearing the wish of one who may not be refused: your ancestor and ours, Gabalawi!" said Gabal in a resounding voice.

Effendi looked searchingly at Gabal, amazed. Huda got up, looking worried, and placed her hand on Gabal's shoulder. "Gabal, what has happened to you?"

"I'm fine, my lady," said Gabal, smiling.

"Fine!" Effendi was thunderstruck. "You are fine? Where is your mind?"

"Listen to my story and judge for yourself," said Gabal very serenely.

He told them the story he had told the Al Hamdan, and when he had finished, Effendi, who had been studying his face distrustfully the whole time, spoke. "The lord of the estate has never left his house since he isolated himself."

"But I met him in the desert."

"Why didn't he inform me directly of his wishes?" he asked mockingly.

"That is his secret and he knows what he is doing."

Exasperated, Effendi laughed. "You truly are a snake charmer, but you aren't satisfied playing tricks with snakes—no, you want to trifle with the whole estate!"

"God knows I have not lied," said Gabal, losing none of his calm. "Let's take it to Gabalawi himself for his judgment, if you can arrange that, or else the Ten Conditions."

Effendi's anger exploded. His face turned pale and his limbs shuddered as he screamed, "You thief! You fraud! You will not escape from your black fate, not even if you hide on the mountaintop!"

"Oh, how terrible!" exclaimed Huda. "I never expected you to bring me so much misery, Gabal."

"Is all this happening only because I have demanded legitimate rights for my people?" asked Gabal incredulously.

"Shut up, you fraud!" shouted Effendi as loudly as he could. "You hashish addict! You alley of hashish addicts, you sons of dogs! Get out of my house, and if you ever rave like this again you'll be condemning yourself and your people to be slaughtered like sheep!"

"I warn you," said Gabal, glowering, "you are going to feel the wrath of Gabalawi."

Effendi attacked Gabal and struck his broad chest as hard as he could, but Gabal bore it with patient immobility. Then he turned to the lady. "I will show him respect for your sake," he said, and turned his back on them and left.

39

Hamdan's people expected imminent catastrophe. Only Tamar Henna marred the unanimity, saying that because Gabal was leading the Al Hamdan this time, the lady would not allow them to be exterminated. But Gabal himself did not share Tamar Henna's view; he said that if the estate were threatened by any newcomer, neither he nor any other person, not even those closest to Effendi, could do anything. Gabal reminded them that it was their ancestor's will that they be strong and endure their misfortunes bravely. Daabis said that Gabal had enjoyed privilege and that he had spurned it of his own choice out of respect for them, so it was not right for any of them to abandon him; resorting to force might fail, but it could not make their lives any worse than they were now. The truth is that the Al Hamdan were fearful and their nerves were tense, but they found in despair a certain strength and resolve, and repeated the saying "We may win, and cannot lose." Only Ridwan the poet kept sighing, "If the lord of the estate wished, he could establish justice, acquit us honestly and save us from certain disaster." Gabal got angry when he heard this. He went to see him, impassioned and glowering, shook him by the shoulders until Ridwan nearly fell off of his chair. "Is this what poets have come to, Ridwan?" he shouted. "You tell tales of heroes and sing to the rebec, but when things turn serious you slither back into your holes and spread indecision and defeat. God's curse on cowards!" He turned to the others. "Gabalawi has honored no other people of this alley as he has honored you. If he did not consider you his own family, he would not have sought me out and talked to me, but he has lit our path and promised his support. By God, I am going to fight them, even if I am alone." But he did not look alone. Every man supported him, and every woman, and they all awaited the ordeal as if unmindful of the consequences. Gabal took over the leadership position in the neighborhood spontaneously, as events dictated, without any design or planning on his part, nor with any opposition from Hamdan, who was happy to abandon a position that would become the target of hostility for an unknowable period. Gabal did not confine himself to the house: he went out—against Hamdan's advice—to go for his accustomed walks. He expected trouble at every step, but no gangster showed him the slightest trace of it, much to his great surprise. The only explanation he could think of was that Effendi must have kept the news of their meeting a secret in the hope that Gabal too would keep quiet about his demands, so that the matter would end as if it had never been. He saw in this policy the lady's sorrowful face and her faithful motherhood. He was afraid that her love would be harder on him than her husband's rudeness, and he thought for a long time over what he must do to shake the ashes from the coals.

Strange things came to pass in the alley. One day a woman's screams for help were heard from a basement; it seemed that a snake had glided between her feet and slithered out into the street. Men volunteered to search out the snake, and went into her house with their sticks. They searched for the snake until they found it, and pounded it until it was dead, then threw it out into the dirt of the street, where boys seized it and played with it excitedly. There would have been nothing strange about this incident in the alley, but barely had an hour passed before another scream was heard from a house at the head of the alley, near Gamaliya. And before night fell there was an outcry in Hamdan's neighborhood: some people had seen a snake which had vanished before anyone could chase it, and all their efforts to find it were in vain. At this point Gabal himself volunteered to find it, using the craft he had gained from Balqiti. The people of Hamdan talk of how Gabal stood naked in the courtyard, and of the secret language he used to address the snake until it came out to him willingly. These events might have been forgotten by the following morning had they not happened all over again in the homes of prominent people. It was reported, and believed, that a snake had bitten Hammouda the gangster as he was crossing the hallway of his house, and the man screamed in spite of himself until his friends heard him and came to the rescue; and then the gossip started. People would talk about the snakes, and then talk about them again; in the meantime, the snakes' strange activity continued. Some of the customers in Barakat's hashish den saw a snake among the ceiling posts; it emerged for about half a minute and then disappeared, and they jumped up, terrified, and ran away. News of the snakes drowned out the poets' tales in the coffeehouses, and it seemed that their activity went beyond all decent bounds when a huge snake appeared in his excellency the overseer's house. Although the house's many servants dispersed into every corner to search out the hiding snake, they found no trace of it. The overseer and the lady were so obsessed with fear that they gave serious thought to leaving the house until they could be assured it was free of snakes. While that house was turned upside down, screams and commotion were heard from the house of Zaqlut, protector of the alley. The gatekeeper went to see what was happening, and came back to inform his master that a snake had bitten one of Zaqlut's sons, then vanished. Everyone was frantic with fear. Cries of help from people seeing snakes were heard from every house, and the lady decided to leave the alley. Old Hassanain, the gatekeeper, said that Gabal was a snake charmer, and that snake charmers knew how to hunt down snakes; he swore that he had drawn a snake out of one of the Al Hamdan people's houses. The color drained from Effendi's face and he said nothing, but the lady ordered the gatekeeper to summon Gabal. The gatekeeper looked at his master, waiting for permission to go, and Effendi mumbled a few exasperated, indistinct words. The lady asked him whether it was better to send for Gabal or to abandon their house, and then he gave the old man permission to go, trembling with bitterness and rage. Crowds of people gathered between the overseer's house and Zaqlut's, as prominent people had been deputized to go to the overseer, led by gangsters: Zaqlut, Hammouda, Barakat, al-Laithy and Abu Sari. All the people talked of nothing but the snakes.

"Something has happened on the mountain to drive the snakes down here into our houses," said Abu Sari.

"All our life the mountain has been our neighbor and nothing has ever happened," shouted Zaqlut, who seemed to be fighting with himself, since he could find no one else to fight.

Zaqlut was agitated over what had happened to his son, and Hammouda was still limping from the wound on his leg; fear had seized all of them. They said that their houses were no longer safe to live in, and that all the people had come out into the alley.

Gabal came with his bag and greeted them all, then stood politely and confidently before the overseer and the lady.

The overseer was unable to look at him, but the lady spoke to him. "We have been told, Gabal, that you can get the snakes out of our homes."

"I have learned that among other things, ma'am," said Gabal evenly.

"I have summoned you to cleanse our house of snakes."

"Does his excellency the overseer give me leave?" asked Gabal, looking at Effendi.

Hiding his rage and misery, the overseer muttered, "Yes."

Here al-Laithy stepped up at the secret suggestion of Zaqlut and asked, "And our houses, and everyone's house?"

"My craft is at the command of all," said Gabal.

There was a chorus of thanks, and Gabal's large eyes scanned their faces for several moments before he spoke. "Perhaps there is no need for me to tell you that everything has its price—this is the way it goes in our alley."

The gangsters looked at him in surprise.

"Why are you shocked?" he asked. "You protect these neighborhoods and are paid collection money, and his excellency the overseer runs the estate in exchange for having the revenues at his disposal!"

It was clear that the difficulty of the situation did not permit their eyes to express what was in their hearts. Zaqlut spoke up again. "What do you want in return for your work?"

"I will not ask for money," said Gabal calmly. "But I am asking for your word of honor that you will respect the Al Hamdan's honor and their rights to the estate."

Silence fell, and the air seethed with repressed hatred. The lady's unease mounted and the overseer stared at the ground.

"Don't think that I'm threatening you with what truth and justice require you to do for your oppressed brothers. The fear that has driven you out of your houses is only a brief taste of what your brothers swallow every day of their miserable lives."

Their eyes shone with rage, as fleetingly as lightning flashes in a cloud, and was smothered instantly.

"I can bring you a Rifai Sufi to charm out the snakes," shouted Abu Sari, "if we can stay out of our houses for two or three days until he comes from his village."

"How can everyone in the alley stay out of their homes for two or three days?" asked the lady.

Effendi was thinking with all his strength and trying to control the feelings of rage and resentment that blazed in his heart. He finally addressed Gabal. "I give you the promise you ask. Begin your work."

The gangsters looked startled, and while circumstances did not permit them to say what they were thinking, their hearts were seized with murderous purpose. Gabal ordered everyone to move back to the end of the garden, leaving the open space and house to him. He took off his clothes, now as naked as the day the lady rescued him from the ditch filled with rainwater. He moved from place to place, from room to room, at times whistling softly or murmuring indistinctly.

Zaqlut came near the overseer and spoke to him. "He's the one who sent the snakes to our houses."

The overseer motioned him to be quiet and muttered, "Let him get rid of his snakes.'

A snake that had been hiding in the light shaft now obeyed Gabal, and he drew another out of the room used for estate business. He draped the snakes around his arms and he appeared with them in the hall, then put them in his bag. He put on his clothes and stood waiting until all the people came forward.

"Let's go to your houses and cleanse them," he said to them. He turned to the lady and said gently, "If it weren't for my people's misery, I would never have laid down a single condition to help you."

He went to the overseer and saluted him. "A free man's promise must be kept," he said boldly, and then walked out; and all the people followed him in silence.

40

Gabal succeeded in ridding the alley of snakes, before the very eyes of all its people. Every time a snake obeyed him, the cheers and delighted trilling resounded, until the alley's goings-on could be heard from the mansion to Gamaliya. When he finished his task and went home, youths and small boys surrounded him and sang, clapping rhythmically, "Gabal, defender of the poor! Gabal, conqueror of serpents!"

The singing and clapping continued even after he left, and this produced a violent reaction in the gangsters' souls; in no time Hammouda, al-Laithy, Abu Sari and Barakat went out to the celebrants and began cursing and abusing them, slapping and kicking them until they broke up and fled to their homes, leaving the street to its dogs, cats and flies. The people wondered what was the secret of this attack—how could they repay Gabal's good deed by attacking his supporters? Would Effendi keep his promise to Gabal, or was the gangsters' attack the beginning of an arrogant new campaign of revenge? These questions ran through Gabal's mind, and he sent for the men of Al Hamdan to come to the house where he was staying, so that they might deal with the matter together.

At that very same time, Zaqlut, consumed with fury, was meeting with the overseer and his wife. "We won't leave one of them alive," he was insisting.

The delight was plain on Effendi's face, but the lady asked, "What about the word of honor the overseer gave?"

Zaqlut scowled until his face became uglier than any human face. "People obey strength, not honor," he said.

"They will always say that we——" she began angrily.

"They can say whatever they want—when have they ever kept quiet about us or about you anyway? Every night their hashish dens are loud with their wisecracks and jokes against us, but when we go out in the streets they stand up submissively. They submit out of fear of our clubs, not out of admiration for our honor."

Effendi glared at her exasperatedly. "Gabal is the one who masterminded the snake plot so that he could force his conditions on us. Everyone knows that! Who is going to ask me to respect a promise I made to a sneaking, deceitful swindler?"

"Remember, my lady," said Zaqlut tonelessly, his face obstinately hideous, "if Gabal succeeds in getting the Al Hamdan's rights to the estate, no one in the alley will rest until he's got his rights too, and if that happens the estate will be lost, and we'll all lose."

Effendi gripped the worry beads in his hands so tightly that the beads crackled. "Don't leave one of them alive!" he shouted at Zaqlut.

And so the gangsters were summoned to Zaqlut's house, and were followed by their close associates. Word got around in the alley that something terrible was in store for the Al Hamdan; the windows filled with women, and the streets jammed up with men. Gabal had prepared his plan. The Al Hamdan men crowded into the courtyard of the middle house, armed with clubs and baskets of stones, while the women were posted on the roof and in various rooms. Each of them had an assigned task, and any slip in the planning or any error in carrying out the plan would mean nothing less than their eternal ruin. So they took their places around Gabal with the utmost anguish and tension. Their state of mind did not escape Gabal's attention, so he reminded them of Gabalawi's support and his promise that the strong would triumph. He found their spirits trusting, some from faith and others from fear.

Ridwan the poet leaned over to Hamdan's ear and said, "I am afraid our plan will not suceed. I think the best plan would be to close the gate and fire away from the roof and windows!"

Hamdan shrugged irritably and said, "We'd just condemn ourselves to a siege until we'd die of starvation!" He went over to Gabal and asked him, "Wouldn't it be better to leave the gate open?"

"Leave it as it is, otherwise they'll get suspicious."

A cold wind whipped up, howling and chasing the clouds across the sky, and they wondered whether it would rain. There was an outcry from the throng outside that drowned out the meowing of the cats and the dogs' barking. Tamar Henna called out in warning, "The devils are here!"

Zaqlut had, in fact, left his house surrounded by gangsters and followed by their hangers-on, their clubs in hand. They strode along slowly to the mansion, then turned toward the Al Hamdan neighborhood and were met by cheers and applause. Those who cheered and applauded were different groups: a small number were delighted at the prospect of a battle and longed to see bloodletting, while others hated the Al Hamdan because they claimed a status that no one else conceded to them. Most resented the gangsters and hated injustice, but hid their feelings and pretended to support them out of fear or hypocrisy. Zaqlut ignored them; he kept walking until he stood before the building where Hamdan lived.

"If there is any man among you, let him come out!"

"Give us a new promise," came Tamar Henna's voice from behind the window, "that you won't deceive the one who comes out."

This reference to the promise enraged Zaqlut. "Don't you have anyone in there but that slut?"

"God have pity on your mother, Zaqlut!" shouted Tamar Henna.

Zaqlut barked the order for his men to attack the gate. Some men attacked the gate, and others threw stones at the windows so that no one would dare to open them and use them for defense. The attackers massed at the gate and pushed against it with their shoulders with strength and determination. They kept pushing hard until the doors began to shake, redoubled their energy until the doors quaked and rocked, then retreated briefly to throw themselves powerfully against it, slamming against it once so hard that it burst into pieces. The courtyard could be seen at the end of the long extended passage, and there stood Gabal and the men of the Al Hamdan, their clubs upraised. Zaqlut waved his hand in an obscene gesture and emitted a derisive laugh, then charged down the passage with his men behind him. Scarcely had they gone halfway when the ground suddenly gave out under them, and they fell to the bottom of a deep pit. With startling speed, windows on both sides of the passage flew open and water flooded out of jugs, pots, basins and waterskins as the men of the Al Hamdan advanced speedily and loosed their baskets of stones into the pit. For the first time, the alley heard shrieks issuing from their gangsters, saw blood spouting from Zaqlut's head and clubs crushing the heads of Hammouda, Barakat, al-Laithy and Abu Sari as they thrashed around in the muddy water. Seeing what was happening to their bosses, their followers fled, leaving the gangsters to their helpless fate. The cascades of water and stones intensified, and the clubs beat down unmercifully. The people heard cries for help coming from throats that had never uttered anything but curses and threats.

"Don't leave one of them alive!" yelled Ridwan the poet as loudly as he could.

The muddy water was now mixed with blood; Hammouda was the first to perish, though al-Laithy's and Abu Sari's wails were loud. Zaqlut's hands clutched at the wall of the pit as he tried to spring out, and hatred gleamed in his eyes. He was beginning to overcome his weakness and exhaustion, and the moans he puffed out were like the lowing of cattle, but the clubs rained blows on him and his hands released the walls; he fell back and collapsed face up in the water, each of his fists clutching mud. Silence reigned over the pit, from which there was no movement or sound; its surface was colored with mud and blood. The men of Al Hamdan stood panting and watching. The gathering of people crowded around the entrance to the passage, staring bewilderedly into the pit.

"This is the punishment for oppressors!" shouted Ridwan the poet.
The news spread like fire throughout the alley. The crowds said that

Gabal had destroyed the gangsters just as he had destroyed the serpents! Everyone hailed him in voices like thunder. Their fervor warmed their bodies; they paid no attention to the cold wind, and acclaimed him as the new leader of Gabalawi Alley. They demanded the gangsters' bodies so that they might mutilate them; they clapped, and some even danced, but Gabal never for a moment stopped thinking. Everything was arranged in his head.

"Now, to the overseer's house!" he shouted to his people.

41

In the moments preceding the exodus of Gabal and his people from the building, their spirits exploded like fierce volcanoes.

Women left their houses and joined the men. They all attacked the gangsters' homes and assaulted the inhabitants with their hands and feet until they ran for their lives, clutching their cheeks and the backs of their heads, screaming and sobbing. All the furniture, food and clothing in the houses was swept away and everything breakable was smashed, the wood and glass especially, until the scene was one of garbage and rubble. The enraged crowds ran toward the overseer's house and massed up against its locked gate, where one of them led the rest in waves of chanting as loud as thunder: "Bring out the leader! And if he doesn't come—"

The shouts were followed by cheers and scornful applause. Some of them headed for the mansion to call on their ancestor, Gabalawi, to come out of isolation to correct the injustices they and the whole alley had suffered. Others banged at the overseer's gate with their fists and shoved it with their shoulders, inciting the hesitant and respectful among them to help break it down. At this critical moment, Gabal appeared, leading the men and women of his family as they walked with determination and pride after the clear victory they had achieved. The people made way for them, cheering and trilling joyfully until Gabal motioned for them to be silent; the roar of their voices diminished slowly and gradually until there was silence, and once more they could hear the whipping wind whistling past their ears. Gabal looked around at their watchful faces.

"People of our alley, I salute you and I thank you."

A second roar of voices rose until he raised his hand requesting silence.

"Our job will be complete only when you have dispersed peacefully."

"We want justice, leader of our alley!" some of them shouted.

"Go in peace," he said in a voice that each of them could hear. "The will of Gabalawi will be done."

There was a burst of cheers for Gabalawi and his son Gabal, who stood there, his gaze prompting the crowd to disperse. They would have liked to stay where they were, but, caught in his gaze, they felt that they could only leave. They left, one by one, until the street was empty. At that point Gabal went to the overseer's gate and knocked.

"Open, old Hassanain!" he called.

"The people—the people," quavered the man's voice.

"There is no one here but us."

The door opened and Gabal stepped in, and his family entered behind him. They passed through the covered passage to the terrace and saw the lady standing dejectedly before the hall door. Effendi appeared at the threshold of the door, his head bowed, and his face so ashen that he might have been wrapped in a white shroud. They muttered among themselves at the sight of him.

"I'm in a terrible state, Gabal," Huda wailed.

Gabal pointed scornfully at Effendi. "If the machinations of this disreputable man had succeeded, we would all be mutilated corpses by now."

The lady sighed audibly in reply but said nothing.

Gabal stared harshly at the overseer. "Now you see how servile you are without strength or power, no gangster to protect you, no courage to guide you and no honor to intercede for you. If I were to stand aside and leave you to the people of our alley, they would tear you apart and trample you."

A spasm of fear shook the man and he seemed hunched over and shrunken, but the lady took a step toward Gabal and spoke urgently. "All I want to hear from you are the gentle words I'm used to hearing. We are in a nervous state that deserves compassionate treatment from your honor."

Gabal frowned to conceal how touched he was. "Had it not been for the respect I have for you, things would have gone very differently."

"I don't doubt that, Gabal. You are a man who does not let people down."

"How much easier it would have been," said Gabal sadly, "for justice to have been done before any drop of blood was shed!"

Effendi made a vague gesture that illustrated his feebleness and self-absorption.

"What's done is done," said the lady. "From now on you will find that we listen better!"

Effendi apparently wished to break his silence at any cost. "There is a chance of making good the errors of the past," he said weakly.

All ear waited attentively, eager to discover the state of the tyrant whose power was gone. They watched him, gloating a little, disapproving and endlessly curious. Effendi was encouraged by his having spoken up, and went on. "Today you are truly worthy to occupy Zaqlut's place."

"I have no wish to be a criminal." Gabal scowled. "Find someone else to protect you. I want only the full rights of the Al Hamdan."

"They are yours without diminution, and you may manage the estate if you like."

"You always wanted to, Gabal," said Huda hopefully.

"Doesn't the whole estate belong to us?" shouted Daabis from among the crowd of the Al Hamdan.

A murmuring sounded from the Al Hamdan, and the faces of the overseer and his wife turned as pale as death.

"Gabalawi commanded me to restore your rights, not to usurp the rights of others," said Gabal in a stern and powerful voice.

"And who told you that the others won't try for their rights?" asked Daabis.

"That is no concern of mine," snapped Gabal. "You only hate tyranny when it's used against you!"

"Yes, you are a noble man, Gabal!" cried the lady emotionally. 'How I hope you will come back to my house!"

"I will live among the Al Hamdan," said Gabal firmly.

"That's not good enough for you!"

"When we come into our own, we will raise it up to be as good as the mansion itself—that is the wish of our ancestor Gabalawi!"

The overseer looked up at Gabal's face with a trace of reluctance and asked, "Does what the people of alley have done today threaten our security?"

"What goes on between you and them is no concern of mine," said Gabal dismissively.

"If you respect our covenant," Daabis put in, "none of them will dare to challenge you."

"Your rights will be restored, with witnesses!" said the overseer enthusiastically.

"You will dine with us this evening," said Huda hopefully. "This is a mother's wish!"

Gabal was aware of the meaning of this declaration of friendship from the overseer's house, and he was unable to spurn it. "You will have your wish, lady," he said.

42

The days that followed shone with delight for the Al Hamdan, or the Al Gabal, as they were now called. Their coffeehouse opened its doors, and Ridwan the poet sat cross-legged on his bench to pluck the rebec's strings. Liquor flowed in rivers, and huge clouds of hashish smoke rose to the rafters of every room. Tamar Henna danced until she was nearly thin. They thought nothing of saying outright who had killed Qidra, and lavished imaginative halos of light upon the tale of Gabalawi's meeting with Gabal. For Gabal and Shafiqa these were the sweetest days of their lives.

"How wonderful it will be to have Balqiti live with us!" he told her.

"Yes," said Shafiqa, who was suffering through the last months of a pregnancy, "so that he can give his blessing to his grandchild."

"You are all my happiness, Shafiqa," said Gabal gratefully. "Sayida will find a good husband among the Al Hamdan."

"Say Al Gabal like everyone else does—you are the best man this land has ever known."

"Adham was better than all of us." He smiled. "How he yearned for a good life where a man would have nothing to do but sing. But his great dream will be realized for us."

He saw Daabis dancing drunkenly amidst a crowd of the Al Gabal, and when Daabis saw him approaching he shook his club exuberantly. "You don't want to be a gangster? I'll be the gangster!"

"There will be no gangsters among the Al Hamdan," Gabal shouted loudly enough for everyone to hear. "But they must all be tough against anyone who turns against them."

Gabal walked to the coffeehouse and everyone followed him, stumbling from drunkenness. Gabal was delighted.

"In all this alley, you people are the most beloved of your ancestor," he told them. "You are the undisputed masters of the alley, so let love, justice and respect prevail among you, and no crime will ever be committed among you."

Drumming and singing could be heard from the homes of the Al Hamdan, and lights from parties of rejoicing shone throughout their nieghborhood, while the rest of the alley was sunk in its usual darkness, while its young people gathered at the outskirts of the Al Hamdan neighborhood to watch from afar. Then some somber-faced men of the alley showed up at the coffeehouse, where they were received warmly, invited to sit down and given tea. Gabal surmised that they had not come solely for courtesy, and he was proven right by the words of Zanati, the oldest of the visitors.

"Gabal, we all share one alley and one ancestor, and today you are master of this alley and its strongest man. It would be better for justice to prevail in all the neighborhoods, instead of in the Al Hamdan neighborhood alone."

Gabal said nothing, and disinterest showed in the faces of his people.

"It is in your power to bring justice to the whole alley," the man persisted.

Gabal had never been interested in the others of the alley, and neither had his people, who had felt superior to them even in the days of their affliction.

"My ancestor entrusted me with my own," said Gabal gently.

"But he is the ancestor of us all, Gabal."

"There are different opinions about that," said Hamdan. He looked at their faces carefully to see the effect of his words, and saw that they looked even more depressed. "He acknowledged *our* relationship with him through the meeting in the desert!"

For a moment Zanati looked as if he wanted to say, "There are different opinions about that," but he was too demoralized to say it. He asked Gabal, "Does our poverty and shame please you?"

"No," said Gabal without enthusiasm. "But it has nothing to do with us."

"How does it have nothing to do with you?" insisted the man.

Gabal wondered by what right this man spoke to him this way, but he did not get angry. He found that part of him almost felt sympathy for the man; but another part of him disapproved of getting involved in new troubles for the sake of others—and who were these others?

Daabis provided the answer when he shouted at Zanati. "Have you forgotten the way you treated us in the time of our affliction?"

The man lowered his gaze for a moment before speaking. "Who was able to state his opinions, or make his sympathies public, when the gangsters ruled? Did the gangsters spare anyone who didn't treat people the way they wanted them to be treated?"

Daabis curled his lip arrogantly to show his skepticism. "You envy us because of who we are in this alley, and you always have, even before there were any gangsters!"

Zanati bowed his head despondently and said, "God forgive you, Daabis!"

"Be grateful to Gabal for not turning against you out of revenge!"

Torn by conflicting thoughts, Gabal took refuge in silence; he was wary of offering help, but did not want to refuse openly. The men saw that they were contending with angry rebuke from Daabis, an ominous silence from Gabal and cold stares from the eyes of the others. They rose from the table in disappointment, and went back to where they had come from. Daabis waited until they had disappeared, then made a crude gesture with his right fist and shouted, "Tough luck, you pigs!"

"Gloating is beneath our dignity!" snapped Gabal.

43

It was a memorable day, the day Gabal received his people's share of the estate. He seated himself in the courtyard of the house—the scene of his triumph—and summoned the Al Hamdan to him. He counted the number of individuals in each family and distributed the money equally among them, and he did not treat himself any differently.

Perhaps Hamdan was not completely content with this equality, but he expressed this feeling indirectly. "It is not justice to cheat yourself!" he told Gabal.

"I took two shares, mine and Shafiqa's," said Gabal, frowning.

"But you are the leader of this neighborhood."

"A leader should not rob his people," said Gabal so that everyone could hear.

Daabis looked as though he were waiting anxiously for an argument, then said, "Gabal is not Hamdan and Hamdan is not Daabis and Daabis is not Kaabalha!"

"You want to divide one family into masters and servants!" Gabal objected angrily, but Daabis stuck by his view.

"We have among us a coffeehouse owner, a wandering peddler, and a beggar—how can they be equal? I was the first one to defy the siege, and was chased by Qidra. I was the first to meet you in your exile, and the first to support you after that, when all our people were hesitant!"

"A man who praises himself is a liar," shouted Gabal, whose anger was mounting. "By God, people like you deserve the suffering they get."

Daabis wanted to keep arguing, but saw the fiery anger in Gabal's eyes and desisted, leaving the courtyard without saying another word. That evening he went to bleary-eyed Itris' hashish den and joined the others where they sat in a circle, smoked and mulled over his problems. He wanted to find a diversion, so he invited Kaabalha to gamble. They played ticktacktoe, and in less than half an hour he had lost his share of the estate money.

Itris laughed as he changed the water in the hashish pipe. "Bad luck, Daabis! It's your fate to be poor, whether Gabalawi wants it or not."

"Riches aren't lost as easily as that," Daabis muttered darkly; losing had obliterated his drugged daze.

Itris drew a breath through the pipe to check the amount of water in it, then said, "But they're gone now, brother!"

Kaabalha carefully smoothed out the bills, then raised his hand to tuck them inside his shirtfront, but Daabis prevented him with one hand while gesturing with the other for Kaabalha to return the money.

"It's not your money anymore," snarled Kaabalha. "You have no right to it!"

"Let it go, you trash!"

Itris watched them uneasily and said, "Don't fight in my house."

"This trash isn't going to rob me!" shouted Daabis, grasping Kaabalha's hand even more tightly.

"Let go of my hand, Daabis, I didn't rob you."

"You earned it doing business, you mean?"

"Why did you want to gamble?"

Daabis slapped him hard and said, "My money, before I break your bones."

Abruptly Kaabalha pulled his hand away, and Daabis, maddened with fury, jammed his finger into Kaabalha's right eye.

Kaabalha screeched and jumped to his feet, covering his eye with his hands, leaving the money to fall into Daabis' lap. He staggered with pain, then collapsed and began to writhe and wail in agony. The seated smokers looked around at him, while Daabis gathered the money and stuffed it back into his shirt.

Then Itris came close to him and spoke in an appalled voice. "You put his eye out!"

Daabis was frightened for a moment, then got up suddenly and went out.

Gabal stood in the courtyard of his triumph surrounded by a crowd of the men of Al Hamdan, anger pulsing in his eyes and the corners of his mouth. Kaabalha squatted with a bandage swathed tightly over his eye, and Daabis stood to bear Gabal's fury in silence and fear.

Hamdan spoke softly to Gabal to soothe his anger. "Daabis will give the money back to Kaabalha."

"Let him give him back his eyesight first!" shouted Gabal at the top of his voice.

Kaabalha wept.

"If only it were possible for sight to be restored," said Ridwan the poet plaintively.

Gabal's face was as dark as a thundering and flashing sky. "But it is possible to take an eye for an eye."

Daabis stared apprehensively into Gabal's face, and gave the money to Hamdan. "I had lost my mind from rage. I didn't mean to hurt him!"

Gabal watched Daabis' face wrathfully for long moments, then spoke in a terrible voice. "An eye for an eye, and the criminal loses."

Looks of consternation were exchanged. Gabal had never been seen angrier than he was today, and events had proven the force of his anger, such as his outburst the day he had left his privileged home, and his fit the day he killed Qidra. Truly his wrath was extreme, and when he was angry nothing could deter him from satisfaction.

Hamdan was about to speak, but Gabal spoke first. "Gabalawi did not choose you for his love so that you might fight one another. We will have a life based either on order or on chaos that will do away with everyone; and that is why you are going to lose your eye, Daabis."

Daabis was consumed with terror and shouted, "No one is going to lay a hand on me, even if I have to fight all of you."

Gabal made for Daabis like a wild bull and struck him so hard in the face with his fist that he fell and lay motionless. He picked him up, still unconscious, and clasped him from behind, grasping him around his arms and chest. He turned to Kaabalha and spoke in a tone of command. "Get up and take your rights."

Kaabalha got up but stood uncertainly. Screams could be heard from Daabis' home. Gabal watched Kaabalha sternly and shouted at him. "Approach, before I bury you alive."

Kaabalha moved toward Daabis, and drove his index finger into his right eye until it flopped out; everyone saw it happen. The pitch of the screams from Daabis' home increased, and some of Daabis' friends, such as Itris and Ali Fawanis, began to cry.

"You cowards and evildoers!" shouted Gabal. "By God, you only hated the gangs because they were against you. As soon as any of you get the least power, you lose no time in harassing and attacking others. The only cure for the devils hidden deep inside you is to beat them unmercifully—pitilessly! Either order or ruin!"

He departed, leaving Daabis with his friends. This incident had a profound effect. Before, Gabal had been a beloved leader; his people thought of him as a gangster who did not want that title or the outward trappings of gangs. Now, he was feared and dreaded. People whispered about his cruelty and oppression, but there were always others to turn their words against them and remind them of the other side of his cruelty: his compassion for those who had been injured, and his genuine desire to establish an order that would safeguard the law, justice and brotherhood among the Al Hamdan. This last view found new support every day in the things that the man said and did, so that even people who had an aversion to Gabal came to like him; those who had feared came to believe; those who turned away from him were inclined to him; and everyone jealously guarded the order he had set up, and abided by it.

Honesty and security prevailed in his days, and he remained a symbol of justice and order among his people until he left the world, without having ever deviated from his path.

This is the story of Gabal.

He was the first to rise up against oppression in our alley, and the first to be honored by meeting Gabalawi after his isolation. He attained such a degree of power that no one could contend with him, yet he shunned bullying and gangsterism and self-enrichment from protection rackets and drug dealing. He remained a model of justice, power and order among his people. True, he did not concern himself with the other people of our alley. Perhaps he secretly despised them or scorned them as the rest of his people did, but he never wronged them or harmed them, and he set an example for all to follow.

Good examples would not be wasted on our alley were it not afflicted with forgetfulness.

But forgetfulness is the plague of our alley.

Rifaa

44

It was nearly dawn. Every living creature in the alley had gone to bed, even the gangsters, the dogs and the cats. Darkness lingered in the corners as if it would never leave. Amid the perfect silence, the gate of the House of Triumph in the Al Gabal neighborhood was opened with extreme caution, and two figures slipped out of it, moving quietly toward the mansion, and they followed along its high wall out to the desert. They stepped warily, and looked back every now and then to make sure that no one was following them, and pressed on into the desert guided by the light of the scattered stars until Hind's Rock appeared to them as a blotch of darkness blacker than its surroundings. They were a middle-aged man and a pregnant young woman, each carrying an overstuffed bundle. When they reached the rock, the woman sighed wearily. "Shafi'i, I am tired," she said.

The man stopped walking and spoke crossly. "May God afflict those who tired you! But rest."

The woman set her bundle down on the ground and sat upon it, resting her large belly on her lap. The man stood for a moment to look around, then sat down on his bundle. Breezes laden with the fresh scent of dawn wafted in their direction, but the woman was preoccupied. "Where will I have my baby, do you think?" she asked.

"Anyplace, Abda, would be better than our accursed alley," Shafi'i said unhappily.

He raised his eyes to the mass of the mountain that loomed from the far north to the far south.

"We'll go to Muqattam Marketplace, where Gabal went in his time of affliction, and I'll open a carpentry shop and work just as I did in the alley. I have two hands as good as gold, and enough money for a good start."

The woman drew her veil closer over her head and shoulders and said sadly, "We'll be living in exile, like people who have no family, when we are of the Al Gabal, the best people in the alley!"

The man spat with contempt and said bitterly, "Best people in the alley! What are we but cowering slaves, Abda? Gabal and his glory days are gone. We got Zanfil, may God send him to Hell, who is against us instead of being for us, who swallows up our money and destroys anyone who complains."

Abda could deny none of this. It was as if she were still living through those bitter days and sad nights, but feeling reassured by her distance from the misery of the alley, she turned tenderly to her heart's happy memories, and she sighed deeply. "There is no other alley like ours, for all the bad things in it. Where would you ever find another mansion like our ancestor's? Or neighbors like we had? Where could you hear the tales of Adham and Gabal and Hind's Rock? God's curse on those evil creatures!"

"They clubbed anyone for the flimsiest reason, and the others stalked around us like fate itself, with their arrogant faces!"

He remembered the horrible Zanfil and how he had taken him by the collar and shaken him so violently that his ribs nearly broke, then rolled him in the dirt in front of everybody, only because he had talked about the estate just once! He stamped his foot at the memory and spoke up. "That damned criminal kidnapped Sayidhum's baby, Sayidhum the head-meat seller, and the baby was never heard from again. He had no pity for a one-month-old! And you wonder 'Where will I have my baby?' You'll have your baby in a place where they don't massacre children."

Abda sighed and spoke gently, as if to soften the meaning of her words. "I just wish you could be satisfied with the same things that satisfy other people."

He frowned angrily, masked by the darkness. "What have I done, Abda? Nothing but wonder what happened to Gabal, and Gabal's covenant, and where is the power of justice, and what brought the Al Gabal back to poverty and humiliation? He wrecked my shop and beat me up, and would have killed me if it hadn't been for the neighbors. If we had stayed in our house until you gave birth, he would have pounced on the baby just as he did with Sayidhum's.

She shook her head sadly. "Oh, if only you had been patient, Shafi'i! Didn't you hear people say that surely someday Gabalawi will come out of his isolation to save his grandchildren from oppression and disgrace?"

Shafi'i exhaled a long breath and snapped, "That's what they say! And I've heard them say it since I was a boy, but the truth is that our ancestor has shut himself up in his house, and that the overseer of his estate monopolizes the estate revenues, except what he pays out to gangsters for his protection. Zanfil, the supposed protector of the Al Gabal, takes his share and buries it in his belly, as if Gabal had never appeared in this alley, as if he had never taken the eye of his friend Daabis to pay for the eye of poor Kaabalha."

The woman was silent, floating in that sea of blackness. Morning would find her among a strange people. The strangers would be her new neighbors. Her child would be born into their hands. The child would grow up in a strange land, like a limb cut from a tree. She had been reasonably happy among the Al Gabal; she had brought food to her husband in his shop, and at night sat by the window to hear old blind Gawad play the rebec. There was no lovelier music than that, and no lovelier story than Gabal's—the night he met Gabalawi in the dark and Gabalawi told him, "Be not afraid." He then helped Gabal, loved and aided him until he triumphed. And he had gone joyfully home to his alley—was anything sweeter than a homecoming after exile?

Shafi'i's face was turned up to the sky and its watchful stars, as he gazed at the first rays of light over the mountain, like a white cloud on the horizon of a black sky.

"We should move. We want to get to Muqattam before sunup," he warned.

"I still need rest."

"May God afflict those who tired you."

How wonderful life would be without Zanfil. Filled with blessings, pure air, the star-studded sky, delightful feelings—but there was also the overseer, Ihab, and the gangsters Bayoumi, Gaber, Handusa, Khalid, Batikha and Zanfil. It was possible for every house to become like the mansion, and for their cries to turn to song, but the miserable people longed for the impossible just as Adham had longed for it before them. And who were these poor people? Men whose backs were swollen from beating, whose buttocks were inflamed from kicks. Their eyes were tormented by flies, and lice infested their heads.

"Why has Gabalawi forgotten us?"

"God knows," the woman murmured.

"Gabalawi!" shouted the man in mingled grief and anger.

His voice echoed back to him.

"Trust in God," he told her.

Abda stood, and he took her hand. They trudged south, toward Muqattam Marketplace.

45

"Here is our alley," said Abda, joy plain in her eyes and her smile. "And here we are coming home to it after our exile—thanks be to Almighty God!"

Shafi'i smiled and wiped his forehead with the sleeve of his cloak. "It's wonderful to be home!" he said gravely.

Rifaa listened to his parents, his serene, handsome features reflecting surprise mingled with sorrow, and spoke almost reprovingly. "Have you already forgotten Muqattam and our neighbors?"

His mother smiled and brought the edge of her wrap over her hair, which was graying with age. She realized that the lad loved his birthplace as much as she loved hers, and that with his naturally gentle and friendly disposition he could not forget friendships.

"Good things are never forgotten," she answered him, "but this is your original home. Your people are here, the best people in the alley. You will love them, and they will love you. How wonderful Gabal's neighborhood will be now that Zanfil is dead."

"Khunfis won't be any better than Zanfil," Shafi'i warned them.

"But Khunfis has no grudge against you."

"Gangsters' grudges form as fast as mud after rain."

"Don't think that way," said Abda urgently. "We have come back here to live in peace. You'll open your shop, and we'll make a living. Don't forget that you lived under gang protection in Muqattam. People do everywhere."

The family continued their journey toward the alley, led by Shafi'i carrying a sack, and behind him Abda and Rifaa, who was carrying an enormous bundle. Rifaa was a good-looking lad: tall and slender, with an innocent face that radiated warmth and gentility: a stranger to the earth he walked upon. His eyes lovingly contemplated everything around him until they were drawn to the mansion that stood alone at the head of the alley, and the tops of the trees swaying above the wall. He gazed at it for a long time. "Our ancestor's house?" he then asked.

"Yes," said Abda delightedly. "Remember what I told you about it? Your ancestor is there, the owner of all the land and everything on it. All goodness is his, and all gratitude is due to him. If it weren't for his isolation from us, the alley would be full of light."

"In his name, Ihab the overseer plunders our alley," Shafi'i added mockingly, "and the gangsters attack us."

They proceeded toward the alley, along the southern wall of the mansion. Rifaa's eyes hung on the locked house. The house of Ihab, the estate overseer, came into view, its gatekeeper seated on a bench by the open gate. Before him stood the house of the alley's gangster, Bayoumi, in front of which was parked a horse-drawn cart filled with bushels of rice and baskets of fruit; servants were making several trips to carry these into the house. The alley seemed to be a playground for barefoot boys, while in front of the doorways families were spread out on the ground or on reed matting, cleaning beans or chopping greens, talking and telling jokes, scolding and snapping at one another with loud shouts and shrieks of laughter. Shafi'i's family headed for Gabal's neighborhood, and encountered an old blind man in the street, slowly feeling his way with his stick.

Shafi'i lowered the sack from his back and approached him, his features aglow with pleasure, until he stood before him. "Peace upon you, Gawad the poet!" he cried.

The poet stopped and cupped his ear attentively, then shook his head in puzzlement. "And peace upon you! I know that voice!"

"Have you forgotten your friend Shafi'i the carpenter?"

The man's face lit up with delight. "Shafi'i, by God!" He opened his arms and the men embraced warmly until passersby stared at them and two wicked boys imitated their embrace. Gawad squeezed his friend's hand. "You left us twenty years ago or more, a lifetime ago! How is your wife?"

"Fine, Gawad," said Abda. "I hope you are well. This is our son Rifaa. Kiss the dear poet's hand."

Rifaa approached the poet gladly, took his hand and kissed it.

The man patted him on the shoulder and explored his head and the features of his face curiously. "Marvelous—marvelous!" he said. "You are just like your ancestor!"

The praise lit up Abda's face, and Shafi'i laughed. "You wouldn't say that if you saw how skinny he is."

"Close enough. There is only one Gabalawi. What does the lad do?"

"I have taught him carpentry, but he's a pampered only child. He spends a little time in my shop and then the rest of the day he wanders in the desert and on the mountain."

"A man never settles down until he's married." The poet smiled. "Where have you been, Shafi'i?"

"In Muqattam."

"Just as Gabal did," the man said with a deep laugh, "but he came back a snake charmer, and you come back a carpenter as you were when you left. Anyway, your enemy is dead, even if his replacement is no better."

"They're all the same," Abda put in quickly. "But all we want is to live like peaceable people."

Some men recognized Shafi'i and hurried over to him. They all embraced him and there was a clamor of welcomes, while Rifaa resumed his infatuated examination of his surroundings; his own people were alive and breathing around him, which considerably lightened the gloom that had clouded his heart since he had left Muqattam Marketplace. His eyes roamed around until they settled on a window in the first house, out of which a girl was looking intently at his face. When their eyes met, she lifted her gaze to the horizon. One of his father's friends noticed this and whispered, "Aisha—daughter of Khunfis. One look at her could start a massacre!"

Rifaa blushed.

"He's not that kind of boy," his mother said. "He's just seeing his alley for the first time."

A man with a bull's muscular bulk came out of the house, swaggering in his flowing galabiya, a coarse mustache bristling over his mouth. His face was scarred and cratered. "Khunfis . . . Khunfis," people whispered to one another. Gawad took Shafi'i by the hand and guided him toward the house.

"God's peace on the protector of the Al Gabal. May I present our brother Shafi'i the carpenter. He has come home to his alley after a twenty-year absence!"

Khunfis stared into Shafi'i's face but ignored the hand offered him for several moments before extending his own, though even then his face did not soften. "Welcome," he murmured coolly.

Rifaa considered him resentfully. His mother whispered to him to go and introduce himself; which he did unwillingly, and put out his hand.

"My son, Rifaa," said Shafi'i.

Khunfis gave Rifaa a look of aversion and disdain, which the people understood as contemptuous of the boy's gentleness, so out of place in this alley. He shook his hand indifferently and turned to Rifaa's father. "So, have you forgotten the way things go in our alley?"

Shafi'i understood what was meant, but did not show his irritation. "We are at your service anytime, sir."

"Why did you leave your alley anyway?" Khunfis asked, searching his face suspiciously.

Shafi'i was silent a moment as he tried to think of the right answer.

"Fleeing Zanfil?" he was asked.

"It wasn't for doing anything unforgivable," Gawad the poet said promptly.

"You can't flee from *me* when I'm angry," Khunfis told Shafi'i in a tone of warning.

"You'll find us to be very fine people," said Abda hopefully.

Shafi'i and his family passed among their friends to the walk of the House of Triumph to move into the empty rooms to which Gawad guided them. A girl of insolent beauty came into view from a window that overlooked the walk; she stood combing her hair before a glass window, and when she saw the new arrivals she asked coquettishly, "Who's the dreamboat?"

Everyone laughed.

"A new neighbor for you, Yasmina," said one man. "He'll live in the walk right in front of you."

"God give us more men!" She laughed.

Her eyes passed briefly over Abda but settled firmly and admiringly on Rifaa, who was even more taken aback by her stare than by that of Aisha the daughter of Khunfis. He followed his parents to the door of their home, across from Yasmina's on the other side of the walk. He heard Yasmina's voice singing, "Mama, what a pretty boy!"

46

Shafi'i opened his carpentry shop at the entrance of the House of Triumph. Abda went out shopping early in the morning, and Shafi'i and his son Rifaa went to work. They sat at the threshold of the shop, waiting for business. The man had enough money to last a month or a little more, so he was not worried. He peered down the passage roofed with residences that led out to the wide courtyard.

"This is the blessed courtyard where Gabal drowned our enemies."

Rifaa gazed at it with dreaming eyes and a smile.

"And right here is where Adham built his hut and the events of his life actually took place; where Gabalawi blessed his son and forgave him."

Rifaa's comely smile broadened, and his eyes were lost in a dream. All beautiful memories were born here. Were it not for the passage of time, the footprints of Gabalawi and Adham would still be here, and the air would still carry their breath. From these windows the water had gushed onto the gangsters in the pit; from Yasmina's window water had cascaded onto the enemy. Today the window emitted only intimidating gazes. Time satirizes even the sublimest things. Gabal had waited inside the courtyard with weak men, but he had triumphed.

"Gabal triumphed, Father, but what good was his victory?"

"We have promised not to think about it. Have you seen Khunfis?"

"Oh, sir!?" called a flirtatious voice. "You—the carpenter!"

The father and son exchanged grimaces, and the father got up and craned his neck to see Yasmina looking out her window, her long braids loose and swinging.

"Yes?"

"Send up your boy to get my table. It needs to be repaired," she said in a voice eager with fun.

The man resumed his seat and told his son, "Trust in God."

Rifaa found the apartment door open for him. "Ahem," he said, and she gave him leave to come in, so he went in. He found her in a brown robe trimmed in white around the collar and the swell of her breasts. Her legs and feet were bare. She was silent for a moment as if to appraise the effect of her appearance on Rifaa, and when she saw that his eyes were steady and untroubled, she pointed to a small table standing on three legs in a corner of the room.

"The fourth leg is under the sofa," she said. "Please repair it and refinish the table."

"Yes, ma'am," he said pleasantly.

"How much?"

"I'll ask my father."

"What about you?" she said aggressively. "Don't you know how much that costs?"

"He's the one who decides that."

"Who's going to fix it?" she asked, looking intently into his face.

"I will, but he'll supervise and help me."

She laughed indifferently. "Batikha, the youngest gangster here, is younger than you are, but he can take over a whole wedding procession, and you can't even repair the leg of a table by yourself!"

"Well, no matter," said Rifaa, in a voice that made plain his wish to end the conversation, "the table will come back to you like new." He picked up the fourth leg from underneath the sofa, lifted the table onto his shoulder and headed for the door. "Good day."

When he put it down in front of his father in their shop, the man examined it and spoke with a trace of exasperation. "To tell the truth, I would have preferred that our first work come from someone more decent."

"She's not bad, Father," said Rifaa innocently, "but she seems to be lonely."

"There is nothing more dangerous than a lonely woman!"

"Perhaps she needs guidance!"

"Our business is carpentry, not guidance," snapped Shafi'i. "Pass me the glue."

That evening Shafi'i and Rifaa went to the Gabal Coffeehouse. Gawad the poet was sitting cross-legged on his bench drinking his coffee. Thick-lipped Shaldum, the coffeehouse owner, sat at the entrance, and Khunfis occupied the seat of honor amid a halo of his admirers. Shafi'i and his son made their way to the gangster to greet him respectfully, then took empty seats near Shaldum. Shafi'i promptly took the pipe and offered his son a glass of cinnamon brew flavored with hazelnuts. The coffeehouse air was lazy. A knotted cloud of smoke rose to the roof, and the motionless air was overlaid with the scent of molasses-cured tobacco, mint and cloves; the men's luxuriantly mustached faces were pale and heavy-lidded. There was coughing and hawking, filthy jokes and harsh laughter, and from down the alley came the shouts of boyish songs.

Children of Gabalawi, charm our snakes!
Are you Christians or are you Jews?
What do you eat? We eat dates.
What do you drink? We drink coffee.

A cat crouching by the coffeehouse door sprang under a bench, and there was a rustling sound before she reappeared, racing toward the alley, her teeth closed over a mouse. Rifaa set down his glass of cinnamon brew in disgust and raised his eyes just in time to see Khunfis spitting; then Khunfis bellowed at Gawad the poet, "When are you going to start, old man?"

Gawad smiled and nodded, then took up the rebec and plucked the opening melodies on its strings. He began with one salutation to Ihab the overseer, a second to Bayoumi, the protector of the alley, a third to Gabal's successor, Khunfis, and went on from there.

"And Adham sat in the estate office, receiving new tenants, and was looking into the ledger when he heard the last man's voice announce his name.

" 'Idris Gabalawi.'

"And Adham looked up in fright and saw his brother standing before him."

The poet went on with the tale in an air of quiet reverence. Rifaa listened raptly. This was the poet, and these were the tales. How often had he heard his mother say, "Our alley is the alley of tales." And truly these tales were worth his love. Perhaps they would compensate for the loss of the games of Muqattam and his privacy, and be a repose for his heart, so scorched with a mysterious love, as mysterious as that locked mansion. There was no sign of life there apart from the tops of the sycamore, berry and palm trees. What signs of life were there from Gabalawi, other than trees and tales? What proof was there that he was his descendant, other than the resemblance Gawad the poet had discerned with his hands? Night was coming on, and Shafi'i was smoking his third pipe. The cries of peddlers and shouts of children had died away in the alley, leaving only the rebec melodies, drumbeats from afar, and the shrieks of a woman being beaten by her husband. Adham had now met his fate at the hands of Idris. Out in the desert, followed by sobbing Umaima. Just as my mother left the alley with me stirring in her belly. A curse on all bullies. And on all cats, when mice breathe their last in their jaws, and on every mocking look and cold sneer, and on whoever welcomes his homecoming brother by telling him, "You can't flee from me when I'm angry," and on all terrorists and hypocrites. By now there was nowhere for Adham but the desert, and the poet was singing one of Idris' drunken songs. Rifaa leaned over to his father's ear and said, "I want to visit other coffeehouses."

"Our coffeehouse is the best in the alley," said Shafi'i, surprised.

"What do the poets there say?"

"The same stories, but the way they tell them there you'd never know it."

Shaldum heard their whispers and leaned over to Rifaa. "Our people are the biggest liars in this alley, and poets are the worst liars of all. In the next coffeehouse you'll hear that Gabal said he was from the alley, when he just said that he was from the Al Hamdan, by God."

"A poet will say anything to please his audience," said Shafi'i.

"You mean he wants to please the gangs!" whispered Shaldum.

The father and son left the coffeehouse at midnight, when the darkness was so intense as to be palpable. Men's voices came out of nowhere, and a cigarette glowed in an invisible hand like a star falling to earth.

"Did you enjoy the story?" the father asked.

"Yes, what wonderful stories."

"Gawad loves you," the father said with a laugh. "What was he telling you during the break?"

"He invited me to visit him at home."

"How quickly you come to love people, but you are a boy who learns slowly."

"I have a whole life for carpentry," Rifaa said in a tone of apology, "but for now I want to visit all the coffeehouses."

They felt their way to the passage, where Yasmina's house resounded with the noise of a drunken brawl and a singing voice: "You in the embroidered cap, who made it? You stitched my heart and now it's yours."

"She's not as lonely as I'd thought," Rifaa whispered to his father.

"There's a lot of life you've missed, being so solitary," his father said, sighing.

They climbed up the stairs slowly and cautiously, and abruptly Rifaa said, "Father, I'm going to visit Gawad the poet."

47

Rifaa knocked at the door of Gawad the poet, at the third house in the Al Gabal neighborhood. Screams of abuse rose from the courtyard, from women who had gathered there to wash clothes and cook. He looked from over the railing of the circular passage that surrounded the courtyard of the house from above. The main fight was between two women, one of whom stood behind a wash bucket, waving her soap-lathered arms, while the other stood at the opening of the passage, sleeves rolled up, answering the obscenities with even more shocking words and jutting out her pelvis contemptuously. The other women had separated into two groups, and their shrieks clashed until the courtyard walls echoed with their hateful curses and filthy libels. He started at what he saw and heard, and turned toward the poet's door, shocked. Even women, even cats, let alone the gangsters. Claws on every hand and poison on every tongue, fear and hatred in every heart. Pure air was only for the Muqattam Desert or the mansion, where Gabalawi alone was blessed with peace! The door opened on the blind man's questioning face. Rifaa greeted him and the man's features broke into a smile as he made room for him to enter.

"Welcome, my boy."

As soon as Rifaa entered he was met with the strong smell of incense —it was like the breath of an angel. He followed the man to a small square room with cushions around the walls and embroidered reed mats spread over the floor. Through the slats of the closed shutters the afternoon air was as tawny as honey. The ceiling around the suspended light was decorated with pictures of birds, especially doves. The poet sat down cross-legged on a cushion, and Rifaa sat beside him.

"We were making coffee," the man said.

He called his wife, and a woman with a tray of coffee appeared.

"Come, Umm Bekhatirha, this is Rifaa, the son of our friend Shafi'i."

"Welcome, my boy," she said. She was in the middle of her sixth decade, erect and strong, with a piercing gaze and a tattoo above her chin.

Gawad motioned toward their guest. "He listens to everything, Umm Bekhatirha. He's crazy about stories. People like him really excite poets and please them. The others fall asleep from smoking hashish!"

"To him the stories are new, but they've heard them before," she said playfully.

"That's one of your demons talking," said the poet crossly. He turned to Rifaa. "This woman is a very fine exorcist."

Rifaa watched her eagerly and their eyes met as she offered him a cup of coffee. How he had loved the ceremonies expelling demons in

Muqattam Marketplace. His heart had followed them with delight; he would stand in the street with his head raised to the windows, and try to see the incense gliding through the air and the dancers' rocking heads.

"Didn't you learn anything about our alley when you lived abroad?" the poet asked.

"My father told me about it, and so did my mother, but my heart was there, and I didn't really think about the estate and its problems. I was amazed at how many victims it had claimed—I tended to have my mother's view, to prefer love and peace."

Gawad shook his head sadly. "How can love and peace live among poverty and gangsters' clubs!"

Rifaa did not reply; not because there was no answer, but because for the first time his eyes lit upon a strange picture on the right-hand wall of the room. It was painted in oils on the wall itself, like the pictures that ornamented the coffeehouse walls. It depicted a tremendous man, and beside him the houses of the alley, tiny as children's toys.

"Who is that in the picture?" the boy asked.

"Gabalawi," said Umm Bekhatirha.

"Has anyone seen him?"

"No, no one of our generation has seen him," said Gawad. "Even Gabal could not see him clearly in the desert darkness, but the painter drew him from the descriptions of him in the stories."

"Why did he shut his doors against his descendants?" Rifaa asked with a sigh.

"Old age, they say. Who knows what time has done to him? By God, if he opened his gates, no one in this alley would stay in his squalid house."

"Can't you—"

"Don't trouble yourself about him," Umm Bekhatirha interrupted. "When the people of our alley start talking about the estate owner, they get to talking about the estate itself, and that leads to every kind of tragedy."

He shook his head, at a loss. "How can anyone not trouble himself with such a fabulous ancestor?"

"Let's do as he does—he doesn't trouble himself with us."

Rifaa raised his eyes to the picture. "But he met Gabal, and spoke to him."

"Yes, and when Gabal died, Zanfil came, and then Khunfis, and . . . heavens! Nothing has ever changed."

Gawad laughed. "This alley needs someone to rid it of its devils just as you rid people of their demons."

"Those people are the real demons, ma'am," said Rifaa smiling. "If you had seen the way Khunfis welcomed my father!"

"I have nothing to do with them. My demons give in to me the way snakes obeyed Gabal. I have all the Sudanese incense and Ethiopian amulets and power-giving chants."

"Where did you get your power over demons?" asked Rifaa earnestly.

She held him in a wary gaze and said, "It is my profession, just as your father's profession is carpentry. It came to me from the Giver of all talents!"

Rifaa finished the last drop of his coffee and was about to say something when Shafi'i's voice rose in a shout from the alley. "Rifaa! Boy! Lazy boy!"

Rifaa went to the window, opened it and looked out until his eyes met his father's. "Just a half hour more, Father!"

The man heaved his shoulders in what looked like despair and went back to his shop. As Rifaa closed the window, he saw Aisha standing in her usual pose by her window, just as he had first seen her, gazing intently at him. He imagined that she smiled at him, that her eyes spoke to him. He hesitated a moment, then closed the window and sat down again.

Gawad was laughing. "Your father wants you to be a carpenter, but what do you want?"

Rifaa thought about it. "I have to be a carpenter like my father, but I love stories, and these secrets about demons—tell me more, ma'am!"

The woman smiled and seemed inclined to grant him a little of her knowledge. "Every person has a demon which is his master, but not every demon is evil or has to be exorcised."

"How can we tell one from another?"

"His deeds tell us. You, for example, are a good boy, and your demon deserves only goodness—but this is not the case with the demons in Bayoumi and Khunfis and Batikha!"

"What about Yasmina's demon, does it need to be exorcised?" he asked innocently.

"Your neighbor?" Umm Bekhatirha laughed. "But the men of Al Gabal want her as she is."

"I want to know these things," he said, intensely serious. "Don't hold anything back."

"Who could deny anything to this good boy?" said Gawad.

"It would be nice if you visited me as your time allows," said Umm Bekhatirha, "but only on condition that it doesn't anger your father. People will ask what this good boy wants with demons; but know that the only illness men have is demons."

Rifaa listened and gazed at the picture of Gabalawi.

48

Carpentry was his living and his future, and there seemed to be no escape from it. If it did not make him happy, what would make him happy? It was better than slaving behind a handcart or carrying baskets, or other lines of work, like being a thug or gangster—how hateful, how detestable they were. Umm Bekhatirha had stirred his imagination as nothing ever had, except for the picture of Gabalawi painted on the wall of the room in the poet Gawad's house. He begged his father to have a picture like it painted in their house or in the shop, but his father told him, "We have better uses for that kind of money, and it's only a fairy tale, so what good is that?" All Rifaa could do was say, "I wish I could see him!" His father laughed heartily and chided him, "Wouldn't it be better to see to your job? You're not always going to have me here, and you have to prepare for the day when you'll have the responsibility of your mother, your wife and children, all by yourself." But Rifaa thought about everything Umm Bekhatirha had done and said, as he had never thought about anything before. What she said about demons seemed to him supremely important. He forgot none of it, even in the happy times he spent visiting all the alley coffeehouses, one after the other. Even the same stories did not make the same profound impression that Umm Bekhatirha's stories did. Every man had a demon that was his master, and just as the master was, the slave became; that was what Umm Bekhatirha said. How many evenings had he spent with the old lady listening to the drumbeat and watching the taming of the demons. Some ailing people were brought to the house, powerless and still, and others were carried in shackled because of their evil. The right incense was burned, for every condition had its own incense, and the appropriate drumbeat, as every demon demanded its own beat, and then the wonders occurred. We know that every demon has his cure, but what is the cure for the overseer and his gangsters? Those evil things mock exorcism, while perhaps it was created solely for them! Killing was the way to be rid of them, while demons submitted to sweet incense and lovely melodies. How can an evil demon be captivated by beauty and goodness? How strange what we learn from demons and exorcisms! He told Umm Bekhatirha that he wished from the bottom of his heart to pursue the secrets of exorcism. She asked him, *Do you crave riches?* He answered her that he did not want riches, only to purge the alley. The woman laughed, saying that he was the first man who wanted that job; what fascinated him about it? He assured her, *The wisest thing in your work is that you defeat evil with goodness and beauty.* His soul was soothed when she began to divulge to him her secrets. To declare his delight, he went up to the roof of the house in the rapture of daybreak to witness the awakening of light, but the mansion, rather than the stars, the silence or the cock, preoccupied his mind, and he gazed at the mansion slumbering among the tall trees and wondered, *Where are you, Grandfather? Why don't you appear, even for a moment? Why don't you come out, even once? Why don't you speak—just one word? Do you not know that one word from you could change our alley? Or do you like what is going on here? How beautiful are the trees around your house! I love them because you do. Look at them, so that I can read your looks upon them.* His father scolded him when he told him of his notions, and said, "What about your work, you lazy boy! Boys your age are roaming every neighborhood trying to find a living, or making the whole alley tremble when they lift their clubs!"

One day when the family was assembled, after lunch, Abda spoke to her husband with a smile. "Tell him!"

Rifaa saw that this involved him and looked expectantly at his father, but the man addressed his wife. "First you tell him what you have to say."

Abda gazed proudly at her son. "Glad news, Rifaa. Lady Zakia, the wife of our protector Khunfis, visited me! I returned her visit, of course, and she received me warmly and presented her daughter Aisha to me—a girl as beautiful as the moon. And then she visited me again and brought Aisha with her."

Shafi'i glanced furtively at his son as he raised his coffee cup to his mouth, to see the effect of this story on him. He shook his head at the difficulty that awaited him, and spoke grandly.

"This is an honor accorded to no other house in the Al Gabal neighborhood. Imagine that the wife and daughter of Khunfis should visit this house of ours!"

Rifaa lifted his eyes to his mother in bewilderment.

"How elegant their house is—the soft chairs, the fabulous carpet! The curtains that hang from the windows and doors."

"All that luxury came from the Al Gabal's usurped wealth!"

Shafi'i stifled a smile and said, "We have promised not to talk about that."

"Let's just remember that Khunfis is the master of the Al Gabal and that the friendship of his family is an answered prayer!" said Abda earnestly.

"Congratulations on your new friend," said Rifaa crossly.

The mother and her husband exchanged a meaningful look.

"The fact that Aisha came with her mother told me something."

"Told you what, Mother?" asked Rifaa, feeling depressed.

Shafi'i laughed and made a despairing gesture with his hand and turned to Abda. "We should have told him how we got married!"

"No!" exclaimed Rifaa. "Father, no!"

"What do you mean? What's wrong with you, acting like a virgin girl?"

"It is in your hands," said Abda with hopeful urgency. "You can make us part of the running of the Al Gabal's estate. They will welcome you if you go to them; even Khunfis will welcome you. If the woman weren't sure of her influence with him, she wouldn't have come here. You can have status that the whole alley will be jealous of from one end to the other."

"Who knows," laughed his father. "Someday you might be overseer of the Al Gabal's estate, or one of your sons might be."

"Are you actually saying this, Father? Have you forgotten why you were driven out of this alley twenty years ago?"

Shafi'i blinked, a little confused. "Today we live like everyone else. We must not ignore an opportunity that comes begging to us."

Rifaa stammered and spoke as if to himself. "How can I marry into a demon's family when all I want to do is expel demons?"

"I never expected to make anything more than a carpenter of you," shouted Shafi'i menacingly, "and now luck offers you an important rank in our alley—but you want to be an exorcist like some black woman! What a scandal! What evil eye is afflicting you? Say that you will marry her, and spare us your jokes."

"I will not marry her, Father."

"I will visit Khunfis to ask him for the match," said Shafi'i, ignoring him.

"Don't do it, Father," shouted Rifaa vehemently.

"Tell me why you are doing this, boy," his father asked him impatiently.

"Don't be hard on him," Abda begged her husband. "You know how he is."

"Don't I know! Our alley will condemn us for his weakness."

"Go easy on him so he'll think about it."

"Boys his age are already fathers and the ground trembles under their steps!" He stared at him, furious, and went on exasperatedly. "Why does all the blood leave your face? You come from the loins of men!"

Rifaa sighed. He was depressed enough to cry. *The bonds of father-hood are broken by anger. A house may become at times a gloomy prison. What you desire is not in this place or among these people.*

"Don't torture me, Father" he said hoarsely.

"You're the one torturing me, just as you have ever since you were born."

Rifaa bowed his head until his face was hidden from his parents. His father dropped his voice and calmed his anger as much as he could.

"Are you afraid of marriage? Wouldn't you like to get married? Tell me what is in your heart—or I'll go to Umm Bekhatirha. Maybe she knows more about you than we do!"

"No!" cried Rifaa sharply. He stood abruptly and left the room.

49

Shafi'i went down to open up the shop but did not find Rifaa there as he had expected. He did not call out for him. It was, he reasoned, wiser to affect coolness over his absence. The day passed, crawling slowly by, the light of the sun left the land of the alley and the sawdust mounted around Shafi'i's feet with no sign of Rifaa. Evening came and he closed the shop, deeply troubled and angry. As usual, he headed for Shaldum's coffeehouse and took his seat, and when he saw Gawad the poet coming in alone he was surprised and said, "So where is Rifaa?"

"I haven't heard from him since yesterday," the man replied, feeling his way to his bench.

"I haven't seen him since he left us after lunch," said Shafi'i uneasily.

Gawad raised his gray eyebrows and sat cross-legged on the bench, tucking the rebec by his side, wondering, "Did anything happen between you?"

Shafi'i did not answer him, but quickly got up and left the coffeehouse. Shaldum was taken aback by Shafi'i's agitation and spoke up with amusement.

"Such a drama our alley hasn't seen since Idris built his hut in the desert! When I was young, I used to run away from the alley for days and no one would ask about me. When I'd come back, my father, God rest his soul, would shout, 'What brings you back here, you little bastard?'"

"The point is, he wasn't positive you were his son," was Khunfis' comment from where he was listening in the heart of the coffeehouse.

The place erupted in laughter, and most of them congratulated Khunfis on his elegant witticism. Shafi'i headed home, and when he asked Abda, "Has Rifaa come back?" she was seized with anxiety. She said that she had thought he was in the shop as usual. She grew even more concerned when he told her that Rifaa had not gone to the poet Gawad's house.

"So where did he go?"

They heard Yasmina's voice split the air as she called a fig seller. Abda gave Shafi'i a suspicious look, but the man shook his head tiredly and gave a brief bark of dry, ironic laughter. "A girl like that can figure men out!"

Shafi'i went to Yasmina's house driven only by despair. He knocked at the door and Yasmina opened it herself. When she recognized him, she tossed her head in surprise and triumph. "You!" she said. "Well, well, how surprised should I be?"

The man lowered his eyes at her diaphanous blouse. "Is Rifaa here?" he asked dejectedly.

"Rifaa!" she said, even more surprised. "Why?" Shafi'i's embarrassment mounted, and she indicated the inside of her house. "Look for him yourself."

But the man turned to go.

"What, has he come of age today?" she asked sarcastically.

He heard her addressing someone within: "These days people are more worried about their boys than their girls."

Shafi'i found Abda waiting for him in the passage.

"We'll go to Muqattam Marketplace together," she told him.

"That boy!" he shouted angrily. "This is what I get after a day of hard work?"

They took a mule-drawn cart to Muqattam Marketplace and asked about him at their old neighbors', and they asked old friends, but discovered no trace of him. While he used to disappear for hours in the afternoon or early evening in seclusion or on the mountain, no one imagined that he would stay out in the desert until this hour of the night. They returned to the alley as they had left it, but in an even more anguished state. People gossiped about Rifaa's disappearance, especially when it went on for days. He became a joke in the coffeehouse, at Yasmina's house and throughout the Al Gabal neighborhood. Everyone ridiculed his parents' anguish. Perhaps Umm Bekhatirha and old Gawad were the only ones who shared the parents' grief. "Where has the boy gone?" asked Gawad. "He isn't this kind of boy; if he were, we wouldn't grieve." Once when Batikha was drunk he yelled, "Little boy lost, good people!" as if he were calling a lost toddler; the whole alley laughed and the small boys repeated it. Abda was sick with grief. Shafi'i worked distractedly in his shop, his eyes red from lack of sleep. Khunfis' wife, Zakia, stopped visiting Abda and ignored her in the street.

One day Shafi'i was absorbed in sawing a board when Yasmina shouted at him as she came in from an errand. "Shafi'i! Look."

He saw her pointing to the end of the alley, into the desert. He left the shop, still holding the saw, to see what she was pointing to, and saw his son Rifaa walking shyly toward the building. He dropped the saw in front of the shop and hurried to his son, examining him with surprise. Then he snatched him by the upper arms.

"Rifaa!" he shouted. "Where have you been? Don't you know what your absence meant for us? For your poor mother, who nearly died from worry?"

The boy said nothing, and his father perceived how emaciated he was.

"Were you ill?"

"No. Let me see my mother," said Rifaa a little confusedly.

Yasmina came up to them and asked doubtfully, "But where were you?"

He did not look at her. Boys gathered around him, and his father led him home. They were quickly followed by Gawad and Umm Bekhatirha.

When his mother caught sight of him she jumped from the bed and clutched him to her. "God forgive you," she said weakly. "How could you do this to your mother?"

He took her hand between his and sat her down on the bed, then sat beside her. "I'm sorry."

His father lifted his glowering face, which hid the exulting relief within him as a black cloud conceals the moon, and scolded him. "All we were trying to do was make you happy!"

"Did you think we would force you to get married?" asked Abda, her eyes filled with tears.

"I am tired," he said sadly.

"Where were you?" everyone asked at once.

"I was depressed with life, so I went to the desert. I had to be alone and to go to the desert. I never left the desert except to buy food."

His father slapped his forehead and shouted, "Is that what normal people do?"

"Let him alone," said Umm Bekhatirha kindly. "I know about these conditions. You shouldn't force someone like him to do anything he doesn't want to."

"His happiness was our only hope, but fate took its course. How thin you are, my boy!"

"Tell me one thing," said Shafi'i in exasperation. "Has anything like this ever happened in our alley before?"

"To me, there is nothing strange about him, Shafi'i, believe me," said Umm Bekhatirha reprovingly. "He's a wonderful boy."

"We're the talk of the whole alley," Shafi'i muttered dejectedly.

"There's no other boy in the whole alley like him!" said Umm Bekhatirha angrily.

"That's the whole problem," said Shafi'i.

"By the unity of God," exclaimed Umm Bekhatirha, "you don't know what you're saying, or understand what others say!"

50

The sight of the carpentry shop now suggested activity and success. On one side of the table Shafi'i stood sawing wood, and on the other Rifaa clasped the adze or hammered nails, while underneath the table the heap of sawdust reached the middle of the can of glue. Window shutters and the leaves of doors leaned against the walls, and in the middle of the room stood a stack of new crates of light, polished wood, needing only paint. The smell of wood filled the air, along with the sound of sawing, hammering, sanding and the gurgle of the water pipe as four seated customers smoked and chatted by the door.

"I'll really try your skill with this sofa, and God willing your next job will be furniture for my daughter's wedding," Higazi said to Shafi'i. He turned to his friends. "I'm telling you again, the times we are living in, if Gabal came back, he'd lose his mind."

They all nodded sadly as they puffed away, and Burhoum the gravedigger smiled at Shafi'i. "Why don't you want to make me a coffin? Doesn't everything have its price?"

Shafi'i stopped sawing for a moment to laugh. "Absolutely not! A coffin in the shop would scare customers away."

"That's true," Farhat agreed. "Damn death and all that."

"Your problem," Higazi resumed, "is that you're too afraid of death. That's why Khunfis can control you, and Bayoumi can rule you, and Ihab can rob you."

"Aren't you afraid of death, too?"

Higazi spat. "It's a fault we all have. Gabal was strong, and with strength and action he won for us rights that cowardice has lost."

Rifaa abruptly stopped hammering and took the nails from his mouth. "Gabal wanted to win our rights through fairness. He resorted to force in self-defense."

Higazi laughed derisively and asked, "Tell me, boy, can you hammer nails without force?"

"People are not wood, sir," said Rifaa very earnestly.

His father gave him a look and went back to his work.

"The truth," Higazi went on, "is that Gabal was one of the toughest gangsters this alley ever knew, and how he tried to make the Al Gabal be like him!"

"He wanted them to protect the whole alley, not just their own people," Farhat added.

"And what are they now but mice, or rabbits?"

"What colors do you want, Higazi?" asked Shafi'i, wiping his nose on the back of his hand.

"Choose a color that won't get dirty too quickly. That's better for cleanliness." He resumed talking to his friends. "The day Daabis took Kaabalha's eye, Gabal took *his* eye. Through power he established justice."

"We have no lack of power," said Rifaa with an audible sigh. "Every hour of the day and night we see people beating up people, fighting and murdering. Even women bare their nails and blood flows, but where is the justice? How obscene it all is."

They were all silent a moment, then Hanura spoke for the first time. "This little teacher looks down on our alley! He's too soft, and it's your fault, Shafi'i."

"Me?"

"Yes. He's a spoiled boy."

Higazi turned to Rifaa and laughed. "Better than this you should find yourself a bride!"

There was loud laughter and Shafi'i frowned. Rifaa blushed.

"Power—power," Higazi resumed. "Without it, there is no justice."

"The truth is that our alley needs mercy," insisted Rifaa despite the way his father glared at him.

Burhoum the gravedigger laughed and said, "Do you want to ruin me?"

Again they roared with laughter. This was followed by fits of coughing until Higazi spoke up, his eyes the red tint of glue. "In the old days Gabal went to ask for justice and mercy from Effendi, who sent him Zaqlut and his men instead, and had it not been for clubs—no, not mercy, clubs—Gabal and his people would have perished."

"Please, everyone! The walls have ears. If they hear you, no one will listen to a word you have to say," Shafi'i warned.

"He's right," said Hanura. "What are you but good-for-nothing hashish addicts? There's no good in you—if Khunfis passed by now, you'd all prostrate yourselves in front of him." He turned to Rifaa. "Don't take offense, my boy, hashish addicts have no shame. Haven't you ever tried hashish, Rifaa?"

"He doesn't like parties. If he takes more than two puffs, he either chokes or drops off to sleep."

"What a fine boy," said Farhat. "Some people think he's an exorcist because of his attachment to Umm Bekhatirha, and others think he's a poet because he loves old stories so much."

"And he hates hashish parties the same way he hates marriage!" laughed Higazi.

Burhoum called the coffeehouse boy to take the pipe away, then they got up quietly, their little party at an end.

Shafi'i abandoned his saw and gave his son a look of rebuke. "Don't make yourself the talk of those people."

Boys showed up to play in front of the store. Rifaa walked around the table to stand before his father, then took his hand and withdrew with him to a far corner of the shop where no one could listen. He seemed agitated and uneasy, but his lips were set determinedly. There was a strange light glowing in his eyes that made his father's eyes questioning.

"I cannot be silent after today," Rifaa said.

His father was irritated; how maddening this dear child was. He squandered his precious time in Umm Bekhatirha's house. He spent long hours all alone at Hind's Rock. When he spent as little as an hour in the shop he caused trouble with his talk.

"Are you tired?"

"I cannot hide from you what I have in my soul," said Rifaa with the strange calm that had replaced his unease.

"What is it?"

"Yesterday," said Rifaa, drawing nearer, "after I left the poet's house at midnight, I felt like I had to get away—I went to the desert. I walked in darkness until I got tired, then I chose a place under the mansion wall overlooking the desert, and sat down, and leaned my back against the wall."

The concern was clear in the man's eyes, and prompted him with one look to resume his story.

"I heard a strange voice speaking—as if someone were talking to himself in the dark. I was gripped by this wonderful feeling that it was the voice of our ancestor, Gabalawi."

The man stared at his son's face. "The voice of Gabalawi?" he stammered. "What made you imagine that?"

"I didn't imagine anything, Father. You'll have proof. I got up as soon as I heard the voice, and turned toward the house. I backed up so that I could see it but I saw nothing but darkness."

"Thank God!"

"But listen, Father! I heard the voice say, 'Gabal carried out his mission and I think well of him, but things have gotten worse—it is more abominable than it was before!' "

Shafi'i felt his heart burning, and sweat trickled down his forehead. "How many people have sat where you did, under that wall, and they never heard a thing."

"But I did, Father."

"It might have been someone lying down in the darkness!"

"The voice came from the mansion," said Rifaa with a resolute shake of his head.

"How did you know that?"

"I called out, 'Grandfather, Gabal is dead, and others have replaced him. Help us!' "

"I hope to God no one heard you," said Shafi'i crossly.

"Gabalawi heard me," said Rifaa, his eyes bright. "I heard him say, 'What an abomination, for a boy to ask his old grandfather to do something. It is the beloved son who should act.' I asked him, 'What can I do against those gangsters? I am weak.' He answered me. 'The weak man is a fool who does not know his strength, and I have no love for fools.' "

"You think that you had this conversation with Gabalawi?" asked Shafi'i with something like panic.

"Yes, by the Lord of Heaven!"

Shafi'i moaned. "Dreams bring the worst disasters!" he lamented.

"Believe me, Father, I know what I am saying."

"Give me hope that perhaps you don't," the man sighed.

"I know now what is wanted of me," said Rifaa, his face shining with rapture like a sweet song.

Shafi'i struck his forehead in despair. "Something is wanted of you, yet?" he shouted.

"Yes. I am weak but I am not a fool. It is the beloved son who should act!"

"Your acts will be shameful," cried Shafi'i, feeling that his heart was being pounded with a hammer. "You will perish and destroy us with you!"

"They only kill those who covet the estate," Rifaa said with a smile.

"What do you covet besides the estate?"

"Adham used to long for a good, full life," said Rifaa in a voice brimming with confidence, "and Gabal too. He sought his rights to the estate only in search of that good, full life, but we were corrupted by the idea that this life will never be worthwhile for anyone unless the estate is divided among everyone. So everyone got his share and invested it, so that he was delivered from hard work, and was freed for a good, full life. But how trivial the estate is to one who can appreciate this life without it —and that is possible for whoever wishes. We can do without it from this moment on!"

Old Shafi'i sighed, somewhat relieved. "Did Gabalawi tell you that?"

"He said he had no love for fools. He said that a fool was a person who did not know his own strength, and that I would be the last one to fight for the sake of the estate. The estate is nothing, Father, and the happiness of a full life is everything. Nothing stands between us and happiness but the demons hiding within us, and it is not for nothing that I should love the treatment of demons and improve on it. Perhaps the will of the Lord of Heaven has compelled me to it.''

Shafi'i relaxed after this torment, but the torment had exhausted him and he sank down on his saw and stretched out his legs, resting his back against the leaf of the window waiting to be repaired, then turned to his son a little ironically. "Why," he asked, "have we not achieved a full life, when we had Umm Bekhatirha before you were even born?"

"Because," said Rifaa confidently, "she waits for sick rich people to come to her—instead of going herself to the poor."

Shafi'i looked into the corner of his shop and spoke with doubt in his voice. "Look at the work we have. What does tomorrow have in store for us, thanks to you?"

"Every good thing, Father," said Rifaa joyously. "Healing the sick won't upset anyone but the demons."

A light glowed in the shop from a mirror by the door that reflected the rays of the sinking sun.

51

That night the uneasiness spread to Shafi'i's house. Although Abda heard the story composedly and knew only that Rifaa heard his ancestor's voice speaking to him and that after that he had decided to visit the poor to cleanse them of demons, she was racked with unease and kept dwelling on the consequences. Rifaa was outside. At the farthest end of the alley—far from the Al Gabal neighborhood—there was a wedding loud with the sounds of drums, pipes and women's joyful trilling. Wanting to face the truth, the woman said sadly, "Rifaa does not lie."

"But he might have been deceived by delusions," said Shafi'i. "It could happen to any of us."

"What do you see in what he heard?"

"How should I know!"

"There's nothing impossible about it—after all, our ancestor is alive."

"We're finished if the word gets around."

"Let's keep it a secret," she said hopefully, "and thank God that it's people rather than the estate that concern him. As long as he doesn't harm anyone no one will harm him."

"How many people in our alley are harmed and they hurt no one!" said Shafi'i tonelessly.

The wedding melodies were drowned out by a clamor that broke out in the passageway. They looked down from the window and saw crowds of men in the passage, and by the light of a lantern one man held they made out the faces of Higazi, Burhoum, Farhat, Hanura and others, and all of them were talking or shouting, and their voices intermingled as the noise level rose. Then a voice bellowed, "The honor of the Al Gabal is at stake! We will allow no one to stain it."

"Our son's secret is discovered!" Abda whispered tremulously into her husband's ear.

Shafi'i drew back from the window and moaned, "My instincts have never been wrong." He walked out of the house unmindful of danger, and his wife followed right behind him. He cut through the throng, calling out, "Rifaa! Where are you, Rifaa?" The man did not see his son in the space lit by the lantern, nor did he hear his voice, but Higazi came up to him and spoke loudly, to be heard above the din. "Is your son lost again?"

"Come listen to what's going on—how evil people are playing with the Al Gabal again!" shouted Farhat.

"Say 'There is no god but God,'" cried Abda anguishedly. "Be tolerant!"

There was a crescendo of angry voices, some of them shouting, "This woman is crazy!" Others yelled, "She doesn't know the meaning of honor!"

Terror gripped Shafi'i's heart. "Where is the boy?" he implored Higazi.

Higazi struggled through the crowd to the gate and shouted at the top of his lungs, "Rifaa! Come here, boy, and talk to Shafi'i."

Now Shafi'i was confused. He had been under the impression that his son was being held in the corner of the passage, but here was Rifaa, appearing in the beam of light. His father grabbed his arm and pulled him back to where Abda stood. In no time a lamp appeared, in Shaldum's hand, as Shaldum came in with Khunfis behind him— Khunfis, whose face was contracted in a scowl of hostility. Everyone looked at the gangster. Silence fell.

"What do you want?" asked Khunfis in a voice brimming with rage.

"Yasmina has disgraced us!"

"Let a witness speak!" said Khunfis.

A donkey cart driver names Zaituna stepped forward until he stood opposite Khunfis. "A little while ago, I saw her coming out of the back door of Bayoumi's house," he said. "I followed her here and asked her what she had been doing in the gangster's house. I saw that she was drunk—the smell of liquor on her breath filled the passageway. She broke loose from me and locked the door after her. Now, ask yourselves what a drunken woman was doing in a gangster's house."

Shafi'i and Abda's nerves relaxed, and Khunfis' tensed; this man knew that his prestige was faced with a severe test. If he failed to punish Yasmina he would lose his standing with the Al Gabal, and if he let these angry people attack her, he would be forced into a confrontation with Bayoumi, the protector of the whole alley. What could he do? The men of Al Gabal were streaming from their houses and crowding into the courtyard and the alley in front of the House of Triumph, making Khunfis' position even more difficult.

"Kick her out of Al Gabal!" angry voices shouted.

"She should be lashed before we kick her out!"

"Kill her!"

There was a shriek from Yasmina, who was secretly listening in the darkness beyond her window. All eyes turned on Khunfis, as Rifaa was heard to ask his father, "Wouldn't it be more fitting for them to vent their rage on Bayoumi, who violated her?"

This infuriated most of them, including Zaituna, who answered him. *"She's* the one who went to *his* house!"

"If you don't have any sense of honor, then just shut up," someone else shouted.

His father rebuked him with a glare, but Rifaa persisted. "Bayoumi didn't do anything the rest of you don't do."

"She is from the Al Gabal," screamed Zaituna frenziedly at him. "She is not for others!"

"This boy is stupid and has no sense of honor."

Shafi'i poked Rifaa to silence him.

"Let's hear Khunfis!" shouted Burhoum.

The fury in Khunfis' heart boiled up and nearly choked him. Yasmina was screaming for help. Anger was spreading, and dark, invasive stares were fixed on the girl's house. Yasmina screamed until Rifaa's heart broke and he could not stand it anymore. He broke away from his father's arm and made his way to Yasmina's house. "Mercy!" he cried urgently. "Have mercy on her weakness and fright!"

"You weakling! You woman!" shouted Zaituna.

Shafi'i too shouted to him passionately, but Rifaa ignored him to answer Zaituna. "God forgive you!" He turned to the throng. "Do whatever you want to me, but have mercy on her! Don't her cries for help hurt your hearts?"

"Don't pay any attention to this clown!" Zaituna turned to Khunfis. "We want to hear from you, sir."

"Do you want me to marry her?" asked Rifaa.

The shouts of rage were interrupted by hoots of mockery.

"All we care about is that she gets her punishment," said Zaituna.

"I will take care of her punishment," said Rifaa desperately.

"We'll all take care of it."

Khunfis saw deliverance from his predicament in Rifaa's suggestion. While he was not convinced by it in his heart, it was the best chance he had. He scowled fiercely to hide his weakness. "The boy has bound himself to marry her, in front of us all. He has his wish."

Zaituna's eyes rolled, blinding him with rage. "This cowardice destroys our honor!"

Suddenly Khunfis' fist smashed his nose, and Zaituna fell back, wailing as the blood spouted from his nostrils. Everyone saw that Khunfis would protect his weak position by terrorizing anyone who stood against him. His eyes moved among the faces whose fear was plain in the lantern light. There was no sign of sympathy for the man whose nose had been shattered; Farhat even scolded him, saying, "Your problem is that you talk too much." Burhoum told Khunfis, "Without you we would never have found a solution!" Hanura told him, "Your anger saved us, sir." They began to disperse, leaving only Khunfis, Shaldum, Shafi'i, Abda and Rifaa. Shafi'i went over to Khunfis to greet him, and put out his hand, but the other, overcome with rage, struck it away with the back of his hand and Shafi'i stepped back, gasping. His son and wife hurried to his side as Khunfis left the passage, cursing the men and women, the Al Gabal and Gabal himself. Shafi'i soaked his hand in warm water, and Abda massaged it.

"You see? Zakia must have been turning her husband against us!"

"The coward forgot that our idiot son saved him from Bayoumi's club," lamented Shafi'i.

52

Rifaa had been the focus of all his parents' hopes; how terribly these were dashed now. The boy's marriage to Yasmina would reduce him to nothing. Even before it happened the family was the talk of the town. Abda wept secretly until it made her ill, and Shafi'i frowned as gloomily as fate had frowned upon him, but they tried to keep it from Rifaa and avoided showing anger. Perhaps Yasmina limited the damage of the whole misadventure with her behavior afterward, when she ran to Shafi'i's house and threw herself weeping at the feet of the man and his wife to pour out some of the gratitude that flooded her heart, sincerely and fervently proclaiming her repentance. There could be no going back on the match after the young man had publicly bound himself to it before the Al Gabal; Shafi'i and his wife accepted that fact and reconciled themselves to it. Their hearts were torn in two by the desire to observe tradition by celebrating Rifaa's wedding with a procession, and the desire to limit it to a reception at home, to avoid exposing a procession to the mockery of the Al Gabal, who among themselves talked of nothing but their total disapproval of the marriage.

"How often have I dreamed of seeing the wedding procession of Rifaa, my only child, wend its way through the neighborhoods," sighed Abda, wistfully expressing her stifled emotions.

"Nobody from the Al Gabal will want to take part in it," snapped Shafi'i.

"It would be better to go back to Muqattam Marketplace than stay here among people who don't like us!" Abda said, scowling.

"We won't go outside the alley, Mother," said Rifaa, who was sunning his legs under the window.

"I wish we had never left there!" Shafi'i exclaimed, adding, to his son, "Weren't you sad, the day we came back here?"

"That was then, this is now," Rifaa said, smiling. "If we went back, who would deliver the Al Gabal from their demons?"

"The demons can keep them forever for all I care!" growled Shafi'i. He paused. "You yourself are going to bring into this house a—"

"I'm not going to bring anyone into this house," Rifaa interrupted him. "I'll go and live in their house."

"Your father didn't mean that!" said Abda.

"But I mean it, Mother. The new house isn't far—we could shake hands from the windows every morning!"

Despite his depression Shafi'i decided to celebrate the wedding day, though just barely. He hung decorations in the passageway and over the doors of the two families' houses, and brought in a singer and a cook. He invited all their friends and acquaintances to come, but only old

Gawad, Umm Bekhatirha, Higazi and his family and some of the very poor, who mainly wanted to be fed, accepted the invitation. Rifaa was the first lad ever to be wed without a procession. The family crossed the passage to the house of the bride, and the performer sang listlessly, what with the small number of guests. While they ate, Gawad the poet extolled Rifaa's noble-mindedness and morality. He said that he was a wise, chaste, pure-hearted lad, but that he was in an alley that valued only bullying, clubs and adultery. Then came the voices of some boys standing out in front of the house, singing:

Rifaa, Rifaa, you little louse,
Who told you to do what you did?

Then they cheered and yelled. Rifaa looked at the ground while Shafi'i turned pale. "Dogs—sons of bitches!" fumed Higazi, but old Gawad said, "How degraded this alley is, but let us never forget the goodness in it. How many gangsters have ruled here? But we remember only Adham and Gabal fondly."

He urged the entertainer to sing something to drown out the heckling outside, and the party continued, struggling against leaden silence, until everyone went home. No one was left in the house except Rifaa and Yasmina, who was the soul of beauty in her wedding dress. Rifaa wore a roomy silk galabiya, an embroidered turban and bright yellow leather shoes. They were sitting on a sofa, facing their pink bed. The dresser mirror reflected the basin and ewer under the bed; she clearly was expecting his assault, or at least the preliminaries for his awaited assault, but he kept gazing at either the hanging lamp or the colored mat. When she had waited a long time and wanted to break the heavy silence that had fallen, she spoke to him tenderly. "I will never forget your kindness. I owe you my life."

He looked at her kindly and said, "We all owe our lives to someone," in a tone that suggested that he did not wish to stay on the subject.

How noble he was! The night of the incident he had refused to give her his hands to kiss; now he did not want to be reminded of the good thing he had done. There was nothing to compare with his goodness unless it was his patience. But what was he thinking about? Was he unhappy that his goodness had driven him to marry someone like her? "I'm not as bad as people think. They loved me and despised me for the same reason."

"I know," he consoled her. "How unjust our alley is."

"They're always so boastful of being descended from Adham," she said resentfully. "At the same time, they brag about their crimes."

"As long as it is possible to exorcise demons, we will get closer to happiness."

She did not see what he meant, but suddenly she realized how ridiculous it was to be sitting this way, and she laughed. "What kind of talk is this for our wedding night!" She lifted her head a little grandly, as if she had forgotten all her gratitude, drew her wrap off her shoulders and threw him a look that smoldered with seduction.

"You will be the person our alley is proudest of," he said hopefully.

"Really?" said Yasmina, "I have wine here."

"I had some with dinner—it was enough."

"I have some good hashish," she said after a little perplexed thought.

"I've tried it, but I didn't like it. I can't stand it."

"Your father is a real addict!" She snickered. "I saw him one time coming out of Shaldum's den. He didn't know whether it was day or night!"

He smiled but said nothing, and she turned away from him, defeated and bursting with anger. She got up and went to the door, turned around and came back to stand under the lamp, which backlit her lovely body through her flimsy dress. She gazed into his calm eyes until despair came over her and she asked, "Why did you save me?"

"I can't stand seeing a person being tormented."

This enraged her. "That's why you married me? That's all?"

"Don't go back to being an angry person!"

She bit her lip in what looked like remorse and spoke softly. "I thought you loved me."

"I do love you, Yasmina," he said simply and truthfully.

"Really?" she mumbled, the surprise plain in her eyes.

"Yes—I love every living creature in our alley!"

"I understand." She sighed dejectedly and stared at him suspiciously. "You'll stand by me for a few months and then divorce me."

His eyes widened. "Don't think that way anymore!"

"I don't understand you! What's in this for you?"

"True happiness."

"I experienced that often enough before I even saw you!"

"There is no such thing as happiness without honor."

"But we're never made happy by just honor," she said, laughing in spite of herself.

"No one here knows true happiness," he said sadly.

She walked heavily to the bed and sat languidly on the edge, and he came toward her. "You're like everyone here," he said gently. "All you can think of is lost time."

Her exasperation was plain in her face. "God help me to solve your mysteries."

"They will solve themselves when you get rid of your demons."

"I'm happy with myself the way I am!" she snapped.

"That's what Khunfis and the others say!" He sighed.

She exhaled sharply. "Are we going to talk about this all night?"

"Sleep. Pleasant dreams!"

She sat back and then threw herself on her back, looking him in the eyes and then at the empty space beside her.

"Rest easy—I'll sleep on the sofa."

She had a fit of laughter, but did not give in to it for long. "I'm afraid your mother will visit us tomorrow and warn you against wearing yourself out!" she sneered, looking over to enjoy the sight of his shamed face.

But he was gazing straight at her with pure and untroubled eyes. "I want to deliver you from your demon!"

"Leave women's work to women!" she shouted angrily, and turned her face to the wall. Her chest heaved with fury and despair. Rifaa reached up to the lamp and lowered the wick, then blew it out. The light died, and darkness fell.

53

The days following the marriage saw tireless activity in Rifaa's life.
He hardly ever went near the shop, and had it not been for the love and
pity of his father he would have had nothing to live on. He invited every
one of the Al Gabal he met to rely on him to cleanse them of their
demons and secure for them a pure happiness they had never dreamed of
before. The Al Gabal whispered that Rifaa bin Shafi'i was not right in
the head and had to be considered hopelessly insane. Some pointed to
his peculiar behavior. Others said it was because of his marriage to a
woman like Yasmina, and people talked of nothing else in the coffeehouse, in homes, among the handcarts and in the drug dens. And how
shocked Umm Bekhatirha was when Rifaa bowed down to whisper in
her ear, with his characteristic sweetness, "Won't you allow me to save
you?"

"Who told you I have an impure demon?" she asked, smiting her
chest. "Is that what you think of the woman who loved you as a son?"

"I offer my services only to people I love and respect," he said
earnestly. "You are a source of goodness and holiness, but you are not
free of a covetousness that drives you to traffic in sick people. If you were
saved from this master of yours, you would do good free of charge!"

The woman could not refrain from laughing.

"Do you want to ruin me completely? God forgive you, Rifaa."

People retold Umm Bekhatirha's story with shouts of laughter; even
Shafi'i laughed mirthlessly at it, though Rifaa had an answer for him.

"Even you yourself need me, Father, and it is only right that I
should start with you."

The man shook his head sadly and pounded the nails with a force
that betrayed his irritation. "God give me patience," he said.

The youth tried to sway him, but the man asked in a tormented tone, "Isn't it bad enough that you've made us the talk of the alley?"

Rifaa retreated dispiritedly to a corner of the shop under his father's skeptical gaze.

"Seriously," Shafi'i asked, "did you make the same appeal to your wife that you made to us?"

"She was like you two," said Rifaa regretfully. "She did not want happiness."

Rifaa went out to Shaldum's den in the dilapidated ruin behind the coffeehouse, and found Shaldum, Higazi, Burhoum, Farhat, Hanura and Zaituna around the hearth. They looked up at him curiously.

"Welcome to Shafi'i's boy," said Shaldum. "So marriage has taught you the value of a drug den?"

Rifaa laid a little package of *kunafa* pastry on the table and took a seat. "I brought you this as a gift."

"Welcome—thank you," said Shaldum, passing the pipe.

But Burhoum laughed and spoke up boorishly. "And then he's going to throw us an exorcism party to cleanse us of our demons!"

"Your wife has a demon called Bayoumi," called Zaituna with an angry nasal twang, drilling Rifaa with a hateful stare. "Cleanse her if you can!"

The men gasped, and all their faces plainly showed embarrassment. Zaituna pointed to his smashed nose. "Thanks to him I lost my nose."

Rifaa did not seem angered. Farhat looked at him sadly. "Your father is a good man and a fine carpenter, but when you act this way you hurt him and humiliate him. The man had scarcely got over your marriage when you abandoned the shop to go and save people from demons! May God heal you, my boy."

"I am not sick. I want you all to be happy."

Ziatuna held a draw from the pipe for a long moment, staring harshly at Rifaa, then spat out the smoke and asked, "Who told you we were unhappy?"

"We are not as our ancestor wanted us to be."

Farhat laughed. "Leave our ancestor alone. How do you know he hasn't forgotten us?"

Zaituna fixed him with a look of contemptuous rage, but Higazi kicked him and warned, "Respect this group—don't even think of starting trouble!" He wanted to improve the general mood, so he nodded and gave his friends a special cue, and they began to sing.

My sweetheart's ship is coming across the water.
How sadly the sails hang over the water.

Rifaa left, and some of them looked sorrowfully after him. He went back to his house, his heart broken. Yasmina met him with a serene smile. She used to scold him for the way he acted, which made him—and, by extension, her—something of a joke; but she had given up scolding him as futile. She endured her life, though she did not know how it would come out, and even handled it with grace. Someone came up to the door and knocked; it was Khunfis, protector of the Al Gabal, and he came in without being asked. Rifaa welcomed him, and Khunfis clapped him on the shoulder with a hand as powerful as a mad dog's jaws. Without preliminaries, Khunfis asked, "What did you say about the estate at Shaldum's?"

Yasmina was frightened and the blood drained from her face, but Rifaa, though he was like a bird in an eagle's talons, spoke calmly. "I said our ancestor wants us to be happy."

Khunfis gave him a violent shake. "Who told you that?"

"It's one of the things he told Gabal."

"He talked to Gabal about the estate," said Khunfis, gripping his shoulder even more tightly.

"The estate means nothing to me," Rifaa replied. Bearing the pain exhausted him. "The happiness I have been unable to give anyone yet has nothing to do with the estate, or with liquor or hashish. I have said that everywhere in the Al Gabal neighborhood and everyone heard me say it."

He shook him again. "Your father used to be rebellious, but then he was sorry. Don't be like him or I'll crush you like a bedbug." He gave Rifaa a shove that landed him on his back on the sofa, then left.

Yasmina ran to help Rifaa up and massage the shoulder he had turned his head to in pain. He seemed half conscious, and murmured as if to himself. "It was my grandfather's voice I heard."

She watched his face with pity and terror, wondering if he had truly lost his mind. She did not repeat what he had said; she was assailed by an anxiety she had never felt before.

One day when he left the house his path was blocked by a woman not of the Al Gabal. "Good morning, Rifaa, sir," she said hopefully.

The note of respect in her voice took him by surprise, as did the "sir." "What do you want?" he asked.

"I have a son who is disturbed," she said submissively. "Please cure him!"

Every one of the Al Gabal despised the people of the alley, and he hated the idea of putting himself in the service of this woman; it would double his own people's contempt for him. "Couldn't you find an exorcist in the alley?"

"Of course," she said, choking up, "but I'm a poor woman."

His heart was touched, and he was fascinated that she had turned to him, he who had met with only derision and contempt from his own people. He looked at her resolutely. "I am yours to command," he said.

54

Yasmina was looking from the window enjoying the new view. Boys were playing in front of the house and *doum*-fruit peddlers were crying their wares, while Batikha grabbed a man by the collar and began to slap him across the face. The man pleaded with him, but in vain.

Rifaa was sitting on the sofa clipping his toenails. "Do you like our new house?" he asked her.

"We have the alley below us here," she said, turning to him. "There, we had only that dark passage to look out on."

"I wish we still had that passage," said Rifaa sadly. "It was a blessed passage. That was where Gabal triumphed over his enemies, but there was no way I could go on living among people who made fun of everything we did. Here, the poor are good people, and being a good person is much more important than being one of the Al Gabal."

"And I have hated *them* since they decided to banish me," said Yasmina disdainfully.

Rifaa smiled. "So why do you tell the neighbors that you're of the Al Gabal?"

She laughed, revealing her pearly teeth, and boasted, "So they'll know I'm better than they are."

He laid his scissors on the sofa and put his feet down on the reed mat.

"You would be a better and more beautiful person if you got over your snobbery. The Al Gabal are not the best people in our alley. The best people are the kindest ones. I used to be wrong like you, and only cared about the Al Gabal, but only people who try sincerely to find happiness deserve it. Look at how these good people come to me and are cleansed of demons!"

"But you're the only one here who works for free!"

"If it weren't for me, the poor would have no one to heal them. They can be healed, but they can't afford it. I never had friends until I came to know them."

She decided not to quarrel, but looked angry.

"Oh, if you would only trust me the way they do! Then I could rid you of what spoils your pleasure in life."

"Do you find me that unpleasant?"

"Only a person who loves her demon without even knowing it."

"What a terrible thing to say to me!"

"You are one of the Al Gabal." He smiled. "All of them refused to submit to my remedy, even my own father."

There was a knock at the door; a new customer had arrived, and Rifaa prepared to receive him.

The truth is that these were the happiest days of Rifaa's life. Everyone in this new neighborhood called him "sir," and they said it sincerely and lovingly. They knew that he expelled demons and gave health and happiness for free, only to please God. No one before him had ever acted so nobly, which was why the poor people loved him as they had never loved anyone before. Of course, the protector of the new neighborhood, Batikha, did not love him, both because of his kind ways and because he could not pay any protection money, but at the same time he had no pretext for attacking him. Everyone he healed had a story to tell. Umm Daoud, who in a nervous fit had bitten her small child, was today a model of serenity and mental health. Sinara, who had no hobby but quarreling and picking fights, was now gentle and mild-mannered, the embodiment of peace. Tulba the pickpocket had sincerely repented and became the coppersmith's apprentice. Uwais, of all people, got married. Rifaa chose four of those he had treated, Zaki, Hussein, Ali and Karim, as friends, and they became like brothers. None of them had known friendship or love before they knew him. Zaki had been dissolute, Hussein a hopeless opium addict, Ali a gangster and Karim a pimp, but they became good-hearted men. They would meet at Hind's Rock, amid the desert and the pure air, to exchange tales of fellowship and happiness and to gaze at their physician through eyes brimming with love and loyalty. They all dreamt of a happiness that might fold the alley in its white wings.

One day Rifaa asked them a question as they sat watching the red glow of the quiet dusk. "Why are we happy?"

"You," said Hussein impetuously. "You are the secret of our happiness."

"Rather because we have been cleansed of our demons," said Rifaa with a grateful smile. "We have been freed of the hatred, ambition, hostility and other evils that are destroying the people of our alley."

"Happy even though we are poor and weak, and we have no part of the estate, and no muscle," Ali said.

Rifaa shook his head sadly. "How much people have suffered because of the lost estate and blind power. Curse, with me, power and that property!"

They cursed them all at once, and Ali picked up a stone and threw it with all his strength toward the mountain.

"Ever since the poets told how Gabalawi had Gabal make the houses of his people to be like the mansion in its beauty and majesty, people have coveted Gabalawi's power and glory. It made them forget his other attributes, so that Gabal was unable to change their hearts by obtaining their right to the estate. When he left this world, the strong took over, the weak became bitter and everyone suffered. While I open the gates of happiness without any estate, power or rank."

Karim embraced Rifaa and kissed him.

"And tomorrow, when the strong sense the happiness of the weak, they will know that their power, glory and usurped wealth are worthless."

There were words of agreement and love from his friends. The breeze carried a shepherd's song to them from deep within the desert.

A single star shone in the sky. Rifaa looked into his friends' faces. "But I cannot care for the people of our alley all alone. The time has come for you to do it for yourselves, for you to learn the mysteries of saving the sick from demons."

The delight was plain in their faces.

"That was our greatest hope," cried Zaki.

"You will be the keys to the happiness of our alley," Rifaa said, smiling.

When they went back to their neighborhood they found it glittering with lights for a wedding in one of the houses. The crowds saw Rifaa and welcomed him with handclapping.

Batikha, enraged, left his seat in the coffeehouse, cursing and swearing, slapping people at random, then went to Rifaa and spoke crudely. "Who do you think you are, boy?"

"A friend of the poor, sir."

"Then get out of here, and walk like the poor, not like a bridegroom leading a parade. Have you forgotten that you're an outcast, and Yasmina's husband, and just a stupid exorcist?"

He spat angrily, and the people dispersed amid a mood of anxiety, but the sound of joyful trilling from the wedding drowned everything else out.

55

Bayoumi, protector of the alley, stood behind the gate of his back garden that opened onto the desert. The night was young, and the man watched and listened. When a hand knocked softly at the gate, he opened it and a woman slipped into the garden; in her black cloak and veil, she was like a part of the night itself. He took her hand and led her through the garden paths, avoiding the house, until they came to the reception hall, where he pushed open the door and entered; she followed. He lit a candle and put it on a windowsill, and the hall seemed not to be there. The sofas stood along the sides, and in the center, inside a circle of cushions, lay a wide tray holding a water pipe and its accessories. The woman threw off her cloak and veil, and Bayoumi drew her to him with a warmth that penetrated to her bones until she gave him a pleading look. She broke nimbly away from him and he sat down on a cushion and laughed softly. He began to probe the coal ashes with his fingers until he found a live coal. She sat beside him and kissed his ear, pointing to the pipe. "I'd nearly forgotten that smell."

He started to kiss her cheek and neck profusely, then tossed a lump of hashish in her lap.

"No one smokes this in our alley but the overseer and little old me!"

Sounds of a furious battle, of cursing, the blows of sticks crashing together and breaking glass sounded from the alley; then running footsteps, a woman's shrieks and the barking of a dog. Worried curiosity lit up the woman's eyes, but the man, oblivious, began to cut up the lump of hashish.

"It wasn't easy, my coming here," she said. "I go from the alley to Gamaliya, so no one will see me, and from Gamaliya to al-Darasa, and from al-Darasa to the desert, until I get to your back door."

He bent over her, not interrupting the work of his hands, and smelled her armpit delightedly. "I have no problem visiting you in your house."

"If you do, none of the cowards will give you any trouble." She smiled. "Even Batikha will pat down the sand for you to walk on. Then they'll work off their anger on *me*." She toyed with his thick mustache and said playfully, "But you sneak out to this place for fear of your wife."

He dropped the lump and encircled her with his arm, pulling her close so tightly that she moaned.

"God help us from the love of gangsters!" she whispered.

He released her as he lifted his head and threw out his chest like a rooster. "There is only one gangster. The rest are his children."

She played with the chest hair that curled out of his shirt collar, and said, "Gangster over others but not over me."

He tweaked her breasts lightly. "You are the crown on my head." He reached behind the tray and grasped a jug. "Great stuff!"

"It has a strong odor my dear husband might smell," she said regretfully.

He drank deeply from the jug until he had enough, and lined up the hashish, frowning. "Some kind of a husband he is! I've seen him so many times, wandering around like a lunatic—the first-ever male exorcist in this bizarre alley!"

"I owe him my life," she said, watching him smoke. "That's why I'm patient with him. There's no harm in him, and it's so easy to fool him."

He offered her the pipe and she took the stem in her mouth eagerly and sucked at it avidly, exhaling the smoke with her eyes closed, her senses already stuporous. Then he took his turn smoking, drawing intermittent puffs and murmuring between each puff.

"Leave him . . . he's wasting . . . your time . . . stupid . . . boy."

She shrugged disparagingly. "My husband has nothing to do in this world but rid poor people of demons."

"And you don't rid him of anything?"

"Never, I swear! One look at his face and there's nothing to be said."

"Not even once a month?"

"Not even once a year—he's distracted from his wife by other people's demons!"

"So let the demons keep him! What good does it do him?"

She shook her head in confusion. "None. If it weren't for his father we would have died of starvation by now. He thinks he's obliged to please the poor people and save them."

"And who obligated him?"

"He says this is what Gabalawi wants his children to do."

Interest shone in the slits of Bayoumi's eyes, and he set the pipe down on the tray. "He said that's what Gabalawi wants?"

"Yes."

"Who told him what Gabalawi wants?"

The woman felt anxious and annoyed—she was afraid of spoiling the mood or discussing something dangerous. "That's how he interprets his sayings as the poets sing them."

He began to finger a new lump of hashish. "What a bitch of an alley, and the Al Gabal are the worst part of it—they produce most of these quacks, and spread strange news about the estate and the Ten Conditions, as if Gabalawi were their ancestor alone. Yesterday their quack Gabal came with a lie and used it to steal the estate, and today this simpleton is interpreting things that cannot be interpreted. He'll say that he heard them from Gabalawi himself."

"All he claims to do is expel demons from poor people," she said uneasily.

The gangster snorted contemptuously. "For all we know, the estate could have a demon!" He raised his voice to a pitch that did not suit the secrecy of their meeting. "Gabalawi is dead or as good as dead, you bastards!"

Yasmina was afraid of ruining the mood and missing this opportunity. She moved her hand to her dress and then slowly took it off. The man's features softened after their sullenness, and he gazed at her with gleaming eyes.

56

The overseer looked tiny in his cloak. The worry was clear in his round white face, the exhaustion that depressed his eyelids, the premature old age in his eyes and the wrinkles worn under them by ardent lusts. Bayoumi's fat face did not reflect the inner satisfaction he enjoyed at his master's unease, unease that reflected the momentousness of the news he had brought him, and, by extension, the momentous role he fulfilled in the service of the overseer and the estate. He was speaking to the overseer. "I had to trouble you with this in spite of myself. I could not take action without consulting you in any matter having to do with the estate. On the other hand, this simpleminded troublemaker is from the Al Gabal, and we have an agreement whereby none of us may attack any of them except with your permission."

Ihab, the overseer, asked gloomily, "Has he really claimed he spoke to Gabalawi?"

"I've heard it from more than one source. The people he treats believe it, even if they make a great secret of it."

"Maybe he's crazy, the same way Gabal was a quack, but this filthy alley loves madmen and quacks. What do the Al Gabal want now that they've plundered the estate, with no right to? Why doesn't Gabalawi talk to someone besides them? Why doesn't he come to me? I'm his closest relative. He's confined in his room and the gate of his mansion is opened only when his possessions are brought to him. He sees no one and no one sees him except his slave girl, but how easy it is for the Al Gabal to meet him or hear from him!"

"They won't be satisfied until the whole estate is theirs," said Bayoumi hatefully.

The overseer's face was pale with anger, and he jumped to his feet to give orders, but then changed his mind and asked, "Did he say anything about the estate, or did he confine his activities to expelling demons?"

"Like Gabal, who confined his activities to expelling snakes," sneered Bayoumi, adding jeeringly, "What does Gabalawi have to do with demons?"

"I don't want the same curse on me that did Effendi in," said Ihab decisively as he stood up.

Bayoumi summoned Gaber, Handusa, Khalid and Batikha to his den and told them that it was up to them to cure the madness of Rifaa, the son of Shafi'i the carpenter.

"For this you summoned us here?" asked Batikha crossly.

Bayoumi nodded, and Batikha slapped his hands together in amazement. "Hah! The gangsters of the alley meet to talk about a creature that's neither man nor woman!"

Bayoumi threw him a look of contempt. "He has pursued his activities before your very eyes and ears, and you sensed no danger. And of course you never heard any of his claims about hearing from Gabalawi."

They exchanged fiery looks through the spreading smoke, and Batikha spoke in bafflement. "Son of a bitch! What's this, Gabalawi and demons! Was our ancestor an exorcist?"

They started to laugh, but quickly desisted when they noticed Bayoumi's terrible scowl. "Batikha, you are stoned," he said. "Gangsters get drunk and smoke hashish, but sniffing cocaine is beneath them!"

"Sir," said Batikha in self-defense, "at Antar's wedding I was the target of twenty men's clubs—my face and neck were covered with blood, but my own club never fell from my hands."

"Let's leave it to him to deal with as he chooses," said Handusa urgently. "Otherwise he'll lose his standing. I wish he could find some way besides attacking the simpleton. Attacking someone like that would only degrade us."

The alley slept, its people unaware of what was being contrived in Bayoumi's den. The next morning Rifaa left his house, and when he saw Batikha standing in his way, he greeted him. "Good morning, Batikha, sir."

"A bad morning to you and your mother," growled the man, throwing him a look of revulsion. "Get back in your house and don't come out or I'll break your head."

"What has angered our protector?" asked Rifaa, surprised.

"You're talking to Batikha now, not Gabalawi," he stormed. "Just get going."

Rifaa was about to speak, but the gangster slapped him so hard that he fell back against the wall of the house. A woman saw the incident and screamed until her voice filled the alley and other women imitated her. Cries to aid Rifaa rose into the air. In no time crowds ran to the scene, among them Zaki, Ali, Hussein and Karim; then came Shafi'i, and Gawad the poet, feeling his way with his cane, and before long the place was crowded with Rifaa's followers, both men and women. Batikha, who had expected none of this, was surprised, but lifted his hand and brought it down on Rifaa's face. He took the blow without defending himself, but the crowd shouted in confusion, for they were seized with an intense agitation; some of them pleaded with Batikha to leave him alone, while others enumerated Rifaa's virtues and good deeds. Many of them asked why he had been attacked, and they protested loudly.

Batikha's anger flared up. "Have you forgotten who I am?"

The truth is that the crowd's love for Rifaa, which had moved them to congregate unconsciously, was what emboldened them to respond to Batikha's warning.

"Our protector, the crown on our head," said a man in the front row of the crowd, "we have come only to ask your pardon for this good man."

"You are our protector and we obey you," shouted a man from the middle of the demonstration, emboldened by the size of the crowd and his location in it. "But what has Rifaa done?"

"Rifaa is innocent, and woe to anyone who harms him!" shouted a third man, at the rear of the crowd, reassured that he was invisible to the gangster's eyes.

Batikha's fury shot up, and he raised his club over his head. "You women!" he bellowed. "I'll teach you a lesson!"

The women's voices sounded from all corners until the alley was convulsed with screams, and every angry throat hurled bloody threats. Bricks landed at Batikha's feet, barring him from taking a step. The man found himself in a terrible spot such as he had never experienced, not even in a nightmare. Death would be easier than asking any of the other gangsters for help, and the downpour of bricks was threatening him with death. He showed his leadership by his silence, and sparks flew from his eyes as the bricks continued to fly and the crowd still menaced him. Nothing like this had ever happened to any of the gangsters before.

Abruptly Rifaa went over to stand before Batikha, and held up his hands to the people until silence fell.

"Batikha has done nothing wrong," he called in a powerful voice. "I am to blame!"

Their faces showed their skepticism but no one uttered a word.

"Go home before he gets angry with you."

Most of the people understood that he wanted to spare the gangster's honor and thus end the crisis, so they dispersed, followed by others who were merely confused. The rest sped away out of fear of being alone with Batikha, and the neighborhood was left empty.

57

Tension in the alley rose after the incident. What frightened the overseer more than anything was the thought that the alley would assume that their solidarity gave them the power to resist gangsters. So it was imperative—in his view—to get rid of Rifaa as well as those who stood by him, though this could only happen with the collusion of Khunfis, the protector of the Al Gabal, in order to avoid the outbreak of open warfare in the alley. The overseer told Bayoumi, "Rifaa is not as weak as you think. He has followers who were able to save him in spite of the gangster. What would happen if the whole alley followed him the way his neighborhood does? He'll put his demons aside and announce that the estate is his real aim!" Bayoumi shook Batikha violently by the shoulders and spewed his wrath out at him. "We gave this business to you alone, and what did you do! You're a disgrace to all of us!" Batikha ground his teeth angrily and said, "I'll get rid of him for you, even if I have to kill him," and Bayoumi shouted, "The best thing for you to do is to vanish from this alley forever!" He sent a messenger to Khunfis summoning him to a meeting, but Shafi'i blocked Khunfis' way. He was more frightened than he had ever been in his life. He had tried to persuade his son to go back to the shop and abandon the work which had brought him so much hardship, but he failed in his effort and went back disappointed. When he heard that Khunfis had been summoned to meet Bayoumi, he blocked his path and told him, "Khunfis, sir, you are our protector and defender. They are asking for you to turn Rifaa over to them, but don't turn him in. Promise them what they want, but don't turn him in. Just give me the order and I'll leave the alley and take him with me, by force if necessary. Just don't turn him in!" Khunfis said very cautiously, "I know better than anyone what to do, and where the Al Gabal's interests lie." The truth is that Khunfis had been deeply worried for Rifaa's sake ever since hearing of the incident with Batikha, and thought that it was he himself, not the overseer or Bayoumi, who should be wary.

So he went to Bayoumi's house and met with him in the reception hall. The gangster told him freely that he had called him there in his capacity as the protector of the Al Gabal so that they might have a meeting of the minds about Rifaa.

"Don't take him lightly," Bayoumi said. "These incidents prove how strong his influence is."

Khunfis agreed, but pleaded that "no one should attack him in front of me."

"We are men, and our interests are the same," said Bayoumi. "We attack no one in our own houses. This boy is coming now, so that I may examine him in your hearing."

And Rifaa came. With his radiant face, he greeted the two men and sat where Bayoumi indicated, on a cushion before them. Bayoumi stared searchingly into his calm, beautiful face, marveling at how this meek child had become the source of these dreadful convulsions.

"Why did you leave your neighborhood and your people?" he asked Rifaa coarsely.

"None of them paid any attention to me," Rifaa said simply.

"What did you want from them?"

"To cleanse them of the demons that corrupted their happiness."

"And are you responsible for the people's happiness?" asked Bayoumi, his voice distorted with rage.

"Yes, for as long as I can achieve it," said Rifaa with frank innocence.

"They have heard you expressing disdain for majesty and power." Bayoumi scowled.

"In order to prove to them that happiness is not in their delusions but in what I do."

"Doesn't that express contempt for those who possess majesty and power?" asked Khunfis angrily.

"No, sir," he replied, untroubled by the man's anger. "But it does express a warning that happiness is something else, other than power and majesty."

Bayoumi studied him with a penetrating gaze. "They have heard you say that this is what Gabalawi wants for them."

Concern showed in Rifaa's limpid eyes. "They say that!"

"What do you say?"

For the first time, he hesitated. "I speak as much as I understand."

"Atrocities come from such stupidity," sneered Khunfis.

"But they say that you repeat to them what you heard from Gabalawi himself!" said Bayoumi, narrowing his eyes.

Confusion appeared in his eyes and he hesitated for a second time before answering. "That is how I understood what he told Adham and Gabal!"

"What he told Gabal does not need interpreting!" screeched Khunfis furiously.

Bayoumi's malice intensified, and he thought to himself, *You are all liars, and Gabal was the first liar among you, you thieves.*

"You say that you heard Gabalawi," he said, "and you said, 'This is what Gabalawi wants.' No one may speak in Gabalawi's name except the overseer of his estate and his heir. If Gabalawi wanted to say anything he would have said it to *him*. He is in charge of his estate and the executor of its Ten Conditions. You simpleton, how can you despise power, majesty and wealth in the name of Gabalawi when these are his own attributes?"

Rifaa's gentle features disclosed his pain. "I speak to the people of our alley, not to Gabalawi. They are the ones afflicted by demons. They are the ones tortured by problems."

"What are you but simply someone incapable of power and majesty," Bayoumi shouted at him. "That's why you curse them—and to raise your pathetic rank among the stupid people of our alley above the rank of people with prestige, and when they follow you, you use them to steal power and majesty!"

Rifaa's eyes widened in surprise. "My only aim is the happiness of the people of our alley."

"You sly little son of a bitch! You delude people into thinking they're sick, that we're all sick, that no one is sane in this alley but you!"

"Why do you despise happiness when you are so close to having it?"

"You sly little son of a bitch! Happiness coming from someone like you is cursed!"

"Why do people hate me," sighed Rifaa, "when I have never hated anyone?"

"You don't fool us the way you fool those stupid people," Bayoumi shouted at him. "Forget your lies and understand that I may not be disobeyed. Thank God that you are in my house; otherwise you might not be leaving here so healthy."

Rifaa stood despairingly, took his leave and went out.

"Leave him to me," said Khunfis.

"The fool has many followers," Bayoumi cautioned him. "We don't want a massacre."

58

After leaving Bayoumi's house, Rifaa headed for his own house. The skies were swathed in autumn mist, and a mild breeze was in the air. The whole alley was crowded around the lemon stalls; it was pickling season, and there was a roar of storytelling and laughter. Some boys had got into a fight and were pelting each other with dirt. Several people greeted Rifaa, but he was also spattered with dirt, so he went on to his house, dusting off his shoulders and his turban. He found Zaki, Ali, Hussein and Karim waiting for him, and they embraced as they did whenever they met, and he told them—and his wife, who joined them—what had gone on between him and Bayoumi and Khunfis. They listened carefully and worriedly, and by the time he finished his story all their faces were grim. Yasmina asked herself: So what would be the outcome of this trying situation? Was there a solution that would save this good man from ruin without threatening her happiness? All their eyes were curious. Rifaa rested his head somewhat wearily against the wall.

"An order from Bayoumi is not something to take lightly," said Yasmina.

"Rifaa has friends," said Ali, the most impetuous of them all. "They defeated Batikha, and he vanished from the alley!"

"Bayoumi is not Batikha!" Yasmina scowled. "If you challenge Bayoumi, you've spoken your last words!"

"Let's listen to our master first!" said Hussein, turning to Rifaa.

"Don't even think of fighting," said Rifaa, his eyes nearly closed. "Anyone who struggles for people's happiness cannot take lightly the shedding of their blood."

Yasmina's face was radiant. She hated the idea of widowhood, fearing that she would be watched again, and thus unable to get away to her wonderful other man.

"The best thing you can do is to spare yourself that mess," she assured him.

"We will never stop our work," Zaki protested. "We'll leave the alley."

Yasmina's heart pounded with fear as she imagined living far from her lover's alley, and she spoke up. "We are not going to live like lost strangers, far from our alley."

Every gaze hung on Rifaa's face. Slowly he moved his head to face them and said, "I don't want to leave our alley."

There was a sudden long, impatient knocking on the door, and Yasmina opened it. The seated men heard the voices of Shafi'i and Abda asking for their son. Rifaa got up and greeted his parents with hugs. They all sat down, and Shafi'i and his wife were out of breath; their faces expressed the unpleasant news they brought.

"My boy," the father was saying before they knew it, "Khunfis has given you up. Your life is in danger. My friends tell me that the gangster's men are surrounding your house."

"Our house," said Abda, drying her bloodshot eyes. "If only we'd never come back to this alley that sells lives for nothing!"

"Don't be afraid, ma'am," said Ali. "All our neighbors are our friends, and they love us."

"What have we done to deserve punishment?" sighed Rifaa.

"You're from the Al Gabal, whom they hate," said Shafi'i anxiously. "How my heart has suffered fear ever since you first mentioned Gabalawi!"

"Only yesterday they fought Gabal because he claimed the estate," marveled Rifaa, "and now they're fighting me because I disdain the estate!"

Shafi'i made a despairing gesture with his hand. "Say whatever you like about them, but it won't change them one bit. All I know is that you are lost if you leave your house, and I doubt whether you're safe even if you stay in it."

For the first time, fear stole into Karim's heart, but he hid it with a firm will and spoke to Rifaa. "They are lying in wait for you outside. If you stay here they will come for you, if they're the gangsters of our alley that I know. Let's escape to my house over the rooftops, and think there about what to do next."

"From there you can escape from the alley in the dark," shouted Shafi'i.

"And let everything I've built up be demolished?"

"Do what he says," his mother begged him, crying. "Please, for your mother!"

"Resume your work across the desert somewhere, if you want," said his father sharply.

Karim got up, looking concerned. "Let's make a plan. Shafi'i and his wife will stay a little longer, then go to the House of Triumph as if they were coming home after a normal visit. The lady Yasmina will go out to Gamaliya as if to go shopping, and when she comes back you will slip out to my house. That's easier than escaping over the rooftops."

Shafi'i liked the plan.

"We must not waste a single minute," said Karim. "I'll go and check out the roofs."

He left the room, and Shafi'i rose and took Rifaa by the hand. Abda ordered Yasmina to pack some clothes in a bundle.

Yasmina began to pack a few clothes, with a constricted chest and wounded heart, a tempest of hatred gathering inside her. Abda kissed her son, hugged him and tearfully murmured a few incantations to protect him from the evil eye. Rifaa left, pondering his situation with a sorrowing heart. How he loved people with his heart; how he had labored for their contentment; how he had suffered their hatred. Would Gabalawi condone failure?

"Follow me," Karim, now back again, was saying to Rifaa and his companions.

"We'll follow you," said Abda, overcome with weeping, "maybe in a little bit."

"God bless you and protect you, Rifaa," said Shafi'i, trying hard not to cry.

Rifaa hugged his parents, and then turned to Yasmina.

"Pull your cloak and veil around you tightly so that no one will recognize you." He leaned closer to her ear. "I can't stand to think of any hand harming you."

59

Yasmina left the house swathed in black, Abda's parting words ringing in her ears: "Goodbye, daughter, may God keep you and protect you. Rifaa is in your hands. I will pray for both of you day and night." Night was beginning to fall; the coffeehouse lamps were being lit, and boys were playing in the light shed by the handcart lanterns. At the same time, cats and dogs were fighting—as they always did at that time of day —around the heaps of garbage. Yasmina walked toward Gamaliya with no room for mercy in her passionate heart. She did not hesitate, but was filled with fear, and imagined that many eyes were watching her. She had no sense of composure until she had left al-Darasa for the desert, and felt truly safe only when she was in the reception hall, in Bayoumi's arms.

When she pulled the veil away from her face, he looked at her attentively. "Are you afraid?"

"Yes," she answered, panting.

"No, you're a lot of things but not a coward. Tell me, what's wrong?"

"They fled over the rooftops to Karim's house, and they'll leave the alley at dawn."

"At dawn, sons of bitches!" muttered Bayoumi scornfully.

"They talked him into going away. Why don't you let him go?"

"Long ago, Gabal went away, then came back," he said with a smile of mockery. "These vermin don't deserve to live."

"He renounces life," she said distractedly, "but he does not deserve death."

"The alley has enough madmen," he said, his mouth distorted in disgust.

She looked at him earnestly, then lowered her gaze, and whispered, as if to herself. "He saved my life once."

"And here you are handing him over to his death," said Bayoumi with a coarse laugh. "An eye for an eye, and the one who started it loses!"

She felt an alarm as painful as a sickness, and glanced at him rebukingly. "I did what I did because I love you more than my life."

He stroked her cheek tenderly. "We'll be free. And if things get hard for you, you have a place in this house."

She felt a little better. "If they offered me Gabalawi's mansion without you, I wouldn't take it."

"You are a loyal girl."

The word "loyal" pierced her, and the sickening sense of alarm came back to her. She wondered if the man was mocking her. There was no more time for talk, and she got up. He stood to say goodbye to her, and she stole out the back door. She found her husband and his friends waiting for her, and sat beside Rifaa.

"Our house is being watched. It was wise of your mother to leave the lamp lit in the window. It will be easy to get away at dawn."

"But he's so sad," Zaki said to her, looking sorrowfully at Rifaa. "Aren't there sick people everywhere? Don't they need healing too?"

"There is a greater need for healing where the disease is out of control."

Yasmina looked at him pityingly. She said to herself that it would be a crime to kill him. She wished that there was one thing about him that deserved punishment. She remembered that he was the one person in this world who had been kind to her, and that his reward for that would be death. She cursed these thoughts to herself, and thought, *Let those who have good lives do good.* When she saw him returning her look, she spoke up as if commiserating with him. "Your life is worth so much more than this damned alley of ours."

"That's what you *say*," Rifaa said, smiling, "but I read sadness in your eyes!"

She trembled, and said to herself: God help me if he reads minds as well as he casts out demons!

"I'm not sad, I'm just afraid for you!" she said.

"I'll get supper ready," said Karim, getting up.

He came back with a tray and invited them to sit down, and they seated themselves around it. It was a supper of bread, cheese, whey, cucumbers and radishes, and there was a jug of barley beer. Karim filled their cups. "Tonight we'll need warmth and morale."

They drank, and Rifaa smiled. "Liquor arouses demons, but it revives people who have got rid of their demons." He looked at Yasmina beside him, and she knew the meaning of his look.

"You'll free me of my demon tomorrow, if God spares you," she said.

Rifaa's face shone with delight, and his friends exchanged congratulatory looks and began to eat their supper. They broke the bread, and their hands came together over the dishes. It was as if they had forgotten the death that surrounded them.

"The owner of the estate wanted his children to be like him," said Rifaa. "But they insisted on being like demons. They were foolish, and he has no love for foolishness, as he told me."

Karim shook his head regretfully, and swallowed. "If only I had some of the power he used to have, things would be the way he wants them to be."

"If, if, if, what good does 'if' do us!" said Ali crossly. "We must *act.*"

"We have never failed," said Rifaa firmly. "We have fought the demons ruthlessly, and whenever a demon departs, love takes its place. There is no other goal."

Zaki sighed. "If only they had let us do our work, we would have filled the alley with health, love and peace."

"It's incredible that we're thinking of fleeing when we have so many friends!" Ali objected.

"Your demon still has roots deep inside you." Rifaa smiled. "Don't forget that our aim is healing, not killing. It is better for a person to be killed than to kill."

Rifaa turned abruptly to Yasmina and said, "You're not eating or paying attention!"

Her heart contracted with fear, but she fought down her agitation. "I'm just marveling at how cheerfully you all talk, as if you were at a wedding!"

"You'll get used to being cheerful when you're cleansed of your demon tomorrow." He looked at his brothers. "Some of you are ashamed of conciliation—we are the sons of a nation that respects only power, but power is not confined to terrorizing others. Wrestling with demons is hundreds of times harder than attacking the weak, or fighting the gangsters."

Ali wagged his head sadly. "The reward of good deeds is the terrible situation we find ourselves in now."

"The battle will not end as they expect," said Rifaa decisively. "And we are not as weak as they imagine! All we have done is shift the battle from one field to a different one, only our battlefield now calls for more courage and tougher force."

They resumed their dinner, thinking over what they had heard. He seemed to them just as calm, reassured and strong as he was handsome and meek. In the long lull came the voice of the local poet, reciting: "One noon Adham sat in Watawit Alley to rest, and fell asleep. A movement woke him, and he saw boys stealing his cart. He got up and threatened them, and one boy who saw him warned his friends with a whistle; they overturned the cart to distract him from going after them. The cucumbers tumbled all over the ground while the boys dispersed like locusts. Adham was so enraged that he forgot his decent upbringing and screamed obscenities at them, then bent down to retrieve his cucumbers from the mud. His anger redoubled with no outlet, so he asked emotionally, *Why was your anger like fire, burning without mercy? Why was your pride dearer to you than your own flesh and blood? How can you enjoy an easy life when you know we are being stepped on like insects? Forgiveness, gentleness, tolerance have no place in your mansion, you oppressor!* He seized the handles of the cart and set out to push it as far as he could get from this accursed alley, when he heard a taunting voice. 'How much are the cucumbers, uncle?' Idris stood there with a mocking grin." Then there was a woman's shout, over the poet's voice, crying, "Little boy lost, good people!"

60

Time passed, with the men in conversation and Yasmina in torment.
Hussein wanted to look around out in the alley, but Karim opposed the
idea; someone might see him and get suspicious. Zaki wondered
whether Rifaa's house had been attacked, and Rifaa pointed out that all
they could hear was the lament of the rebec and the cheering of
the street boys. The alley was leading its usual life, and there was no sign
that any crime was being planned. Yasmina's mind was such a whirlpool of worry that she was afraid her eyes would give her away. She
wanted her torment to end any way possible and at any cost; she
wanted to fill her belly with wine until she no longer knew what was
happening around her. She said to herself that she was not the first
woman in Bayoumi's life and she would not be the last; that stray dogs
always collected around piles of garbage; only let this torment end at
any cost. With the passage of time, silence slowly overcame the racket,
and the voice of the children and cries of the peddlers died down,
leaving only the lament of the rebec. A sudden revulsion at these men
seized her, for no other reason than that, in a way, it was they who
tormented her.

"Should I prepare the pipe?" asked Karim.

"We need clear heads!" said Rifaa firmly.

"I thought it would help us pass the time."

"You're too afraid."

"It looks like there's no need to be afraid at all," Karim protested.

Yes, there had been no incidents, and Rifaa's house had not been
attacked. The melodies had fallen silent and the poets had gone home.
They could hear the sounds of doors slamming, the conversations of
people going back to their houses, laughter and coughing, and then
nothing. They continued to wait and watch until the first cock crowed.

Zaki got up and went to the window to see the street, then turned to them.

"Quiet and emptiness. The alley is just the way it was the day Idris was kicked out."

"We should go," said Karim.

Yasmina was overcome with anguish, wondering what would become of her if Bayoumi was late for the appointment, or had changed his mind. The men got up, each carrying a bundle.

"Farewell, hellish alley," said Hussein, leading the way out. Rifaa gently guided Yasmina ahead of him, and followed with his hand on her shoulder, as if afraid of losing her in the darkness. Then came Karim, Hussein and Zaki. They slipped out of the apartment door one by one, and ascended the stairs, using the railing as a guide in the total blackness. The darkness on the roof seemed less intense, though not a single star could be seen. A cloud absorbed all the light of the moon concealed behind it, and its surface reflected the scudding clouds.

"The walls of the roofs almost touch," said Ali. "We can give the lady help if she needs it."

They followed, and as Zaki—coming last—arrived, he felt a movement behind him and turned to the door of the roof, where he detected four phantoms. "Who is there?" he asked in alarm.

They all halted and turned around.

"Stop, you bastards," said Bayoumi's voice.

Gaber, Khalid and Handusa fanned out from his right and left, and Yasmina gasped. She slipped away from Rifaa's hand and moved toward the door of the roof. None of the gangsters stopped her.

"The woman has betrayed you," said Ali dazedly to Rifaa.

In a moment they were surrounded. Bayoumi began to examine them at close range, one by one, asking, "Who's the exorcist?"

When he found him, he grabbed him by the shoulder with an iron hand and sneered. "The demon's companion! Where did you think you were going?"

"You don't want us here," said Rifaa indignantly. "We're leaving."

After a brief sarcastic laugh, Bayoumi turned to Karim. "You—what good did it do, hiding them in your house?"

Karim gulped with a dry mouth, and his muscles trembled. "I didn't know of any trouble between you and them!"

Bayoumi struck him in the face with his free hand, and he fell to the ground, but quickly jumped up again and ran, terrified, toward the adjacent roof. Suddenly Hussein and Ali ran after him, but Handusa pounced on Ali and kicked him in the stomach. He fell down, groaning from his depths. At the same time, Gaber and Khalid went after the others, but Bayoumi said contemptuously, "There's nothing to fear from them. Neither of them will say a single word, and if they do they're dead."

Rifaa, whose head was bent toward Bayoumi's fist by the terrible grip, said, "They have done nothing to deserve punishment."

Bayoumi slapped him and taunted, "Tell me, didn't they hear from Gabalawi the way you did?" He pushed Rifaa in front of him and said, "Walk in front of me and don't open your mouth."

He walked, resigned to his fate. He descended the dark stairs carefully, and the heavy footfalls followed him. He was so overcome by the darkness, confusion and evil that threatened him that he could scarcely think of those who had fled or betrayed him. A profound and absolute sadness seized him, eclipsing even his fears. It seemed to him the darkness would prevail over the earth. They came out into the alley and crossed the neighborhood, in which, thanks to him, no sickness remained. Handusa went before them to the Al Gabal neighborhood, and they passed under the closed-up House of Triumph, until he imagined that he could hear his parents' hesitant breaths. He wondered for a moment about them, and imagined that he heard Abda crying in the quiet night, but he was speedily brought back to the darkness, confusion and evil that threatened him. The Al Gabal neighborhood seemed like a collection of colossal phantom hulks shrouded in darkness; how intense the darkness was, how deep its sleep. The footfalls of the executioners in the pitch-blackness and the creaking of their sandals were like the laughter of devils playing in the night. Handusa turned toward the desert, opposite the mansion wall, and Rifaa raised his eyes to the mansion, but it was as dark as the sky. There was a figure at the end of the wall.

"Khunfis?" asked Handusa.

"Yes," said the man.

He joined the men wordlessly. Rifaa's eyes were still raised to the mansion. Didn't his ancestor know his situation? One word from him could save him from the claws of these monsters and spare him from their plot. He was capable of making them hear his voice, just as he had made Rifaa hear it in this place. Gabal had been in a predicament like this, and he had been delivered, and triumphed. But Rifaa passed the wall and heard nothing but the footfalls of these evil men, and their regular breathing. They pressed on into the desert, where the sand made their steps heavy. Rifaa had a feeling of banishment in this desert as he thought back on how the woman had betrayed him and how his friends had sought refuge in flight. He wanted to turn back to the mansion, but abruptly Bayoumi's hand shoved at his back and he fell on his face.

"Khunfis?" called Bayoumi, lifting his club.

"With you to the end, sir," said Khunfis, also lifting his club.

"Why do you want to kill me?" Rifaa asked despairingly.

Bayoumi slammed his club down on his head, and Rifaa cried out, then called out from the depths of his soul, "Gabalawi!"

In the next instant, Khunfis' club came down on his neck, and then the clubs took turns.

Then there was silence, broken only by his death rattle.

Their hands began to dig furiously in the sand in the dark.

61

The killers left the desert, heading for the alley, and quickly vanished in the darkness. Four human shapes rose to stand at a spot near the scene of the crime, and could be heard sighing and weeping quietly.

"Cowards!" one of them shouted. "You held me back and wore me out, so he died undefended."

"If we had obeyed you, we would all have been lost, without saving him," another told him.

"Cowards!" Ali repeated. "You are nothing but cowards."

"Don't waste time talking," sobbed Karim. "We have a terrible job to finish before morning."

Hussein raised his head and trained his tearful eyes on the sky, and muttered anxiously, "It will be dawn soon. Let's be quick."

"A man whose life was as short as a dream—but in him we lost the most precious thing we knew in life!" wept Zaki.

"Cowards," muttered Ali through his clenched teeth as he headed toward the scene of the crime.

They followed him, and all knelt in a half circle to examine the ground searchingly.

"Here!" shouted Karim abruptly, like a man stung. He sniffed his hand. "This is his blood!"

"And this fresh area is where he's buried," shouted Zaki at the same moment.

They crowded around him and began to scoop the sand away with their hands. No one in the world was more wretched than they, because of the loss of their cherished one, and their helplessness at his death. Karim experienced a moment of madness and said simplemindedly, "Maybe we'll find him alive!"

"Listen to the delusions of cowards," snapped Ali, his hands still working.

Their noses were full of the smell of dirt and blood. A dog howled from the direction of the mountain.

"Slow down," called Ali softly. "This is his body."

Their hearts pounded, and their hands relented slightly as they heartbrokenly felt the edges of his clothing, then they began to weep loudly. They all helped to draw the corpse out of the sand, and gently lifted it up as the cocks in the alleys and lanes began to crow. Some of them said to hurry, but Ali reminded them that they would need to fill up the hole. Karim took off his cloak and spread it on the ground, and they laid the body on it. They all helped to refill the hole. Hussein removed his cloak and covered the body with it, then they took it up and marched toward Bab al-Nasr. The darkness was lifting over the mountain, revealing clouds, and the dew fell on their tearful faces. Hussein led them along the way to his tomb until they arrived there, and they preoccupied themselves silently with opening the tomb. The light of day spread gradually, until they could see the shrouded body, their bloodstained hands, and eyes red from weeping; then they lifted up the body and descended with it into the tomb's interior. They stood humbly around it, pressing their eyes to stop the unseen tears that flowed.

"Your life was a brief dream," said Karim in a voice choked with tears. "But it filled our hearts with love and purity. We did not imagine that you would leave us so quickly, let alone that you would be murdered by a member of our infidel alley, which you healed and loved; our alley, which wanted only to murder the love, mercy and healing that you represented. It has brought a curse upon itself until the end of time."

"Why do the good die?" sobbed Zaki. "Why do the criminals live?"

"If it had not been for your love that lives on in our hearts," moaned Hussein, "we would have hated people forever!"

"We will never know peace until we expiate our cowardice," added Ali.

As they left the tomb, heading back into the desert, the light was dyeing the horizons with the melting hue of a red rose.

62

None of his four companions appeared in Gabalawi Alley again.
People thought they had left the alley secretly, after Rifaa, out of fear of
the gangsters' retribution. But the friends lived at the edge of the desert
in a state of frayed nerves, wrestling with all their might against the
oppression of their pain and sharp regret. Rifaa's passing pained their
hearts more than death, and being deprived of his company was a lethal
torment; none of them had any further hope in life than to mourn
Rifaa's death properly by keeping his message alive and seeing to the
punishment of his killers, as Ali insisted they must. While it was true that
they could not return to the alley, they hoped to accomplish what they
wished outside it. One morning the House of Triumph awoke to Abda's
cries, and the neighbors hurried to her to hear the news.

"They killed my son Rifaa," she shouted hoarsely.

The neighbors were shocked into silence, and looked to Shafi'i,
who was drying his eyes.

"The gangsters killed him in the desert," he said.

"My son, who never hurt anyone in the world," wept Abda.

"Does our protector Khunfis know about this?" some of them
asked.

"Khunfis was one of the killers," said Shafi'i angrily.

"Yasmina betrayed him—she led Bayoumi to him," wept Abda.

Horror was plain in their faces.

"So that's why she's been staying in his house after his wife left,"
someone said.

The news spread through the Al Gabal neighborhood, and Khunfis
came to Shafi'i's house.

"Are you crazy?" he shouted. "What have you been saying about
me?"

Shafi'i stood before him unafraid, and said sternly, "That you took part in killing him, when you were his protector!"

Khunfis pretended to be angry. "Shafi'i, you are crazy!" he shouted. "You don't know what you're saying. I won't stay here, so I won't be forced to punish you!"

He left the house frothing at the mouth. The news spread to Rifaa's neighborhood, where he had lived after leaving the Al Gabal's. The people were shocked, and raised their voices, raging and weeping, but the gangsters went out into the alley and patrolled it up and down, clubs in their hands and trouble blazing in their eyes. Then the news spread that sands west of Hind's Rock had been found blotched with Rifaa's blood. Shafi'i and his best friends went to look for the corpse there. They searched and excavated but found nothing. The people were frenzied and anxious at the news, and many of them expected trouble in the alley. The people of Rifaa's neighborhood wondered what he could have done to have been killed. The Al Gabal said, *Rifaa was killed, and Yasmina is living in Bayoumi's house.* The gangsters infiltrated by night the place of Rifaa's murder and dug up his grave by torchlight, but they found no trace of the corpse.

"Did Shafi'i take it?" Bayoumi asked.

"No," said Khunfis. "My spies have told me he found nothing."

"It's his friends," shouted Bayoumi, stamping his foot. "It was a mistake to let them escape. Now they're fighting us behind our backs."

When they returned, Khunfis leaned close to Bayoumi's ear and whispered, "Your keeping Yasmina is giving us problems."

"Admit that you're a weak leader in your territory," said Bayoumi, exasperated.

Khunfis bid him an exasperated farewell. The tension had mounted in the Al Gabal and Rifaa neighborhoods, and the gangsters continued to attack any complainers. The alley was so thoroughly terrorized that its people hated going out unless it was unavoidable. One night—when Bayoumi was in Shaldum's coffeehouse—some of his wife's relatives sneaked into his house with the intention of attacking Yasmina, but she became aware of them and fled in her nightgown into the desert. They chased her, and she ran like a crazed thing through the darkness even after her pursuers had given up the chase, and kept running until she could scarcely breathe, and had to stop. She panted violently, threw her head back and closed her eyes, until she had regained her breath, then looked behind her and, though she saw nothing, shied at the idea of going back to the alley by night. She looked ahead and saw a faint, faraway light that might be from a hut, and made for it, hoping to find there a place to stay until morning. It took her a long time to get there, but it did seem like a hut, so she went up to the door and called out to the people inside. Suddenly she found herself facing her husband's most intimate friends: Ali, Zaki, Hussein and Karim.

63

Yasmina froze where she stood and looked from one face to another; they seemed to her like a wall blocking her escape in a nightmare. They stared at her with aversion, and the aversion in Ali's eyes had an iron severity.

"I'm innocent," she shouted instinctively. "By the Lord of Heaven, I'm innocent. I went with you until they attacked us, and ran away the same as you did!"

They scowled.

"And who told you we ran away?" asked Ali hatefully.

"If you hadn't run away," she quavered, "you wouldn't be alive now. But I am innocent. I didn't do anything. All I did was run away!"

"You ran to your master, Bayoumi," said Ali through clenched teeth.

"Never. Let me go. I am innocent."

"You'll go into the belly of the earth!" shouted Ali.

She tried to escape, but he jumped at her and grabbed her shoulders tightly.

"Let me go, for his sake—he never loved killing or killers!"

His hands closed around her neck.

"Wait until we've thought about this," said Karim uneasily.

"Be quiet, cowards!" he shouted, grasping her neck with all of the rage, hatred, pain and remorse at war inside him. She tried in vain to free herself from his grip; she clutched his arms, kicked him and shook her head, but all her effort was lost and in vain. Her strength gave out, her eyes bugged out and then she began to spit blood. Her body convulsed violently, and then was still for good. He let go of her, and she fell at his feet, a corpse.

The next morning, Yasmina's body was found dumped in front of Bayoumi's house. The news spread like the dust of a hot sandstorm and everyone, men and women alike, ran toward the gangster's house. There was a huge din of competing comments, but everyone kept his true feelings secret. The gate of Bayoumi's house flew open, and the man rushed out like a raging bull and began to club everyone he could. Everyone ran away terrified and took shelter in homes and coffeehouses while the man stood in the empty alley cursing and threatening, and striking the dirt, the walls and the empty air.

The same day, Shafi'i and his wife abandoned the alley. It seemed that every trace of Rifaa had vanished.

But there were things that spoke of him constantly, such as Shafi'i's home in the House of Triumph, the carpentry shop, Rifaa's house in the neighborhood that was called "the hospice," the site of his death west of Hind's Rock and most of all his loyal companions, who stayed in contact with his admirers and taught them the mysteries of his way of cleansing souls of demons to treat the sick; thus, they were certain, they were restoring Rifaa to life. Ali, however, could not rest unless he was punishing criminals.

"You have nothing to do with Rifaa!" Hussein once scolded him.

"I know Rifaa better than any of you do," said Ali sternly. "He spent his short life in a violent struggle against demons."

"You want to go back to gangsterism—the most hateful thing in the world to him."

"He was a leader, bigger than any gangster, but his gentleness fooled you," cried Ali fervently.

Each of them went on to promote his own view, in total sincerity. The alley retold Rifaa's story, with all the facts, which most people had not known. It was reported that his body had lain in the desert until Gabalawi himself came and got it; now it was concealed in the soil of his own fabulous garden. The perilous events were just trailing off there, when the gangster Handusa vanished mysteriously. His mutilated corpse was discovered dumped in front of the house of Ihab the overseer. The overseer's house was just as convulsed as Bayoumi's had been, and the alley went through a terrible period of fear. Violence fell like rain on anyone who had had any relation, or imagined relation, with Rifaa or any of his men. Clubs crushed heads and feet trampled bellies, words pierced hearts and hands inflamed necks. Some people locked themselves in their houses, and some abandoned the alley altogether; some, contemptuous of the danger, were executed in the desert. The alley, covered in blackness and gloom, was loud in its screams and wails, and smelled of blood, but strangely, this did not impede further actions. Khalid was killed as he left Bayoumi's house before dawn, and the rage of the terror mounted to madness, but our alley was awakened from its last sleep one night by a tremendous fire that destroyed the house of the gangster Gaber and killed his family.

"Rifaa's crazy people are everywhere, like bedbugs!" shrieked Bayoumi. "I swear to God, they are going to be killed, even in their houses!"

Word got around the alley that their houses were to be attacked at night, and people were practically insane with fear. They ran out of their houses in a frantic mob, carrying sticks, chairs, cooking-pot lids, knives, clogs and bricks. Bayoumi planned to strike before things got completely out of control; he lifted his club and came out of his house surrounded by a ring of his followers.

Ali appeared for the first time, leading the rioters with some other strong men. As soon as he saw Bayoumi coming, he ordered bricks to be thrown, and a swarm of bricks as thick as locusts landed on Bayoumi and his men, and the blood began to spout. Bayoumi pounced like a madman, screaming like a savage, but a rock struck the top of his head, and he stopped, and in spite of his rage, his strength and his boldness, he staggered, and then fell down, his face a mask of blood. His followers were quick to flee, and waves of angry rioters swept into the gangster's house; the sounds of smashing and breaking could be heard by the overseer in his house. Mischief reigned as punishment was meted out to the remaining gangsters and their followers and their houses were laid waste. The danger mounted, and total chaos was near when the overseer summoned Ali, and Ali came to meet him. Ali's men held off from further revenge and destruction, awaiting the results of this meeting, and things calmed down and people cooled off.

The meeting produced a new covenant in the alley. The followers of Rifaa were recognized as a new community, just like Gabal's, with its own rights and prerogatives, and Ali was appointed overseer of their estate, and their protector. He would receive their share of the revenues, and distribute them on the basis of total equality. All those who had fled the alley during times of trouble now returned to the new community, led by Shafi'i and his wife, Zaki, Hussein and Karim. Rifaa enjoyed respect, veneration and love in death that he had never dreamed of during his lifetime. There was even a wonderful story, retold by every tongue and recited to rebec tunes, particularly of how Gabalawi lifted up his body and buried it in his fabulous garden. All Rifaa's followers agreed on that and they were unanimously loyal and reverent to his parents, but they differed on everything else. Karim, Hussein and Zaki insisted that Rifaa's mission had been limited to healing the sick and despising power and majesty; they and their sympathizers in the alley did as he had done. Some went further and refrained from marriage, to imitate him and live their lives his way. Ali, however, retained his rights to the estate, married and called for the renewal of their community. Rifaa had not hated the estate itself, but only to prove that true happiness was achievable without it, and to condemn the vices inspired by covetousness. If the revenue was distributed justly, and put toward building and charity, then it was the greatest good.

In any case, the people were delighted with their good lives, and welcomed life with radiant faces; they said with confident security that today was better than yesterday, and that tomorrow would be better than today.

Why is forgetfulness the plague of our alley?

Qassem

64

Almost nothing in the alley had changed. Feet that were still bare left their deep prints in the dirt. Flies still lingered in garbage and on people's eyes. Faces were still tired and haggard, clothes were ragged, obscenities were exchanged like greetings and ears were numb with lies and hypocrisy. The mansion still sat behind its walls, immersed in silence and memory, with the overseer's house to the right and the protector's house to the left; then there was Gabal's neighborhood, and Rifaa's, in the middle of the alley. The rest of the alley, sprawling down to Gamaliya, was inhabited by uncouth people of uncertain lineage— "Desert Rats," as they were called—the most lost and miserable people in the alley. Now, at this time the overseer was Sayid Rifaat, and he was like every other overseer. The protector was Lahita, a short, thin man whose appearance did not suggest power, but in a fight his speed, severity and deadliness transformed him into a lick of flame. He had become protector after a series of battles that had made blood flow in every street. The protector of the Al Gabal was called Galta, and his people still prided themselves on being the closest to Gabalawi, as having the best community, and because their man, Gabal, was the first and last to whom Gabalawi had spoken, and the first he had favored. As a result, they were very unpopular. The protector of the Al Rifaa was Hagag, and he had very little resemblance to Ali; he was more like Khunfis and Galta and other usurpers. He embezzled estate revenues, beat anyone who complained and exhorted his people to follow Rifaa's teaching to despise power and majesty! Even the Desert Rats had their protector, named Sawaris, but he was not trustee to any estate. This was the way life was, and all those who wielded clubs, as well as the poets with their instruments, said that it was a just system that observed Gabalawi's Ten

Conditions, with the overseer and protectors to administrate and supervise it. In the Desert Rats' territory, old Zachary, the potato seller, was
renowned for his goodness, and was distinguished among his people by
his distant kinship with Sawaris, the local gangster. He would make the
rounds of the alley's neighborhoods, pushing his cart and hawking potatoes. In the middle of his cart stood the little stove that exhaled the
fragrant, delicious smoke that attracted the boys of Rifaa and Gabal as
well as boys from Gamaliya, Atuf, al-Darasa, Kafr al-Zaghari and Bait al-
Qadi. Zachary had been married for long years without being blessed
with a child, but at around this time his loneliness was beguiled by an
orphan boy, Qassem—Zachary's nephew—after his parents died. The
man did not find the child a burden, for life, especially in their part of
the alley, was nearly as cheap as the lives of the dogs, cats and flies that
found their sustenance in dumps and garbage heaps. Zachary loved
Qassem as he had loved his father, and when his wife became pregnant
after the boy had joined their family, he saw Qassem as a good omen and
felt even more tenderly toward him. His love did not diminish when he
was blessed with a son of his own, Hassan. Qassem grew up nearly alone,
as the day passed with his uncle far from their neighborhood and his
aunt busy with her house and baby, but his world broadened as he grew.
He played in the courtyard of their building or out in the alley, and
made friends with other boys from his own neighborhood, and from
Rifaa and Gabal. He went out to the wasteland to play around Hind's
Rock, explored every part of the desert and climbed up the mountain.
He and his young friends peered up at the mansion, proud of his grandfather's prestige, but he was never able to know what to say when some
people spoke of Gabal and the others of Rifaa, or what to do when their
talk turned gloating or malicious or quarrelsome. How often he gazed at
the overseer's house, puzzled and awestruck; how often he looked long-
ingly and hungrily at the fruit in the trees. One day he saw the gatekeeper nodding off, so he slipped stealthily into the garden without
seeing anyone, and without anyone seeing him. He began delightedly
walking down the paths, picking guavas from off the lawns and eating
them lustily, until he found himself before the pool, where his eyes did
not leave the column of water spouting from the fountain. Over-

whelmed with delight, he took off his clothes, slipped into the water and began to plunge around, beat his hands on the surface of the water and rub his body with it, oblivious to everything around him. The next thing he knew, a sharp voice shouted angrily, "Othman, you bastard, come here, you blind son of a blind man!" He turned his head toward the source of the sound and saw a man wrapped in a red cloak, standing on the terrace and pointing at him with a trembling finger, his face blazing with rage. He started for the edge of the pool and climbed to the garden bank, leaning on his elbows, and then saw the gatekeeper hurrying toward him. He made for the bower of jasmine adjacent to the wall, forgetting his clothes where he had taken them off. He ran to the gate, rushed into the alley, and Othman chased him, catching up with him in the middle of the neighborhood. He snatched him by the arm and stopped, panting, and Qassem's bellows rose until they filled the alley. In no time his aunt came, carrying her baby, and Sawaris came out of the coffeehouse. His aunt was taken aback at his appearance, and took him by the hand.

"For shame," she told the gatekeeper, "you've terrified the boy. What has he done and where are his clothes?"

"His excellency the overseer saw him swimming in the fountain!" shouted the gatekeeper haughtily. "The little devil should be flogged. The rascal got in while I was sleeping. Why don't you give us a rest from your little devils!"

"We are sorry. The boy is an orphan. You are right," said the woman urgently, taking him from the man's hand. "I'll punish him for you, but please, sir, can't we have his only clothes back?"

The gatekeeper made an exasperated gesture and turned his back on her as he started home.

"Thanks to this vermin *I* have been cursed and insulted—dirty little devils! This stinking alley!"

The woman went back to the building holding Hassan on her hip, hauling Qassem by the hand as he gulped and cried.

65

Zachary gazed at Qassem with satisfaction.

"You are not a child anymore, Qassem. You are almost ten," he said. "The time has come for you to start working."

Qassem's dark eyes shone with delight. "How often I've hoped you'd take me with you, uncle!"

"You wanted to play, not work," the man laughed. "But today you are a bright boy and you can help me."

The lad ran to the handcart, trying to push it, but Zachary prevented him.

"Be careful the potatoes don't fall out, or we'll starve to death," said his uncle's wife.

Zachary caught the cart handles in his hands.

"Walk in front of the cart and call out, 'Fabulous potatoes, roasted potatoes,' and watch everything I say and do. You'll be taking potatoes up to customers who live upstairs. Just keep your eyes open in general."

"But I *can* push it," said Qassem, gazing regretfully at the cart.

The man pushed the cart and said, "Do as I told you and don't be stubborn. Your father was a fine man."

The cart descended toward Gamaliya, with Qassem shouting in a voice as high as a whistle, "Fabulous potatoes, roasted potatoes!" Nothing could touch his delight as he set out into strange neighborhoods and worked like a man. When the cart reached Watawit Alley, Qassem looked around him and told his uncle, "This is where Idris blocked Adham's path!"

Zachary nodded disinterestedly.

"Adham was pushing a cart, just like you!" Qassem continued, laughing.

The cart made its daily rounds, from al-Hussein to Bait al-Qadi, and from Bait al-Qadi to al-Darasa, while Qassem stared with astonishment at the pedestrians, the shops and the mosques, until they came to a small square his uncle told him was Muqattam Marketplace. The boy contemplated it admiringly.

"Is this really Muqattam Marketplace? This is where Gabal fled; this is where Rifaa was born!"

"Yes," said Zachary without enthusiasm. "Neither one of them is ours!"

"But we are all children of Gabalawi," said Qassem. "Why aren't we like them?"

Zachary laughed. "At least we're poor like them!"

The man steered his cart toward the fringes of the marketplace on the edge of the desert, directly toward a sheet-metal hut which seemed to be a shop selling worry beads, incense and amulets. An old man with a long white beard sat on a hide out in front of it. Zachary stopped the cart at the hut and warmly shook hands with the old man.

"I have all the potatoes I need today," the man said.

"To me, sitting with you is better than making money," said Zachary as he sat down beside him.

The old man looked at the boy curiously. "Come here, Qassem, and kiss Yahya's hand."

The boy approached the old man, took his skinny hand and kissed it politely. Yahya ruffled Qassem's thick hair and considered his handsome face.

"Who is the boy, Zachary?"

"The son of my late brother," said Zachary, stretching his legs out in the sun.

He had the boy sit beside him on the hide, and asked him, "Do you remember your father, boy?"

"No, sir," said Qassem, shaking his head.

"Your father was a friend of mine, and he was a fine man."

Qassem raised his eyes to the merchandise, gazing at the colors. Yahya reached over to a nearby shelf and selected an amulet, then hung it around the boy's neck.

"Keep it, and it will keep you from all harm."

"Yahya was from our alley," said Zachary. "From the Rifaa neighborhood."

Qassem looked at Yahya. "Why did you leave our alley, sir?"

"The Rifaa gangster got mad at him a long time ago and he decided to leave," Zachary said.

"You did the same thing Shafi'i, Rifaa's father, did!" said Qassem in surprise.

Yahya laughed a long, toothless laugh and said, "You knew that, my boy? How well the people of our alley know the stories—what's wrong with their heads, that they never learn?"

The coffeehouse boy came with a tea tray, which he set down in front of Yahya, and left. Yahya drew a small package from the breast of his clothes and began to unwrap it.

"I have something valuable here," he said contentedly. "Its effects will last until morning!"

"Let's try it," said Zachary, sounding interested.

"I've never heard you say no," laughed Yahya.

"How can I refuse pleasure?"

They divided the piece and began to chew it. Qassem watched them, fascinated, until his uncle laughed. The old man began to sip his tea. "Do you dream of becoming a gangster, like the people of our alley?" he asked Qassem.

"Yes," said Qassem, smiling.

Zachary cackled, then added apologetically, "Forgive him, Yahya. You know that in our alley either a man is a gangster or he offers them his head to smack."

"God rest your soul, Rifaa," sighed Yahya. "How did our infernal alley produce you!"

"It was his end, as you know."

"Rifaa did not die on the day of his death." Yahya frowned. "He died the day his successor turned into a gangster!"

"Where is he buried?" Qassem asked with concern. "His people say that our ancestor buried him in his garden. The Al Gabal say that his body was lost in the desert."

"The damned villains!" shouted Yahya angrily. "They still feel hatred for him, even today!" More composed, he asked, "Tell me, Qassem, do you love Rifaa?"

The boy looked cautiously over at his uncle but said simply, "Yes, sir, I love him very much."

"Which would you love more, being like him or being a gangster?"

Qassem turned to him two eyes which showed both perplexity and amusement. He moved his lips to speak but said nothing.

"Let him be content to sell potatoes, like me," laughed Zachary.

Silence fell among them as the marketplace went into an uproar over a donkey which had flung itself to the ground, overturning the cart it was fastened to; the lady passengers hopped out of it, while the driver rained blows on the donkey.

"We have a long journey," said Zachary, getting up. "Peace, Yahya."

"Bring the boy with you whenever you visit," said Yahya. He shook Qassem's hand and ruffled his hair. "You're remarkable."

66

The only place in the desert that offered shelter from the raging sun was Hind's Rock. That is where Qassem sat on the ground with no companions but the sheep. He wore a clean blue galabiya—as clean as a shepherd's galabiya can be—with a thick turban to shield his head from the sun, and old, frayed leather slippers on his feet. He was lost in his thoughts part of the time, and the rest of the time watched the ewes, rams, nanny goats and kids. His staff lay at his side. Muqattam loomed near, looking huge and gloomy from where he sat, as if he were the sole creature under the limpid dome, challenging the wrath of the sun, pained but unyielding. The desert rolled on to the horizon, burdened with heavy silence and burning air. When he had worn out his thoughts, dreams and youthful, evanescent suppositions, his gaze roamed

to the flock, taking in their play and sport, their fights and their ro-
mances, their movement and their idleness, especially the kids and baby
lambs, who excited his love and sentimentality. He marveled at their
black eyes; their stares made his heart beat faster, as if they were speaking
to him. He spoke to them in turn, and compared the affectionate care he
gave them with the insults the people of the alley got from the arrogant
gangsters. He paid no attention to the condescending view of shepherds
in the alley, convinced from the very start that a shepherd was better
than a bully, a phony or a beggar. Anyway, he loved the desert and the
pure air, and enjoyed the companionship of the Muqattam, Hind's
Rock and the dome of the sky with its strange moods—and shepherding
always brought him to Yahya. The first time Yahya saw him as a shepherd, he asked, "From a potato seller to a shepherd?"

"Why not, sir?" asked Qassem, not embarrassed. "It's a job that
hundreds of idle men in my neighborhood begrudge me!"

"Why did your uncle let you go?"

"My cousin Hassan got bigger, and he has more right to go with
Uncle on his rounds than I do. And tending sheep is better than begging!"

Not a day passed without him visiting his teacher. He loved him,
and was enthralled by his conversation; he had found in him a man
immersed in the lore of his alley, its present and its past. He knew
everything the poets sang of and more, and even knew what was often
deliberately ignored. "I tend sheep from every neighborhood," Qassem
told Yahya. "I have sheep from Gabal, and some from Rifaa, and from
the rich people in our own neighborhood. And the marvel is that they
all graze together in brotherhood, something unknown among their
bigoted owners in our alley!" He also told him that "Humam was a
shepherd. And who are the people that despise shepherds? Beggars and
slobs, and the unemployed. At the same time, they respect the gangsters,
and what are the gangsters but shameless, bloodthirsty thieves. God
forgive the children of the alley!"

Once, he told him jokingly, "I'm poor and happy. I don't lift my
hand to hurt anyone, and even my sheep get only affection from me. So,
am I not like Rifaa?"

"Rifaa! You, like Rifaa!" The man stared at him in horror. "Rifaa spent his life saving his brothers from demons, so that they could be good!" Then the old man laughed. "You are a boy crazy about women, you lurk in the dark for the desert women!"

"Is there something wrong with that, sir?"

"It's your own business, but don't say you're like Rifaa!"

Qassem considered this a moment, then said, "Wasn't Gabal like Rifaa, one of the good children of Gabalawi? He was, sir, and he fell in love and married, and he gained his people's rights in the estate, and distributed them justly."

"But his only goal was the estate!" said Yahya sharply.

The boy thought this over and then said plainly, "But civility, justice and the law were other goals of his."

"So you think Gabal is better than Rifaa?" asked Yahya indignantly.

His dark eyes filled with confusion, and Qassem hesitated for a long time before saying, "They were both good men, and how rare good people are in our alley. Adham, Humam, Gabal and Rifaa—that's it. But gangsters—we have so many!"

"And Adham died heartsick, Humam was murdered and Rifaa was murdered!" said Yahya sadly.

Those were indeed the good men the alley had produced. Brilliant lives and bad ends, Qassem whispered to himself as he sat in the shadow of the great rock. A burning desire to be like them rose in his heart. The gangsters—how degraded their deeds were. A mysterious sadness entered him, and unease gripped him. He said to himself, to allay his fear: How many people, how many deeds, this rock has witnessed—the passion of Qadri and Hind, the murder of Humam, the meeting of Gabal and Gabalawi, Rifaa's talk with his ancestor. But where were the deeds and where were the people? Only fond memories, but they were more precious than a flock of goats and sheep! And this rock witnesses our great ancestor when he roams these horizons all alone, doing his own will, as wrongdoers are terrified. So how is he, in his isolation?

At the end of the day he got up, stretched and yawned. He whistled melodiously and waved his staff. The sheep bleated and began to gather and troop off in a mass toward town. He felt hungry; he had eaten nothing all day long but a small fish and a small loaf of bread, but a good dinner awaited him at his uncle's house. He quickened his pace until he caught the first glimpse from afar of the mansion and its high walls, its shuttered windows and the tops of the trees. What was the garden like, the garden that the poets sang of, for which Adham had died pining? As he drew closer to the alley, its chaotic noise reached his ears. He passed opposite the great wall into the alley as the air filled with darkness. He made his way between mobs of frolicking boys flinging mud at one another, his ears assaulted by peddlers' cries, women's gossip, the sarcasm and obscenities of the idle, the shrieks of lunatics, and the bells on the overseer's vehicle, while his nose was filled with the strong smell of tobacco laced with honey, rancid garbage and the lovely aroma of garlic and coriander sauce. He ascended to the buildings of Gabal to bring its sheep home and did the same in Rifaa, and then had only one ewe left, belonging to Lady Qamar, the only lady who owned property in the Desert Rats' neighborhood. She lived in a two-story house with a medium-size courtyard; a palm tree grew in the center, and a guava tree in the corner. He walked into the courtyard driving Naama in front of him, meeting the slave woman, Sakina, with her frizzy, graying hair on his way. He greeted her, and she greeted him back with a smile. "How is Naama?" she asked in her coppery voice.

He told her how much he liked the ewe, and left it with her, turning back, when the lady of the house appeared, entering the courtyard from the alley. She stood before him, her cloak wrapped around her full body, her dark eyes looking at him tenderly over the black veil that covered her lower face. He stood aside and averted his gaze, and she spoke to him with refined amiability.

"Good evening."

"Good evening, ma'am."

The woman now walked more slowly, looking carefully at Naama, and then at him. "Naama is getting fatter every day, thanks to you!"

"Thanks to God, and your good care," he said, touched by her affectionate looks even more than by her kind words.

"Give him some dinner," said Lady Qamar, turning to Sakina.

He lifted his hands to his head in thanks. "You're very kind, ma'am."

He was rewarded with another look from her as he said goodbye and left. He went away deeply moved by her warmth and sympathy, as he was whenever good luck permitted him to meet her. It was the kind of sympathy he had never experienced, except in what he had sometimes heard of the mother's love he had never known. If his mother had lived, today she would be about the same age as this woman in her forties. How strange this affection seemed in his alley, so proud of its power and violence. Even more wonderful was her reticent beauty and the copious delight it imparted to his soul. It was nothing like his passionate adventures in the desert, with their blind, raging hunger and brief melancholy satisfaction. He hurried to his uncle's house, his staff over his shoulder, hardly able to see what was in front of him, so great was his excitement. He found his uncle's family assembled on the balcony overlooking the courtyard, waiting for him. He sat with the three of them around the low table which held a meal of falafel, leeks and watermelon. Hassan, now sixteen, was so tall and strong that Zachary dreamed of seeing him someday become protector of the Desert Rats. When dinner was ended, the woman cleared the table, Zachary went out and the two friends stayed on the balcony until a voice called to them from the courtyard: "Qassem!"

They both got up, and Qassem answered, "We're coming, Sadeq."

Sadeq met them, radiant with joy. He was about the same age and height as Qassem, but slenderer. He worked as an assistant to a coppersmith in the first shop in the Desert Rats' neighborhood, close to Gamaliya. The friends headed for the Dingil Coffeehouse, and as they entered they were spotted by Taza the poet, who sat cross-legged on his bench toward the front. Sawaris sat near Dingil at the entrance, and the young men went over to the gangster and greeted him humbly despite the pride Qassem and Hassan felt at being related to him. They took their seats on one bench, and a boy speedily came to take their usual order; Qassem loved a pipe and mint tea. Sawaris surveyed Qassem disdainfully and asked bluntly, "What's with you, boy, all neat like a girl?"

Qassem blushed. "There's nothing wrong with being clean and neat, sir," he said apologetically.

"At your age it's stupid!" sneered Sawaris.

Silence fell in the coffeehouse, as if its customers, silverware and walls were all listening in on the gangster. Sadeq looked kindly at his friend, knowing how easily hurt his feelings were, and Hassan hid his face behind his glass of ginger drink, so that the gangster would not see his anger. Taza took up his rebec and began to pluck melodies from its strings; after saluting Rifaat the overseer, Lahita the gangster, and Sawaris, protector of this neighborhood, he began his chant.

"Adham imagined that he heard footfalls. Slow, heavy footfalls that stirred misty memories, as a strong, sweet smell may defy perception and definition. He turned his face to the entrance of the hut and saw the door open, then saw it blocked by a huge form. He started in surprise, and peered through the dark, his hopes enclosed by fears, then a deep moan escaped him. 'Father?' he murmured. He seemed to be hearing the old voice: 'Good evening, Adham.' His eyes swam with tears. He tried to get up but could not. He felt a delight, a bliss that he had not known in twenty years."

67

"Wait, Qassem," said the slave Sakina. *"I have something for you."*

Qassem stood where the ewe was tethered to the trunk of the palm tree, waiting for the slave, who had gone inside, his heart thumping; he told himself that any good the slave's voice promised him had to come from a nobler good in the heart of the lady of this house. He felt a keen longing to see her look at him, or to hear her voice, which would blissfully cool his body, which had burned in the desert all day long.

Sakina came back out with a package and handed it to him. "A pastry. Eat it in good health!"

He took it and said, "Please thank the generous lady of the house for me."

Then her voice came from behind the window, saying kindly, "The thanks are God's, my good man."

He waved his hand in thanks, without looking, and left, repeating her words, "my good man," with almost drunken delight. The shepherd had never heard these words before. And who had pronounced them? The only respectable lady in his miserable neighborhood! He gave the darkening alley a loving look and said to himself, "Our alley may be miserable, but it still has a few things that can give happiness to weary hearts!" He was jerked out of his reverie by a voice shouting, "My money! My money's been stolen!" He saw a turbaned man in a loose white galabiya running toward the opening of the alley, coming from the fringe of their neighborhood. Everyone in the alley turned toward the screaming man, the children ran to him and the merchants and people sitting in doorways craned their necks to see him. Heads emerged from windows and from the ground, through cellar trapdoors. Customers came out of the coffeehouse and surrounded the man on all sides. Qassem noticed a man nearby, scratching his back with a wooden stick through the neck of his galabiya, watching the scene through expressionless eyes.

"Who is the man?" Qassem asked him.

"An upholsterer who worked in the overseer's house."

Sawaris, the Desert Rats' gangster, Hagag, the gangster of Rifaa, and Galta, the gangster of Gabal, closed in on the man and quickly ordered everyone to move back. They all immediately retreated several steps.

"The evil eye got him!" said a woman from her window in a building in the Rifaa neighborhood.

"Yes!" said another woman, from her window in one of the closest buildings in Gabal. "Everyone has been jealous of the money he was going to get for upholstering the overseer's furniture. God keep us from the evil eye!"

A third woman, standing in front of a gate and picking lice from a boy's head, said, "And, my God, he was laughing when he left the overseer's house. He didn't know he was going to be shouting and crying! Damn money!"

"He stole all the money I had!" screamed the man in his loudest voice. "A week's pay, and even more, money for my house and shop and children—twenty pounds and change! Goddamn bastards!"

"Whoa! Everyone shut up!" said Galta, the gangster of Gabal. "Shut up, you animals! The alley's reputation is at stake here, and in the end the gangsters will get the blame."

"By your God," said Hagag, the gangster of Rifaa, "no one's going to be blamed. But how do we know he lost his money in our alley?"

"I swear I'll divorce my wife!" the man shouted hoarsely. "I was robbed in your alley—I got the money from the gatekeeper of his excellency the overseer, and at the end of the alley I felt my breast pocket and it was all gone!"

A babble of voices rose, and Hagag shouted, "Shut up, you stupid beasts! Listen, man, where did you notice that your money was gone?"

The man pointed to the end of the Desert Rats' territory.

"In front of the coppersmith's shop, but actually no one came near me there."

"So he was robbed before he entered our area," said Sawaris.

"I was in the coffeehouse when he passed by," said Hagag, "and I didn't see anyone in our neighborhood go near him."

"There are no thieves in Gabal!" said Galta angrily. "We are the finest people in this alley!"

"That's enough, Galta," said Hagag crossly. "You're wrong about the finest people in the alley too."

"No one can deny it."

"Don't push me!" Hagag thundered. "Goddamn peasant beliefs."

"A thousand curses, a thousand curses on peasant gutterisms that are below us!" shouted Galta just as angrily.

"Please! My money was lost in your alley," wept the upholsterer. "I'm sure you're all fine people, but what about my money? What about me, poor Fangari?"

"We must start a search," said Hagag sharply. "We'll search every pocket, every man, every woman, every child and every corner."

"Go ahead and search," said Galta contemptuously. "You'll find the criminal, and it won't be one of us."

"The man left the overseer's house, and passed first of all through Gabal," said Hagag. "So let's start the search in Gabal."

Galta snorted.

"Not while I'm alive. Remember who you are, Hagag, and who I am."

"Listen, Galta, I have more knife scars on my body than you have hairs!"

"I don't have any room left for hair on my body!"

"Don't wake the devil in me!"

"I'm ready for all the devils in the world."

"What about my money?" shrieked Fangari. "Isn't this bad for you, that people will say I was robbed in your alley?"

This angered one woman, who shouted, "Watch out, you ugly creep, you'll ruin our reputation!"

Someone said, "Why wouldn't the money have been stolen in Desert Rat territory? Most of them are thieves and beggars."

"Our thieves do not steal in our own alley!" Sawaris proclaimed.

"How do we know that?"

"That's all the insolence we need," said Sawaris, his eyes reddening with rage. "The search will find the thief, or it's the end of this alley!"

"Start with the Desert Rats!" several voices called.

"Anyone who goes beyond a routine search, I'll smash his face with my club," shouted Sawaris. He lifted his club, and his men gathered around him. Hagag lifted his own club, and Galta retreated to his own territory and did the same. The upholsterer withdrew, weeping, to a doorway. It was nearly night. Everyone was expecting a bloody battle when Qassem came out into the middle of the alley and raised his voice.

"Wait! Blood won't find the lost money! They will say, in Gamaliya, in al-Darasa and Atuf, that if you go into Gabalawi Alley you'll be robbed, even if you have the protection of its overseer and all the alley's protectors!"

"What does the shepherd want?" asked one of the men from Gabal.

"I have a solution for getting the money back for its owner without a fight," said Qassem magnanimously.

"I would appreciate that," said the upholsterer, running to Qassem's side.

"It will restore the money to its owner without exposing the thief," Qassem told the crowd.

Silence fell, and all eyes settled very intently on Qassem, who spoke up again. "Let's wait until it's dark—that will be very soon. Don't light even one candle in the alley, and let's all walk from one end of the alley to the other, so that suspicion won't be on any one neighborhood. In the meantime, whoever has the money will be able to put it down in the dark, without giving himself away. We will find the money, and the alley will be spared the tragedy of a battle."

The upholsterer grabbed Qassem's arm in humble supplication, and shouted, "Yes, this is the solution, please accept it, for my sake." "It's a good idea!" someone called. "It's a good chance for the thief to save himself and the alley." A woman trilled with joy. The people looked from one gangster to the others, not knowing whether to be hopeful or afraid; none of the proud and touchy gangsters wanted to be the first to give his agreement, so the people of the alley could only wonder whether reason would prevail, or whether the clubs would be swung to shed blood.

A voice known to all of them suddenly rang out: "Listen!"

All heads turned to the source of the voice, to where the protector of the whole alley, Lahita, stood, not far from his house. Silence fell, and everyone waited breathlessly for him to speak again.

"Accept the idea, you filthy gypsies," he said contemptuously. "If you weren't so stupid, you wouldn't need a shepherd to save you."

A murmur of relief ran through the crowd, and the women trilled shrilly with joy. The pounding of Qassem's heart intensified. He saw Qamar's house; knowing that her dark eyes were watching him from behind one of the two windows that looked out on the alley filled him with a splendid happiness. He savored a sense of great triumph thus far unknown to him. Everyone waited for night, looking up at the sky out into the desert, following the gradual descent of darkness. Their surroundings began to disappear from sight, and their faces to be hidden as the people turned into mere shapes. The two paths around the mansion that led out into the desert were closed off by blackness. The phantom shapes began to move, walking toward the mansion, then quickly crossed the alley to Gamaliya and headed from there to their own neighborhoods. At this point Lahita shouted in his most commanding voice, "Lights!"

The first light to come on was in Qamar's house in the Desert Rat district, the handcart lanterns were lit, then the coffeehouse lamps, and once more the alley existed. A group of people went to scour the ground by lamplight, and shortly one of them sang out, "Here is the wallet!"

Fangari raced over to the light and snatched up the wallet, counted his money and hurried toward Gamaliya without looking back, leaving behind him a loud roar of laughter and women's trilling. Qassem found himself the center of attention, the recipient of congratulations, jokes and every kind of commentary, tossed his way like roses. When Qassem, Hassan and Sadeq went to their local coffeehouse that evening, Sawaris greeted him with a smile of welcome. "A pipe for Qassem, on the house!"

68

Blushing, bright-eyed, smiling and with a light heart, he went into Qamar's courtyard to fetch Naama, the ewe. "Here I am," he called, and was untying Naama's tether at the bottom of the steps, when he heard the door to the women's quarters creak open, and the lady's voice. "Good morning."

"God give you a very good morning, ma'am," he said earnestly.

"Yesterday you did a great thing for our alley."

"God was my guide," he said, dancing with joy inside.

"You taught us that wisdom is better than violence," she said in a melodious voice that gave away her admiration.

And your love is better than wisdom, he said to himself.

"Thank you," he said.

There was a smile in her voice when she said, "We saw you tending the men of Gabalawi the way you tend your flock. Be safe; goodbye."

He left with the ewe, and with every building he passed he added kids, billy goats, nanny goats or sheep to his caravan. He heard many pleasantries, and even the gangsters who had always ignored him now returned his greetings. He moved down the path alongside the mansion wall, behind a wide column of sheep, on his way to the desert. He was met by a blazing sun high over the mountain, and the hot breath of the bright morning air. Some shepherds came into view at the foot of the mountain, a man in ragged clothes playing a pipe passed by and a flock of kites circled under the clear dome of the sky. With every breath he took, he smelled the pure and immaculate air; the massive mountain seemed to him to harbor great treasures of promised hopes. As he surveyed the desert with a marvelous feeling of relaxation, an expansive happiness took hold of him, and he began to sing.

Sweet, beautiful and Upper Egyptian,
My arm's tattooed with your inscription!

His eyes moved over Hind and Qadri's rock, the sites where Humam and Rifaa had died, and where Gabal encountered Gabalawi. Here were the sun, the mountain, the sand, grandeur, love and a heart bursting with love, and yet he asked what it all meant, both the part that was history and that which was to come; the alley with its feuding neighborhoods and puffed-up gangsters and the stories that were told in every coffeehouse—with differences.

Shortly before noon he drove his sheep toward Muqattam Marketplace, went into Yahya's hut and sat down.

"What's this I hear about what you did in our alley yesterday?" the old man called.

Qassem hid his shyness by taking a sip of tea.

"It would have been better for you to let them all fight and kill one another," Yahya added.

"You don't really mean that," said Qassem, his eyes still lowered.

"Avoid having admirers or else you'll provoke the gangsters," Yahya warned.

"Do gangsters feel provoked by people like me?"

"Who would ever have imagined that a traitor would betray Rifaa?"

"What's the comparison between the great Rifaa and me?"

When Qassem was ready to leave, the old man bid him goodbye, saying, "Always keep the amulet I gave you."

That afternoon, he was sitting in the shade behind Hind's Rock when he heard Sakina's voice calling, "Naama!" He jumped up and looked around the rock, and saw the slave standing by the ewe's head, petting her snout. He greeted her with a smile.

"I have an errand in al-Darasa," she said in her coppery voice, "and I came this way, for a shortcut."

"But it's such a hot route!"

"That's why I'm taking a break in the shadow of the rock." She laughed.

They sat close to one another in the shade where he had left his staff.

"When I saw what you did yesterday," Sakina said, "I knew your mother really prayed for you from her heart before she died."

"Don't you pray for me?" he said, smiling.

She looked away with her sly face. "I pray for a nice wife for someone like you!"

"Who will be satisfied with a shepherd?" He laughed.

"Luck works miracles, and now you're the equal of any protector, without having to shed any blood."

"I swear—your tongue is sweeter than a honeydew melon."

She gave him a frank stare with her weak eyes. "Should I tell you something wonderful to do?"

"Yes," he said, suddenly excited.

With African candor she said, "Try your luck and propose to the lady in our neighborhood."

Everything suddenly seemed different. "Who do you mean, Sakina?"

"Don't pretend you don't understand. There is only one lady in our neighborhood."

"Qamar!"

"No one else."

"Her husband was a great man. I'm only a shepherd!" he said unsteadily.

"But when luck laughs, everyone may laugh along, even the poor."

"What if my proposal angers her?"

Sakina stood up. "No one knows when a woman will be happy or angry. Trust God. You take care of yourself," she said as she left.

He raised his face to the sky and closed his eyes, as if overtaken by drowsiness.

69

Zachary and his wife stared perplexedly into Qassem's face, and so did Hassan, as they sat out on the porch of their lodging after dinner.

"Say anything but that," his uncle said. "I've known you to be a model of good sense and honor, even though you're poor, even though we're poor. What has happened to you?"

A burning desire for information brightened his aunt's eyes.

"I have support for this—her slave is the one who brought it up with me."

"Her slave!" his aunt gasped, her eyes pleading for more.

His uncle laughed briefly, showing his bewilderment, and said dubiously, "Maybe you misunderstood."

"No, uncle," said Qassem calmly, to hide his irritation.

"I understand it!" exclaimed his aunt. "The slave said it because the lady said it!"

"There is no man better than Qassem," said Hassan, moved by his well-known love for his cousin.

" 'Fabulous potatoes, roasted potatoes,' " muttered Zachary, shaking his head. "But you have no money!"

"He tends her ewe, and she can't ignore that," said his aunt. She laughed. "Make sure you never slaughter a ewe for the rest of your life, in honor of Naama, Qassem!"

"The grocer Uwais is Qamar's uncle, and he's the richest man in the neighborhood," said Hassan thoughtfully. "He'll be our in-law, the way Sawaris is our relative—what could be better!"

"Qamar is related to Lady Amina, the overseer's wife—through her late husband, who was related to Amina," said Hassan's mother.

"That's what makes it so hard," said Qassem uneasily.

Then Zachary spoke with sudden enthusiasm, as if guessing at the rise in prestige they would all derive from the anticipated match.

"Talk the way you did the day the upholsterer was robbed. You're brave and you're wise. We'll go to the lady together to talk about it, *then* we'll talk to Uwais. If we begin with Uwais, he'll send us to the mental hospital!"

Everything transpired just as Zachary had planned, and soon Uwais was sitting in the reception room of Qamar's house, stroking his bushy mustache to conceal his restlessness as he waited for her to come in. Qamar entered, wearing a simple dress and a brown scarf covering her head. She greeted him politely and took a seat, a look of calm resolution in her eyes.

"You've really confused me!" Uwais said. "Only recently you refused the hand of Mursi, my business assistant, because you said he wasn't good enough for you, and today you're happy with a shepherd!"

"Uncle," she said, blushing modestly, "he is a poor man, of course, but there isn't anyone in our neighborhood who doesn't testify to his goodness, and his family's."

Uwais frowned. "Yes, but the same way we testify to a servant's being reliable or clean. Fitness as a husband is something else!"

"Uncle," she said politely, "show me any man in our alley as well-bred as he is—show me just one who doesn't brag about his acts of bullying, savagery or meanness!"

The man almost exploded with anger, but remembered that he was dealing not only with his niece but with a woman who owned a substantial share of his business, so he spoke with polite urgency. "Qamar, if you wished, I could marry you to any gangster in the alley. Lahita himself would want you, if you agreed to share him with his other wives."

"I don't like these gangsters, or that kind of man anyway. My father was a good man, like you, and with all he had to endure from them, he passed his hatred of them on to me. Qassem is a well-bred man who lacks nothing but money, and I have enough money for two."

Uwais sighed and looked at her for a long time before making his last try. "I have a message for you from Lady Amina, the wife of his excellency the overseer. She told me, 'Tell Qamar to come to her senses. She's moving toward a mistake that will make us the talk of the alley.' "

"That lady's orders don't interest me," said Qamar sharply. "It's too bad she doesn't know whose doings *have* made them the talk of the alley."

"She's only worried about your honor."

"Oh, uncle, don't think that she worries about us at all, or even remembers us! Since my husband died ten years ago, I've never even crossed her mind."

He paused a long moment, clearly embarrassed, then said with evident difficulty, "She also says that it is not right for a woman to marry a man who does not deserve her, especially when he constantly visits her house!"

Qamar immediately rose to her feet, her face pale with anger. "Let her watch her tongue!" she exclaimed. "I was born here, I grew up here, I was married and widowed in this alley, everybody knows me, and my reputation is perfect among everyone here!"

"Of course, of course—she was only indicating what might be said."

"Uncle, let's drop the subject of this lady—she's nothing but a headache. I have told you, because you are my uncle, that I have agreed to marry Qassem. It will be with your consent and in your presence!"

Uwais thought this over silently. He had no power to prevent her, and it would not be wise to anger her so much that she might pull her money out of his business. Sad and confused, he stared at the space between his feet. He opened his mouth to say something, but only a cryptic mumble came out. Qamar still gazed at him with steady patience.

70

Zachary gave his nephew a few pounds—most of them borrowed—to put himself in order before the wedding.

"If I could, I'd give you all the money you needed, Qassem," he said. "Your father was a good brother to me, and I still remember his generosity to me on my wedding day."

Qassem bought a galabiya, some underwear, an embroidered turban, some yellow leather slippers, a bamboo cane and a snuffbox. After daybreak he went to the baths and had a steam bath, plunged into the bath, went to the masseur, bathed and was perfumed with incense, then stretched out in a little cell to sip tea and dream of happiness.

Qamar took charge of the wedding party. She prepared the roof of her house for the women, invited a famous lady singer and hired the most skillful cook in the neighborhood. A pavilion was set up in the courtyard for the male guests and their singer. Qassem's family and friends came, and the neighborhood men arrived with Sawaris at the head of them. Glasses of barley beer and twenty pipes were passed around, until the bright lamps were indistinct in the smoke, and the glorious aroma of hashish spread everywhere. Every corner of the house rang with the women's trilling, cheers and laughter, and, light-headed from drinking, Zachary bragged, "We are a fine old family, a noble family!"

Uwais held in his anger at this as he sat between Sawaris and Zachary, saying only, "Well, you are related to Sawaris!"

"God bless Sawaris!" bellowed Zachary.

The musicians immediately struck up for Sawaris, who managed a smile and a wave. The gangster had, in the past, been exasperated by Zachary's insistently bringing up their distant kinship, but his feelings changed when he learned of Qassem's marriage to Qamar. He had decided secretly not to release Qassem from paying protection money.

"Everybody loves Qassem," Zachary resumed. "Who in our alley does not love him?" Then, as if he had read something untoward in Sawaris' stare, he added, "If it hadn't been for his wisdom the day of the robbery, the heads of our Rifaa and Gabal neighbors would have had nothing to save them from the club of our protector, Sawaris!"

Sawaris' features relaxed, and Uwais agreed with what Zachary had said. "That's true, by the Lord of the heavens and the earth!"

"The time for playful union nears," the singer crooned.

Qassem seemed to grow more uncomfortable, and Sadeq, as usual, noticed quickly, and handed him a fresh glass of beer, which he drank to the last drop, down to the dregs, still holding the pipe in his other hand. Hassan had had so much to drink that the patterns on the pavilion's fabric danced before his eyes, and this did not escape Uwais' notice.

"Hassan drinks too much for someone his age," he told Zachary.

Zachary got up, glass in hand, and told his son in a confiding tone, "Hassan, don't drink like that."

He answered "like that" by swallowing a whole glass in a confusion of laughter and gaiety. Uwais' anger writhed within him, and he said to himself, "If it weren't for my niece's silliness, what you've drunk tonight would cost you a thousand times what you have!"

At midnight, Qassem was summoned for the wedding procession, and all of the men headed for the Dingil Coffeehouse, led by Sawaris, the head of the procession and its protector. The street outside the house was crowded with boys, beggars and cats who had been drawn there by the smells from the kitchen. Qassem sat between Hassan and Sadeq, and

Dingil welcomed them and told his boy, "A happy night! Get my own pipe for these fine young men."

Then all the prosperous men offered pipes to everyone there, at their own expense.

The singers showed up, followed by the drummers and horn players, and Sawaris got up and commanded, "Let's begin the procession."

Plump Ka'abura led the procession, wearing a galabiya with nothing on underneath, dancing barefoot and balancing a club on his head. The singers were next, then Sawaris, then the bridegroom and his parade of friends, with lines of torchbearers flanking everyone. The singer began, in a pleasant voice.

> *First, oh! these eyes of mine.*
> *Second, oh! these hands of mine.*
> *Third, oh! these feet of mine.*
> *What entangled me first with my love were my eyes.*
> *When I greeted my love it was with my hands.*
> *Now I'm guided along to my love by my feet!*

Shouts of pleasure rose from all the drunken and drugged mouths as the procession wound its way to Gamaliya, Bait al-Qadi, al-Hussein and al-Darasa, and the night passed, unheeded by the happy partygoers. The procession went back the way it had come, gay and noisy. It was the first procession ever to come off peacefully: no club was raised and no blood was shed. Zachary's rapture reached its peak, and he snatched his stick and began to dance. He played with the stick and swayed haughtily, swung now his head, now his chest, then his middle. His exuberant dance steps were, by turns, warlike and suggestive; he spun around for his finale, amid cheers and handclapping.

With that, Qassem left for the women's quarters. He saw Qamar sitting in the middle of two rows of her guests, and walked to her amidst waves of excited trilling. He took her hand and she stood up, and they walked out, led by a dancer who seemed to be giving them their final lesson, until they were alone in the bridal chamber. With the door closed, they were completely cut off from the outside world, now plunged into silence, except for faint whispers or footsteps. In one glance, Qassem saw the rose-colored bed, the cozy sofa and the ornate carpet, things he had never dreamed of, and then his eyes settled on the woman, who was sitting down, taking the jewels out of her hair. She seemed stately, soft-skinned and radiantly beautiful; the walls gazed down on her with a pearly light. He saw everything through his restlessness, excitement and overflowing happiness. He came near her in his silk galabiya, his body giving off heat mingled with the smell of liquor, until he stood before her, looking down at her; her eyes were cast down, as if in expectation. He took her face between his palms, and was about to say something, but seemed to change his mind. He leaned over her until her hair trembled under his breath, then kissed her forehead and cheeks.

His nose detected the scent of incense wafting in from behind the door, and he heard Sakina's voice reciting some obscure incantation.

71

Days and nights of love, devotion and relaxation passed—how sweet is the happiness of this world. The only reason he ever left the house was to avoid embarrassment, lest people say that he had not left his house since his wedding. His heart overflowed to the point of drunkenness, with every kind of delight, as he enjoyed all the love, tenderness and attention he had ever wanted. He became fond of cleanliness, seeing everything in this place orderly, finding the very atmosphere perfumed with incense, and a woman who saw him only when she was beautified, her face clearly radiant with love. One day as they sat side by side in the sitting room, she said to him, "To me, you're like a meek little lamb— you don't ask for anything, you don't give orders or scold anyone, when everything in this house belongs to you!"

He brushed away a lock of her hennaed hair. "I've come to a point when I have all I need!"

She pressed his hand hard. "I always knew in my heart that you were the best man in our neighborhood, but your good manners sometimes make you look like a stranger in your own house. Don't you know that that hurts me?"

"You're talking to a man that good luck brought from the hot sands to the paradise of this happy home."

She tried to look serious, but her smile won out as she said, "Don't think you're going to get any rest in my house. Any day now you're going to take my uncle's place managing my property. I wonder if you'll take that on."

"It's play, compared with being a shepherd."

He did take over the management of her property, which was spread everywhere from the Desert Rats' territory to Gamaliya. Dealing with quarrelsome tenants called for great ingenuity, but his tact helped everything go as smoothly as possible. The job required only a few days of his time each month, and apart from that he had leisure he had never known before. Perhaps the greatest triumph he scored in his new life was winning the confidence of his wife's Uncle Uwais. He had shown him respect and attention from the very start, and volunteered to help him out in some of his business tasks, until the man got used to him and reciprocated Qassem's warmth and respect. One day Uwais could not help telling him straight out, "Really, some thoughts are terrible. Do you know that I used to think you were one of this alley's philanderers! And that you would exploit my niece's affection just to get her money and squander it away whoring around, or use it to marry some other woman! But you've proven yourself to be a trustworthy and wise man. She made a good choice."

In the coffeehouse, Sadeq laughed delightedly and said, "Treat us to a pipe, the way big men like you have to!"

And Hassan said, "Why don't you take us to a bar?"

"I have no money except what I get for managing my wife's property, or for the jobs I do for Uwais," Qassem now answered them.

Sadeq was astonished, and told him, "A woman in love is a plaything in a man's hand!"

"Unless the man is in love too!" said Qassem angrily. He stared at him rebukingly. "You're like all the others in this alley, Sadeq. They think love is just another way of exploiting others."

Sadeq smiled sheepishly. "That's how weak people think," he said apologetically. "We aren't as strong as Hassan, or even as strong as you, and I have no ambition to be a gangster—and in our alley, either you beat people or you get beaten!"

"What a strange alley," said Qassem, dropping his sharp tone to show that the apology was accepted. "You're right, Sadeq, the state of this alley is enough to make you despair."

"Oh, if only it were really the place other people think it is!" Hassan said, smiling.

Sadeq agreed. "They say, 'Gabalawi Alley! That's the place for real men.' "

Melancholy filled Qassem's face, and he stole a sidelong glance at where Sawaris sat, in the front of the coffeehouse, to make sure that he was out of earshot before he spoke. "As if they've never heard about our misery."

"People worship power—even its victims do!"

Qassem thought a few moments. "The thing is that power that does good, like the power of Gabal or Rifaa, is different from the power of bullies and criminals."

"Adham cried to him, saying, 'Carry your brother!' " said Taza the poet, continuing his story, "and Qadri wailed, 'I can't.' 'You were able to kill him!' 'Father, I can't.' 'Don't call me Father! Anyone who kills his own brother has no father, no mother and no brother.' 'I can't.' Adham's grip closed more tightly on him. 'It's the killer's job to carry his victim.' "

The poet picked up the rebec and began his chant.

"Right now, you are living the life Adham dreamed of!" Sadeq said to Qassem.

"But with every step I take, I find something sad or disturbing," said Qassem, protest written clearly on his face. "Adham never dreamed of leisure or wealth except as a way to real happiness."

All three of them were silent for a while, until Hassan said innocently, "That kind of real happiness will never exist."

"Unless everybody has a chance at it," said Qassem with a dreamy look in his eyes.

He thought this over, how he enjoyed money and leisure, but the misery of others spoiled his happiness. He submissively paid protection money to Sawaris; that was why he wanted to do something with his leisure time, almost to escape from himself, or from this cruel alley. Perhaps had Adham got what he wished for, and become like Qassem, he might have grown weary of happiness and yearned for work.

It was at about this time that strange symptoms began to befall Qamar; Sakina said that they were signs of pregnancy. Qamar could scarcely believe her. Her hope of pregnancy was her greatest dream, so she was consumed with joy, and Qassem's heart was filled with bliss: he spread the news in every corner where he had loved ones. It was learned in his uncle's house, the coppersmith's shop, Uwais' grocery and Yahya's hut. Qamar went to great lengths to give herself proper care, and she told Qassem in a very meaningful tone of voice, "I have to avoid any strain."

He smiled, understanding what she meant. "Sakina will have to take care of all the household duties, and I will have to be patient!"

"I could kiss the ground you stand on, I'm so grateful!" she said in an almost childishly exuberant tone.

He went to the desert to visit Yahya, but stopped at Hind's Rock, passed into its shade and sat down. He saw at some distance a shepherd tending his sheep, and his heart flooded with emotion. He wished he could tell him, "Man is not made happy by power alone; in fact it doesn't make him happy at all." But wouldn't it be better to say that to powerful men like Lahita and Sawaris? How tenderly he thought of the people of his alley, who dreamed futilely of happiness; it was never long before time threw their dreams away with the trash that filled the garbage heaps. Why not savor the happiness he had, and close his eyes to what lay around him? Perhaps this question had once perplexed Gabal, and later Rifaa—it would have been possible for them to savor comfort, and enjoy peace and quiet for as long as they lived. What is the secret of the torment that stalks us? He pondered this, gazing at the sky over the mountain, clear except for small bits of cloud, like the scattered petals of a white rose. He lowered his head in what seemed like exhaustion, and something moving caught his eye: a scorpion scurrying toward a rock. He quickly lifted his staff and brought it down on the scorpion, crushing it; he stared at it a long time in revulsion, then got up and resumed his journey.

72

Qassem's household welcomed a new life, and the poor of the neighborhood shared their joy. She was named Ihsan, after the mother he had never known, and with her birth, the house came to know new kinds of crying, dirtiness and sleeplessness. She also gave it new delight and contentment. But why did the father's mind and gaze sometimes wander, as if pursued by cares? It made Qamar deeply thoughtful and uneasy, until she asked him one day, "Are you not well?"

"Of course I'm well."

"But you're not yourself."

"God knows how I am," he said, looking away.

She hesitated a moment before asking, "Is it something about me that's not right?"

"There isn't anyone I love as much as you," he said firmly, "not even our precious baby."

"Maybe it's the evil eye." She sighed.

"Perhaps." He smiled.

She felt sorry for him and burned incense for him, and prayed for him from the bottom of her heart. One night she was awakened by Ihsan's crying, and did not find him by her side. At first she thought he had not come home after his evening in the coffeehouse, but when the baby stopped crying, the woman realized that the alley was immersed in the profound silence that prevailed only well after the coffeehouses had closed. Doubtful, she got up, went to the window and looked out at the total darkness that enveloped the slumbering alley. She went back to the baby, who had now started crying again, and gently offered her her breast, wondering what could have made him this late, for the first time in their life together. Ihsan fell asleep, and Qamar again left her bed for the window. When she heard nothing, she went out into the hall and woke up Sakina. The slave sat up dopily, but jumped anxiously out of bed when her mistress told her why she had come to talk to her. The slave immediately decided to go to Zachary to ask about her master. Qamar wondered what could have kept him in his uncle's house until this hour, and her own answer shattered her hope, but she did not prevent Sakina from going. Perhaps something unexpected was afoot; or at least his uncle might offer her help in her bewilderment. When Sakina had left, she began to wonder, again, what was keeping him. Did it have something to do with the change in his moods? Or with his excursions into the desert in the afternoons and evenings?

Sakina roused Zachary and Hassan with her cries. Hassan said that Qassem had not spent the evening with him; Zachary asked when his nephew had left the house, and Sakina told him it had been early in the afternoon. The three of them left the building, and Hassan went next door, coming back with Sadeq, who said uneasily, "It's nearly dawn! Where could he have gone?"

"Maybe he fell asleep at Hind's Rock," said Hassan.

Zachary ordered the slave to go back to her mistress and tell her that they were going to search for him as best they could, then the three set out toward the desert. Feeling the damp of the autumn night, they tightened their turbans around their heads. They were guided by the late month's crescent moon, shining from a star-studded patch of sky from which the clouds had receded. "Qassem! Qassem!" shouted Hassan in a voice that split the air like a shooting star, and his voice echoed back repeatedly from the direction of Muqattam. They quickened their pace until they reached Hind's Rock, then fanned out around it, searching, but they found no trace of him.

"Where has he gone?" asked Zachary in his deep voice. "He wouldn't be playing a trick, and he has no enemies."

"And there's no other reason he'd have to run away!" murmured Hassan perplexedly.

Sadeq remembered that the desert was not spared the presence of bandits and his heart sank in his chest, but he said nothing.

"Might he be at Yahya's?" Zachary asked weakly.

"Yahya!" the two young men shouted together, given relief from despair.

"What could have brought him there?" Zachary asked sadly.

They began walking in silence toward the edge of the desert, thinking black thoughts, and hearing from afar the crowing of cocks, but the darkness was unrelieved because of the heavy clouds. Sadeq made a sound like a soft sigh, and he said, "Qassem, where are you!" Their journey seemed futile, but they kept going until they stood before Yahya's sleeping hut. Zachary went up to the door and knocked with his fist until he heard the old man's voice: "Who's at the door?"

The door opened, and the figure of Yahya appeared, leaning on his stick.

"Pardon us," said Zachary apologetically. "We have come to ask about Qassem."

"I've been expecting you!" said the old man calmly.

His answer buoyed their spirits at first, but the anxiety quickly returned.

"Have you heard from him?" asked Zachary.

"He's asleep, inside."

"Is he all right?"

"God willing!" Then, with deliberate matter-of-factness, he added, "He's all right now. Some of my neighbors were coming home from Atuf, and they found him at Hind's Rock—he was unconscious. They carried him here, and I spattered his face with perfume until he woke up, but he was very tired, so I let him sleep—he fell asleep again in no time."

"I wish you had let us know," said Zachary rebukingly.

"They brought him at midnight," said Yahya with unchanged calm. "I couldn't find anyone to send to you."

"He must be ill," said Sadeq uneasily.

"He'll be fine when he wakes up," said the old man.

"Let's wake him up and check on him," said Hassan.

"We'll have to wait until he wakes up on his own," said Yahya firmly.

73

He sat in the bed, his back propped up against a pillow, pulling the blanket up over his chest, a thoughtful look in his eyes. Qamar was sitting cross-legged by his feet, holding Ihsan at her breast. The baby was moving her hands constantly, and making soft, strange, undecipherable sounds. A thread of smoke rose from the incense burner in the middle of the room, twisted, then broke and diffused its fragrance, as if confiding a delicious secret. The man stretched his hand out to the bedside table for the glass of caraway drink, sipped at it slowly and replaced it, empty except for the dregs. The woman whispered sweetly to the baby and cuddled her, but the uneasy glances she stole at her husband showed that her baby talk and dandling were only a mask for her feelings.

"How are you now?" she finally asked.

He turned his head instinctively toward the closed door of the room, then toward her. "It's not sickness," he told her calmly.

"I'm glad to hear that," she said, confusion in her eyes. "But tell me what in God's name *is* wrong with you!"

"I don't know!" he said, after hesitating a few moments. "No, that isn't what I should say. I know everything, but—the truth is, I'm afraid that our days of peace are over."

Suddenly Ihsan began to cry, and Qamar quickly gave her her breast and looked at him with a searching and anxious gaze. "Why?"

He sighed and pointed to his chest. "I have a big secret here, too big for me to keep alone."

"Tell me about it, Qassem!" she lamented, even more worried.

He shifted a little as he sat, his eyes serious and purposeful. "I'll tell it, for the first time. You're the first person to hear it, but you have to believe me. I'm only telling the truth. Last night something really strange happened there, by Hind's Rock, while I was alone in the night and the desert."

He swallowed hard, and she encouraged him with a loving look.

"I was sitting and watching the crescent moon go down, which was covered up by the clouds pretty quickly, and then it was so dark that I was thinking of getting up, when all of a sudden I heard a voice nearby: 'Good evening, Qassem.' I was shaking from the surprise, because there hadn't been any sound or movement before that. I looked up and saw the figure of a man standing one step away from where I was sitting, but his face couldn't be seen. I could make out his white turban, and the cloak he was wrapped up in. I hid my exasperation, and told him, 'Good evening! Who are you?' He answered me—who do you think he said he was?"

Qamar shook her head apprehensively and said, "Go on—I can't wait."

"He said, 'I am Qandil.' I was amazed, and I told him, 'Forgive me, I—' But he interrupted me, and said, 'I am Qandil, servant of Gabalawi'!"

"What did he say?" the woman cried.

"He said, 'I am Qandil, servant of Gabalawi.' "

The mother's sudden movement pulled her breast away from the baby's mouth, and her face contracted, about to cry, but the woman readjusted herself and said, her face pale, "Qandil, the servant of Gabalawi? No one knows anything about his servants. His excellency the overseer prepares all the things the mansion needs, his servants bring them to the mansion, and Gabalawi's servants take them in the garden."

"Yes, that's what people in our alley say, but this is what he told me."

"Did you believe him?"

"I stood up as fast as I could, partially to be polite, and partially to be ready to defend myself if I had to. I asked him how I was supposed to know he was telling the truth, and he told me, very calmly, very sure of himself, 'Follow me, if you want, so that you can see me go into the mansion.' So I was reassured, and said to myself that I'd believe him so that he'd explain himself. I didn't hide the fact that I was very happy to meet him. I asked him about our ancestor, how he was doing and what he did."

"You two talked about all that?" Qamar interrupted, stunned.

"Yes, I swear to God, but listen! He said that our ancestor was fine, but he didn't say anything more. So I asked him if he knew what was happening in our alley. He said that Gabalawi knew everything—that the dweller in the mansion watches every small thing that goes on in our alley, and that was why he had sent him to me!"

"To you!"

Qassem frowned restlessly. "That's what he said. I let something slip out that showed how surprised I was, but he didn't pay any attention. He said, 'Maybe he chose you because you showed wisdom the day of the robbery and because of your honesty in your house. He wants to inform you that all the people of the alley are equally his grandchildren, that the estate is their inheritance on an equal basis and that gangsterism is an evil that must be eliminated. And that the alley must be an extension of the mansion.' Then there was silence, as I had lost the power of speech. I looked up, and my eye caught the highest clouds as they pulled apart and showed the crescent moon. I asked him politely, 'Why is he telling me that?' And he answered, 'So that you can do it yourself.' "

"You!" gasped Qamar.

"That's what he said," Qassem went on, his voice trembling. "I was going to ask him to explain, but he saluted me and went away, and I did follow him, until it seemed to me that I saw him go up to the highest wall of the mansion, facing the desert, on a very high ladder, or something like that. I just stood there—I was amazed. Then I went back to where I had been before. I wanted to go to Yahya's, but I blacked out, and only came to in his hut."

Silence again descended upon the room. Her dazed eyes never left his face. Sleep slowly closed Ihsan's eyes as she suckled, and her head drooped against her mother's forearm, so Qamar laid her gently on the bed and resumed watching her husband with anxious eyes and a pale face. Sawaris' coarse voice rose from the alley cursing a man, along with the man's shouts and groans as he was being slapped and beaten; then Sawaris' voice again, raised in warnings and threats as he walked away, and the man's cry of rage and despair: "Gabalawi!" Qassem asked his soul, burdened with his wife's looks, *What do you think of me?* The woman said to herself, *He is telling the truth, he has never lied to me; why would he make up such a story? He is trustworthy. He is not interested in my money, though he could have got it safely. So why would he want the estate's money, which would be so dangerous to try to get!* Were their days of peace really over?

"I'm the first person you've divulged the secret to?"

He nodded.

"Qassem, our life is one life. I don't care about myself as much as I care about you. Your secret is dangerous, and you know what its consequences are. But think, really try to remember, and tell me, was it real, what you saw, or perhaps a dream?"

"It was real and true. It was not a dream," he said determinedly, and a little resentfully.

"They found you unconscious?"

"That was after the meeting!"

"Maybe you were confused," she said tenderly.

He sighed, more pained than he had ever been, and said, "I didn't confuse anything. The meeting was as clear as a sunny day!"

"How do we know," she said, after hesitating somewhat, "that he was really Gabalawi's servant and his messenger to you? It might have been any drunk or drug addict from the alley—there are so many of them!"

"I saw him go up to the mansion wall," said Qassem stubbornly.

"In our whole alley, there's no ladder tall enough to go halfway up that wall!" She sighed.

"But I saw him!"

She was like a mouse in a trap, but she did not give up. "It's only that I'm afraid for you. You know what I mean. I'm afraid for our house and our daughter and our happiness. I have to ask myself: Why did he come to you in particular? Why doesn't he carry out his will himself, when the estate is his, and he's lord over everybody?"

"Why did he go to Gabal or Rifaa?" he asked in turn.

Her eyes widened, and the corner of her mouth contracted, like that of a child about to cry. She looked away, frightened.

"You don't believe me," he said. "I'm not asking you to believe me."

She burst into tears, and abandoned herself to her sobs as if to escape from her thoughts. Qassem leaned toward her, reached his hand out to hers and pulled it toward him. "Why are you crying?"

She looked at him through her tears, gulping and sobbing. "Because I believe you. Yes, I believe you, and I'm afraid our days of peace are over!" Then in a soft, pitying voice: "What are you going to do?"

74

The air of the room was heavy with tension and anxiety. Zachary was frowning and thoughtful, while Uwais stroked his mustache, and Hassan seemed to be talking to himself. Sadeq's eyes were locked on the face of his friend Qassem; Qamar sat alone in a corner of the reception room, praying God to guide them all to reason and righteousness. Two flies hovered around their empty coffee cups. Qamar called for Sakina to clear away the tray, and the slave came and took it, and reclosed the door behind her.

Uwais took a breath and said, "This secret is going to wreck our nerves!"

A dog yelped in the alley, as if he had been hit with a stone or a stick, a peddler's voice rose, in a singsong pitch for dates, and an old woman cried miserably, "O Lord, enough of this life."

Zachary turned to Uwais. "Uwais, you're the biggest and most eminent of any of us—you tell us what you think!"

The man shifted his gaze between Zachary and Qassem. "The truth is that Qassem is a fine man, but his story has made me dizzy!"

"He is a truthful man," said Sadeq, who had been eager to speak the whole time. "I challenge any person to think of one lie he has ever told. I believe him—I swear it to you on my mother's grave!"

"Me too," said Hassan enthusiastically. "He'll always find me right beside him."

For the first time, Qassem smiled gratefully, and looked at his cousin's strong body admiringly, but Zachary gave his nephew a look of disapproval. "This is not a game. Think of our life and our safety."

Uwais nodded vigorously to show his agreement. "That is the truth. No one has ever before heard what we've heard today."

"Gabal and Rifaa heard things like this, and more!"

Uwais stared at him in surprised revulsion. "Do you think you're like Gabal and Rifaa?"

Pained, Qassem lowered his eyes, and Qamar looked at him affectionately. "Uncle!" she said. "Who knows how these things happen?"

He resumed stroking his mustache, and Zachary spoke. "What good is there in thinking he's like Gabal or Rifaa? Rifaa died a terrible death, and Gabal would have been killed if his people hadn't joined forces with him. Who's with you, Qassem? Have you forgotten that they call our neighborhood the Desert Rat territory? Or that most of the people are either beggars or other poor unfortunates?"

"Don't forget that Gabalawi chose him above everyone else, even above the gangsters," said Sadeq vigorously. "I don't think he'll abandon him if things get hard."

"That's what they said about Rifaa in his time, and he was murdered an arm's length from Gabalawi's house!" said Zachary hotly.

"Don't raise your voice," Qamar cautioned.

Uwais glanced furtively at Qassem, thinking, *What strange things to have heard and said. This shepherd my niece has made into a gentleman! I believe he's truthful and trustworthy, but is that enough to make him a Gabal or Rifaa? Do great men come this simple? What if these dreams come true?*

"It looks like Qassem isn't moved by our warnings. So what does the lad want? Is he troubled that our community should be the only one with no share in the estate? Qassem—do you want to be a gangster and overseer here?"

"That is not what I was told," said Qassem, agitation rising in his face. "He said that all the people of the alley are his grandchildren, that the estate belongs to all on the basis of equality and that the gangsters are evil!"

Excitement flashed in Sadeq's and Hassan's eyes, and Uwais was shocked.

"Do you know what that means?" Zachary asked.

"Tell him!" said Uwais angrily.

"You are challenging the power of the overseer and the clubs of Lahita, Galta, Hagag and Sawaris!"

Qamar's face turned pale, but Qassem said calmly, almost sadly, "That's right."

Uwais emitted a laugh which echoed in indignant looks from Qassem, Sadeq and Hassan, but Zachary paid no attention.

"We will all be destroyed. We'll be crushed like ants. No one will believe you. They didn't believe the ones that met Gabalawi, or heard his voice, or talked with him—how will they believe someone who was sent one of his servants?"

"Never mind those stories," said Uwais in a new tone of voice. "No one saw the meeting between Gabalawi and Gabal, or Gabalawi and Rifaa—the stories are told that way, but no one saw them. Even so, it was good for the people. Gabal got its exalted status, and Rifaa too; our neighborhood deserves to be like them, doesn't it? All of us come from the loins of that man hiding in his mansion. But we have to approach this very wisely and be careful. Qassem, remember your community— forget about 'grandchildren' and 'equality' and what's good and what's evil. It will be easy to get Sawaris to join us; he's your relative, and we can work with him to get us a share of the estate revenues."

Qassem glowered angrily. "Uwais, you want one thing and we want something else. I don't want to haggle, or share in the revenues. I have firmly decided to do the will of our ancestor, as I was told."

"God help us," Zachary groaned.

Qassem's scowl did not dissolve. He remembered his anxieties, his solitary times and his conversations with his teacher Yahya; how release had come to him from the hand of a servant he had never known before; how new adventures beckoned on the horizon; how Zachary thought only of safety, Uwais only of income; how life would be good only when they faced the adventure-crowded horizon.

"Uncle," he said with a sigh, "I had to begin by asking your advice, but I won't ask you for anything."

"*I'm* with you," said Sadeq, pressing his hand.

Hassan made a fist. "And I'm with you, with you through good and bad."

"Don't be misled by childish talk!" said Zachary irritably. "When the clubs are raised, people like all of you will be hiding. And who will you be risking death for? There are just animals and vermin in our alley. You have a guaranteed carefree, easy life. Come to your senses; enjoy your life."

Qassem asked himself what this man was saying. It was as if he were listening to some of the voices within himself, which said, *Your daughter —your wife—your house—yourself. But you made the same choice as Gabal and Rifaa; let your answer be the same as theirs.*

"I've thought about it a long time, uncle, and I've chosen my way," he said.

Uwais smacked his hands together resignedly. " 'There is no power and no strength save in God!' The strong will kill you and the weak will just jeer at you!"

Qamar looked helplessly back and forth between her uncle and her husband's uncle, sorry for her husband's disappointment and at the same time fearful of the consequences of his standing by his opinion.

"Uncle," she said, "you are the leader of all the prominent people. You could help him through your influence."

"What is it you want, Qamar?" Uwais asked disapprovingly. "You have money, a daughter and a husband. What does it matter to you whether the estate is divided among everyone or the gangsters take it?

We regard as mad anyone who wants to be a gangster—what do you think of someone who wants to be overseer of the whole alley?"

Qassem sprang to his feet, deeply wounded. "I don't want anything like that. I want the good things our ancestor wants for us."

Uwais tried to conciliate him with a forced smile. "Where is our ancestor? Let him come out into the alley, even if his servants have to carry him on their shoulders. Let him execute the terms of his estate any way he wants. If he were to speak, do you think anyone in the alley, no matter how powerful he is, could lift a finger toward him, or even an eye?"

"And if the gangsters jump on us to murder us, would he make one move, or even care if we die?" Zachary concluded.

"I won't ask anyone to believe me or help me," said Qassem very despondently.

Zachary got up and went to him, putting his hand warmly on his shoulder. "Qassem, it was the evil eye. I know all about this kind of mischief. People have been talking so much about your intelligence and good fortune that the evil eye lit on you. Seek protection in God from the devil, and know that today you are one of the finest people in our community. You can, if you want, go into business with some of your wife's money. Enjoy your wealth. Forget all of this in your head, and be happy with the good things God has given you."

Qassem bowed his head sadly, then raised it to face his uncle and spoke with wondrous determination. "I won't forget anything in my head, even if the whole estate were mine alone."

75

WHAT ARE YOU GOING TO DO? FOR HOW LONG WILL YOU THINK *and wait? What are you waiting for? Your relatives didn't believe you, so who will believe you? What good is sorrow? What good is sitting alone by Hind's Rock? The stars don't answer, neither do the darkness and the moon. Do you hope to meet the servant again? What new thing do you expect from him? You stare into the darkness, around the site where, it is said, your ancestor met Gabal. You stood for such a long time by the huge wall, at the place where, it is said, he spoke to Rifaa. But you did not see him or hear his voice, and his servant has not returned. What are you going to do? This question will stalk you the way the desert sun stalks shepherds. It will constantly tear away your peace of mind and the pleasures of happiness. Gabal was like you, but he triumphed. Rifaa knew his own way, and kept to it until he was murdered, then he triumphed. What are you going to do?*

"How you neglect your beautiful little girl," Qamar chided him. "She cries, and you ignore her. She plays, but you don't play with her."

He smiled at the little face, scenting her sweet breath, which soothed the inferno of his thoughts. "She's so dear!" he said.

"Even the hour we do spend together, you're not really there—like we're no longer part of your world."

He moved closer to her on the couch, where they all sat, and kissed her cheek, then kissed the baby's face all over. "Don't you see how much I need you?" he said.

"You have my whole heart and all the love, affection and friendship in it, but you have to be easier on yourself."

She lifted the child into his arms, and he cuddled and rocked her tenderly, listening to her otherworldly chants. Suddenly he said, "If God gives me victory, I will not exclude women from getting income from the estate."

"But the estate is only for males, not females," said Qamar in surprise.

He gazed into the dark eyes in the little face. "My ancestor said, through his servant, that the estate belongs to everyone, and women are half our alley. It's amazing our alley doesn't respect women, but it will respect them when it respects justice and mercy."

Love and solicitude were clear in Qamar's eyes. She said to herself: He talks about victory, but where is this victory? How she longed to advise him to take a safe, peaceful course, but her courage let her down. She wondered what the future held for them. Would she have the luck of Shafiqa, Gabal's wife, or be afflicted with Abda's fate—or Rifaa's! Gooseflesh covered her body, and she looked away lest he see anything questionable in her eyes.

When Sadeq and Hassan came to go to the coffeehouse with Qassem, he suggested that they visit Yahya so that he might introduce them. When they reached his hut they found him smoking the pipe, and the air redolent of the rich savor of hashish. Qassem introduced his friends, and they all sat down in the entryway of the hut, where the full moon beamed like happiness through a small window.

Yahya looked at the three faces in mild astonishment, as if asking: Are these really the ones who are going to turn the alley upside down? He repeated to Qassem what he had already told him. "Be careful that no one should know your secret until you're ready."

They had a pleasant round at the pipe. The bright moonlight from the window illuminated Qassem's head and fell on Sadeq's shoulder, and the coals blazed in the brazier in the dim hall of the hut.

"How should I get ready?"

The old man laughed. "Anyone chosen by Gabalawi has no need to ask the opinion of an old man like me!" he joked.

There was silence broken only by the gurgle of the pipe, until the old man spoke up again. "You have your uncle, and your wife's uncle. There's no good or harm in your uncle, but you can bring the other one over to your side if you promise him something."

"What should I promise him?"

"Promise to make him overseer of the Desert Rats."

"No one is to be above anyone else when it comes to the estate revenue," said Sadeq loyally. "It is everyone's legacy on the basis of equality. That's what Gabalawi said."

"What a strange old man!" chuckled Yahya. "It was power with Gabal, and mercy with Rifaa, and now he has something else!"

"He owns the estate," said Qassem. "He has the right to substitute or change the Ten Conditions!"

"But you have a terrible task, my boy. It concerns the whole alley, not just any neighborhood."

"That's what Gabalawi wanted."

Yahya had a long fit of coughing that left him weak, and Hassan volunteered to take over handling the pipe. The man stretched his legs out and sighed deeply. "So will you use force, like Gabal, or love, like Rifaa?"

Qassem's hand explored his turban. "Force when necessary, and love at all times."

Yahya nodded and smiled. "The only problem you have is your concern with the estate. That will cause you endless trouble."

"How can people live without the estate?"

"The same way Rifaa did," said the old man grandly.

"He lived with the help of his father and his friends," said Qassem seriously, but politely. "He left behind him friends not one of whom could imitate him. The fact is that our miserable alley needs cleanness and dignity."

"Do those come only with the estate?"

"Yes, sir, with the estate and with an end to gang rule. That is how to win the respect that Gabal won for his neighborhood, and the love that Rifaa called for—and the happiness that Adham dreamed of."

"What have you left for the one coming after you?" laughed Yahya.

Qassem thought this over for a while. "If God gives me victory, the alley will not need anyone else after me."

The pipe made the rounds like an angel in a dream, the water singing in its glass filter. Yahya yawned and asked, "What will be left for any one of you if the estate is divided out equally?"

"But we want the estate in order to capitalize on it, and that way the alley will be like an extension of the mansion!" said Sadeq.

"What kind of preparations have you made?"

The radiant moon disappeared behind a passing cloud, and they sat in darkness, but within a minute the radiant light reappeared.

Yahya looked at Hassan's burly body. "Can your cousin defeat the gangsters?"

"I'm seriously thinking of consulting an attorney," Qassem suddenly said.

"What attorney will agree to threaten Rifaat the overseer and his protectors?" yelled Yahya.

Despondent thoughts invaded their drugged stupor. The three friends went home, discouraged. Qassem suffered terribly in his solitude; he was so driven by worry and care that one day Qamar told him, "We shouldn't be so worried about people's happiness that we make ourselves miserable!"

"I have to be worthy of the good opinion in which I'm held," he said sharply.

What are you going to do? Why don't you step back from the edge of the abyss? The abyss of despair, filled with silence and stagnation, a graveyard of dreams covered with ashes. His loveliest memories and favorite melodies had turned against him. Tomorrow was already wrapped in yesterday's shroud.

But one day he summoned Sadeq and Hassan. "It's time to begin," he told them.

Their faces were jubilant.

"Tell us," Hassan said.

"I've done my thinking, and come to a decision. We are going to set up an exercise club!" Surprise tied their tongues, but he smiled. "We'll have it in the courtyard of my house. Exercising is a big pastime in most of the neighborhoods."

"What does that have to do with our mission?"

"Like a weight-lifting club? What does that have to do with our mission?" asked Sadeq in his turn.

Qassem's eyes were brilliant. "The young will come to us, in love with strength and games, and we will choose the most trustworthy and mature of them."

Their eyes widened.

"We'll be a team—and what a team we'll be!"

"Yes. And we'll get young men from Gabal, and from Rifaa!"

They were happy enough to sing, and as he walked, Qassem almost seemed to dance.

76

Qassem sat near the window, watching the festival in the alley. How wonderful feast days are in our alley!

The water carriers had sprayed the ground using waterskins; the donkeys' necks and tails were adorned with artificial flowers. The space danced with the vivid colors of children's clothes and balloons, little flags flew from the handcarts, and shouts, cries and cheers mingled with the sound of pipes. Donkey carts tilted by with men and women dancing on them. The shops were closed, and the coffeehouses, bars and drug dens were crowded. Everyone, everywhere, was smiling brilliantly and wishing one another a happy holiday. Qassem sat in new clothes with Ihsan standing cradled in the crook of his arm, exploring his features with her small hands and clutching at his cheeks with her fingernails.

"What entangled me first with my love were my eyes," sang a voice under the window.

He suddenly recalled his joyous wedding procession, and his heart softened. He was a man who loved music and entertainment; how Adham had longed for the leisure to sing in that garden of song! And what was this man on the feast day singing? "What entangled me first

with my love were my eyes." The man was right. Since his eyes had
looked up in the darkness to Qandil, his heart, mind and will had not
been his own. Here was the courtyard of his house, turned into a club
for strengthening minds and purifying souls. Like the rest of them, he
lifted weights and was learning fencing. The muscles of Sadeq's arms
filled out, as his leg muscles already had, thanks to his coppersmithing
work. Hassan was huge, a giant, anyway. And the others, how splendid
was their enthusiasm; Sadeq had wisely advised him to invite the unemployed and beggars to his club, and in no time they were as enthusiastic
about the exercises they did as they were about the things he said.
Perhaps there were not many of them, but they were so eager that they
were stronger than any force twice their number. "Ad! Ad!" cried Ihsan,
and he gave her a series of kisses. The edge of his galabiya was damp
underneath her. From the kitchen he heard the rapping of the mortar
and pestle, the voices of Qamar and Sakina and the meowing of the cat.
A donkey cart passed under the window, loaded with clapping singers.

Recite a prayer for the soldier boy.
He threw off his fez for a job as a saint!

Qassem smiled, remembering the night Yahya had sung this hymn
stoned on hashish. *Oh, if things would only straighten themselves out, all
you'd have to do is sing, alley of mine! Tomorrow the club will be filled with
strong and reliable helpers; tomorrow, with them, I will challenge the overseer,
the gangsters, and all obstacles, so that there will be nothing in the alley but a
merciful ancestor and his dutiful grandchildren. Poverty, filth, beggary and tyranny will be wiped out. The vermin, flies and clubs will disappear. A feeling of
safety will prevail, with gardens and singing.* He awoke from his daydreams
to the sound of Qamar's voice scolding Sakina in an angry outburst. He
listened for a moment, surprised, and then called his wife. The door
quickly opened, and Qamar came out, pushing the slave in front of her.
  "Look at this woman! She was born in our house, like her mother
before her, but she's not afraid to spy on us!"

He looked disapprovingly at Sakina until she cried out in her coppery voice, "I'm not a spy, master, but my lady is so mean!"

There was a panic in Qamar's eyes that she failed to hide. "I saw her smile and tell me, 'God willing, by the time the feast comes next year, Qassem will be master of the whole alley, just as Gabal was in Al Hamdan Alley.' Ask her what she meant by that."

Qassem frowned, worried. "What do you mean, Sakina?"

"I mean what I said," the slave answered with her natural daring. "I'm not a servant like the rest of them, working here today and somewhere else tomorrow. I'm a daughter of this house, and it was not right to hide a secret from me."

The man and his wife exchanged a look; he motioned at the child, and she came and took her away from him. He ordered the slave to sit down, and she sat at his feet.

"Is it right to tell strangers to this house your secret, while I was kept in the dark?"

"What secret are you talking about?"

"Qandil's talk with you at Hind's Rock!" she said with the same boldness.

Qamar gasped, but Qassem motioned the slave to continue.

"The same as happened with Gabal and Rifaa before. You aren't any less than they are, sir, you are a master. Even when you were a shepherd, you were a master. I was the go-between that brought you together, don't you remember? I should have been told before anyone else. How can you trust outsiders and not trust your Sakina? God forgive you both, but I pray for your victory, yes, I pray for your victory over the overseer and the gangsters. Who doesn't want that for you?"

"You had no right to spy on us!" shouted Qamar, rocking the baby in nervous jerks. "We won't forget about it either."

"I didn't mean to spy, God is my witness," Sakina insisted with genuine heat. "But I heard, from behind the door, some talk that I listened to. I couldn't help it. No one could have closed their ears to that. What breaks my heart, ma'am, is that you don't trust me. I'm not a spy. You're the last person I'd ever betray, and who would I be spying for anyway? God forgive you, ma'am."

Qassem was watching her very closely, with his eyes and heart. When she was finished, he spoke calmly. "You are loyal, Sakina. I don't doubt your loyalty."

She stared at him, curious and hopeful, and said, "Long life to you, sir, I am loyal."

"I know loyal people," he said softly. "Treason will never grow in my house, as it did in the house of my brother Rifaa. Qamar, this woman is as loyal as you are. Don't worry about her. She is ours, and we are hers, and I will never forget that she was my messenger of happiness."

"But she was eavesdropping," said Qamar in a voice that sounded a little mollified.

"She wasn't eavesdropping. Our voices were carried to her by God's will," Qassem said, smiling. "The same way Rifaa heard his ancestor's voice without trying. Bless you, Sakina."

The slave snatched his hand and covered it with kisses. "I'd die for you, sir. By God, may you triumph over your enemies and our enemies until you reign over the whole alley."

"Reigning isn't what we want, Sakina."

She laid out her hands in prayerful supplication. "May God give you everything you want!"

"Amen." He smiled at her. "You'll be my messenger, if I need a messenger, and that way you can be part of our mission."

The woman's face gleamed with joy, and her eyes spoke clearly of her pride.

"If God wills that the estate should be shared, as we want, no woman will be deprived, whether she be a lady or a servant." As she was still tongue-tied with surprise, he added, "Gabalawi said that the estate is everyone's, and you, Sakina, are a granddaughter of Gabalawi, just like Qamar, equally."

The woman's face beamed with delight, and she looked gratefully at her mistress. From the alley came the tune of a dancer's pipe. Someone shouted, "Lahita, happy holidays!" Qassem turned toward the street and saw a procession of gangsters riding fine horses all adorned, being welcomed by people's shouts and cheers. They headed toward the desert to compete, in accordance with their holiday custom, in races and fencing matches. No sooner had their procession passed by than Agrama appeared in the alley, staggering drunkenly. Qassem smiled at the sight of the boy, whom he considered one of the most faithful members of the club, and followed him with his gaze as he stood exactly in the middle of the Desert Rats' neighborhood and began to shout, "I'm tough!"

"Prince of the Desert Rats!" called a jeering voice from a nearby building in Rifaa.

Agrama turned his two bloodshot eyes up at the window. "It's our turn now, bitch!" he shouted drunkenly.

A crowd of boys, drunks and swaying drug addicts gathered around him, loudly singing, trilling, drumming and piping in a loud uproar.

"Listen!" a voice shouted. "It's the Desert Rats' turn. Don't you want to hear that?"

"One grandfather for everyone!" Agrama called, staggering. "One estate for everyone. Goodbye to gang rule."

Then he vanished in the crowd, and Qassem jumped up, grabbed his cloak and ran out of the room, saying, "God damn alcohol!"

77

"*Avoid appearing drunk in public,*" said Qassem earnestly, frowning, as he sat by Hind's Rock, looking into the faces of his close friends, all members of the club: Sadeq, Hassan, Agrama, Shaaban, Abu Fisada and Hamroush. The mountain loomed loftily behind them, the portents of night descending on it. The desert was empty except for a shepherd leaning on his staff, far off to the south.

Agrama's head was bowed. "I wish I had died before doing that," he said sadly.

"It was a mistake that apologies can't fix," said Qassem coolly. "The important thing for me now is to find out how much of an impression your folly has had on our enemies."

"Everyone heard him, that much is sure," said Sadeq.

"I saw that for myself in the Gabal Coffeehouse, where one of my Gabal friends invited me to meet some people," said Hassan gloomily. "I heard a man talking loudly about what Agrama did—yes, and he was laughing mockingly, but I think it's possible his story will make people suspicious, and I'm afraid it will be told and retold until one of the gangsters hears it."

"Don't exaggerate, Hassan," sighed Agrama.

"Exaggerating is better than ignoring it, otherwise we might not be ready for them!"

"We swore that we wouldn't fear death!" said Agrama.

"The same way we swore to keep the secret!" said Sadeq sharply.

"If we perish now, all our great hopes will be squandered," said Qassem.

Their depression mounted as darkness fell, until Qassem spoke again. "Well, let's make a plan."

"Let's make a plan assuming the worst," said Hassan.

"Which means fighting," said Qassem gloomily.

They all nodded and exchanged looks in the shadows. The stars gradually appeared over their heads, and a wind blew in whose billows traces of the day's heat lingered like evil intentions.

"We will fight to the death," said Hamroush.

"And things will be the way they've always been!" said Qassem crossly.

"They would beat us in no time," said Sadeq.

"Luckily, you're related to Sawaris," Abu Fisada said to Qassem, "and your wife is related to the overseer's wife. Besides, Lahita was a friend of your father's when they were young."

"That might postpone fate, but it won't stop it," said Qassem coolly.

"Don't you remember that at one time you were thinking of getting a lawyer?" asked Sadeq hopefully.

"And we were told that no lawyer would dare challenge the overseer and the gangsters."

"There's a lawyer in Bait al-Qadi known for his courage," said Agrama, trying to mitigate his sin.

"The thing I'm most afraid of is that we'd be proclaiming our hostility with a suit. Maybe our fears of the consequences of what Agrama said are premature,"said Sadeq, as if he had changed his mind.

"Let's consult the lawyer about it," said Agrama. "We'll arrange with him to delay filing the suit until we're forced to. We'll find someone to take care of it for us, even if it's someone from outside the alley."

Qassem and the others agreed to this as a precautionary measure, and immediately got up and went to the office of Shanafiri, the lawyer in Bait al-Qadi. The sheikh met with them, and Qassem explained their case, telling him that their intention was to postpone filing the suit for a time, and in the meantime he could study the subject and prepare to take all the necessary steps. Contrary to their expectations, he agreed to take the case, and collected an advance on his fee, and they left him highly satisfied. They went their different ways, the friends going back to the alley while Qassem went to see Yahya. They sat in the entryway of the hut, smoking and chatting. Yahya seemed sorry at what had happened, and advised Qassem to be cautious and alert.

After that Qassem went home, and when Qamar opened the door to him, there was something in her face that alarmed him. He asked her what was wrong.

"His excellency the overseer has summoned you!"

"When?" His heart was pounding.

"The last time was ten minutes ago."

"The last time!"

"He's sent three messengers in the last few hours!" Her eyes swam with tears.

"That isn't what I expect from you," he said.

"Don't go," she sobbed.

He pretended to be calm. "Going is safer than disobeying, and remember, those thieves never attack people in their own homes."

Ihsan began crying within, and Sakina rushed to her. "Don't go until I can talk to Lady Amina."

"That would not be worthy of us," he said firmly. "I'll go right now. There's no reason to be afraid—none of them know anything about me."

She held him. "He's summoned you, not Agrama. I'm afraid some of them have informed on you."

He pulled away from her tenderly. "I've told you from the beginning that our days of peace are over. All of us know that we'll have to face harm sooner or later. Don't be so sad. Take care until I come back."

78

The gatekeeper came back out of the overseer's house and told Qassem, with mild rudeness, "Come in."

He walked ahead and Qassem followed, making every effort to master his emotions. The sweet smell of the garden wafted to him, but he did not look around until he found himself in front of the reception hall. The gatekeeper moved to the side, and Qassem entered, firm-hearted to a degree he had never seen in himself before. He looked ahead of him and saw the overseer sitting on a sofa at the far end of the hall. There were two other men seated on chairs, one on the overseer's right and the other to his left. He could not see who they were, and it did not occur to him to pay attention to them. He approached the overseer where he sat until he stood an arm's length away, and raised his hand in greeting.

"Good evening, Your Excellency the overseer."

He noticed, unintentionally, that the man at his right was Lahita; he meant only to glance at the other, but stared in spite of himself, for the shock nearly paralyzed him: the man was none other than Sheikh

Shanafiri, the lawyer! He understood the gravity of the situation, that his secret was discovered, that the despicable lawyer had betrayed his trust and that he had stepped into a trap. Despair struggled in his heart with rage and exasperation. He knew that cunning and deceit would not save him, so he decided to be strong and defiant. He could not retreat a single step; he had to advance, or at least hold his ground. He remembered this situation in the days that followed; he dated from this day the birth of a new person within himself, whose existence he had never imagined. He was pulled from the whirlpool of thoughts by the overseer's coarse voice.

"You are Qassem?"

"Yes, sir," he said, and sounded natural.

"Are you surprised to see this learned man here?" he asked, without inviting him to be seated.

"No, sir," he said in the same tone of voice.

"Are you a shepherd?" the overseer asked mockingly.

"I haven't been a shepherd for more than two years."

"What is your job now?"

"I manage my wife's property."

A brief, sarcastic nod was his answer, and then the overseer gestured for the lawyer to speak.

"You might be surprised to see me here, since I'm your lawyer," the sheikh said to Qassem, "but the overseer's rank supersedes all such considerations. My conduct gives you an opportunity to repent, which is better than getting mixed up in some antagonism that would lead to your ruin. His excellency the overseer has permitted me to inform you that I have interceded with him on your behalf for a pardon, if you ask his forgiveness. Please appreciate my good intentions. Here is the advance fee—I'm returning it to you."

Qassem stared at him harshly.

"Why didn't you tell me the truth when I was in your office?"

The lawyer was surprised at his boldness, but the overseer stepped in. "You are here to answer questions, not ask them."

The lawyer stood up and asked permission to leave, then went out, pulling his cloak around him to hide his agitation.

The overseer fixed Qassem with a cruel stare and spoke as if cursing. "How did you allow yourself to be seduced into trying to sue me?"

He was being trapped into either fighting or being killed. He did not know what to say.

"Talk. Tell me what you are doing. Are you crazy?"

"Praise God, I am sane," said Qassem despondently.

"That certainly isn't obvious to me. Why did you dare to do such an evil thing? You haven't been poor since that crazy woman decided to accept you as her husband. What did you want from your deed?"

Qassem took the offensive, the better to control his anger. "I don't want anything for myself."

The overseer glanced at Lahita as if to call his attention to the strange things he was hearing, then redirected his eyes angrily back to Qassem. "Then why did you do what you did?" he shouted.

"All I wanted was justice," said Qassem.

The man's eyes narrowed with hatred. "Do you think that your wife's kinship with my lady can protect you?"

"No, sir," said Qassem, lowering his eyes.

"Are you a gangster, capable of challenging all the other gangsters in the alley?"

"No, sir."

"Admit that you are crazy, and get out!" the man yelled.

"Praise God, I am sane."

"Why did you dare to file a suit against me?"

"I wanted justice."

"For whom?"

"For all," answered Qassem, his eyes thoughtful.

The overseer looked searchingly, skeptically at Qassem's face. "What business is that of yours?"

"It would satisfy Gabalawi's conditions," said Qassem, almost drunk with courage.

"You Desert Rat!" screamed the overseer. *"You* speak of Gabalawi's terms!"

"He is our ancestor, the ancestor of all of us."

The overseer jumped to his feet in a rage and whipped Qassem

across the face with his fly whisk, using all his strength. *"Our* ancestor!"
he shouted. "Not one of you even knows who his own father is, but you
have the insolence to say 'our ancestor'! You thieves! You rats! You trash!
You persist in your insolence, and depend on this house to protect you
and your wife, but even a dog in this house loses his protection when he
bites the hand of his benefactors."

Lahita stood up to calm the overseer's agitation. "Have a seat, sir. It
is not right for this insect to spoil your peace of mind."

Rifaat sat down, his lips trembling with rage. "Even the Desert Rats
have designs on the estate, and have the insolence to say 'our ancestor.' "

"It's clear that what people say about the Desert Rats is right," said
Lahita, taking his seat. "Unfortunately for our alley, it is going straight to
Hell." He turned to Qassem. "Your father was one of my oldest friends
—don't make me kill you."

"He deserves something more terrible than death for what he's
done!" shouted the overseer. "If it weren't for my lady, he'd be among
the dead already!"

Lahita resumed questioning Qassem. "Listen to me, my boy. Tell
me who's behind you."

"Who are you talking about, sir?" asked Qassem, whose face still
stung where the fly whisk had lashed it.

"Who pushed you to file that suit?"

"No one but myself."

"You were a shepherd before fate smiled on you. What more do you
want?"

"Justice. Justice, sir."

"Justice!" shrieked the overseer, grinding his teeth. "You dogs, you
trash, that's your password whenever you decide to rob and plunder."
He turned to Lahita. "Make him confess!"

Lahita addressed Qassem in a tone of mingled solemnity and menace. "Tell me who is behind you!"

"Our ancestor," said Qassem with unseen provocation.

"Our ancestor!"

"Yes. Read his conditions and you will see that he is the one
behind me."

Again Rifaat jumped to his feet. "Get him out of my face!" he shouted. "Throw him out!"

Lahita stood up and took Qassem by the arm. He walked him to the door, grasping his arm in an iron fist, which Qassem bore patiently, and then whispered in his ear, "Do yourself a favor and come to your senses. Don't force me to drink your blood."

79

When Qassem went into his house, he found Zachary, Uwais, Hassan, Sadeq, Agrama, Shaaban, Abu Fisada and Hamroush. They looked at him in sympathetic silence. He sat down beside his wife.

"Didn't I tell you?" said Uwais.

"Please, uncle, let him catch his breath," Qamar scolded.

"The worst hardships are the ones you cause yourself!" he said anyway.

Zachary studied Qassem's face carefully. "They insulted you, nephew. I know you as well as I know myself. You didn't need all this."

"If it weren't for Lady Amina, you wouldn't have come back alive," said Uwais.

Qassem scanned his friends' faces. "That dirty lawyer betrayed us," he said.

Their faces hardened, and they exchanged anxious looks. Uwais was the first to speak. "Disband now, while you can, and thank God that you got away."

"What do you say, cousin?" Hassan asked.

Qassem thought a moment. "I can't lie to you: death threatens us. I will excuse any of you who don't want to help me."

"Let it end here," said Zachary.

"I will not abandon it, whatever the consequences may be," said

Qassem with quiet determination. "I will never be less faithful to my ancestor and the people of this alley than Gabal or Rifaa were."

Uwais got up angrily and left the room, saying, "He's crazy. God help you, niece."

Sadeq stood and went straight to Qassem and kissed his forehead. "What you've said gives me back my spirit."

"The people of our alley kill one another over a coin, or for no reason at all," said Hassan urgently. "Why should we be afraid of dying, when we have something worth dying for?"

Sawaris' voice sounded in the alley, calling Zachary, who stuck his head out the window and told him to come in. In a moment he entered the room and sat down, scowling darkly. He looked at Qassem. "I didn't know there was a protector in this alley besides me!"

"It's not as you've been told," said Zachary worriedly.

"What I was told was worse than that.".

"The devil has played with our children's minds," said Zachary plaintively.

"Lahita made me listen to some pretty rough things because of your nephew," said Sawaris coarsely. "I had thought he was a levelheaded boy, but he's completely crazy. Now, listen. If I'm too easy on you, Lahita will come and punish you himself, but I will not let anyone expose me to ridicule. So don't go too far, and God help anyone who decides to be stubborn."

Sawaris began to watch Qassem's friends, and let none of them go near his house; he humiliated Sadeq and punched Abu Fisada to enforce his orders, and asked Zachary to advise Qassem to stay inside his house until the trouble was forgotten. Qassem found himself a prisoner in his own house, as no one but Hassan visited him, but there was no power that could imprison the news of the alley. Whispers of the excitement in the Desert Rats' territory made their way to Gabal and Rifaa: the lawsuit almost filed against the overseer, rumors about the Ten Conditions, even of a meeting between Qassem and Gabalawi's servant Qandil. People were stirred up with every possible emotion, and the accusations and sardonic jokes flew.

"The alley is whispering about all this," Hassan told Qassem one day. "In the hashish dens you're all they're talking about."

Qassem turned to him a face clouded with worry and deep thought, as it had been for days. "We've become prisoners. Time is passing, and nothing is being done."

"No creature is expected to be superhuman," said Qamar soothingly.

"Our brothers are as fired up as they can be," said Hassan.

"Is it true that in Gabal and Rifaa they say I'm crazy and a liar?"

"Cowardice corrupts men," said Hassan, sounding pained and looking away.

Qassem shook his head in bewilderment. "Why do people of Gabal and Rifaa call me a liar, when they have people who've met Gabalawi or spoken to him? Why do they call me a liar, when they should be the first to believe me and support me?"

"Cowardice is the curse of our alley. That's why they're such hypocrites with the gangsters!"

They heard Sawaris' voice in the street, rising like a bull's bellow of curses and insults. The family looked out the window and saw Sawaris, who had Shaaban by the collar and was shouting at him.

"What are you doing here, you son of a whore?"

The boy tried vainly to slip out of his grasp. Sawaris had him by the neck with his left hand while he struck him repeatedly on his face and head with his right.

Enraged, Qassem left the window and ran to the door, ignoring Qamar's pleas. In under a minute he was standing before Sawaris. "Leave him alone, Sawaris," he said resolutely.

The man did not stop brutally beating his prey. "Just behave yourself, or I'll have even your enemies crying over you."

Qassem grabbed his right hand and gripped it hard, shouting furiously, "I won't let you kill him, do what you want."

Sawaris let Shaaban go, and the boy fell unconscious on the ground. He snatched a basket of dirt from off the head of a passing woman and dumped it over Qassem's head. Hassan would have pounced on him had not Zachary's arm encircled him just in time. Qassem removed the basket from his head; his face was covered with dirt, and the dirt poured from his head and clothing until he was filthy. A fit of coughing seized him; Qamar screamed, Sakina shouted and Uwais came running. Men, women and children poured through doorways toward the scene, amid a rising babble of voices. Zachary was restraining his son Hassan with all his might, and looked into his bugged-out eyes with a plea and a warning.

Uwais approached Sawaris. "I'll take the blame for this, Sawaris."

"Mercy, Sawaris," shouted several voices.

"With all these friends and relatives, Sawaris is lost, and turned into a woman instead of a gangster!"

"God forgive us, Sawaris, you're our master and we fear you!" said Zachary.

Sawaris walked off to the coffeehouse, the men lifted up Shaaban, Hassan brushed the dirt off of Qassem's face and clothing and everyone present could—now that Sawaris was gone—express their sympathy.

80

That evening, one of the buildings in the Desert Rats' neighborhood emitted a ragged cry of mourning, and in moments it was echoed by dozens of voices in the building. Qassem looked out of the window and asked Fatin, the nut seller, what was happening. "Long life to you," the man said, "Shaaban is dead." Stunned, he left the house, heading for Shaaban's building, which was only two houses down from his. There he found the courtyard dark but crowded with the residents of the lower-level apartments who had come to offer words of comfort, sorrow and anger, while the halls of the upper floors rang with voices.

"He didn't die, Sawaris killed him!" a woman was heard to shout violently.

"God damn you, Sawaris!"

"Qassem killed him! He makes up lies, and our men get killed!" cried a third.

Qassem's heart contracted with sorrow. He moved through the darkness up to the second floor, where the deceased's family lived. He saw, by the light of a fixed lamp in the entryway wall, his friends Hassan, Sadeq, Agrama, Abu Fisada, Hamroush and others.

Sadeq came to him, weeping, and embraced him without a word, his face haggard in the dim light. "His death will not go unavenged," he said.

Agrama approached Qassem and whispered in his ear. "His wife is in a very bad state. She even accused us of killing him."

"Poor thing," Qassem whispered back.

"The murderer must be killed," said Hassan vengefully.

"What witness would come forward in this alley?" said Abu Fisada irritably.

"We can kill just as well as anyone else," said Hassan.

Qassem jabbed Hassan to quiet him. "It would be wisest not to walk in his funeral, but we'll all meet in the graveyard."

Qassem headed into the dead man's apartment; Sadeq tried to prevent him, but he brushed him aside and entered. He called Shaaban's wife, and she came, looking surprised; she gazed at him tearfully, then her eyes hardened. "What do you want?"

"I've come to offer my condolences."

"You killed him," she said sharply. "We could have done without the estate, but we needed him."

"God give you patience, and confound evildoers," he said gently. "We are your family, whenever you need family. His blood will not be lost."

She stared at him distrustfully, then turned and left him. With her withdrawal there was an outburst of wailing and sobbing, and he left, downcast and worried.

When morning came, the people saw Sawaris sitting at the entrance of the Dingil Coffeehouse, showing passersby a face triumphant in its menace and criminality. People greeted him more warmly than usual to hide their bitterness. They shied away from taking part in the mourning ceremony, instead staying in their shops, behind their carts or on the ground. The bier was carried out at noon, escorted only by family and friends, but Qassem joined them, ignoring the gangster's burning looks. The dead man's brother-in-law grew angry.

"You kill a man and walk in his funeral!" he snapped at Qassem.

He kept his silence and patience until someone else asked him roughly, "Why did you come?"

"To fight, the way my friend fought, God rest his soul," said Qassem firmly. "He was brave. You're not like him. You know who the killer is, but you aim your anger at me."

Most of them fell silent. The women massed behind the men, barefoot, hurrying forward in black, throwing dirt on their heads and smiting their cheeks. The funeral moved through Gamaliya toward Bab al-Nasr. When the burial ceremonies were concluded, the mourners went home, except for Qassem, who walked slowly until he fell far behind them. Then he went back to the grave and found his friends waiting for him. His eyes were full of tears, and all of them were tearful and sobbing. He dried his eyes with his hand. "Whoever wants to be safe is free to go."

"If we wanted to be safe, you wouldn't have found us around you," said Hamroush.

Qassem placed his hand on the grave marker. "His loss has hurt me. He was brave and zealous. He was treacherously killed when we needed him most."

"A treacherous gangster murdered him, but some of us will live to see the last gangster in this alley dead," said Sadeq.

"But we mustn't die the way our late friend did," said Hamroush. "Think of the future, and how we can triumph!"

"And how we can meet to talk."

"The only company I had in my prison was my thinking about just that, and I've made up my mind. It won't be easy, but it's unavoidable."

They all asked him at once, and he went on. "Leave the alley. Each of us has to put his own things in order and leave. We'll emigrate, the way Gabal did long ago, and as Yahya did recently. We'll set up our club in a safe place in the desert, until we've gotten stronger and have more people."

"It's a good idea," said Sadeq.

"We can cleanse the alley of gangsters only by force. We can only enforce Gabalawi's conditions by force. Justice, mercy and peace can prevail only by force. Our power will be the first just power, not a power to oppress."

They listened with heedful hearts. They looked at Qassem and at the grave marker behind his back, and it seemed to them that Shaaban was listening with them, and giving his blessing.

"Yes, force will solve these problems," said Agrama emotionally. "Just power, not power to oppress. Shaaban was on his way to see you when he ran into Sawaris; if we had been with him, the gangster would have run into a force he couldn't have beaten. God damn fear and disunion!"

For the first time, Qassem drew a happy breath of relief. "Our ancestor has put his trust in us. Surely he knows some of his children deserve it."

81

Qassem went back to his house at midnight, but he found Qamar awake and waiting for him. She was even more than usually affectionate and attentive, and it hurt him to think of her waiting up for him until that hour. Then he saw that her eyes were tired and red after crying, much as the sun leaves an aurora.

"Have you been crying?" he asked dispiritedly.

She did not answer, as if absorbed in the cup of warm milk she was preparing for him, so he spoke again. "Shaaban's death has upset all of us. God rest his soul."

She answered him suddenly. "I already did my crying for Shaaban, but now I was crying when I thought of that man attacking you. You're the last person who deserves to have dirt thrown on his head and face."

"It's not very much compared to what happened to our poor friend."

She sat beside him and offered him the cup. "It really hurt me," she stammered, "what was said about you."

He smiled, pretending that was unimportant, and lifted the cup to his lips, but she went on resentfully. "Galta is assuring the people of Gabal that you have designs on the estate, to claim it all for yourself. Hagag is telling all the people of Rifaa the same thing. They're both spreading rumors that you say degrading things about Gabal and Rifaa."

He did not hide his concern. "I know that. I also know that if it weren't for you I wouldn't even be alive today."

She rubbed his shoulder affectionately, recalling for no reason their past days, when their conversations had no end and their happiness knew no limit; the delights of the radiant nights after Ihsan was born. Today she possessed nothing of him, and he possessed nothing of himself. She even hid the occasional pains of her illness from him; he scarcely gave a thought to himself, so how could she worry him about her? She was too ashamed to overburden him, to help his enemies without meaning to. Who could possibly reassure her about him, when the days of their lives were passing by as quickly as their days of peace? God help you, alley of ours.

"I never lose hope, even in dark times," Qassem continued. "I have so many good friends, even if I seem alone. One of them challenged Sawaris—who would ever have dared do that before? And the rest are like him. Courage is the most important thing for the people of this alley, if they aren't going to be trampled down for the rest of their lives. Don't tell me to take the safe path; the man who was killed was killed on his way to my house. You wouldn't be happy for your husband to live with the humiliation of cowardice."

Qamar smiled, and replaced the empty cup. "The gangsters' wives trill with joy when there are fights, which are evil; how can I be less happy than they are when what I have is good?"

He saw that her sadness was more profound than it had first seemed to him. He stroked her cheek lovingly and said comfortingly, "You are everything to me in this world. You are my best friend in life."

She smiled, summoning the serenity that she needed before she could sleep.

Sadeq's disappearance took Shantah the coppersmith by surprise. He looked for him at his house, but found no trace of him or any of his family. Nor could Abdelfatah, the salt-cured-fish seller, find any trace of his employee, Agrama, anywhere in the alley. Abu Fisada did not show up at Hamdoun's snack shop, though he had not notified him of any absence. And where was Hamroush? Hassuna the baker said that he had vanished, as if the very flames of the oven had consumed him. Others, too, had gone and not come back. The news spread through the Desert Rats' neighborhood, and its echoes reached the rest of the alley, until people in Gabal and Rifaa sneered that the Desert Rats were deserting, and soon Sawaris would have no one to collect protection money from. Sawaris summoned Zachary to the Dingil Coffeehouse.

"Your nephew is the best person to help us find out where these people have gone," he warned him.

"Please, Sawaris, don't blame him," said Zachary. "Days, weeks and months have gone by, and he has not left his house."

"Children's games!" raged the gangster. "I have only brought you here to warn you what might happen to your nephew."

"Qassem is one of your own family. Please don't give his enemies anything to gloat over."

"He is his own enemy, and he is my enemy. He thinks he's a modern-day Gabal, and that curse is the fastest way to Bab al-Nasr."

The cemetery was at Bab al-Nasr.

"Patience, Sawaris, we are all under your protection."

On his way home, Zachary met Hassan coming back from Qassem's house, and he began to unload on him all of the anger Sawaris had left him with, but Hassan interrupted him. "Please be patient, Father. Qamar is ill—very ill, Father."

The whole alley learned of Qamar's illness, even the overseer's house. Qassem stayed with her, at the extreme limit of sorrow and depression, shaking his head bewilderedly and saying, "With no warning, you lie down, helpless!"

She spoke to him weakly. "I was hiding my condition from you, to spare your heart, which has been so burdened with troubles."

"I should have shared your pain with you from the beginning," he said in utter despair.

Her pale lips parted in a smile, like a wilted flower on a dry stalk. "I'll be healthy again, like before," she said.

That was his prayer, but what was this cloudiness in her eyes, the dryness over her skin and this ability to hide pain? *All this for you. O God, keep her in Your mercy, and spare her for me, and have compassion on the child's crying, which will never cease.*

"Your tolerance toward me has made me unable to tolerate myself."

She smiled again, in seeming rebuke. Umm Salem was brought in to burn incense for her, Umm Atiya to prepare her some dressings and Ibrahim the barber to bleed her, but Umm Ihsan seemed to resist recovery.

"I would do anything to ransom you from your pain."

"May no harm come to you," she answered in a voice as weak as silence. Then she went on: "I love you so much."

The way she looks makes the whole world black in my eyes, he said to himself.

"A sensible man like you is the last person to need consoling," she said.

Male and female visitors came, but the place got too confining for him and he went up to the roof. Women's voices floated out of the windows of the buildings, curses mingled with peddlers' cries from the street, and a child's crying, which at first he took to be Ihsan's, until he saw the child wriggling in the dust on a neighboring roof. Darkness was falling slowly. A flock of pigeons flew back to their dovecote, and a solitary star winked on the horizon. He pondered the meaning of the strange look in Qamar's eye—it was as if she could not see—the twitching of one side of her mouth, the blue tint that had come over her lips, and his overwhelming feeling of anguish. He stayed there for a few hours and then went down, meeting Sakina in the hall, holding Ihsan in her arms.

"Go in softly so she doesn't wake up," she whispered.

He lay down on the sofa facing the bed, in the dim light shed by a lamp on the windowsill. There was no sound outdoors but the lament of the rebec, followed by the voice of Taza the poet.

"The grandfather said calmly, 'I have decided to give you a chance no one from outside here has ever had: to live in this house, to marry into it and to begin a new life in it.' Humam's heart beat in a rapture of joy, and he said, 'Thank you for your kindness.' 'You deserve it.' The boy's gaze alternated between his grandfather and the carpet before he asked anxiously, 'My family?' 'I have clearly told you what I want,' Gabalawi reproached him. 'They deserve your forgiveness and your affection,' Humam pleaded."

Qamar, asleep, made a sudden movement, and he jumped off the sofa to her. He saw a new luster in her eyes instead of the cloudy look, and asked her what was wrong.

"Ihsan!" she cried in a strong voice. "Where is Ihsan?"

He sped out of the room, and returned with Sakina, who was carrying the sleeping baby in her arms. Qamar pointed to Ihsan, and Sakina brought her near so that she could kiss her cheek. Qassem sat at the foot of the bed, and she looked down at him.

"Mine's greater," she whispered.

He leaned over her. "What do you mean?"

"I've given you great pain but mine's greater."

He bit his lip. "Qamar, I'm so sad, because I can't do anything to lighten your pain."

"I'm afraid for you, after."

"Don't talk about me," he said, intensely sad.

"Qassem, go. Be with your friends. You'll be killed if you stay behind."

"We'll go together."

"Not the same way," she said with some difficulty.

"You don't want to give in to me the way I'm used to."

"Oh, that was in the past."

It seemed as if she were resisting some great pressure, and she beckoned with her hand. He leaned more closely over her, until he felt her breath; she squirmed and strained forward as if appealing for help. Her chest fell in, and exhaled a harsh, rattling sigh.

"Sit her up, she wants to sit up!" shouted Sakina.

He took her in his arms to sit her up, but she emitted a moan, like a mute farewell, and her head dropped against his chest. Sakina rushed the child out of the door, and then the silence was shattered by her screams.

82

In the morning, Qassem's house and the street in front of it were crowded with mourners. The ties of kinship commanded a deep-seated respect in the alley (which, however, enjoyed not one of its many benefits), so Sawaris had to come to offer condolences, and the Desert Rats were quick to follow behind. The overseer, Rifaat, had to come to offer condolences, and he was immediately followed by Lahita, Galta and Hagag, and everyone in the alley followed them. The funeral was joined by huge throngs such as the alley had never seen before except at gangsters' funerals. Qassem showed a wise man's composure despite his hidden agonies. Even at the moment of the burial, all of his senses and his faculties wept, but not his eyes. All of the mourners left until only Qassem, Zachary, Uwais and Hassan remained at the burial site.

Zachary patted Qassem on the arm. "Be brave, nephew," he said sadly. "God be with you."

Qassem slumped slightly and sighed deeply. "My heart is buried in the earth, uncle," he murmured.

Hassan's face contracted sympathetically, and the graveyard was perfectly silent.

"We should be going," said Zachary, taking a step.

But Qassem stood where he was, and protested, "Why did they come?"

Zachary understood what he meant. "We should thank them anyway."

"Make a new beginning with them," Uwais added, encouraged. "They've taken a step, and it calls for steps from you. Fortunately, what's been said about you outside our neighborhood is not taken very seriously here!"

He was immersed in silence and sorrow, and did not want a discussion with him. At this point a group led by Sadeq appeared, as if they had been waiting for the mourners to leave; it was a large group but Qassem knew them all, and they hugged him until tears came into his eyes. Uwais rolled his eyes at them irritably, but they ignored him.

"Now there's nothing to keep you in the alley," Sadeq told Qassem.

"His daughter, his house and his property are there," Zachary objected sharply.

"I had to stay in the alley," said Qassem meaningfully, "and thanks to that, your numbers have grown!"

He looked at the faces turned to him, as if citing their multitude to prove the truth of what he said. He had persuaded most of them to emigrate and join his companions when he had slipped out of his house every night after the alley was asleep to visit those in whom he recognized friendship and a good preparedness to accept what he told them.

"Will we have to wait long?" Agrama asked.

"Until you have enough people."

Agrama turned to him, aside, and said, "My heart bleeds for you. No one understands your terrible loss better than I do."

"Yes, you're right," said Qassem emotionally. "It is very hard."

"Hurry and join us, because you're alone now," he said, watching him sympathetically.

"Everything in its good time."

"We should be getting back," said Uwais loudly.

The friends embraced, and Qassem and the others went home. For days he was alone in his house, so depressed that Sakina worried about the harmful consequences of his sorrow. But he continued his secret nightly excursions with unflagging energy. The number of persons disappearing continued to mount, and people wondered about them, bewildered. Everyone in the rest of the alley ridiculed the Desert Rats and their protector even more; they said that Sawaris' turn to flee would come any day now.

"This makes me very nervous," Zachary warned him one day. "The consequences could be frightening."

There was no choice but to wait, however. These were busy and dangerous days, in whose scowling passage Ihsan provided the only smile. She was learning how to stand by grabbing on to the arms of chairs, looked at him with her innocent face and spoke to him in the language of the sparrows and nightingales. He enjoyed watching her face lovingly, and said to himself, "She will be a beautiful girl, but it is more important to me that she be as good and loving as her mother." His delight was the dark eyes in Qamar's round face, which would remain a lasting sign of the loving relationship that fate had ended. He wondered whether he would live long enough to see her be a beautiful bride; or would it be her fate to have only painful memories of the house of her birth?

One day there was a knock at the door, and when Sakina asked who was there, a youthful voice called, "Open up, Sakina."

She opened the door to see a girl of twelve or more, oddly muffled up in a cloak and wearing a veil over her face. Surprised, Sakina asked her what she wanted, but she hurried to Qassem's room.

"Good afternoon," she said rapidly, and removed the veil to reveal a brown, moon-round face with lovely features that exuded sprightliness.

"Welcome—sit down—welcome, welcome," said Qassem, amazed.

"I am Badriya. My brother Sadeq sent me," she said, sitting down on the edge of the sofa.

"Sadeq!" said Qassem attentively.

"Yes."

He watched her curiously, then asked, "What made him do something so risky?"

"No one would ever recognize me in this cloak," she said with an earnestness that made her seem even prettier.

He saw that her body was mature for her age, and nodded, reassured. She resumed speaking, even more earnestly.

"He wants to tell you to leave the alley immediately. Lahita, Galta, Hagag and Sawaris are plotting to kill you tonight."

He frowned, alarmed, and Sakina groaned.

"How did he find that out?"

"Yahya told him."

"But how did Yahya know?"

"A drunk let the secret out in a bar where there was a friend of Yahya's. That's what my brother said."

He looked at her silently, until she got up and began to pull her cloak over her nubile body, and then he got up too.

"Thank you, Badriya. Hide yourself carefully, and give my regards to your brother. Go in peace."

She drew the veil across her face. "What should I tell him?"

"Tell him that we'll meet before morning."

She shook his hand and left.

83

Sakina's face was pale, and her eyes expressed panic. "Let's get out of the house now!" she shouted, and jumped up to get going.

"Bundle up Ihsan and wrap her in your cloak. Go out as if you have an errand, but go to Qamar's grave and wait for me there."

"What about you, sir?"

"I'll follow along at the right time."

Her eyes wavered between concern and confusion.

"Hassan will take you to the place where we'll stay," he reassured her.

In seconds, she was ready to leave. He kissed Ihsan again and again.

"We entrust you to the safekeeping of Him who never dies," the woman told him as she headed for the door.

He stood at a crevice in the window blinds to keep an eye on the road, and watched the slave walk toward Gamaliya until she disappeared in the curve of the street. His heart pounded as he gazed at the crook of her arm that contained the precious bundle. His eye moved over the neighborhood, and saw some men who were followers of the gangsters, some sitting in the Dingil Coffeehouse and others standing idle here and there; he could barely make out their features in the steadily falling darkness. All indications were that they were preparing, but were they waiting for him to go out for his nightly excursion, if they had discovered that secret, or would they attack his house when the night was nearly over? Now they were carefully spreading out, lest their mission be discovered. They were creeping through the dusk like insects, their very breath exhaling the smell of crime. Would he meet Gabal's fate, or Rifaa's? This was the situation in which Rifaa had found himself that dark night: he had hidden in his house with a heart full of good intentions, while the lower floor was invaded by heavy feet, whose owners' very skin smelled of blood lust. When will you have shed enough blood, miserable alley? He paced back and forth in the room until he heard a tap at the door and Hassan's voice calling him.

Hassan entered with his powerful body and eyes reflecting unease. "There are strange, suspicious movements in the alley," he said.

"Has my Uncle Zachary come home from his walk?" Qassem asked, ignoring his remark.

"No, but I was saying that there's something suspicious out there. Look out of the window blind."

"I saw what you're worried about, and I know what's going on. Sadeq warned me in time by sending his little sister to me. If he's right, the gangsters will try to kill me tonight, and that's why I sent Ihsan away with Sakina. They're waiting for you at Qamar's grave. Go get them, and then all of you go to our brothers' headquarters."

"What about you?"

"I'll escape and follow you."

"I will not leave you alone," said Hassan resolutely.

"Do what I told you, now," said Qassem urgently, with a hint of vexation. "I'll escape using a trick, not force. Your strength won't help me if we should meet any resistance, and by going, you'll protect my daughter, and you'll be able to put some of our men at the beginning of the roads from Gamaliya up to the mountain. They may be able to help me, if I need them when I escape."

Hassan acceded to his wishes, shook his hand firmly. "No one has a brain like yours. You probably have a good plan," he said.

He was answered with a smile of reassurance, and Hassan went away gloomily. It was not long before Zachary arrived, panting; Qassem was sure that he was on his way back from Yahya's with the news. He spoke first. "Sadeq sent me word of the news."

"I just found out a little while ago, when I passed by Yahya's, and I was afraid you hadn't heard," the man said, plainly upset.

"I'm sorry for being the cause of all these upsets," said Qassem contritely, and made him sit down.

"I've been waiting for something like this. I had noticed a change in how Sawaris was acting toward me, but I deceived myself. Now I see all those devils everywhere, like locusts. And you're all alone and have no way of escaping."

Qassem straightened up determinedly and said, "I will try, and if I fail, there are men on the mountain who will not be beaten."

"What's that compared to your life or your child?" asked Zachary morosely.

"I'm surprised that you're not leading my followers!"

"Come with me to Sawaris," he went on, as though he had not heard. "We'll negotiate with him, and promise him what he wants."

Qassem laughed briefly to deride his uncle's suggestion without answering it. Zachary turned to the window to look out to the street, which seemed dark and dreadful.

"Why did they choose tonight?" Qassem asked him.

"The day before yesterday, one of the Al Gabal announced that your cause would be a good thing for everyone, and it's said that one of the Al Rifaa said the same thing. Perhaps that's what made them decide to move quickly."

"See, uncle? Qassem beamed. "I am the enemy of the overseer and the gangsters, but the friend of our alley, and everyone will see that."

"Think now of what is in store for you."

"Here is my plan. I'll escape over the rooftops as far as your house, leaving my lamp burning to mislead them," said Qassem earnestly.

"Someone might see you."

"I won't go until it's dark and people aren't sitting out on their roofs."

"And if they attack your house before then?"

"They won't do that until everyone in the alley is asleep."

"They may have become more reckless than you think."

"In that case, I'll die." Qassem smiled. "Who can postpone his appointed time?"

The man raised a face that bespoke urgency, but it met a calm and confident smile that was like determination personified. "They might search my house," he said in despair.

"Luckily, they aren't aware that news of their plots have reached us, and I'll escape first, God willing."

They exchanged a long gaze, more eloquent than tears, then embraced. When Qassem found himself alone, he shook off his emotions and went to the window to watch the street. Everything was as usual in the neighborhood, with children playing around the handcart lanterns, the coffeehouse packed and sociable, the roofs resounding with women's conversations; the coughing of smokers, interspersed with their insults and obscenities, and the rising lament of the rebec. There was Sawaris, in the doorway of the coffeehouse, with the messengers of death occupying the corners. *Scions of treachery, thieves of men, ever since Idris' burst of cold laughter, you have been passing on a legacy of crime and sinking the alley in a sea of darkness. Isn't it time the captive bird is freed?* Time passed slowly and heavily, but it eventually drew the soirees to an end. The roofs were silent, the street was empty except for the carts and the children, the coffeehouses were abandoned and for a time there were the voices of shadowy shapes heading home. Hallucinating drunks came back from Gamaliya and hashish dens put out their fires, leaving only the companions of death out in the dark. "It is time to act," he told himself. He hurried to the steps and climbed to the roof, then went to the dividing wall between his roof and the roof of the neighboring house, crossed it easily, and was about to run on when a figure stood in his way and said, "Stop." He realized that the roofs were occupied by killers; that his encirclement was complete. He turned to retreat, but the other man pounced at him and seized him in his powerful arms. Qassem summoned all of his strength, which was redoubled by fear, and surprised him with a punch in the stomach that released the arms around him. A kick in the stomach doubled him over, and then he collapsed, moaning, and did not rise again. There was a muffled cough from the third or fourth roof down, and he changed his mind about advancing. He withdrew, worried, to his roof, and stood at the steps, listening; he could hear footsteps coming up. They were massing at the door of his apartment; they smashed against it. It flew open and was almost ripped from the frame, and they rushed inside. He went down quickly, not losing a second, ending up in the courtyard. He hurried to the door, and saw a figure moving outside the house, jumped on him and grabbed him around the throat, butted him with his head, kicked him in the stomach and shoved him away. He fell on his back, motionless. Qassem headed for Gamaliya, his heart thumping. Now they saw that the house was empty, and they might go up to the roof, where they would find their supine friend; others might be on their way down to follow him. He passed his uncle's house without stopping, and when he neared the end of the alley he began to run. Where the alley opened into Gamaliya, a figure jumped out into his path and shouted in a voice like thunder to alert others, "Stop, son of a bitch!" He raised a club before Qassem could get out of the way, but a second figure appeared from around the bend, bashed the man over the head with a cane, and he dropped, screaming.

"Let's run as fast as we can," the second figure said.

Qassem and Hassan ran through the darkness, paying no attention to rocks or potholes.

84

At the opening of Watawit Alley, Sadeq joined them. At the end of it
they found Agrama, Abu Fisada and Hamroush around a four-wheeled
horse-drawn cart. They all got in, and the horse galloped off, driven by
the cabman's whip. Despite the darkness, the cart raced along, giving off
rattling and clopping sounds in the stillness of the night like a string of
small explosions, and they looked back, fearful and apprehensive.

"They'll head for Bab al-Nasr," said Sadeq in an attempt to reassure
them. "They think you'll hide in the desert, near the graveyards."

"But they know that you don't live in the graveyards."

The speed of the cart made the difference, however, and it gave
them the feeling they really were far from danger.

"You did a very good job of organizing everything," said Qassem
with relief. "Thanks to you, Sadeq. If it hadn't been for your warning,
I'd be among the dead now."

Sadeq pressed his hand in silence. The cart sped on until Muqattam
Marketplace appeared in the starlight, shrouded in solitude and darkness,
except for the lamplight shining from Yahya's hut. They cautiously drove
the cart to the middle of the square, left it, and walked to the hut.
Almost immediately the old man's voice sounded, asking who was there;
Qassem answered, and the voice rose again, in thanks. The two men
embraced warmly.

"I owe you my life," said Qassem.

"It was just a coincidence," said the old man, laughing, "but it
happened in a way that saved the life of a man who is the most deserving
of life. Hurry to the mountain—it will be the best base for you."

Qassem grabbed his hand and looked gratefully and affectionately at
face by the light of the lamp.

"Today you are like Rifaa or Gabal," the old man said. "I will return to our alley when you have triumphed."

They headed east from the hut, penetrating deep into the desert, toward the mountain. They were led by Sadeq, who knew the route better than any of them. There was a glow mingled with the darkness that heralded the approach of dawn, and the dew was falling from the sky. From afar came the crowing of a cock, a newcomer's screech at the birth of a new day. They reached the foothills, and followed them south until they found the narrow passage that led up to their new dwelling place on top of the mountain. They climbed behind Sadeq in a line, one by one, because of the narrowness of the path.

"We prepared a house for you in the middle of our houses," Sadeq told Qassem. "Ihsan is sleeping there now."

"We built our houses with sheet metal and burlap," said Agrama.

"They're not a lot worse than our houses in the alley," Hassan joked.

"It's good enough having no overseer or gangsters among us," observed Qassem.

They heard voices.

"Our new alley has woken up—they're waiting for you," said Sadeq.

They looked up and saw rays of light pursuing the remnants of darkness, and Sadeq shouted at the top of his lungs, "Here we are!" and men's and women's heads appeared, there were shouts and trills of joy, and people began to sing, "Put henna on the sparrow's tail!"

"Look at them all!" said Qassem admiringly, lighthearted with joy.

"It's a new civilization on the mountain," said Sadeq proudly. "The population grows every day. All the emigrants from the alley have joined us, with Yahya's guidance."

"The only trouble is that we have to make our livings in faraway neighborhoods, for fear of being discovered by someone from our alley."

When Qassem got to the top, the men greeted him with hugs, the women shook his hand and all voices were raised in welcome, cheers and cries of "God is great!" Sakina was among them, and told Qassem that Ihsan was asleep in the hut that had been prepared as their home. They all walked to the new neighborhood, which was comprised of a square area of huts on a mountain clearing. They cheered and sang, and the horizon was brilliant with exuberant light, like a lake of white roses.

"Welcome to our protector, Qassem!" a man called out.

Qassem's face changed, and he shouted angrily, "No! God's curse on all protection gangs! There is never peace or safety wherever they are found!"

All the new faces were turned to him.

"We will raise clubs the way Gabal did, but to achieve the mercy that Rifaa called for. We will use the estate for everyone's good, until we make Adham's dream come true. That is our mission—not gang rule."

Hassan pushed him gently toward the hut that had been prepared for him, and called out to the crowd, "He didn't close his eyes all last night. Let him get some of the rest he's earned."

Qassem lay down on a burlap sack beside his daughter, and was quickly overcome by sleep. He woke up between noon and the early afternoon, his head heavy and his body weary. Sakina brought Ihsan to him, and placed her in his arms. He began to kiss her lovingly, and the woman offered him a jug of water.

"This water was brought to us from the public pump—the same way Gabal's wife used to fetch it!"

The man smiled; he loved anything that linked him to the memories of Gabal or Rifaa. He looked around his new house to examine the walls, which were covered with burlap and nothing else, and clasped Ihsan to his chest even more tenderly, then stood up and handed his daughter to Sakina. He went out and found Sadeq and Hassan waiting for him, sat between them and said, "Good morning." He looked over the neighborhood, but he saw only women and children.

"The men have gone to al-Sayida and Zainhum to look for work," Sadeq explained, "and we stayed behind to look after you."

His eyes followed the women as they cooked or did washing in front of the huts, and the children as they played here and there.

"Do you think these women are happy?"

"They dream of owning the estate, and the comforts that Lady Amina enjoys," said Sadeq.

He smiled broadly, and then looked slowly from one of them to the other. "What's going on in your heads about our next step?"

Hassan lifted his head over his brawny shoulders and said, "We know exactly what we want."

"But how?"

"We'll wait for our moment, and then attack."

"We should be patient, until most of the people of the alley join us, then attack," Sadeq protested. "That way we can ensure victory on the one hand and low casualties on the other."

"Yes!" said Qassem, his features jubilant.

They sank into a dreamy repose, which was interrupted by a shy voice. "Food!"

Qassem looked up and saw Badriya carrying a platter of beans and loaves of bread. She gazed at him with her laughing eyes, and he could not help smiling.

"Welcome to my little lifesaver."

She placed the platter in his hands. "God give you long life."

She went back to Sadeq's hut, which was next to his. He felt a tenderness and contentment in his heart, and began to eat heartily.

"I have a good amount of money that will help us when we need it," he said as he ate. After a moment he added, "We have to go after everyone in the alley who seems ready to join us. There are so many oppressed people who want us to win, and only fear keeps them from joining us."

The two men shortly left to go where the other men had gone earlier, and he found himself alone. He stood and set out to walk around the place, as if inspecting it. He passed playing children; none of them took any notice of him. The women, however, all greeted him with blessings, and he noticed a very elderly woman with pure white hair, eyes clouded with age and a trembling chin, so toothless that she looked as if she had nearly swallowed her jaws. He greeted her, and she returned his greeting.

"Who are you, mother?" he asked politely.

"Umm Hamroush."

"Welcome, mother of us all—how did you decide to leave our alley?"

Her voice was like the rattle of dry leaves. "The best place is near my son." Then, as if remembering something: "And far from those gangsters." Encouraged by his smile, she said, "I saw Rifaa when I was a girl!"

"Really?" he asked her, very interested.

"Yes, by your life. He was sweet, and handsome, but it never crossed my mind that a neighborhood address would be named for him, or that they'd be telling stories about him to music!"

"Didn't you follow him, like all the rest?"

"No, no one knew about us in our neighborhood. We ourselves didn't know who we were. If it weren't for you, no one would be talking about the Desert Rats at all."

He looked at her closely, and wondered: What must our ancestor look like by now? But he smiled gently at her still, while she said prayers for him for a long time, and then he left. He continued walking until he stood at the top of the passage, at the foot of the mountain. He looked out at the desert below, and then at the horizon. Far off were the roofs and domes, scattered landmarks that now looked like one place. He said that they should be one thing, and that it looked so small from above: Rifaat the overseer and Lahita the gangster seemed meaningless from here. There seemed to be no difference between Rifaat and his Uncle Zachary. *It would be nearly impossible to make your way from where you are to that turbulent alley if it weren't for the mansion, which can be seen from anywhere: our ancestor's house, with its strange wall and tall trees. But he is discredited by age, and dread of him has declined like the sun now sinking toward the horizon. Where are you? How are you? Why is it you no longer seem to be yourself? Those who falsify your commandments are a mere arm's length from your house. These women and children, far away in the mountain—aren't they the closest people to your heart? You will regain your standing when you enforce the terms of your charter without overseers' assassinations or the violence of gangsters; like the return of the sun tomorrow to the highest point in the sky. Without you we would have no father, no world, no estate, no hope.*

A sweet voice woke him from his drowsy thoughts. "Coffee, Qassem, sir."

He turned around to see Badriya holding out a cup in her hand, and he took it.

"Why the trouble?"

"Going to trouble for you is like a vacation, sir."

God rest your soul, Qamar, he thought, and sipped the coffee companionably. Between sips their smiling eyes met. How delicious the coffee tasted on the mountainside, overlooking the desert.

"How old are you, Badriya?"

She bit her lip. "I don't know," she murmured.

"But you know what brought us to this mountain?"

"You!"

"Me?"

"You want to strike the overseer and the gangsters, and make the estate ours. That's what my father says."

He smiled. He saw that he had finished the coffee but had not returned the cup to her, so he handed it to her.

"I wish I could give you part of the thanks you deserve." She blushed, turned away with a smile and ran off.

"Be safe," he managed to say.

85

Late afternoon was the time for fencing, so the men set out to do their strenuous exercises with wooden sticks. That was after they had come back—men and women alike—with a little money and some simple food, after a long and exhausting day of work. Qassem was the most enthusiastic, and he loved seeing his men's zeal and energy in preparation for the crucial day. There were strong men among them, but they harbored a love for him that their hate-torn alley had never known. The sticks resounded, clacked and landed in powerful exchanges, and the boys watched and imitated them while the women relaxed or prepared supper. The line of huts had grown longer with the arrival of new men in the new neighborhood; Sadeq, Hassan and Abu Fisada had proved to be expert recruiters. They lay in wait for the men of the alley where they were most likely to be found, and stayed with them until they had persuaded them to join up. They quit the alley secretly, with a hope in their hearts that they had never known before.

"I can't guarantee that all this activity won't lead our enemies to us," Sadeq would tell Qassem.

"The only approach to us is the narrow passage. They'll be wiped out if they try to come through it."

His lasting happiness was Ihsan when he played with her, rocked her and sang to her, but this was not the case when she reminded him of his late wife; those occasions immersed him in gloom and the hot sighs of yearning. She had been taken from him at the outset of their journey, and left him prey to terrible depression whenever he was alone; or to regret, as when he had been on the mountainside, the day he drank the coffee, the day of the shy smile, as soft as an afternoon breeze. One night, he could not fall asleep, and he fell prey to tormented depression and insomnia in the dark hut. He got out of bed and went outside, strolling in the open space between the huts, under the stars, to breathe in the sweet night air, the mountain air of the summer midnight.

A voice called to him. "Where are you going at this hour of the night?"

He turned and saw Sadeq approaching. "Aren't you asleep yet?"

"I saw you when I was lying in front of the hut, and I like you better than sleep."

They walked side by side to a mountain ledge, and stood there.

"Sometimes I can't stand being alone," Qassem told him.

"I can't ever stand it!" laughed Sadeq.

They watched the horizon, the glittering sky and the earth sunk in blackness.

"Most of your men are married or have families," Sadeq resumed. "They're never lonely."

"What do you mean?" Qassem asked suspiciously.

"Someone like you cannot do without a woman."

"Marry, after Qamar?" The objection in his voice was as strong as his feeling that the man was right.

"If she were able to make you hear her voice, she would say the same thing I'm saying," said Sadeq sincerely.

Qassem was disturbed, though excitement boiled within him. "It's like treason, after her love and caring," he said, almost to himself.

"The dead can do without our loyalty!"

What does this good man intend? To speak the truth or justify my pleasure? But sometimes truth has a bitter taste. You cannot face yourself with the same candor with which you faced conditions in your alley. He who settles these matters in your life is the same one Who set these stars in the sky. The indisputable truth is that your heart is still beating, as it always has. He sighed audibly.

"No one needs a companion as much as you do," said Sadeq.

On the way back to his hut, he saw Sakina standing at the door, looking at him questioningly.

"I saw you go out, when I thought you were fast asleep!" she said worriedly.

So intense were his thoughts that he burst out, with no preface, saying, "Look at the way Sadeq is trying to make me get married!"

"I wish I had said it before he did!" Sakina said, as if snatching a long-awaited opportunity.

"You!"

"Yes, sir. It hurts my heart to see you sitting all alone, lonely and thinking."

"They are all with me," he said, pointing to the sleeping huts.

"Yes, but you have no one for you in your home, and I'm old. I have one foot on the ground and the other in the grave."

He sensed that his hesitation was a sign that he accepted what she wanted, but even so, he did not go into the hut. "I'll never find a wife like her!" he lamented.

"That's true, but there are some very fine girls!"

They exchanged a look in the shadows, and there was silence. Then the slave said, "Badriya! What a sweet girl she is!"

"That young girl!" he said, surprised, his heart pounding.

"She looks pretty ripe to me, when she brings you food or coffee," she said, hiding a sly smile.

"You demon!" he said, turning away from her. "God's curse on your begetters!"

The news echoed joyfully throughout the mountain community. Sadeq nearly danced, his mother made the desert ring with her trilling and Qassem was showered with congratulations. The whole neighborhood celebrated the wedding, without having to hire any professional entertainers. The women danced, Umm Badriya among them, and Abu Fisada sang in his pleasant voice, "I was a fisherman, and fishing for fish is fun."

The wedding procession wound around the huts, lit only by the lights in the heavens. Sakina moved to Hassan's hut with Ihsan, to leave Qassem's hut for the bride and groom.

86

He loved watching—from where he sat on a skin in front of his hut— as Badriya kneaded dough. She was young, of course, but what other woman had her energy and ability? She stretched, weary, and with the back of her hand pushed back the hair that hung over her forehead. She looked desirable in a way that captivated every fold of his heart, and her blushing face showed that she felt his eyes following her, and she stopped her work, pouting. He laughed delightedly, bent over her, grasped her braid and kissed it again and again, then went back to where he had been sitting. He was happy and carefree, as he always was on the rare occasions when he was free of his friends and thoughts. Ihsan was walking from one place to another nearby, watched by Sakina, who was resting on a rock. There was a burst of noise at the head of the passage, and he saw Sadeq, Hassan and some of his companions coming toward him, with a man he knew as Khurda, the Rifaa community's garbage collector. He immediately rose to his feet to welcome them, while the women trilled as they always did when a new man from the alley joined them in the mountain. The man embraced him.

"I am with you," he said, "and I've brought my club with me!"

"Welcome, Khurda," Qassem said. "We don't make any distinction between one community and another here; the alley belongs to all of us, and the estate is for all."

"They all wonder where your place is," laughed the man from Rifaa. "They are expecting trouble from you, but there are many who hope you win." He looked around him, at the huts and the people, and said, sounding impressed, "All of them are with you!"

"Khurda has brought some important news," said Sadeq.

Qassem looked at him quizzically.

"Today Sawaris is getting married for the fifth time," said Khurda earnestly. "His wedding procession will be tonight."

"This kind of chance at getting him will never happen again," said Hassan enthusiastically.

All the men grew excited.

"We'll attack the alley someday, and in the meantime, every gangster we can eliminate will help that attack to go more easily, and the outcome will be more guaranteed," said Sadeq.

Qassem thought this over before speaking. "We'll attack the procession, the way the gangsters do, but always remember that we're attacking it to destroy gang rule."

Shortly before midnight, the men gathered on the mountainside, and stole down, one at a time, behind Qassem, clubs in hand. The sky was clear, with the full moon high and spreading its dreamy light everywhere. They came out into the desert and headed north, behind Muqattam Marketplace, then marched opposite the mountain so as not to stray from the road. As they neared Hind's Rock, they were approached by the figure of a man who had been posted there to spy for them.

"The procession will go toward Hind's Rock," he told Qassem.

"But our processions usually go to Gamaliya," said Qassem, surprised.

"Maybe they're staying away from the areas they think might be close to your base!" said Khurda.

Qassem thought quickly. "Sadeq and some men will go into Bab al-Futuh. Agrama and a few others will go to the desert of Bab al-Nasr. When I call you to attack, attack."

The men broke up into groups, and before they set off, he said, "Concentrate the fight on Sawaris and his followers. The rest will be your brothers tomorrow."

Each group went on its way. Qassem, Hassan and their men hurried north, opposite the mountain, then turned left into the graveyard road until they were hidden behind the gate.

"The procession will gather at the al-Falaki Coffeehouse," said Hassan.

"We have to attack it before it reaches the coffeehouse, so that we don't attack people we have nothing to do with."

They continued to wait in the dark, their nerves taut.

"How well I remember Shaaban's murder," said Hassan abruptly.

"The gangsters' victims can't be counted," said Qassem.

Sadeq whistled, and Agrama answered, and their determination was strengthened.

"If Sawaris is killed, the people of the neighborhood will hurry to join us," said Hassan.

"And if the others come to get us, we'll slaughter them at the passage."

These dreams were like the moonlight. It would be less than an hour before their victory was decisive, or their hopes would evaporate along with the souls from their slain bodies. He imagined that he could see Qandil's silhouette, and hear Qamar's voice. It was as though an eternity had passed since his shepherding days. His fingers closed over his club and he said to himself, *We cannot be defeated.*

He heard Hassan say something. "Don't you hear it?"

He listened more closely, and heard the echoes of music. "Get ready —the procession is coming," he said.

The voices came nearer and became more distinct, then came the horns and drums, the cries and the cheers. Then, by the light of torches, the procession appeared as it moved near, and the accursed Sawaris, surrounded by dancers juggling clubs.

"Should I whistle to Agrama?" Hassan asked.

"When the front of the procession reaches the garlic market," said Qassem steadily.

The procession continued its progress, and the dancing and juggling intensified. One dancer, caught up in the rapture of the dance, leaped into the air and spun around in front of the procession, making an undulant circle with graceful speed. He twirled a spinning club like a fan with his raised hand, and advanced one step after each turn, until he had passed the garlic market. The procession behind him moved very slowly, until the front of it reached the garlic market, and Hassan whistled three times. Agrama and his men poured out of al-Tamayin Lane and fell on the rear of the procession, their clubs leading the way. Confusion scattered its ranks, and there were screams of rage and fear. Hassan whistled three more times, and Sadeq and his men plunged out of Samakin Road onto the middle of procession from the other side, before it had recovered from the first attack. Qassem and his men immediately charged through the gate as one man, to attack the front of the procession. Sawaris and his men recovered from the surprise of the trap, lifted their clubs and joined the dogged fighting. Many of the noncombatants fled, taking refuge in the nearby lanes and alleys as the thwacking of the clubs grew more frenzied, blood streamed from heads and faces, lanterns were smashed and flowers were scattered and trampled. Voices wailed from windows, and the coffeehouses closed their doors. Sawaris fought hard and nimbly, swinging his club like a madman in every direction, and the fighting intensified as their hatred grew as black as the night. Sawaris suddenly found himself face to face with Sadeq.

"You son of a dirty bitch!" he shouted, and aimed a blow at him that struck his face. Sadeq convulsed and staggered, and Sawaris lifted his club and brought it down again; Sadeq took the blow on the club gripped in his hand, but fell to his knees from the force of the stroke. Sawaris was about to deal him the third and final blow, but saw Hassan bearing down on him like a beast to save his friend. He turned toward him, brimming with anger.

"You too, Bin Zachary, son of a whore!" he shouted. He loosed a terrible blow which would have killed Hassan had he not dodged it by jumping aside. As he jumped, he caught Sawaris with the end of his club, wounding him on the neck, and this blow prevented Sawaris from striking again for a few moments. Hassan regained his balance and swung with all his tremendous strength, smiting Sawaris' forehead, which spouted a fountain of blood. At once his hand loosened around his club, and it dropped. He staggered backward, then fell motionless on his back, and a man's voice rang out over the racket of the colliding clubs: "Sawaris is killed!" Agrama got the man above the nose with a blow of his club, and he screamed and retreated, stumbled over a body and fell. The determination of Qassem's men was strengthened, and they redoubled their blows. Sawaris' men began to straggle, horrified by the number of their fallen men, and they began to withdraw, then run away. Qassem's men gathered around him, panting, some streaming with blood and others wounded. By the lamplight diffused through the panes of the coffeehouse doors, they saw the bodies strewn on the ground, some dead, others unconscious.

Hamroush stood over the body of Sawaris. "Now you can sleep in peace, Shaaban!" he cried.

Qassem pulled him aside. "The day of victory is near, the day when the rest of the gangsters will meet the same fate; the day we become masters of our own alley, owners of our estate and dutiful children of Gabalawi."

When they went back to the mountain, the women received them with joyful trilling, and news of the victory spread quickly. Qassem repaired to his hut.

"You're all dusty and bloody. You should have a bath before you sleep," Badriya told him.

When he lay down after his bath, he moaned with pain. She brought him food and waited for him to sit up and eat it, but he was in a state between waking and sleeping. He felt a relaxation that resembled happiness and a feeling of unease that was like sorrow.

"Eat your food," said Badriya.

He looked at her through heavy, dreaming eyes. "You'll see victory soon, Qamar," he said.

He realized his slip of the tongue too late, and saw the change in Badriya's face. He sat up in his bed on the ground. "Your cooking is so good," he said lovingly, if a little embarrassed.

But, frowning, she ignored his show of affection. He took a piece of falafel, and said, "It's my turn to invite you to eat!"

She turned her face away, muttering, "She was old, and not beautiful."

His straight back bowed over in anguish, as if he were collapsing, and he spoke to her with burning sorrow and rebuke. "Don't say anything bad about her. Someone like her should never be mentioned except kindly."

Her head turned vigorously toward him, but she saw the terrible grief on his face, and faltered. She said nothing.

87

The vanquished went home in total disgrace, staying as far away as possible from the lights of Sawaris' house, whose atmosphere still glittered with the joy of the wedding and entertainment. Every man went home. Then, as the bad news spread like fire, many houses became loud with shrieking, and the wedding reception was extinguished as if smothered with dirt. Voices lamented Sawaris, and then the men who had died with him. The tragedy encompassed some men of Rifaa and others of Gabal who had taken part in the procession. Who was the criminal attacker? Qassem, Qassem the sheep boy, Qassem who would have been nothing but a beggar for all his born days if it hadn't been for Qamar! One man swore he had followed Qassem's gang on their way home, until they reached their refuge above Muqattam. Many people wondered whether they would remain on the mountain until they had destroyed the men of the alley. Sleepers were woken up by the shouting and went out into the alley and courtyards.

"Kill the Desert Rats!" shouted one of the men of Gabal angrily.

"They haven't done anything," Galta said, restraining him. "Their protector is dead, and a large number of their men."

"Burn Muqattam!"

"Get Qassem's corpse and feed it to the dogs!"

"I'll divorce my wife if I don't drink his blood!"

"The bastard, the coward, the rat!"

"He thinks he's safe on the mountain!"

"He won't be safe anyplace but in his grave!"

"When I'd give him a coin, he used to kiss the ground!"

"He used to pretend to be nice and friendly toward us, now he's turned on us and killed our men!"

The next day, the whole alley was in mourning. The day after, all the gangsters met at Rifaat the overseer's house. He was boiling with rage and hatred, and spoke with bitter mockery. "Let's shut ourselves up in our alley, to keep death out!"

Lahita was the most humiliated of all of them, but he wanted to belittle the misadventure in order to minimize his responsibility. "What was it but a fight between a protector and some of the men in his territory!" he said.

"They killed one man from my area and wounded three," Galta protested.

"They killed one of ours," said Hagag.

"The real damage is to your reputation, as protector of the alley," said Rifaat slyly to Lahita, who turned pale with anger.

"A shepherd! I swear to God, you must be joking!"

"A shepherd!" repeated the overseer, no less seriously. "He was, but now he's a danger. We took his raving too lightly for too long, and overlooked him out of consideration for his wife, but his mischief is out of control now. He pretended to be poor until he was able to kill his gangster and his followers. Now he's holed up on the mountain, and his ambitions have no limits."

They exchanged angry looks, and the overseer resumed. "He is attracting people, and that is the tragedy of the alley. We cannot ignore that. He is promising the estate to people, even though the estate isn't big enough for its owners, but no one believes that; the beggars don't believe that, and there are enough of them! Our alley is an alley of beggars! He promises to end gang rule, and the cowards love that—and there are enough of them! It's an alley of cowards. The people will always side with the winner. If we do nothing, we're dead."

"He has a bunch of mice around him—we can wipe them out!" exclaimed Lahita.

"But aren't they up there on the mountain?" asked Hagag.

"We can watch the mountain until we find a way in," said Galta. "Just act. If we do nothing—as I said—we're dead."

Lahita grew even angrier, and addressed the overseer solemnly. "Do you remember, sir, that I planned to have him killed, when his wife was alive, and your wife was against it?"

The overseer unlocked his eyes from Lahita's, and spoke almost apologetically. "Remembering mistakes doesn't do any good." There was a long silence before he continued: "Besides, these relationships have been respected in our alley for a long time."

There was an unusually loud clamor outside, as if warning of renewed trouble. Their nerves tensed, and the overseer shouted for the gatekeeper and asked him what was going on.

"They're saying that the shepherd has joined Qassem, and driven all the sheep in the alley along with him!"

"The dog!" shouted Lahita, jumping to his feet. "This alley of dogs! Just wait!"

"What neighborhood was that shepherd from?" the overseer asked.

"From the Desert Rats. His name is Zuqla."

88

"*Welcome, Zuqla.*" Qassem embraced him.

"I was never against you," said the shepherd fervently. "My heart was always with you, and if I hadn't been afraid, I would have been one of the first people to join you. As soon as I heard that Sawaris had been killed—God send him to Hell!—I hurried to you, and I drove all your enemies' sheep ahead of me!"

Qassem looked at the mass of sheep in the clearing between the huts, where the women were watching and chatting delightedly, then laughed. "It is legitimate to take them, considering the property of ours they have stolen in the alley."

In the course of that day, an unprecedented number of people joined Qassem, strengthening the general resolve and bolstering morale. But Qassem woke up early the next morning to a strange uproar. He immediately went outside and saw his men coming toward his hut, quickly and with worried looks on their faces.

"The alley has come for revenge. They are massed below the passage."

"I was the first to go out to work," said Khurda. "I saw them when I was just a few steps away, and I ran back. Some of them chased me and hit me in the back with rocks. I began to shout for Sadeq and Hassan, until a group of our brothers came to the top of the passage. They saw the danger, and threw rocks at the attackers until they withdrew."

Qassem looked over at the opening of the passage and saw Hassan and some of the men standing there, clutching rocks. "We can hold them off there with ten men," he said.

"Coming up there will mean suicide for them," said Hamroush. "Let them come up if they want."

The men and women crowded around Qassem until all the huts were empty. The men brought their clubs, and the women had baskets of bricks that had been kept ready for a day like this. The first rays of light shone from the clear sky.

"Is there any other road to the city?" asked Qassem.

"There is a road to the south, two days' walk from the mountain," said Sadeq grimly.

"I don't think we have more than two days' worth of water," said Agrama.

An uneasy murmur ran through the crowd, especially from the women.

"They have come for revenge, not a siege," said Qassem. "If they surround us, we'll head for the other road to break the siege."

He began to think, keeping his face serene, for every eye was upon it. If they were besieged, they would have the greatest trouble bringing water by the southern road. If his men attacked them, could they be sure of success against such men as Lahita, Galta and Hagag? What destiny did this day have in store for them? He went back to his hut, and returned holding his club. He walked over to Hassan and his men at the opening of the passage.

"None of them will dare to come any closer," said Hassan.

Qassem stepped to the mountain ledge and saw his enemies gathered in a crescent-shaped formation in the desert, far out of rock-throwing range. Their sheer numbers were frightening, but he was unable to make out any gangsters among them. His gaze moved over the empty space to the mansion, Gabalawi's house, immersed in silence, as if oblivious to his children's struggle for his sake. How desperately they needed his supernatural strength, to which this place had submitted in the past. Perhaps he would not be assailed by anxiety, had it not been for Rifaa's murder so near his ancestor's house. He felt an urge, deep inside him, to shout "Gabalawi!" at the top of his voice, as the people of his alley did all the time, but he heard the voices of the women nearby, and turned to look around. He saw the men spreading out over the mountain ledge and watching their enemies, and the women heading for the same spots. He shouted for them to come back, and shouted again when they hesitated. He ordered them to prepare food and do their usual chores, and they obeyed him.

Sadeq came over to Qassem. "That was the right thing to do. The most worrisome thing for me is the power of Lahita's name over us."

"The only thing we can do is strike," said Hassan, shaking his club. "It will be impossible for us to go out and earn livings now that they know our hiding place. The only thing we can do is attack."

Qassem turned his head to look out toward the mansion. "What you say is true. What do you say, Sadeq?"

"Let's wait until nightfall."

"Waiting will only hurt us," said Hassan. "And darkness won't help us in battle."

"So what's their plan?"

"To force us to go down to them."

Qassem thought that over. "If Lahita is killed, victory is assured," he said, looking from one man to the other. "If he falls, Galta and Hagag will battle it out to succeed him."

As the sun rose higher, the gravelly ground blazed with the heat that radiated everywhere.

"Tell me, what will we do?" said Hassan. He meant: about the siege; but before anyone could answer, there was a shout from a woman in the square, immediately followed by other shouts.

"We're being attacked from the other side!" someone shouted.

The men abandoned the ledge and ran toward the southern side of the square. Qassem commanded the defenders at the passage to be even more alert, ordered Khurda to have capable women join the defenders of the passage, then ran, with Sadeq and Hassan on either side of him, to the center of his men in the square. Lahita was visible to all of them, leading a large gang of men coming from south of the mountain.

"He distracted us with his men, so that he could make his way around the mountain, to attack us by the southern road," raged Qassem.

"He is walking into his own death!" shouted Hassan, his massive body swelled up with enthusiasm.

"We must win, and we will win," said Qassem.

His men spread around him like two strong arms as the advancing force came closer, clubs in the air, looking like a patch of thorns. As they came nearer into view, Sadeq said, "Galta isn't with them. Neither is Hagag!"

Qassem realized that Galta and Hagag were leading the siege below the mountain, and guessed that they would attack the passage no matter what it cost them, though he confided his suspicions to no one. He took a few steps forward, brandishing his club, and his men gripped theirs.

Lahita's crude voice rang out. "You'll never get a burial service, you sons of whores!" he shouted.

Qassem and his men sped forward to attack, and the others flung themselves forward like a hail of stones, until their clubs clashed together, and raging and clamor grew loud. At the same time, bricks were launched at attacks below by the women defending the opening of the passage, but every one of Qassem's men was locked in battle with an enemy attacker. Qassem and Dingil fought hard and artfully. Lahita's club landed on Hamroush's collarbone, breaking it. Sadeq and Zainhum fought long and hard, but Hassan lashed out with his furious club, and Zainhum dropped. Lahita struck Zuqla, knocking him over. Qassem was able to wound Dingil on the ear, and the man screamed and retreated, then slumped over. Zainhum made a fierce lunge at Sadeq, but Sadeq speedily made a thrust at his belly that stopped his hands, then made a second thrust that dropped him. Khurda fought off Hafnawi, but Lahita crippled his arm before he could savor his victory. Hassan aimed a blow at Lahita, but he dodged it nimbly and raised his club to strike back. Before he could, Qassem swung his club, and their clubs clashed; like the wind, Abu Fisada came in to deliver a third blow, but Lahita butted him with his head and broke his nose; Lahita looked like a force that could not be resisted. The fighting grew fiercer, with the clubs batting one another relentlessly, a flood of curses and obscenities, and blood spurted in the fiery sun. Each side in turn lost men who dropped to the ground. Lahita burned with rage at this heroic resistance, which he had never expected, and redoubled his forays, his blows and his cruelty. On the other side, Qassem ordered Hassan and Agrama to seize the opportunity to join him attacking Lahita, to destroy the backbone that gave the attackers strength.

One of the women defending the opening of the passage suddenly came to shout, "They're coming up with dough boards for shields!"

The mountain men's hearts froze.

"You'll never get a burial service, you sons of whores!" shouted Lahita.

"Win before the criminals come up!" Qassem shouted to his men.

He went for Lahita, flanked by Hassan and Agrama. The gangster met him with a terrible blow he deflected with his club. Agrama wanted to anticipate him with a blow, but the gangster hit him on the chin, and he sprawled out on his face. Hassan jumped in front of him and they exchanged two blows; Hassan threw himself on him, and they were locked in a deadly struggle. The women at the passage began to scream, and some of them started to flee, endangering the position. Qassem quickly sent Sadeq and several men to the mountain ledge, then charged at Lahita, but Zihlifa blocked his way, and they engaged in violent combat. Hassan pushed Lahita back with all his strength, and he took one step back. He spat in Lahita's eye, roared and kicked him, crippling one of his knees. With lightning speed, Hassan attacked him, hunched low, and butted him in the stomach like a raging bull; the tyrant lost his balance and fell backward. Hassan knelt over him and slammed his club over his neck with both hands, pushing it down with all his strength. Men hurried over to defend their gangster, but Qassem and some of his men fought them off. Lahita kicked his feet, his eyes bulged and his face was bright with blood. He began to choke. Suddenly Hassan leaped up to stand over his powerless adversary, and swung his club in a wild, furious blow, smashing Lahita's skull, killing him.

"Lahita is dead!" he thundered. "Your protector is dead! Look at his corpse!"

Lahita's unexpected death had a violent effect, as the fighters' resolution either flared up or waned, and hope and despair drove the bitter fighting. Hassan joined Qassem in his struggle, and not one of his blows failed. Men sprang out and stood firm, and clubs were swung and then brought down. The dust rose and blew away, and combatants were seized by a bloody daze. Their lungs spewed curses, screams, obscenities, moans and menacing yells. Every few moments a man staggered and fell, or retreated and fled. The field was covered with the fallen, and blood glistened in the sunlight. Qassem turned aside to look over at the opening of the passage, which preyed on his mind, and saw Sadeq and his men passing down stones in baskets with a fervid tension that indicated the approach of mounting danger. He heard the women, his wife among them, as they screamed for help. He saw some of Sadeq's men hefting their clubs in preparation for meeting the enemies who would ascend through the downpour of stones. He assessed the danger, at once started toward Lahita's body, for the battle had moved away from it as the men from the alley had pulled back, and dragged it behind him toward the opening of the passage. He shouted for Sadeq, who hurried to him, and they both took up the corpse and carried it to the beginning of the passage. They heaved it together and threw it, and it landed, then rolled down and stopped at the feet of the climbers holding the boards, throwing them into confusion.

Hagag's voice reverberated as he shouted in rage. "Forward! Climb! Death to the criminals!"

"Forward!" shouted Qassem scornfully, with strange self-control. "This is your protector's corpse, and your other men's corpses are behind me. Forward! We are waiting for you!"

He gave the men and women a sign, and rocks flew like rain until the attackers' vanguard halted and then began to retreat slowly, despite the urging of Hagag and Galta. Qassem could hear the babble of argument, protest and complaint.

"Galta!" Qassem called. "Hagag! Come forward—don't run!"

"Come down, if you are men!" Galta bawled hatefully. "Come down, you women, you bastards!"

Hagag, standing amidst a wave of retreating men, shouted, "I won't live any longer without drinking your blood, you stinking shepherd!"

Qassem picked up a stone and threw it with all his might. The rain of stones continued, and the retreating wave moved more quickly, until almost everyone was carried along. Hassan came up and wiped the streaming blood from his forehead.

"The battle's over," he said. "The survivors have fled south."

"Call the men to follow them!" said Qassem.

"You're bleeding from the teeth and chin!" Sadeq pointed out.

He wiped his mouth and chin with his palm, spread it out and saw that it was bright red.

"They killed eight of us," said Hassan sadly. "Our survivors are badly wounded and won't be able to move."

He looked down through the hail of stones to see his enemies racing through the end of the passage.

"If they had kept coming, they wouldn't have found anyone to resist them here," said Sadeq. He kissed Qassem's bloody chin and said gratefully, "Your brain saved us!"

Qassem ordered two men to stand guard at the top of the passage, and sent others to pursue the retreating force and to reconnoiter, then walked back, between Sadeq and Hassan, as they limped wearily and heavily to the square, on whose surface nothing was left but corpses. It had been a massacre, and what a massacre! Eight of his men had been killed, and ten of his enemies, not counting Lahita. None of his living men had been spared a broken bone or wound. They had made their way back to their huts, where the women began to bandage their wounds, while the huts of the dead were loud with shouts and sobs. Badriya came, grief-stricken, and had them come into the hut so that she could wash their wounds, then Sakina came carrying Ihsan, who was shrieking with tears. The sun, at its zenith, flung its fire below as the kites and crows circled and dipped in the hot air, which reeked of blood and earth. Ihsan did not stop crying, but no one paid attention to her. Even the giant Hassan seemed to be tottering.

"God have mercy on our dead," murmured Sadeq.

"God have mercy on the dead and the living too," said Qassem.

Suddenly awakening to a kind of rapture, Hassan said, "Soon we will have victory, and our alley will say farewell to its age of blood and terror."

"Down with terror and blood," said Qassem.

89

The alley had never known a catastrophe like this. The men returned silent, dazed and feeble, their eyes cast down, as if studying the surface of the ground. They found that news of the defeat had preceded them to the alley, and that their homes resounded with wailing and the smacking of cheeks in mourning. The news spread through every lane and alley, making the alley's imposing reputation the gloating gossip of every vengeful tongue. It came to light that the Desert Rats had entirely evacuated their neighborhood from fear of revenge: the houses and shops were empty, and no one doubted that they had all joined their victorious compatriot, increasing his numbers and strength. Sorrow descended over the whole mourning-dulled alley, but its hot breath dripped with resentment, loathing and lust for revenge. The men of Gabal wondered who would be the next protector of the alley, and everyone in Rifaa wondered the same thing. Distrust spread like dust in a gale. The overseer, Rifaat, learned what mutters were circulating, and summoned Galta and Hagag to a meeting. They came, each surrounded by his toughest men, so that the overseer's reception hall was overcrowded. Each group occupied one side of the hall, as if neither felt safe mixing with the other any longer. The overseer was not slow to see the significance of this, and it made him even more worried.

"You know that we have suffered a catastrophe, but we have survived," he said. "It has not stopped us. We are still capable of achieving victory with our own hands, as long as we maintain our unity. Otherwise we are finished."

"We will strike the last blow," said one of the men of Gabal, "and then we will never have this problem again."

"If they had not taken refuge on the mountain, they would all be dead," said Hagag.

"Lahita engaged them after a long, terrible journey that would have brought a camel to its knees," said a third man.

"Tell me about your unity—how united are you?" asked the overseer irritably.

"We are brothers, by God's grace, and always will be," Galta said.

"That's what you say, but the way you came here in these numbers is a sign of the distrust that divides you."

"That's because of the revenge that we all want," Hagag said.

The overseer stood tensely, and gazed at the rows of somber faces.

"Be frank. You are all watching each other with one eye, and have the other on Lahita's empty position. The alley will never be safe as long as this is the case. The worst thing would be for the thing to be settled with clubs. You would all be ruined, and Qassem would eat you for breakfast."

"God forbid—never!" many of them shouted.

"The alley has only two neighborhoods now, Gabal and Rifaa. We can have two protectors. There is no need to have just one. Let us commit ourselves to that, so that we can act as one against the rebels."

Dreadful moments of silence passed, then several voices spoke in tepid agreement.

"Yes . . . yes."

"We will go along with that," said Galta, "even though we have been the elect of this alley since earliest history."

"We will accept, but no one is doing us a favor," protested Hagag. "There are no masters or servants here, especially since the Desert Rats are gone. Who could deny, after all, that Rifaa was the noblest man this alley ever saw?"

"Hagag!" objected Galta resentfully. "I know what you're getting at."

One of the Al Rifaa was about to say something, but the overseer began to shout angrily. "Tell me! Have you made up your minds to act like men, or not? If any word of your weakness gets out, the Desert Rats will march down the mountain like wolves. Tell me, are you able to agree and stand together, or should I make other plans?"

The answer was scattered.

"Shhhhhh!"

"Shame!"

"The alley is going to lose everything!"

Eventually they all looked at him resignedly.

"You still have better numbers and greater strength, but don't attack the mountain again." Their faces were questioning. "We will imprison them up there on the mountain. We will occupy the two roads that lead to the mountain, and they will either starve to death or be forced to come down to you, and you will kill them."

"Good idea," said Galta. "I pointed that out to Lahita, God rest his soul, but he considered sieges cowardly and insisted on attacking."

"That's the idea," said Hagag. "But we have to delay doing it until the men are rested."

The overseer asked them to commit themselves to brotherhood and cooperation, and they all shook hands and swore they would. In the days that followed, it became clear to anyone who could see that Galta and Hagag were much harder on their followers, to hide the effect of the defeat they had suffered. They spread the word in the alley that if it had not been for Lahita's stupidity, they could have destroyed Qassem easily; his insistence on going up the mountain had exhausted the men and strained their strength and courage—they had met the enemy in terrible shape. The people believed what they were told, and anyone who showed skepticism was cursed, insulted and beaten. No one was allowed to get into discussions about the leading position in the alley, at least publicly, but many people—of both Gabal and Rifaa—debated, in the drug dens, who would replace Lahita after the victory. Despite the agreement and all the oaths, an atmosphere of secret suspicion had taken root in the alley. Every gangster kept himself surrounded, and never went far from his base without a crowd of his men. But preparations for the day of revenge never stopped for a moment. They agreed among themselves that Galta and his men would camp at the Muqattam Road, at the marketplace, Hagag and his men would camp at the Citadel Road, and neither group would leave their positions at all, even if it meant spending the rest of their lives there. Their womenfolk would take over the buying and selling, and would bring them food. In the evening of the day before they were supposed to head out, they gathered in all the drug dens. They brought flasks of wine and liquor, and drank and smoked hashish until late that night. Hagag's men said goodbye to him in front of his building in Rifaa; he was in a state of superb pleasure and relaxation. He pushed open the door and walked down the hallway, humming "First we—" but he never finished. A figure seized him from behind, clapped a hand over his mouth and with the other hand drove a knife into his heart. The body shuddered powerfully in his arms, but, not wanting to let it drop and make a sound, he laid it down gently on the floor, where it did not move in the gloomy shadows.

90

The alley awoke early the next morning to a startling outburst of screams. Windows flew open and heads popped out, and people ran toward the building where Hagag, the protector of the Rifaa community, lived, where a numerous crowd had gathered. Wails of mourning were interrupted by shouts, and the hall of the building was filled with men and women making comments and asking questions; eyes red with weeping warned of truly perilous mischief. The people of Rifaa ran from every building, every house and basement, and before long Galta and his men came. People made way for them until they reached the hall.

"This is the most horrible thing!" Galta shouted. "If only it could have been me instead, Hagag!"

People who were crying stopped crying, the shouters stopped shouting and the morbidly curious stopped asking questions, but he did not hear one kindly word.

"Despicable plots!" he resumed. "Gangsters don't betray one another, but Qassem is a shepherd, a beggar, not a gangster, and I will never rest until I've thrown his corpse to the dogs."

"Congratulations, Galta, you're the new gangster of the alley!" shouted a grief-stricken woman.

His features contracted angrily, and the people near him fell silent, but farther back there was a wave of grumbling.

"Let women keep their mouths shut on this tragic day!"

"Let everyone who's got a mind understand!" the woman said.

The grumbling rose into a lively babble, and Galta waited for this storm to die down before speaking again. "This is a sly conspiracy, carried out at night, to sow dissension among us!"

"Conspiracy!" said another woman. "Qassem and his Desert Rats are on the mountain, and Hagag was killed in his house, among his own people and his neighbors, who want to take over!"

"Crazy bitch! All of you are crazy if you think like that, and if you do, we'll all be killing one another the way Qassem plotted we should!"

A jug landed and shattered at Galta's feet, and he and his men stepped back.

"The son of a whore knew how to sow dissension among us," he said.

He left for the overseer's house, but the clamor only grew after he was gone. Two men—one of Rifaa, the other of Gabal—got into a violent argument, and were immediately imitated by two women. Boys from both neighborhoods started fighting, people began swearing matches from the windows and riot spread through the alley until each neighborhood's men massed with their clubs. The overseer came out of his house, surrounded by his men and servants, and strode out to the dividing line between the two districts.

"Come to your senses!" he shouted. "Anger will blind you to your real enemy, Hagag's killer!"

"Who told you that?" shouted one of the men of Rifaa. "What Desert Rat would dare enter this alley?"

"How could they kill Hagag today, when they needed him so much?" Rifaat shouted.

"Ask the criminals, don't ask us."

"The people of Rifaa will not obey a gangster of Gabal."

"They will pay dearly for his blood."

"Don't serve the conspiracy," said the overseer, "or you'll be seeing Qassem come in here like a plague!"

"Let him come if he wants, but Galta will not rule us as protector." The overseer wrung his hands. "We are finished! We will be ruined."

"Ruin is better than Galta!" they yelled.

A brick was thrown from Rifaa and landed among the assembled men of Gabal. Someone from Gabal responded in kind, and the overseer quickly withdrew. Bricks began to fly in both directions, and in no time a bloody battle had broken out between the two neighborhoods. Cruel blows were struck, and fighting spread to some roofs, where women pelted each other with bricks, stones, dirt and pieces of wood. The clash lasted a long time, despite the fact that the people of Rifaa were fighting without their gangster; but they lost many casualties to Galta's lethal blows. Women's voices now shrieked from windows, a noise that could not be heard above the chaos of the battle, though they could be seen pointing in terror, now to the east end of the alley, now to the other end. The people turned to see what the women were pointing at, and saw Qassem in front of the mansion, leading a band of men with clubs. At the other end was Hassan, leading more men; the place rang with screams of warning, and then everything happened very quickly. As if paralyzed, people stopped throwing punches. On a spontaneous impulse, they intermingled and re-formed, the fighters and the fought, and divided up into two detachments to confront the newcomers.

"I said it was a plot, and you didn't believe me!" shouted Galta furiously.

They prepared for battle, though they were now in the worst state of strain and hopelessness. But Qassem suddenly halted, and so did Hassan, as if they were executing a single plan.

"We do not want to harm anyone," cried Qassem as loudly as he could. "We want no winner and no loser. We are all a people with one alley and one ancestor, and the estate belongs to all."

"It's a new plot!" shouted Galta.

"Don't push them to fight to defend your gang rule. Defend it yourself, if you want to."

"Attack!" bellowed Galta.

He charged at Qassem's men, and his men followed. Others attacked Hassan and his men, but many held back. Some who were wounded or exhausted slipped into their houses, and were followed by the hesitant others. Only Galta and his band of men were left, but even so they plunged into a ferocious battle and fought a desperate defensive fight, battering one another with clubs, heads, feet and hands. Galta concentrated his attack on Qassem with blind hatred. They exchanged violent blows, but Qassem met his adversary's blows with his club, nimbly and cautiously. With their superior numbers, his men surrounded Galta's gang, who fell under dozens of clubs. Hassan and Sadeq set upon Galta as he fought with Qassem; Sadeq struck his club, and Hassan landed his club on Galta's head, then a second time, and a third. The club dropped from his hand, and he bounded up like a slaughtered bull, then collapsed on his face like a gate slamming shut. The battle was over. The crack of clubs and shouts of men fell silent. The victors stood up, out of breath, wiping the blood from their heads, faces and hands, but their mouths were bright with smiles of victory and peace. Wailing could be heard from the windows, Galta's men were scattered on the ground and the brilliant sun shed its fierce rays.

"You have won," Sadeq told Qassem, confident and assured. "God gave you victory; our ancestor does not err when he chooses. Our alley will never mourn again after today."

Qassem smiled serenely and turned resolutely to look at the overseer's house, but all their heads were turned to him.

91

Qassem walked ahead of his men to the overseer's house, and found it
steeped in silence and gloom, its gate and windows locked. Hassan
knocked forcefully at the gate, but no one answered. Some of the men
clustered against the gate and shoved it until both panels flew open, and
Qassem entered, his men following behind. There was no sign of the
gatekeeper or any of the servants. They hurried to the hall, checking all
of the rooms on the way, then searched all three floors, but it was clear
to them that the overseer, his family and his servants had fled the house.
And the truth was that Qassem was not sorry, because deep inside he
had no wish to murder the overseer, in deference to Lady Amina,
without whom he would have been killed at the outset. Hassan and the
others were furious, however, at the deliverance of the man who had
forced poverty and dishonor on the alley for as long as he had ruled it.

This was how Qassem triumphed and became the uncontested master of the alley. He took over the running of the estate, since the estate
had to have an overseer. The Desert Rats went home to their territory,
and were joined by everyone who had emigrated from the alley out of
fear of the gangsters, and chief among these was Yahya. There were forty
days of peace, during which wounds healed, spirits calmed down and
hearts came to feel secure. And one day Qassem stood before the mansion and summoned all the people of the alley to come to him, men and
women, from all the neighborhoods, and they came, anxious and curious, their hearts pounding with every kind of notion. They filled the
square, Desert Rats mingling with all the Al Gabal and Al Rifaa. Qassem
smiled gently and humbly, and yet grandly, and pointed up to the
mansion.

"Gabalawi lives here," he said. "He is ancestor of us all. He knows no distinction between any of his children, between neighborhoods or individuals, between men and women."

Their faces were bright and surprised with joy, especially those faces that had expected to hear the treatise of a man who had conquered and taken over.

"His estate is all around you. It belongs to all of you equally, as he promised when he told Adham, 'The estate will belong to your children.' It is up to us to utilize it the best way possible so that it will provide for everyone, and prosper, so that we may live the way Adham wanted to live, abundantly blessed and nourished, totally secure and truly happy."

The people looked at one another as if they were dreaming.

"The overseer is gone and will never be back, and the gangsters have disappeared; they will never again be seen in our alley. You will never again pay protection money to a tyrant or submit to any barbarous bully. You will live in peace, mercy and love."

His eyes scanned their delighted faces.

"It is up to you whether or not things go back to the way they were. Watch your overseer, and if he betrays you, remove him. If any one of you resorts to violence, strike him. If any person or community claims to be above the rest, punish them. This is the only way you can guarantee that things do not go back to the way they were. God be with you."

That day some people were consoled for their dead, and others for their defeat. Everyone looked to tomorrow as if it were the appearance of the full moon of a spring night. Qassem distributed the estate revenue among everyone justly, after setting aside an amount for building and renovation. Yes, each person's share was small, but he enjoyed unbounded feelings of justice and respect. Qassem devoted his tenure to building, rebuilding and peace. Our alley had never before known the unity, harmony and happiness that it enjoyed. Yes, there were some of the Al Gabal who harbored feelings they did not make public; they whispered among themselves, "Are we of the Al Gabal, and ruled by one of the Desert Rats?" And there were some like them among the Al Rifaa. And indeed there were those of the Desert Rats who succumbed to pride and arrogance, but no voice was raised to disturb the peace while Qassem was alive. The Desert Rats saw in him a kind of man that had never existed before and would never be again. He combined power and gentleness, wisdom and simplicity, dignity and love, mastery and humility, efficiency and honesty. In addition, he was witty, friendly and good-looking, kind and companionable. He had good taste, he loved to sing and he told jokes. Nothing about him changed, though his marital life expanded, as if it were following the same course of renewal and expansion that the estate took. While he loved Badriya, he married a beauty of the Al Gabal and another of the Al Rifaa. He fell in love with a woman of his own clan, and married her too. People said that in this he was looking for something he had lost when he lost his first wife, Qamar. His Uncle Zachary said that he wanted to strengthen his ties with all the different neighborhoods of the alley, but our alley needed no explanation or justification for what he did. The fact is that they admired his vigor even more than they admired his character; in our alley, the love of women is a power in which men lose themselves. They brag about it. It imparts a status that equals that of gangsterdom, in its time, or even surpasses it.

However that may be, our alley had never known its true sovereignty, never felt that it could be independent, without an exploiting overseer or a gangster to humble the people. It had never before known the brotherhood, friendship and peace of Qassem's time.

Many people said that if the plague of our alley had been forgetfulness, it was now free of that plague, and would be free of it forever.

That is what they said.

That is what they said, Gabalawi Alley!

Arafa

92

No one contemplating the state of our alley would ever believe what the poets say in the coffeehouses. Who are Gabal and Rifaa and Qassem? What sign is there, besides the coffeehouse stories, that any of them accomplished anything? All the eye can see is an alley sunk in darkness and poets that sing of dreams. How did this happen to us? Where is Qassem and the united alley, and the estate to be used for everyone's good? Where did this greedy overseer and his insane gangsters come from? You will hear, around the pipe passed from hand to hand in the hashish dens, between the sighs and the laughter, how Sadeq succeeded Qassem as overseer, and followed the same course; how one group saw Hassan was worthier to be overseer, because he had been related to Qassem and since he was the man who had killed the gangsters. They urged Hassan to raise his club, which no one could withstand, but he refused to return the alley to the era of the gangsters. The alley had been divided among itself, however, and now some of the Al Gabal and Al Rifaa began to say out loud what they used to keep secret. When Sadeq left this life, repressed ambitions revealed their ugly faces and hostile looks. The clubs came out of hibernation, and the blood flowed within every neighborhood, and in fights between neighborhoods, until the overseer himself was killed in one of the battles. Things got out of control, security and peace were buried; the people saw no alternative to bringing back a scion of the old overseer, Rifaat, to be overseer, the position over which so many ambitious men were fighting. This was how Qadri came to be overseer, and the neighborhoods resumed their old clannishness, as each was taken over by a gang, and battles raged over who would rule the whole alley, until Saadallah won. He occupied the protector's house and became the first overseer,

while Yusuf took over the Al Gabal, Agag the Al Rifaa and Santuri the
Al Qassem. At first the overseer distributed the estate revenues honestly,
and the rebuilding and renovation activity continued, but before long
greed began to toy with his heart, and the same with the gangsters, as
expected; and they went back to the old system. The overseer took half
the estate income and divided the other half among the four gangsters,
who kept it instead of giving it to its rightful owners. They did not stop
there, but insolently forced their miserable followers to pay protection
money. This brought a halt to construction activity, and stopped work
on houses that were only half or even a quarter finished. It seemed that
nothing had changed since the old days, though the Desert Rats' territory had now become the Al Qassem neighborhood. It was ruled by a
gangster like the others, its buildings were surrounded by huts and ruins,
and its people had gone back to being what they had been in the black
days, enjoying no honor or sovereignty. They were worn down by
poverty, menaced by clubs and constantly being slapped. Filth, flies and
lice were everywhere, and there was no end of beggars, swindlers and
cripples. Gabal, Rifaa and Qassem were nothing but names, or songs
chanted by drugged poets in the coffeehouses. Every group was proud
of its man, of whom nothing was left, and competed to the point of
quarreling and fistfights. Drunken slogans were passed around; going
into a drug den, a man might say, "It's no good," meaning the world,
not the drug den. Another might say, "There's one way out, death—
better God should get you than a gangster's club. The best thing is to
get drunk or smoke hashish." They sang sad popular songs about depression, poverty and disgrace, or chanted filthy, obscene ditties, bellowing them into the ears of the women and men who sought comfort
or amusement even in these low, dark dumps. When one of them felt
especially tormented, he would say, "What's written is written. What
good is Gabal, or Rifaa, or Qassem. We're flies in this world and dirt in
the next." How strange that our alley should have remained the most
favored among all the alleys. Men in neighboring alleys pointed to us
and said admiringly, "Gabalawi Alley!" while we squatted solemnly,
gloomily, as if hypnotized by our cherished memories of the past, or
listening raptly to an unseen voice within us, softly whispering, "It is

not impossible for what happened yesterday to happen again tomorrow, or for the dreams of poets to come true once more, or for darkness to recede from our world."

93

One day, in the early afternoon, the alley spotted a foreign young man walking in from the desert, followed by another who seemed to be a dwarf. He was wearing a gray galabiya and nothing underneath, and a belt around his waist that divided his galabiya in half—the upper half bulged and sagged with the things inside. He wore faded and worn-out red leather shoes, and there was no hat on his thick, disheveled hair. His skin was dark and his eyes were round and alert, with an eager and penetrating look, and there was a certain confidence in the way he moved. He stopped for a moment in front of the mansion, then walked slowly on, followed by his friend. Everyone looked at him as if to say, "A stranger in the alley! How insolent!" He read the same look in the eyes of the peddlers, shop owners, the men sitting in the coffeehouses and women watching from the windows; even in the eyes of the dogs and cats. It seemed to him that even the flies avoided him out of scornful protest. Boys turned provocatively toward him, and some of them walked close to him, while others loaded their slingshots or searched the ground for a stone to throw. He smiled warmly at them and slipped his hand into his breast pocket. He drew out some mints and began to give them out, and the boys came closer to him gladly, sucking the mints and staring at him curiously. He smiled as he spoke to them.

"Is there a basement for rent around here? Come on, men—the one who finds me one will get a bag of mints."

"A thousand misfortunes on you!" snapped a woman sitting on the ground in front of a building. "Who are you to live in our alley?"

"Arafa, at your service." He laughed. "A native of your alley, like the rest of you, coming home after a long absence."

She stared at him closely. "Whose son are you? You must be your mother's favorite."

He laughed very hard, overdoing it slightly, but politely. "Gahsha, of fond memory. Did you know her, dear lady?"

"Gahsha? 'We read the future well!' Her?"

"The very same."

There was a woman nearby, leaning against a wall and following their conversation, picking lice from a boy's head. "You used to follow your mother around back then, when you were a boy," she said. "I still remember you. Everything about you has changed, except for your eyes."

"Yes, by God," said the first woman. "Where is your mother? She's dead! God rest her soul. I used to sit in front of her basket asking about the future, and she'd whisper and see my fortune in the shells she threw, and then she'd tell me. God rest your soul, Gahsha!"

"God bless you," he said gratefully. "God willing, *you* can guide me to a vacant basement."

She peered at him with bleary eyes and asked, "What brings you back here after all this time?"

"Every living thing journeys back to its home and family," he said, imitating the accent of a learned man.

She pointed to a building in Rifaa. "There's a basement there that's been vacant since the tenant died in a fire, God rest her soul. Does that bother you?"

A woman listening from her window laughed. "The demons themselves are afraid of this man," she said.

He lifted his face, which was pleasant with laughter. "My sweet alley! Who is funnier or sweeter than my people? Now I know why my mother told me on her deathbed to come back here." He looked at the woman sitting on the ground. "We're all going to die, my late mother's customer—from fire, drowning, demons or clubs."

He saluted her and walked to the building she had indicated, with everyone watching him.

"We know his mother—who knows his father?" one man said ironically.

"God has not willed that we know," said an old woman.

"He can claim that he's the son of a man of Gabal, or Rifaa, or Qassem, however he wants, or will do him the most good. God rest his mother's soul!"

"Why did you bring us back to this alley?" his companion whispered irritably in his ear.

Arafa smiled still as he answered. "I hear this kind of talk everywhere, and anyway this is our alley, and this is the only alley we can live in. We've done enough wandering around the markets and sleeping in the desert and in slums. Besides, these are good people, even if they have dirty tongues; and pretty stupid, clubs or no clubs. We'll make a good living here. Remember that, Hanash."

Hanash shrugged his narrow shoulders, as if to say, "It's in God's hands."

A drunk blocked their way. "What do we call you?"

"Arafa."

"Arafa what?"

"Arafa ibn Gahsha!"

All the bystanders shook with laughter, delighted at his fatherless humiliation.

"We always used to wonder, back then when your mother was pregnant, who the father could be. Did she ever tell you the truth?"

Arafa masked his pain with even more laughter, and said, "She died before she ever found out herself!" He walked away, leaving them laughing, and news of his return spread through the alley. Before he had rented the basement, a boy from the Al Rifaa neighborhood coffeehouse came to him.

"Agag, the protector of the alley, is asking for you."

He went to the coffeehouse, which was not far from his building. As soon as he came near, a picture painted on the rear wall, above the poet's bench, caught his attention. It was a picture of Agag mounted on his horse, below a likeness of the overseer, Qadri, with his splendid mustache and elegant cloak. Above that was a scene with Rifaa's body in Gabalawi's arms, as the old man was lifting it from the grave to take to his mansion. He studied the picture eagerly but quickly, then entered

the coffeehouse and saw Agag sitting on a bench in the middle of the
right wall, surrounded by his followers and subordinates.

Arafa walked over to him until he stood before the gangster, who
offered him a long, disdainful stare, as if to put him in a trance before
striking. Arafa raised both hands to his head. "Greetings, blessings on
our protector! We seek refuge in you, and rejoice in your presence."

Mockery glinted in the man's narrow eyes. "Pretty words, Gahsha's
boy, but pretty words aren't the only coin we recognize here!"

"I'll have the other kind of coin very soon, God willing," Arafa said,
smiling.

"We already have more beggars than we need!"

"I am no beggar, sir." Arafa laughed, but arrogantly. "I am a magician known to millions of people!"

The seated men exchanged glances, and Agag scowled. "What do
you mean? Are you crazy?"

Arafa stuck his hand into his breast pocket and drew out a delicate
little box the size of a lotus fruit. With his outstretched hand he offered it
submissively to Qadri, who took it disinterestedly and opened it. He saw
a black substance inside and took a close look at it.

"A grain of that in a cup of tea two hours before, well, you know,
no offense, and after that, either you will be happy with your servant
Arafa or you can kick him out of the alley with every curse you know."

For the first time, everybody craned their necks eagerly, and even
Agag could not hide his interest, though he spoke with sham disdain.
"This is your magic?"

"I also have rare incense, exotic herbs, treatments and cures and
charms. My power is best known for sickness, barrenness and debilita-
tion."

"Well, well!" said Agag in what sounded like a threat. "We will be
waiting to see your protection money."

Arafa's heart skipped a beat, but his face grew even more cheerful.
"Everything I own is yours, sir."

Suddenly the gangster laughed. "But you haven't told us who your
father is!"

"Maybe you already know!" said Arafa, still smiling.

Everyone in the coffeehouse laughed, and jeering comments filled the smoke-clouded air. When Arafa had left the coffeehouse, he said to himself resentfully, "Who knows who his father really was? Not you, Agag. Bastards!"

He and Hanash inspected the basement, satisfied. "It's roomier than I'd expected," he said. "It's just right, Hanash. This room will be good for having company, and the one in the back for a bedroom, and the last one for work."

"I wonder which room that woman burned to death in," said Hanash a little uneasily.

Arafa's loud laughter rang against the empty walls. "Are you afraid of demons, Hanash? We work with them the same way Gabal worked with snakes." He looked contentedly around him. "We only have one window in the room on the street. We'll see the street from below through the window with the iron bars. This tomb has one fabulous advantage—it can't be robbed."

"It might be ransacked."

"*Might!*" Then he sighed. "All I do is help people, but all my life I've got nothing but insults."

"Success will make up for all the harm you've suffered," said Hanash, "and the suffering of your late mother."

94

When he had leisure time, he loved to sit on an old sofa and watch what was going on through the window that looked out on the alley. He sat with his forehead against the bars of the window, his eyes level with the surface of the alley, with its rush of feet, wheels, dogs, cats, insects and children. He never saw people's torsos or faces unless he crouched and raised his head. A naked child stood in front of him, playing with a dead rat; an old blind man walked by, carrying in his left hand a wooden platter heaped with seeds, beans, sweets and drowsy flies, and a thick cane in his right; the sound of wailing came from another basement window; two men were fighting, and blood ran down their faces.

He smiled at the naked boy. "What's your name?" he asked gently.

"Una."

"Hassuna, you mean. Do you like your dead rat, Hassuna?"

He threw it at Arafa, and had it not been for the bars it would have hit him in the face. The boy ran away, and Arafa turned to Hanash, who was dozing at his feet.

"You see signs of the gangsters in every inch of this alley, but you don't see a single sign of people like Gabal or Rifaa or Qassem."

Hanash yawned. "We see people like Saadallah, Yusuf, Agag and Santuri, but all we hear about are Gabal and Rifaa and Qassem," he said.

"But they did exist, right?"

Hanash pointed to the floor of the room. "This building is in Rifaa. Everyone who lives in it is of the Al Rifaa. They belong to Rifaa, and every night the poets remind us that he lived and died for love and happiness. And we have breakfast every morning listening to their screaming and fights. That's how they are—men and women both."

Arafa curled his lip, annoyed. "But they did exist, right?"

"And screaming is the least of what goes on in Rifaa. The battles— God help you from them. Only yesterday one of them lost an eye."

"Strange alley!" said Arafa sharply. "Rest in peace, Mother. Look at us, for example. Everybody uses us, and no one respects us! They don't respect anybody." He set his teeth. "Except the gangsters."

Hanash laughed. "It's enough that you're the only person in the alley that everyone does business with—from Gabal, Rifaa and Qassem."

"God damn them all." He was silent a few moments, his eyes bright in the dim light of the basement, then said, "Each of them is so stupidly, so blindly proud of its man—all proud of men of whom nothing is left but their names. And they never make any attempt to go one step beyond that false pride! Bastards. Cowards."

His first customer was a woman of the Al Rifaa, who came in the first week after he had moved into his basement. "How can I get rid of a woman without anyone knowing?" she asked in a subdued voice.

He was alarmed, and looked at her in surprise. "I don't do that, ma'am. If you want medicine for the body or spirit, I am at your service."

"Aren't you a magician?" she asked dubiously.

"In everything that does good for people. For killing, there are other people who do that."

"Maybe you're afraid. But we would be partners, with one secret."

"That wasn't Rifaa's way," he said with gentleness that contained a hint of mockery.

"Rifaa!" she exclaimed. "God have mercy on him. We live in an alley where mercy doesn't do any good. If it was any good, Rifaa wouldn't have been killed."

She left him, in despair, but he was not sorry. Rifaa himself—the best man that ever was—had never found safety in this alley; how could he aspire to it if he began his work with a crime? And his mother! How she had suffered, she who had never harmed anyone. He had to have good relations with everyone, as befitted every decent businessman. He began to frequent all the coffeehouses, and in every one of them he found a customer he knew. He listened to the poets' stories in every neighborhood until they all mingled in his head, and made it spin.

His first customer from the Al Qassem neighborhood was an elderly man, who smiled and whispered to him. "We heard about the gift you gave Agag, the protector of Rifaa."

He smiled at the wrinkled face of the old man, who spoke again. "Give us what you have, and don't be surprised. Believe me, I'm still alive!"

They both smiled at the secret, and the old man was encouraged.

"You're one of the Al Qassem, aren't you? That's what the people in our neighborhood think."

"Do they know who my father is?"

"The Al Qassem are known by their looks!" said the man earnestly. "You are one of us. We are the ones who raised this alley up to the peak of justice and happiness, but, what a pity, it's an ill-omened alley." Then he remembered why he had come. "The gift, please." The old man departed, holding the box close to his weak eyes, with new hope, energy and spring in his feeble gait.

Arafa's most recent visitor was an unexpected one. He was sitting on a cushion in the reception room, behind an incense burner exhaling delicate, bewitching smoke, when Hanash came in with an old Nubian man. "Yunis is the gatekeeper for his excellency the overseer," he said.

Arafa immediately stood up and offered both his hands in welcome. "Welcome! Welcome! It's like a visit from the Prophet! Have a seat, sir!"

They all sat down together, and the gatekeeper spoke with typical Nubian frankness. "Lady Nazira, the overseer's wife, cannot sleep because of bad dreams."

Arafa's eyes showed clear interest, and hope and ambition made his heart beat faster, but he said simply, "That's a temporary condition. It will go away."

"But the lady is very disturbed. She sent me to you to find something that would help."

Arafa felt a happiness and control he had never known in all the wandering life he had been used to with his late mother. "The best thing would be if I could talk to her myself."

"Impossible!" said the gatekeeper sharply. "She will not come to you, and you must not go to her."

Arafa repressed his despair in order to pursue this golden opportunity. "Then I need her handkerchief, or something else of hers."

The gatekeeper bowed his turbaned head and got up to go. When they reached the basement door, the gatekeeper paused, then moved close to Arafa's ear and whispered, "We have heard about your gift to Agag, the protector of Rifaa."

When the gatekeeper had left with the gift, Arafa and Hanash laughed for a long time.

"Whom do you think he took the gift for?" Hanash asked. "For himself, or the overseer, or maybe the overseer's wife?"

"An alley of gifts and clubs!" jeered Arafa. He moved to the window to look out on the alley at night. The opposite wall was silver in the moonlight, the crickets were chirping loudly and the voice of the local poet rose from the coffeehouse.

"And Adham asked, 'When are you going to realize that you and I have nothing to say to one another?' And Idris said, 'Heaven forgive us, aren't you my brother? That's a bond that can never be broken.' 'Idris! You've done enough to me.' 'Sorrow stinks, but we're both bereaved. You lost Humam and Qadri, and I lost Hind—now the great Gabalawi has a whore for a granddaughter and a murderer grandson.' And Adham's voice rose in a roar. 'If the punishment you get isn't as horrible as the things you've done, I hope the world drops into Hell!' "

Arafa turned wearily away from the window. *When will our alley stop telling its tales? When will the world go to Hell? Once upon a time my mother used to say, "If the punishment does not fit the crime, let the world go to Hell!" My poor mother, who dwelled in the desert. But what good have the tales done you, poor alley?*

95

Arafa and Hanash were hard at work in the rear basement room by the light of a gas lamp fixed in the wall. The room was too dark and damp to be habitable, and was all the way in the back of the basement, so Arafa had made it into his workroom. On the floor and in the corners of the room lay collections of paper amulets, dust and lime, plants and spices, dried animals and insects such as mice, frogs and scorpions. There were piles of glass pieces, long-necked bottles, tin cans of fluids and strange, strong-smelling liquids. There was charcoal and a stove, and the shelves that had been installed on the walls held all kinds of vessels, containers and bags. Arafa was absorbed in a mixture of certain substances which he was kneading in a large ceramic vessel. Sweat dripped from his forehead, and every so often he wiped it with the sleeve of his galabiya.

Hanash was reclining nearby and watching closely, ready to obey any order he might be given. He spoke as if to console Arafa, or to curry his favor. "Not even the busiest person in this ill-omened alley works a fraction as hard as you do. Any what's it for? A coin, or a piaster at the most."

"God rest Mother's soul," said Arafa contentedly. "I am the only one who appreciates her. The day she gave me to that strange magician —who could read you every thought you had in your head—my life changed completely. Without her, I would have been a pickpocket, at best, or a beggar."

"Coins," said Hanash, insistent in his chagrin.

"With patience, money comes in. Don't worry about that. Protection rackets are not the only way to riches. And don't forget my exalted position here. Everyone who comes to me depends on me completely, and their happiness is in my hands. That's no small thing. And don't forget, either, the fun of the magic itself, the joy of turning dirty ingredients into something useful, the joy of healing, when people follow your orders. And there are the unknown powers you long to contact, and possess, if you could."

Hanash looked at the stove and suddenly interrupted what his companion was saying. "I should light the stove under the skylight, or we'll choke."

"Light it in Hell, but don't interrupt my thoughts! No idiot in this alley that considers himself educated is able to realize the importance of what I'm doing in this dark, filthy room with its funny smells. They appreciate the use of the 'gift,' but the gift isn't everything. This room can produce marvels that the imagination can scarcely comprehend. Crazy people have no idea of Arafa's true worth. Maybe someday they'll know. Then they'll have to ask for God's mercy on Mother, and not make insinuations against her the way they do now."

Hanash had half stood up, but squatted back down and said resentfully, "All this beauty could be destroyed by some stupid gangster's stick."

"We harm no one," said Arafa sharply. "We pay the protection money. So why would anyone want to hurt us?"

"Why did they want to hurt Rifaa?" laughed Hanash.

"Why are you trying to drive me crazy?"

"You want to get rich, and here only gangsters get rich. You want to be powerful, but here only gangsters are allowed to be strong. You figure it out, brother!"

Arafa was silent, checking to see that he had been right about the ingredients he was mixing, then looked at Hanash, who still looked worried. He laughed. "Mother warned me before you. Thank you, Hanash, but I have come back to the alley with a plan."

"It looks like all you care about anymore is magic."

"Magic is so wonderful," said Arafa, immediately carried away by the happy thought. "There is no limit to its power. No one knows where it ends. Even clubs are like children's toys to someone who possesses magic. You know it, Hanash. Don't be a fool. Imagine if all the children of the alley were magicians!"

"Well, if they were all magicians, they'd all have starved to death!"

Arafa's laughter showed his sharp teeth. "Don't be a fool, Hanash. Ask yourself what they might have done. By God, miracles would have come out of our alley the way curses and insults do now!"

"Yes, if they didn't die of starvation first."

"Yes, and they won't die as long as they have—" He fell silent before he finished what he was saying, and kept thinking intently until his hands stopped working. Then he resumed: "The poet of the Al Qassem says that Qassem wanted to use the estate so that everyone's needs would be met. So they wouldn't have to work. They'd be free for the leisured happiness that Adham dreamed about."

"That's what Qassem said!"

Arafa's eyes were bright and he spoke intensely. "But leisure isn't the ultimate goal! Imagine spending your life free and at leisure. It's a beautiful dream, but it's so ludicrous, Hanash. It would be so much better to be freed from work so that we could work marvels."

Hanash shook his large head, which seemed planted on his body with no neck to speak of, to protest a statement that meant nothing to him. Then, in his serious workplace tone of voice, he said, "Let me light the stove under the skylight now."

"Do it, and put yourself over the flame, because all you deserve is burning."

Arafa left the workroom an hour later. He went to the sofa and sat down to look through the window. After the silence, his ears were assaulted by the clamor of life. He heard the cries of peddlers, women's conversations, shouted jokes and whole anthologies of obscenity, accompanied by wafting smells and the unending stream of pedestrians. Then he noticed something new in front of the wall that faced his window: a portable coffee stand made of a kind of tall cage covered with an old cape. There were boxes of coffee, tea, cinnamon, games, cups, glasses and spoons. An old man sat on the ground fanning the fire to heat the water, while a young girl stood behind the cage, calling out in her warm voice, "Great coffee, men!" The coffee stand was parked at the spot where Qassem and Rifaa met, and it seemed that most of its customers were handcart owners and the poor. Arafa gazed at the girl through the bars. How pretty, that brown face with its black scarf. That dark brown caftan that covered her from her neck to her feet; the hem of it trailed on the ground when she walked to deliver an order or returned with an empty glass. It was modest and decent. How beautiful, her slenderness and honey-colored eyes, if only it were not for the redness of her left eyelid, either from inflammation or from uncleanliness. She was the old man's daughter, that was clear from their faces; he had begotten her in his old age, which is a very common thing in our alley.

"My girl! A cup of tea, if you please!"

She looked over at him, and quickly filled a glass from a pitcher that was half buried in the ashes, then crossed the road to offer it to him.

He smiled as he took it. "Bless you. How much?"

"A nickel piece."

"It's expensive! But for you, nothing is too much."

"In the big coffeehouse," she protested, "they charge half a piaster, and it's exactly what you have in your hand."

She left without waiting for his reply, and he began to sip the tea before it cooled, and without taking his eyes off her. How happy it would make him, having a girl that young. Her only fault was her red eye, and he could treat that easily, though that would require money that he did not yet have. The basement was ready; Hanash could sleep in the hall or the receiving room, if he liked, as long as he cleaned out the bedbugs first. He heard a strange buzz and saw people looking toward the end of the alley. Some of them were saying, "Santuri—Santuri." Straining as much as he could, he looked out between the bars, and saw the gangster coming, surrounded by his gang. When he passed the portable coffee stand, he noticed the girl, and asked one of his men, "Who is the girl?"

"Awatif, the daughter of Shakrun."

The man waggled his eyebrows, satisfied, and headed into his neighborhood.

Arafa felt anxious and unhappy. He waved his empty glass at the girl, and she glided over and took it and the coin from his hand. He motioned with his chin in the direction Santuri had gone. "Doesn't that bother you?"

She laughed as she turned to go. "I'll ask you for help if I need it, but will you help?"

Her scorn cut him; it was sad, not challenging. Just then he heard Hanash calling, and he jumped down to the floor and went inside.

96

Arafa's clientele grew as the days passed, but no customer lifted his heart the way Awatif had done the day he saw her coming toward him in the receiving room. He forgot the learned gravity he assumed in front of his customers, standing up to welcome her. He seated her on a cushion opposite him, and sat down cross-legged, feeling that the world was not large enough to contain his joy. He greeted her with a look that took all of her in, but settled on her left eye, which was nearly hidden beneath an inflamed swelling.

"You've neglected that, girl," he objected. "It's been red since the first day I saw you."

"I just washed it with warm water," she said almost apologetically. "When you're as busy with work as I am, you forget."

"You must never forget your health, especially when it's a question of a precious organ like your beautiful eye!"

She smiled, affected by the praise, while he reached back to a shelf behind him for a vessel. He took a small package from it and held it up to her. "Tie up the contents of this in a handkerchief, hold it over steaming hot water, then bind it over your eye every night until it goes back to being as beautiful as its sister."

She accepted the package, and took a bag from her pocket, asking him with her right eye how much it cost.

He laughed. "Don't worry about that. We're neighbors, and now we're friends."

"But you pay for the tea you drink."

"Actually, I'm paying your father," he said evasively. "He is a venerable man. I wish I knew him! I feel so sorry that he has to work at his age."

"But he's in good health," she said indifferently. "He refuses to sit at home, even though his long life is one of the reasons he is sad. He lived through the events of Qassem's time."

Arafa's face lit up with interest. "Really! Was he one of his followers?"

"No, but he was happy in those days, and he's nostalgic for them now."

"I want to know him, and listen to him."

"Don't get him talking on that subject. I wish he'd forget it forever, for his own good. One time he was in a bar having a drink with some of his friends, and after he got drunk he stood up and said, as loudly as he could, that life should go back to being the way it had been under Qassem, and when he got back to our alley he found Santuri in front of him. Santuri punched and slapped him, and he didn't stop until he was unconscious."

Deeply angered, Arafa thought a moment, then looked slyly at Awatif. "No one is safe with those gangsters around."

She glanced at him fleetingly to see how much he meant by this clear statement. "You're right, no one is safe with them."

He paused, biting his lip hesitantly. "I saw Santuri give you an absolutely insolent look."

She hid her smile with a slight downward turn of her head. "God take him!" she said.

"Doesn't it please a girl to be admired by a gangster like him?" he asked suspiciously.

"He has four wives!"

His heart sank deep within him. "But if he could have another?"

"I've hated him ever since he attacked my father," she said sharply. "And I feel the same way about all the gangsters. They have no hearts. They're so arrogant when they collect the protection money that you'd think they were the ones giving it."

He relaxed, reinvigorated. "Yes, Awatif. And Qassem did the right thing when he got rid of them, but they're back, like inflamed boils!"

"That's why my father longs for Qassem's time."

He suddenly shook his head inattentively. "And there are others, who long for Gabal's times, and Rifaa's, but the past is gone for good."

"You say that because you never saw Qassem, like my father," she said, sounding pleasantly vexed.

"Did you see him?"

"My father told me."

"And my mother told me, but what good is that? It doesn't get rid of gangsters for us. My mother herself was one of their victims, and they even make insinuations about her, when she's dead."

"Really?"

His face clouded, like a glass of clear water suddenly made turbid by its swirling sediment. "That's why I'm afraid for you, Awatif. The gangsters threaten our livings, supplies, love and peace. I'll tell you the truth —from the time I saw that beast looking at you, I knew I would have to get rid of them all."

"They say our ancestor, Gabalawi, wants it that way."

"Where is our ancestor?"

"In the mansion," she said simply.

He spoke quietly, his face showing no sign of mirth. "Yes, your father talks about Qassem, and Qassem talked about our ancestor. That's what we hear. But all we see is Qadri, Saadallah, Agag, Santuri and Yusuf. We need a power to rid us of that torment. What good are memories?"

He was aware that this turn of the conversation risked spoiling their meeting, so he began to speak ardently. "Our alley needs a power, the way I need you!"

She looked at him in disgust, and he smiled with a boldness that came naturally to his predatory eyes.

"A nice, hardworking, beautiful girl," he said seriously, to banish the rising anger of her lowered eyebrows. "So overworked that she forgets her eye until it swells up, then she comes to me, thinking that she needs me. The truth becomes clear to her—that I am the one who needs her."

"I have to go," she said, starting to get up.

"Not in anger, please. Remember, I didn't say anything new. Of course you've noticed my admiration for you these past days. I'm always looking from my window at your coffee stand. A bachelor like me can't live alone forever. My house is full of work—it needs to be looked after. I make more money than I need—someone has to help me spend it."

She left the room, and he stood at the end of the hall to see her out. It was as if she did not want to go without saying goodbye.

"Stay well," she said.

He sang softly to himself.

How proud your cheek, my beauty.
I hope to drink with, and to, my beauty.
And you're the most beautiful thing I see.

Then he strode vigorously into his workroom and found Hanash engrossed in his chores. "What are you doing?"

Hanash showed him a bottle. "It's ready, and perfectly sealed, but you have to try it in the desert."

Arafa took it from him and checked the plug. "Yes, in the desert. Otherwise everyone will find out about it."

"We're starting to make a living, and life is good—don't throw away all the happiness God has given you."

Hanash had begun to feel depressed by life since it started to unravel, in his eyes. Arafa smiled at the thought, and gazed at Hanash.

"She was your mother just as much as mine."

"Yes, but she begged you not to consider revenge."

"You had a different opinion then!"

"We'd be killed before we could take revenge."

Arafa laughed. "I won't hide from you that I stopped thinking of revenge a long time ago."

"Give me the bottle and let me empty it," said Hanash, his face bright.

But Arafa closed his hand over the bottle. "No, let's test it until it's perfect."

Hanash frowned resentfully.

"I mean what I say, Hanash. Trust me, I've changed my mind about revenge, not because our mother begged me, but because I think the gangsters have got to go. Apart from any revenge."

"Because you love that girl," said Hanash pointedly.

Arafa laughed until Hanash could see down his throat. "Love for the girl, love for life, call it what you want. Qassem was right!"

"What do you have to do with Qassem! Qassem was doing what his ancestor wanted."

He made a glum face. "Who knows? Our alley tells its stories, but we are doing vital things here in this room, there's no doubt about that. Where is the safety in our life? Agag will come along tomorrow to rob us of everything we've got, and if I make any move to marry Awatif, I'll have to face Santuri's club. This is the way it is for every man in our alley, even the beggars. What ruins my happiness is what ruins the happiness of the whole alley, and what protects me will protect them. I'm not a gangster, or one of Gabalawi's men, but I possess the wonders in this room, and they give me ten times the power that Gabal, Rifaa and Qassem had, put together." He lifted the bottle in his hand, and made a vigorous motion as if to throw it, then returned it to Hanash. "We'll test it tonight in the desert. Now, smile and get ready to be amazed."

He left the workroom for the window, and squatted on the sofa, looking out at the portable coffee stand. Night was falling gradually, and he could hear her voice hawking coffee and tea. She avoided looking at his window, which showed that she was thinking of him. A smile twinkled on her lips like a star. Arafa smiled, and his whole being smiled, and happiness so flooded his heart that he vowed he would comb his hair every morning. He heard the clamor of people chasing a thief out of Gamaliya, then, from a coffeehouse, the rebec melodies and the voice of the poet beginning the evening's recital.

> First, to Lord Qadri our overseer
> Second, to Saadallah our gangster
> Third, to Agag, our local protector!

This wrested him pitilessly from his dream, and he said, with a certain mutinous weariness, "Now the stories will begin. When will these stories ever end? What good has ever come from listening to them all night long? The poet will sing, and the drug dens will wake up. Alley of sighs."

97

Shakrun's life entered a period of mysterious upset. He sometimes spoke in a very loud voice, as if he were giving a speech. "Age. It's old age," people said pityingly. He got terribly angry for the most trivial reasons, or no reason, and they would again say, "Old age." He remained silent for long periods, even when circumstances called for him to say something, and they said, "Old age." He said things that the alley considered blasphemous, which made people say, a little anxiously, "God spare me from old age." Arafa often watched him with concern and sympathy through the bars. One day he was watching him, and said to himself, "He is a dignified man, in spite of his old rags and dirtiness. The decadence of this alley after Qassem's time is engraved on his gaunt face. It was his bad luck to have lived in Qassem's time, and to have enjoyed justice and safety. He got his full share of the estate revenue, and saw the buildings built in Gabalawi's name, and then stopped on Qadri's orders. In all, he is a courageous man who has lived too long." He saw Awatif coming, her face flawless since her eye was healed. He turned from the man to her and called out with a smile. "Tea, beautiful!"

She brought him the glass, and he spoke before taking it from her to make sure that she stayed.

"Congratulations on being well. You're the rose of this alley."

"Thank God. And you." She smiled.

He took the glass, purposely touching her fingers with his, and she went back, her happy walk illustrating her acceptance of his touch, and her pleasure. What better time to take the decisive step? He was not a man who lacked boldness, though if he did Santuri would have a thousand accounts to settle with him. It was Shakrun's fault, for putting his daughter in Santuri's way! Poor man, pushing his cart had exhausted him until he could do it no longer, so he had opened this ill-omened coffee stand. From afar he heard clamor and shouts, and saw all heads turn toward Gamaliya. In no time a horse-drawn cart appeared, filled with singing, handclapping women, and in the middle of them a bride returning from the public baths. Boys ran toward the cart, cheering and holding on to the sides as it moved toward Gabal. The air was ablaze with shrill trilling, shouted greetings and obscene whispers.

Shakrun stood up as if in anger. "Strike!" he thundered. "Strike!"

Awatif hurried to him and made him sit down, patting him worriedly but lovingly on the back. Arafa wondered whether the man was dreaming, or hallucinating. What was worse than old age? So how could Gabalawi be living? He watched the man until he had quieted down, and then asked him gently, "Shakrun, did you ever see Gabalawi?"

"Idiot," said Shakrun, without looking at him, "don't you know that he has been secluded in his mansion since before Gabal's time?"

Arafa laughed, and Awatif smiled.

"God give you long life, Shakrun," he said pleasantly.

"That was a prayer that was really worth something, back when life was worth something," Shakrun shouted.

Awatif came to take his glass, and whispered to him, "Leave him as he is. He doesn't sleep even one hour a night."

"My heart is with you," he said with ardent concern. Then, before she could start walking away, "I would like to talk to him about you and me."

She warned him with a finger and departed. He consoled himself by watching the children playing hide the onion. Suddenly Santuri appeared, coming from the Al Qassem neighborhood, and instinctively Arafa drew his head back from the bars. What brought him here? Luckily he had moved into the Rifaa neighborhood, and Agag was his protector, Agag who was so besotted with the "gifts." The gangster came closer until he stood before Shakrun's coffee stand, watching Awatif's face closely. "Coffee, no sugar," he said.

A woman's laughter pealed from a window, and another woman was heard to ask, "What brings Qassem's gangster to order coffee from the beggars' stand?"

Santuri seemed indifferent to everything. Awatif gave him the cup, and Arafa's heart flip-flopped in his chest. The gangster waited for the hot drink to cool, showing the girl a shameless smile that revealed his gold teeth. Arafa thought to himself that he would like to beat him with Muqattam Mountain itself.

Santuri sipped his coffee. "It's delicious. Made with your beautiful hands," he said.

She was afraid to smile and just as afraid to frown. Shakrun looked at her, alarmed. The gangster gave her a five-piaster coin, and she reached into her pocket for his change, but he did not wait for it, or look as though he wanted anything. He strolled back to the Qassem coffeehouse. Awatif was confused.

"Don't go to him," Arafa told her in a low voice.

"What about the rest of the money?" she asked.

Despite his feebleness, Shakrun stood up and took the money, then went to the coffeehouse. A moment later he came back and took his seat again. He began to laugh until his daughter came over to him.

"That's enough laughing," she said urgently.

Again he got up, and stood facing Gabalawi's mansion at the end of the alley. "Gabalawi!" he shouted. "Gabalawi!"

Every eye was on him, from the windows and the doors of the buildings, basements and coffeehouses. Children ran to him, and even the dogs stared at him.

"Gabalawi!" Shakrun shouted again. "How long will you be silent and hidden? Your commandments are ignored and your money is being wasted. Look, you're being robbed the same way your grandchildren are being robbed, Gabalawi!"

"Hurray!" yelled the children, and most of the people laughed.

But the old man kept shouting. "Gabalawi, can't you hear me? Don't you know what has happened to us? Why did you punish Idris, when he was a thousand times better than the gangsters in our alley? Gabalawi!"

At this point Santuri came out of the coffeehouse. "Be careful, you senile old man."

Shakrun turned to him angrily. "God damn you, bastard!"

People began to whisper anxiously, "He's a dead man." Santuri walked toward him, blind with rage, and punched him on the side of the head. The man staggered and almost fell, but Awatif caught him. Santuri saw her and went back to his chair.

"Let's go home, Father," the girl said, weeping.

Arafa joined her in holding him up, but the old man tried weakly to push them away from him. He was breathing heavily, and everyone became very somber.

"It's your fault, Awatif," said a woman from a window. "He should have been home."

"What could I do?" asked Awatif, still crying.

"Gabalawi!" gasped Shakrun weakly. "Gabalawi!"

98

It was not yet dawn when a long wail broke the silence, and then the people knew Shakrun had died. It was not an unusual occurrence in the alley. "God send him to Hell," Santuri's followers said. "He was always disrespectful, and his own disrespect killed him."

"Shakrun was murdered," Arafa told Hanash. "The same way a lot of people in this alley are murdered. The murderers don't take the trouble to hide their crimes, and no one dares complain. There are no witnesses."

"It's horrible!" said Hanash in loathing. "Why did we ever come here?"

"It is our alley."

"Our mother left it. It ruined her. It's an accursed alley, it and everybody in it."

"But it is our alley," Arafa insisted.

"As if we're doing penance for sins we never committed."

"Giving up would be the worst sin of all."

"The test with the bottle failed on the mountain," said Hanash despairingly.

"But it will succeed the next time."

Only Awatif and Arafa walked behind Shakrun's bier. Only they had shown up in front of the building. Everyone was surprised to see Arafa the magician taking part in the funeral, and they whispered about the strange audacity of that insane magician.

Even stranger, Santuri joined the funeral procession when it passed through the neighborhood of the Al Qassem. And he did it with such insolent boldness! But it was without a trace of shame. He even spoke to Awatif. "May you live out his years, Awatif."

Arafa realized that this was the man's preface to a further demand. By now the funeral procession had changed in the blink of an eye, as it was hurriedly crowded with every neighbor and acquaintance whom fear had prevented from taking part. Now it filled the whole street.

"May you live out his years, Awatif," Santuri repeated.

She looked at him menacingly. "You kill a man and walk in his funeral."

"Something like that was once said to Qassem," Santuri said loudly enough for everyone to hear.

"Say, 'God is One!'" a babble of scolding voice urged Awatif. "Death is in God's hands alone!"

"My father was murdered by a blow of *your* hand!" Awatif shouted.

"God forgive you, Awatif," said Santuri. "If I had really hit him, he would have died then and there. The truth is that I did not hit him, but I upset him, and everybody will swear to that."

The people vied with one another to corroborate this.

"He just got him excited! He never touched him—may worms eat our eyes if we're lying!"

"God will avenge me!" cried Awatif.

"God forgive you, Awatif," said Santuri with an indulgence that became the stuff of a long-enduring proverb.

Arafa inclined himself to Awatif's ear and said in a near-whisper, "Let the funeral go peacefully." The next thing he knew, one of Santuri's followers, a man named Adad, slapped him across the face and shouted at him.

"You son of a toilet! Who told you to get involved between them?" Arafa turned to him, dazed, and received a blow even harder than the first. Another man slapped him, a third spat in his face, a fourth grabbed him by the collar and a fifth pushed him so hard that he fell on his back. A sixth man kicked him and said, "You'll be buried in a grave if you go to her."

He lay sprawled on the ground, stunned, then collected himself and got up with great pain. He brushed the dirt from his galabiya and his face. A crowd of children had gathered around him and were chanting, "The calf has stumbled, get a knife!" He went back to his basement, hobbling and half crazed with anger.

"I told you not to go!" groaned Hanash when he saw him.

"Shut up! They'll be sorry!" he shouted in impatient rage.

"Please forget that girl," said Hanash with combined gentleness and determination. "If you don't, we're dead."

Arafa was silent for several moments, looking at the floor and thinking. When he lifted his face, it was sullen with dreadful certainty. "You'll see me married to her, sooner than you think."

"This is insanity itself."

"And Agag will lead the wedding procession."

"You're dousing yourself with alcohol and throwing yourself in the fire."

"I will retest the bottle in the desert tonight."

He stayed at home, not going out for days, but kept up his relationship with Awatif by way of the barred window. When the period of mourning had ended, he met her secretly in the hall of her building.

"We should get married immediately," he told her frankly.

The girl was not surprised at his request, but answered sadly, "If I accept, I'll be causing you unbearable troubles."

"Agag has agreed to give us a party. You know what that means," he said confidently.

Steps were taken in total secrecy until everything was ready. The alley learned, without prior notice, that Awatif, daughter of Shakrun, had married Arafa the magician and moved into his house; that Agag, the protector of the Al Rifaa, had witnessed the wedding. Many of the people were stunned, and others asked how that could have happened—how Arafa had dared do it—how Agag had been persuaded to give his blessing. But the people who knew said, "We're in for it now."

99

Santuri met his followers in the Al Qassem coffeehouse. Agag learned of this, and met with his followers in the Al Rifaa coffeehouse. The alley was aware of these meetings, and grew very tense. The peddlers, beggars and children lost no time in evacuating the area between the Al Qassem and Al Rifaa neighborhoods, and the shops and windows were locked up. Santuri and his men came out into the alley, and Agag and his men came out too. Evil emblazoned the air, and its sickening odor spread; only a nudge was needed for a flaming inferno to explode.

"What has made our men so angry?" a good man called out from his roof. "Think, before the blood flows!"

Agag stared at Santuri and broke the terrified silence. "We are not angry. We have no cause for anger."

"You went too far," said Santuri bluntly. "No gangster can approve what you did."

"What did I do?"

"You protected a man who was challenging me," raged Santuri, the words coming from his mouth and his eyes alike.

"All the man did was marry a solitary girl after her father died. I witness the marriage of every Rifaa person."

"He has nothing to do with Rifaa," said Santuri contemptuously. "No one knows who his father is, not even himself. You could be his father, or I could be, or any beggar in the alley."

"But today he lives in my territory."

"All he did was rent a vacant basement!"

"So what!"

"Do you know that you went too far?" shouted Santuri.

"Don't shout," said Agag. "There is no need for us to fight like roosters."

"Maybe there is a need."

"Don't get me started!"

"You watch it, Agag!"

"Damn you, oaf!"

"Damn your father!"

Their clubs were raised, but were frozen by a bellowed command: "For shame!"

Their heads turned toward the source. There was Saadallah, protector of the alley, moving through the crowd of Rifaa until he stood in the area between the two neighborhoods.

"Put down your clubs," he said.

All the clubs were lowered, like the heads of men at prayer. Saadallah looked at Santuri and then at Agag.

"I don't want to hear what any of you have to say. Go home quietly. A massacre over a woman? What kind of men are you?"

The men broke up in silence, and Saadallah went back to his house.

Arafa and Awatif were in their basement, unbelieving that the night would pass in peace. They were listening to what was happening outside with pounding hearts, pale faces and dry mouths. They heard Saadallah's commanding, unanswerable voice, and Awatif sighed deeply. "What a life," she said.

He wanted to breathe some comfort into her heart. He pointed at his temple and said, "I work with this, just like Gabal, and the sly devil Qassem."

She swallowed with a little difficulty. "Will our safety last?"

He drew her to his chest, outwardly amused. "I wish every couple were as happy as we are."

She laid her head on his shoulder, catching her breath, and whispered, "Do you think that's the end of that?"

"No gangster is ever sure of his flank."

She raised her head. "I know that, but I have a wound in me that will never heal until I see him dead."

He knew whom she meant, and looked thoughtfully into her eyes. "For you, revenge is a duty, but it won't lead to anything decisive. Our safety is threatened, not because Santuri wants to attack us, but because the safety of our whole alley is threatened by the attacks of all the gangsters. Even if we beat Santuri, who can guarantee us that Agag won't turn on us tomorrow—or Yusuf the day after tomorrow? It's either safety for everyone, or safety for no one."

She smiled weakly. "Do you want to be like Gabal or Rifaa or Qassem?"

He kissed her hair and breathed in its clove-scented smell, but did not answer.

"They were put to work by our ancestor, Gabalawi."

"Our ancestor, Gabalawi!" he said irritably. "Everybody, when he's down, cries out, 'Gabalawi!'—like your late father. But haven't you heard of grandchildren like us who have never seen their ancestor, and they live all around his locked mansion? Have you heard of any estate owner who lets criminals manipulate his estate this way, and he does nothing about it, and says nothing?"

"It's old age!" she said simply.

"I have never heard of any old man who lived this long," he said distrustfully.

"They say there's a man in Muqattam Marketplace who's more than a hundred and fifty years old. With God, anything is possible."

He was silent, then murmured, "With magic, anything is possible too!"

She laughed at his vanity, and traced her fingers on his chest. "Your magic can heal eyes."

"And do lots of other things."

"What fools we are!" she sighed. "We have such fun talking, as if nothing were threatening us."

He ignored her interruption. "Maybe someday it will be able to get rid of the gangsters themselves, and build buildings, and provide livings to all the people of this alley."

"Do you think that might happen before Judgment Day?" She laughed.

His sharp eyes took on a dreamy look. "If only we were all magicians!"

"If!" She continued: "It didn't take long for Qassem to establish justice, without your magic."

"And it didn't stay established long. But magic never wears off. Don't underrate magic, my honey-eyed dear, it's just as powerful as our love. It creates new life in the same way. But it can't do its work unless most of us are magicians."

"And how will that happen?" she joked.

He thought a long while before answering. "If justice is achieved, if Gabalawi's conditions are implemented. If most of us could dispense with hard labor and devote ourselves to magic."

"Do you want an alley of magicians?" She laughed lightly. "How can the Ten Conditions be implemented when our ancestor is bedridden, and it looks like he is no longer able to get any of his family to do it for him?"

He gave her a curious look. "Why don't we go to him ourselves?"

"Can you get into the overseer's house?" she asked, laughing again.

"No, but maybe I can get into the mansion."

"That's enough joking," she said, slapping his hand. "Let's concentrate on staying alive for now."

"If I liked jokes," he said with a mysterious smile, "I wouldn't have come back to this alley."

Something in his tone of voice frightened her, and she stared at him in alarm. "You mean what you said!" she cried.

He looked at her in silence.

"Imagine if they caught you in the mansion!"

"What's so unusual about a grandson in his grandfather's house?" he asked serenely.

"Tell me that you're joking. Lord! How can you look so serious? Strange. Why do you want to go to him?"

"Isn't meeting him worth the risk?"

"This is just your talk—how has it become an awful fact?"

He rubbed the palm of her hand to calm her thoughts. "Ever since coming back to our alley, only *I* have thought of unthinkable things."

"Why can't we live the way we are now?"

"I wish! They won't let us live the way we are now. And a man has to take care of his own life."

"So we'll escape from the alley."

"I won't escape, when I have magic!"

Tenderly he pulled her close until she was pressed against him, and he stroked her shoulder. "We'll have lots of opportunities for talk," he said. "For now, just rest."

100

HAS THE MAN GONE CRAZY, OR IS HE BLINDED BY VANITY? Awatif wondered as she watched Arafa work and think. For her part, the only thing that spoiled the serenity of her happy days was her desire for revenge against Santuri, her father's murderer. Revenge had been a sacred tradition in the alley since ancient times, but she might have been made to forget even this sacred tradition, however grudgingly, for the sake of the happy life marriage had given her. But Arafa was certain that revenge against Santuri was only a part of a grand project he had promised himself to carry out—as it appeared to her. She did not understand him. Did he think he was one of those men of whom the poets sang? Gabalawi had not asked anything of him, though he did not seem to put much stock in Gabalawi or what the poets said. What was absolutely sure was that he gave magic much, much more of his time and effort than his livelihood required. When he thought, his thoughts far transcended himself and his family, extending to general issues no one else cared about—the alley, gang rule, the overseer, the estate, its revenues, and magic. He dreamed vast dreams of magic and the future, though he was the only man in the alley who rejected smoking hashish, as his work in the back room required alertness and attention. But all this was nothing next to his insane wish to infiltrate the mansion. *Why, husband?* To ask him how things should be in the alley. *You know how things should be in the alley; we all know; why is it necessary to risk death?* I want to know the Ten Conditions of the estate. *The important thing is not to know but to act, and what will you be able to do?* The truth is that I want to see the book that got Adham kicked out, if the stories are true. *What do you want with that book?* Something makes me positive that it's a book of magic. Only magic can explain Gabalawi's deeds in the desert—not muscles or a club, as people think. *What do you need with all these risks, when you're happy, and you make a fine living without them?* Don't think that Santuri has forgotten us. Whenever I go out, I almost stumble over his men's hateful looks. *Magic is enough for you—just forget the mansion.* The book is there: the first book of magic, with the secret of Gabalawi's power, which he begrudged even his son. *It might be nothing like what you imagine.* Or it might be—it's worth the risk.

Then he took the decisive step unambiguously.

"That's how I am, Awatif. What can I do? I'm just the despised son of a wretched woman and an unknown father. Everyone knows that, and makes jokes about it, but I have nothing to worry me in this world but the mansion. It's not so strange for someone who never knew his father to strive with all his might to know his grandfather. My back room has taught me to have no faith in anything I haven't seen with my own eyes and touched with my own hands. I must get inside the mansion. I might find the power I'm searching for, or I might find nothing at all, but whatever I find will be better than the confusion I'm enduring now. I'm not the first person to choose the hard way in our alley. Gabal could have kept his job with the overseer, and Rifaa could have been the best carpenter in the alley, and Qassem could have enjoyed Qamar and her fortune, and lived the life of a distinguished man. But they chose the other way."

"How many people in our alley go racing, on their own legs, to their ruin!" sighed Hanash.

"How few of them had sound reasons," said Arafa sharply.

But Hanash was quick to help his brother. He followed him like his shadow out to the desert in the dead of night. When Awatif despaired of changing his mind, she raised her hands in prayer for him. It was a black night; the crescent moon appeared early, and then disappeared. The brothers walked close to the walls until they reached the back wall of the mansion that overlooked the desert.

"Rifaa was standing right here when he heard Gabalawi's voice," Hanash whispered.

Arafa cast a critical look around him. "That's what the poets say. I'll know the truth of everything."

Hanash pointed to the desert. "And in that desert he spoke to Gabal himself, and sent his servant to Qassem," he said solemnly.

"And in that desert Rifaa was killed, and our mother was raped and beaten, and Gabalawi did nothing!" said Arafa irritably.

Hanash frowned and put his digging tools on the ground. They both began digging under the wall, taking out dirt in a basket. They worked seriously and doggedly, until their chests were filled with the reek of earth. Hanash had been no less industrious than Arafa, and clearly he was driven by the same desire, though he was terribly afraid. Arafa's head cleared the level of the ground by just one inch when he spoke from within the pit. "That's enough for tonight." He vaulted out of the ground on his palms, and said, "We have to cover the top of the hole with wooden planks, then cover that with dirt so that no one will know about it."

They hurried home after that, followed by the dawn, and he thought of the next day; the strange next day, when he would walk through the unknown mansion. Who knew? Perhaps he would meet Gabalawi and even talk to him, interrogate him about the past and the present, about the terms of the estate and the secret of his book. This was a dream that had only come true in the clouds of hashish smoke that were puffed out of the pipe.

In the basement, he found Awatif still awake, waiting up for him. When she saw him, she gave him a chiding but drowsy stare. "Like you're coming back from a graveyard!" she murmured.

"You are sweet," he said merrily, hiding his unease. He threw himself down beside her.

"If I meant anything to you, you'd listen to me."

"You'll change your mind when you see what happens tomorrow."

"I have one chance for happiness out of a thousand for total ruin."

Arafa laughed. "If you could see their hateful looks, you'd be convinced that the peace we enjoy is nothing but a fantasy."

Sudden shouts tore the stillness. They were followed by wails. Awatif scowled. "That's a bad omen."

He shrugged indifferently. "Don't blame me, Awatif. You're partly responsible for what I'm doing."

"Me!"

"I came back to this alley with a secret wish to avenge my mother," he said firmly. "When your father was attacked, that wish for revenge grew into a vendetta against all the gangsters, but my love for you added something new to that, that made it bigger than my original idea—that I should get rid of the gangsters, not for revenge, but so that people can enjoy life. I went to our ancestor's house only for the secret of his power."

She gave him a long look in which he read clearly, in the light, the aching fear that she would lose him as she had lost her father. He smiled warmly to give her courage, while the wailing outside grew more agonized.

101

Hanash gripped Arafa's hand in farewell; his brother was in the deepest part of the pit. Arafa stretched out on his face and began to crawl through the passage, fragrant with the smell of earth, and kept crawling until his head emerged from the ground in the garden of the mansion. His nose was greeted by a wondrous fragrance like the essence of all the essences of rose, jasmine and henna, mingled with the dew of dawn; the fragrance intoxicated him despite his overwhelming sensation of fear.

Here he was, smelling the garden for which Adham had died pining. All he could see of it was sheer darkness under the wakeful stars. It lay in dreadful silence, except for the intermittent whisper of the leaves in the breeze. Finding the ground fresh and damp, he reminded himself to remove his sandals when he stole into the house, so as to leave no mark upon the floor. Where did the gatekeeper, the gardener and all the rest of the servants sleep? He crept on all fours, being very careful not to make any sound that might reach the building whose bulk and outline seemed mountainous in the shadows. Making his way toward the house, he felt an alarm he had never known in his life, though he was used to going out in darkness, and spending the night in the desert and in ruins. He continued to crawl along the wall until his hand touched the first step that led up to the terrace, if the poets could be believed. This was where Gabalawi had pushed Idris out, and expelled him. That was Idris' fate, his punishment for defying his father's orders. What would Gabalawi do to someone who stormed his house to steal the secret of his power? But, slow; no one could possibly expect that a thief could gain entry to the house that had been secure and impregnable throughout time. He crawled around the parapet, then started to mount the steps on his hands and knees, up to the level of the terrace. He took off his sandals and clamped them under his arm, then crawled to the side door that the poets said led to the sleeping chamber. Suddenly he heard a cough—a cough from the garden. He remained below the door, but looked into the garden, where he saw a figure coming toward the terrace. He held his breath, under the impression that the beating of his heart could be heard reverberating. The figure came closer, and began to climb the steps; perhaps it was Gabalawi himself. Perhaps he would catch Arafa committing his crime, just as he had done with Adham long ago, and at almost the same time of day. The figure reached the level of the terrace just a couple of arm lengths from where he hid, but went to the other side of the terrace and lay on something that looked like a bed. His tension eased, leaving in its place a feeling of powerlessness. Perhaps the figure was only a servant who had answered the call of nature and then gone back to sleep; now his snores could be heard. Arafa regained something of his daring, and raised his hand to feel for the doorknob.

He found it and turned it gently, then pushed the door tentatively, and it opened wide enough for him to creep through; then he reclosed it behind him. He found himself in pitch-blackness, so he kept one arm out in front of him to feel for the first steps, which he mounted as lightly as the wind. He came out into a long hall, lit by a lamp set in the opening of a wall, which curved inward to the right, and to the left it ran the length of the house. In the center was the closed door to the sleeping chamber. This turn was where Umaima had stood, and Adham had proceeded from where he stood; and here *he* was, going for the same thing. His chest constricted with growing terror, and he called on his will and daring. It would be ridiculous to turn back. A servant might appear at any moment, and he might be awakened from his madness by a hand seizing him by the shoulder. He must hurry. He proceeded on tiptoe toward the door and twisted the gleaming knob; it turned with his hand. He pushed the door and it opened slowly. He slipped in, closing it behind him. He rested his back against the door in the dark, through which he could see nothing, breathing warily, as if conserving his breath, and trying vainly to see. After a moment he smelled the sweet aroma of incense, which for no reason filled his heart with unease and strange sorrow. He no longer doubted that he was in Gabalawi's sleeping chamber. When would he grow accustomed to the darkness? How could he collect his scattered nerves? Who had stood, long ago, where he was standing now? Why did he feel that he was going to collapse completely unless he recovered all of his strength, resolution and daring? Every movement that was not precisely and carefully made threatened him with death. He recalled the clouds, how they moved along in their course that randomly drew them into strange shapes: a mountain as easily as a tomb. He touched the wall with his fingertips and used it as a guide, moving parallel with it, bent over, until a chair bumped against his shoulder. A sudden movement in the far corner of the room froze his blood; he stayed behind the chair, watching the door through which he had entered. He heard light footfalls, and the rustle of clothing. He expected light to shine into the shadows; to see Gabalawi standing before him. He would fall beseechingly at his feet, and tell him, "I am your grandson. I have no father, and no bad intentions. Do whatever you want with me." Despite the dark, he saw a figure moving toward the door, and saw the door open slowly, and the light of the outer hall filtering in behind it. The figure went out, leaving the door ajar, and turned to the right. He saw from the light of the outside lamp that it was an old black woman with an unforgettably long, thin face. Was she a servant? Was it possible that this room was in the servants' wing? He looked over from the chair to the rest of the room, to see it in the dim light coming in through the door, and made out the shapes of chairs and sofas. It showed him, in the center of the room, the outline of a huge bed with high bedposts and mosquito netting. At the foot of this bed was another, small one; perhaps this was the one the servant had been leaving. This magnificent bed could only be Gabalawi's. He was sleeping there now, unaware of this crime. How he wanted to see him, even from a distance; if only it were not for the partly open door that warned of the woman's return. He looked to his left and saw the door of the little chamber, locked to contain its terrible secret. This was how Adham, may he rest in peace, had seen it long ago. He crawled behind the chairs, forgetting Gabalawi himself, until he had reached the spot in front of the small door. He could not fight the temptation, and raised his hand until his finger entered the keyhole. He pushed down to open the mechanism and pull it toward him, and it yielded. He quickly pushed it back, his heart trembling with fear and a feeling of victory. The dim light disappeared, and once again the room was sunk in darkness. Again he heard the light footsteps and the squeak of the bed as she lay down on it; then there was silence. He waited patiently for the old woman to fall asleep, straining his eyes to study the big bed, but he could see nothing. He was persuaded that it would be insanity to try to communicate with his ancestor, since before that could happen the old woman would awaken and fill the air with her shrieks, and that would be that. He would be content with the perilous book, with its terms of the estate and magic spells his ancestor had used to control the vast void, and the people, in the earliest times. No one before Arafa had ever imagined the book was a book of magic, because no one before him had ever practiced magic. He put his hand up again and stuck his finger in, then pulled the door open and crawled in. He closed it behind him and stood up warily, breathing deeply to relieve his exhausted nerves. Why had Gabalawi begrudged his children the secret of his book? Even the most loved of them all, Adham! There was a secret, no doubt about that, and it would be discovered within seconds, as soon as he lit a candle. Long ago Adham had lit a candle, and here he was, fatherless, lighting one again in the same spot. The poets would sing about this forever. He lit the candle, and saw two eyes looking at him. Despite his confusion, he saw that the eyes were those of an old black man who was lying on a bed facing the inside of the room. And despite his confusion and his terror, he saw that the old man was struggling out of the dreamland between sleep and consciousness; perhaps the sound made by striking the match had stirred him. Involuntarily, unfeelingly, he pounced at him and seized his neck in his right hand, squeezing with all his might. The old man made a violent movement, grabbed his hand and kicked him in the stomach, but Arafa only redoubled the pressure on his neck. The candle fell from his left hand and went out; the room was in darkness. The old man made a final desperate motion in the dark, then was still, though Arafa's frenzied hand did not let up until his fingers felt weak. He then retreated, panting, until his back met the door. The seconds passed. He was in a hell of torment and silence, feeling his strength leave him, feeling that time was heavier than sin. He would fall on the floor or on the corpse of his victim if he did not pull himself together. Escape called him, a power that he could not fight, but how could he step over the body to get the ancient book, the ill-omened book? He did not have the courage to light another match; blindness was preferable. His forearms ached, possibly from the marks of the old man's fingernails, in his futile struggle. His body trembled at the thought. Adham's crime was disobedience; his was murder. He had murdered a man he did not know, and there was no known reason for him to have done it. He had come in search of a power with which to combat the criminals, and, unknowingly, became a criminal. He turned his head in the darkness to face the corner where he thought the book was hung. He pushed the door and slipped in, closing it behind him, and crawled along the wall to the door. He hesitated behind the last chair. All he saw in this house were servants. Where was its master? This crime would stand between the two of them forever. He felt disappointment and failure down to the very depths of his soul. He opened the door gently; the light hurt his eyes, and he imagined that it was attacking him in a furious clamor and boisterous sparkling. He closed the door gently and went away on tiptoe, going down the stairs in pitch-blackness. He crossed the terrace to the garden, his alertness dulled by exhaustion and dispiritedness. The man asleep on the terrace now woke up and asked, "Who's that?" Arafa clung to the wall underneath the terrace, feeling that his terror made him stronger. The voice called out once more, and a cat meowed in reply. He stayed in his hiding place, afraid of moving on to another crime. When all was silent again, he crawled along the earth of the back garden to the wall, and felt around for the opening until he found it, then crawled in, just as he had come. When he reached the end, or almost, he collided with a foot. Then, before he could take in what was happening, the foot kicked him in the head.

102

He leaped at the body above the foot and they fought briefly, until the other man let out a shout of anger that gave away his identity to Arafa.

"Hanash!" cried Arafa in bewilderment.

They helped each other out of the hole up to the ground surface.

"You were gone so long," said Hanash. "I went in to see what I could find out."

"You made a mistake, as usual," said Arafa, breathing with difficulty. "Let's get out of here."

They returned to the sleeping alley. When Awatif saw him, she cried out, "Wash—oh God!—what's this blood dripping from your hand and your neck?"

He trembled but did not answer her. He went in to wash, but almost immediately fainted. When he came to a short while later, with the help of Awatif and Hanash, he was sitting on a sofa between them, feeling that sleep was farther away from him even than Gabalawi was. He could no longer bear the burden of his secret alone, and described to them what had happened during his strange excursion. When he was through, their eyes were fixed on him in terror and despair.

"I was against the idea from the beginning," whispered Awatif, but Hanash tried to ease the impact of the tragedy.

"It would have been impossible to avoid that crime," he said.

"But it's worse than Santuri's crimes, or any of the gangsters'!" said Arafa sadly.

"Don't invite suspicion on yourself," said Hanash.

"But I killed an innocent old man. Who knows, he could have been the servant that Gabalawi sent to Qassem!"

There was a period of silence, like bitter insomnia, until Awatif spoke. "Shouldn't we go to sleep?"

"You two sleep," said Arafa. "I won't be sleeping tonight."

Again silence fell over them.

"Didn't you see Gabalawi or hear his voice?" Hanash asked.

"No," he said sadly, shaking his head.

"But you saw his bed in the dark!"

"The same way we see his house!"

"When you were gone so long, I thought it was because you were talking to him," sighed Hanash.

"Nothing's easier than imagining things outside the house."

"You look feverish. I think you'd better sleep," said Awatif worriedly.

"Where will my sleep come from?" But he felt that she was probably right, as he was very hot and dazed.

"You were just an arm's length away from his testament, but you didn't look at it," Hanash resumed dejectedly.

Arafa's face contracted in pain.

"What a hard and hopeless trip!" said Hanash.

"Yes." Then Arafa added, in a sharper tone, "But it taught me that we shouldn't rely on anything but magic, which we have right in our own hands. Don't you see that I took a chance on a crazy trip, for an idea that was maybe the farthest thing from my mind?"

"Yes, no one but you has ever said that his famous book is a book of magic."

Arafa looked, even more than before, as though he was enduring a terrible state of unrest in his mind and soul. "The test with the bottle will be successful sooner than you think. It will come in very useful if we need it for self-defense."

The terrible silence threatened to reestablish itself, so Hanash spoke. "I wish you knew some magic that would help get you to the mansion and its owner without these risks!"

"There is no end to magic," said Arafa fervently. "All I actually have now are a few medicines and the bottle project, for attack or defense. And the things that are possible—the human mind can't get around them."

"You should never have thought of that adventure," said Awatif crossly. "Gabalawi is from one world, and we're in another world. Talking to him wouldn't have done any good, even if you had done it. Maybe he's forgotten all about the estate and the overseer, and his gangsters and grandchildren and the alley!"

Arafa was angered for no apparent reason, though his bizarre night would have justified even the strangest behavior. "This deluded, ignorant alley!" he said sharply. "What does it know about anything? Nothing! All it has are stories and poets, but did you ever hear of them doing the things they hear about! And they think their alley is the heart of the world. What is it but an asylum for bullies and beggars. In the beginning it was a wasteland for vermin, until your ancestor Gabalawi came here!"

Hanash flinched. Awatif wet a rag to lay on his forehead, but Arafa abruptly pushed her hand away.

"I have something no one else has, not even Gabalawi himself. I have magic, and magic can do for our alley what Gabal, Rifaa and Qassem put together weren't able to do."

"When will you sleep?" pleaded Awatif.

"When the raging fire in my head goes out."

"It's almost sunrise," said Hanash.

"Let it rise!" snapped Arafa. "But it won't rise until magic has destroyed the gangsters, freed people of their demons and brought more happiness than the estate ever could. It will be the legendary music that Adham dreamed of." He sighed deeply, then leaned his head wearily against the wall. Awatif hoped he would fall asleep, but then a voice rang out in the stillness, so loudly that it frightened them, and was followed by shrieks and lamentations.

Arafa jumped to his feet and cried out in terror. "The servant's body has been found!"

"How can you tell the voices are coming from the mansion?" asked Awatif, her throat dry.

Arafa ran outside, and the two of them immediately followed him. They stood in front of the building, their heads turned to the mansion.

The first light of morning was shimmering through the last soft shadows. People opened their windows and poked their heads out, all looking at the mansion. A man was running from the far end of the alley in the direction of Gamaliya, and when he passed them, Arafa asked, "What's happened?"

He answered without stopping: "God's will, after his long life. Gabalawi is dead!"

103

The three of them headed back into the basement. Arafa's feet could barely carry him. He fell on the sofa.

"The man I killed was a miserable-looking black servant. He was sleeping in the side room."

Neither of them said a word. They buried their gazes in the floor to avoid his wild eyes.

"I can see you don't believe me! I swear to you both, I never even went near his bed."

Hanash hesitated for long moments, but sensed that talking was better than silence, so he spoke cautiously. "Maybe you didn't see his face clearly, you were so surprised?"

"Never!" shouted Arafa miserably. "You weren't with me."

"Lower your voice," said Awatif, frightened.

He left them, hurrying into the back room, where he sat in the dark, shaking with fear. What insanity had moved him to make that doomed excursion! Yes—doomed. The earth shook below him and leaked tragedy from its core. This eerie room was the only hope he had left.

The first rays of sunlight glistened, and all the people began to gather in the alley around the mansion. The news was whispered and spread quickly, especially when the overseer made a brief visit to the mansion, after which he went home. The people said that thieves had burglarized the mansion through a tunnel they had dug underneath the rear wall, and killed a faithful servant. When Gabalawi got the news, he suffered a shock that his frail health could not withstand, not at his age; and he gave up the ghost. People's anger was so great that its black smoke prevented them from weeping or screaming. When Awatif and Hanash told Arafa the news, he said, "That shows I was right!"

At once he remembered that he had been the cause of his death anyway, and fell back into a shamed and pained silence.

Awatif did not know what to say. "God rest his soul!" she murmured.

"He didn't exactly die young," observed Hanash.

"But I caused his death!" Arafa said, in the sad tone the poets used. "I'm worse than any of his other descendants, even the evil ones, and there are so many of them!"

"You went with only good intentions," Awatif said, weeping.

"Isn't it possible they might have evidence against us?" asked Hanash uneasily.

"Let's get out of here!" said Awatif.

"If we did that," Arafa said, pointing irritably at Awatif, "we'd give them the clearest proof of our crime."

There were hostile cries from the crowded street.

"We must kill the murderer before we bury the victim!"

"This is the worst generation yet in our alley. Even the worst people respected the mansion, throughout our history—even Idris himself! We'll be cursed until the Judgment Day!"

"The killers aren't from our alley. How could they be?"

"We'll get all the facts about this."

"We'll be cursed until the Judgment Day."

The clamor and lamentation grew more intense, until Hanash's nerves gave out. "How can we stay in the alley after today!"

The Al Gabal suggested burying Gabalawi in the Gabal Cemetery: they considered that they were more closely related to him than any other community, and hated the idea of him being buried in the same cemetery that held Idris and the remains of Gabalawi's other family members. The Al Rifaa asked that he be buried in the same grave he had dug for Rifaa with his own hands. The Al Qassem said that Qassem had been Gabalawi's finest grandson, and that his tomb was the most fitting resting place for the body of the venerable ancestor. There was almost a riot in the alley, with the body going unburied. But Qadri, the overseer, announced that Gabalawi would be buried in the mosque that had been built on the site of the old estate office in the mansion. This solution met with substantial public relief, although the people of the alley regretted that they would be deprived of the sight of his funeral, just as they had always been deprived of the sight of the man himself in life. The Al Rifaa whispered delightedly that Gabalawi would be buried in the grave he had dug for Rifaa with his own hands. No one but themselves believed that old story, and people ridiculed them about it until their protector, Agag, grew angry and nearly got into a fight with Santuri. At that point, Saadallah began to pay attention, and shouted his warning at them.

"I will smash the head of any troublemaker who tries to mar the respect of this sad day!"

Only Gabalawi's closest servants witnessed the washing of the body. They were the ones who shrouded it and placed it on the bier, and carried the bier to the great hall that had witnessed the most momentous events of the family: his handing over the estate management to Adham, and Idris' rebellion against that. Then the overseer and the leaders of Gabal, Rifaa and Qassem were summoned to pray over him, and after that, as the sun sloped toward the horizon, he was placed in his grave. In the evening, everyone in the alley went to the funeral tent. Arafa and Hanash went with the group from the Al Rifaa. Arafa had not slept since committing his crime, and his face was like a corpse's. The people talked of nothing but the greatness of Gabalawi, conqueror of the desert, master of all men, the symbol of power and courage, owner of the estate and the alley, and first father of succeeding generations. Arafa looked sad, but no one could have imagined what was in his heart. The man who had attacked the mansion cared nothing for its glory; he had confirmed his ancestor's existence only with his death! He had turned away from everyone and polluted his hands forever. He asked himself how he could ever atone for such a crime; the exploits of Gabal, Rifaa and Qassem were not enough for that. Getting rid of the overseer and the gangsters, and saving the alley from their criminality, was not enough either. Teaching everyone magic, its arts and benefits, was not enough. Only one thing would do it: to become so proficient in magic that he could bring Gabalawi back to life! Gabalawi, who had been easier to kill than to see. The passage of time would give him strength to heal the terrible wound in his heart. These gangsters and their lying tears. But oh! and oh! again! None of them had sinned as he had. The gangsters sat gloomily, covered with shame and disgrace: other alleys would say that Gabalawi had been murdered in his house while the gangsters sat around smoking hashish. That is why their stares promised revenge; why calamity and death could be read in their eyes.

When Arafa went back to the basement late that night, he drew Awatif to him and spoke with pleading despair. "Awatif, tell me the truth. Do you think I'm a criminal?"

"You are a good man," she said tenderly. "You are the best man I ever met in my life, but you have the worst luck!"

He closed his eyes. "No one has ever been torn apart by the kind of pain I'm feeling."

"Yes. I know that." She kissed him with her cold lips and whispered, "I'm afraid we're cursed."

He looked away from her.

"I'm worried," said Hanash. "They'll find us out today or tomorrow. I don't think they'll find out everything about Gabalawi—his origins, the estate, him and his sons, his contacts with Gabal, Rifaa and Qassem—but they'll find out about his death!"

Arafa took an uncomfortable breath. "Do you have any solution, aside from escaping?"

Hanash said nothing.

"Me, I have a plan," said Arafa. "Though I'd like to reassure myself before putting it into action. I can't act if I'm a criminal."

"You're innocent," said Hanash wearily.

"I am going to act, Hanash. Don't worry about us. It will distract the alley from the crime. Wonders will take place, and the most wonderful thing of all will be that Gabalawi will come back to life."

"Oh!" said Awatif.

"Are you crazy?" Hanash asked, scowling.

"One word from our ancestor, and his good grandchildren worked until they died," he said feverishly. "His death is stronger than his words. A good son has to do all he can. To take his place, to be *him*, do you understand?"

104

Arafa prepared to leave the basement as soon as the last sound in the alley had died away. Awatif walked him as far as the hall, her eyes red with crying. She spoke in a weak and resigned voice.

"I hope you'll be safe."

"Why can't I go with you?" asked Hanash insistently.

"It's easier for one person to escape than for two," said Arafa.

Hanash patted him on the back, but advised him, "Only use the bottle as a last resort."

He nodded in agreement and left, with a glance at the alley, immersed in darkness; then headed toward Gamaliya. He followed a long, circuitous route that took him through Watawit Alley, al-Darasa and the desert behind the mansion, until he reached the wall of Saadallah's house that overlooked the desert from the north. He made for a spot halfway down the wall, and felt the earth there until he found a particular stone. He rolled it aside, then disappeared into the passage he and Hanash had dug so tirelessly, night after night. He crawled on his belly to the end of the tunnel, then worked with his scabby hands to remove the panel that blocked it. He emerged in the garden of the gangster's house, and hid by the wall to look the place over. He saw a closed window that glowed with a dim light. The garden was sunk in sleep and shadow, except for a wakeful light in the window of the reception hall. Every few moments loud noises and crude laughter burst from the hall. He slowly drew a dagger from his shirt and waited eagerly. Time's passing weighed heavier than sin, but the group broke up a half hour after his arrival. The door opened and the men filed out toward the outer gate that opened onto the alley. The gatekeeper preceded them, holding a lantern, closed the gate after them and came back, walking in front of Saadallah toward the terrace. Arafa picked up a stone from the ground in his left hand, and proceeded, crouching low, the dagger in his right hand. He hid behind a palm tree until Saadallah began to ascend the first steps of the flight of stairs. Arafa pounced, sinking the dagger in his back, above the heart. The man yelped, then collapsed on the ground. The gatekeeper turned, terrified, but the stone smashed into the lantern, putting it out. Arafa ran quickly toward the wall where he had come in. The gatekeeper howled, and in no time there were the sounds of running and a confusion of voices inside the house and at the end of the garden. Arafa tripped over a protrusion, perhaps a tree stump, and fell on his face. Pain shot through his leg and elbow, but he mastered the pain, and crawled the rest of the way to the tunnel. The shouts intensified and the footsteps grew louder. He threw himself into the passage and crawled rapidly through it until he came out in the desert. There he stood up, with a moan, and headed east. Before making the turn around the wall of the mansion, he looked behind him, saw figures rushing toward him and heard someone shout, "This way!" He doubled his speed, in spite of the pain, until he reached the end of the mansion's back wall. When he crossed the empty space between the mansion and the overseer's house, he noticed lights like torches and heard shouts. He headed into the desert, for Muqattam Marketplace, feeling sure that the pain would get the better of him sooner or later, that his pursuers' steps were getting closer and their voices clearer in the silence: "Grab him! Surround him!" At this point he took the bottle out of his breast pocket; this was the bottle he had spent months testing. He stopped running, faced the oncoming men and squinted until he could make out the figures before throwing the bottle at them. In less than a second came the reverberation of an explosion such as had never been heard before, followed by screams and moans. He resumed running, even though there were no footsteps behind him now. At the edge of the desert, he flung himself on the ground, panting and gasping. He was still in pain, crippled and alone under the stars. He looked back, but there was nothing but darkness and silence. With his hand he wiped away some of the blood running down his leg, then dried it with sand. He felt that he should go on, whatever the cost, and struggled up, bracing himself with his hands. Ignoring the pain, he walked toward al-Darasa. As soon as he entered al-Darasa, he caught sight of an approaching figure, and watched it, cautious and fearful, but the figure passed by without turning toward him. Arafa sighed with relief and set off for home by the same route he had used to come. When he neared Gabalawi Alley, he heard noises unusual for that latest time of night: a mixture of bellowing voices, weeping and angry cries that warned of unpredictable mischief in the dark. He paused, then proceeded, keeping very close to the walls. With one eye he glanced at one corner of the alley, and saw crowds of people gathered at another, between the overseer's house and Saadallah's. The Al Qassem neighborhood looked deserted and dark. He slipped along by the wall until he was in the building. He flung himself between Awatif and Hanash and showed them his bloody leg. Awatif was horrified and went away, but came back with a basin full of water and began to wash the wound while he gritted his teeth so that he would not cry out in pain. Hanash helped her.

"Their rage is blazing like fire out there," he told her uneasily.

"What did they say about the explosion?" Arafa grimaced.

"The ones who were chasing you described what happened, and no one believed them. They just stood there gaping at the wounds on their faces and necks. The explosion story almost eclipsed the killing of Saadallah!"

"The gangster of this alley is dead," said Arafa. "Tomorrow the rest of the gangsters will start hacking one another to pieces to take his place!" He looked at his wife, absorbed in tenderly bandaging his wound. "The era of the gangsters is about to disappear, and the first gangster to go will be your father's murderer."

But she did not reply. Hanash's eyes glinted worriedly. Arafa rested his head in his hand, the pain was so great.

105

Early the next morning, someone tapped at the basement door, and when Awatif opened it she saw Yunis, the gatekeeper of the overseer's house. She greeted him softly and invited him in, but he stood where he was.

"His excellency the overseer has summoned Arafa, to consult with him urgently!"

Awatif went to tell Arafa. This lofty invitation gave her little of the natural pleasure it would have brought in other circumstances.

After a short delay, Arafa came out dressed in his best clothes: a white galabiya, a speckled turban and clean leather slippers, but leaning on a cane because of an unexpected but pronounced limp. He greeted Yunis with a raised hand. "Here I am."

The gatekeeper set off, and Arafa followed. The alley was overcome with gloom from one end to the other. All eyes were anxious, as if dreading what catastrophes the next day would bring. All the gangsters' hangers-on were consulting with one another in the coffeehouses, amid the sounds of uninterrupted wailing and lamentation from Saadallah's house. Arafa entered the overseer's house behind the gatekeeper and walked down the passage roofed with jasmine trellises until they reached the terrace. He considered the similarities between this house and the mansion; there were so many that he decided the only difference was one of scale. He thought resentfully, *You imitate him in what benefits you, not what benefits everyone else!* The gatekeeper went ahead to announce him, then turned and motioned him in. He passed into the great hall and saw Qadri, the overseer, seated at the far end, waiting for him. He stopped about an arm's length away from him and bowed respectfully from the waist. The overseer seemed, at first glance, tall and powerfully built, with a fat, ruddy face. When he smiled to acknowledge the greeting, his mouth revealed filthy yellow teeth very much out of keeping with his otherwise magnificent appearance. He motioned for him to sit down beside him on the divan, but Arafa sat instead in the nearest chair. "Never mind, Your Excellency."

But the overseer persisted in his invitation, indicating the divan and speaking in a tone that combined kindness and command. "Here. Sit here."

Arafa had no choice but to sit beside him, but at the far end of the divan. *This must be secret business,* he said to himself, and this was confirmed when he saw the gatekeeper lock the hall door. He remained submissively silent, while the overseer gazed at him tranquilly, and then spoke in a quiet and confiding tone. "Arafa. Why did you kill Saadallah?"

Their eyes locked. His joints felt weak, and things began to spin. The future became the past. He saw the man looking at him self-confidently, and did not doubt that he knew everything. It was fate. Qadri gave him no more time, but spoke again, a little sharply. "Don't be afraid! How could you kill someone if you were this fearful? Pull yourself together and answer me. Tell me truthfully why you killed Saadallah."

Arafa hated the sound of the silence, so he spoke, but hardly knew what he was saying. "Sir—me?"

"You little bastard! Do you think I'm raving? Or that I have no proof? Answer me. Why did you kill him?"

Torn with confusion and desperation, he looked meaninglessly all around the hall.

The overseer spoke again, in a voice as cold as death. "There is no way out, Arafa. If the people outside knew about you, they would tear you apart with their teeth and drink your blood."

The wailing from the gangster's house grew louder. His hopes were buried in the dirt. He opened his mouth but said nothing.

"Silence is an easy way out," said the overseer cruelly. "Of course, then I'd just throw you to those savages outside and tell them, 'Here is Saadallah's killer.' Or, if I wanted, 'Here is Gabalawi's killer!' Gabalawi!" he shouted harshly.

"You dig tunnels under back walls. You escaped the first time, and fell down the next time. But why do you kill, Arafa?"

"I'm innocent, Your Excellency, innocent!" said Arafa in despair, but meaninglessly and almost unintentionally.

"If I made the charge against you public, no one would even ask me for proof," said the overseer derisively. "In our alley, rumor is truth, truth is a judgment, and the judgment is death. But tell me, what made you attack the mansion? And kill Saadallah?"

This man knew everything. How? Arafa did not know; but he did know everything. Otherwise why was he accusing him among all the people in the alley?

"Were you going to steal something?"

He closed his eyes in despair, but said nothing.

"Say something!" shouted the overseer angrily. "You son of snakes!"

"Sir."

"Why do you want to steal, when you're doing better than most people?"

"Temptation to evil," he said in a tone of desperate confession.

The overseer laughed triumphantly, while Arafa asked himself bewilderedly, *Why had the man postponed his destruction until now?* Why had he not shared his secret with one of the gangsters instead of summoning him in this strange way? The overseer left him to himself as if to torment him, then finally spoke. "You're such a dangerous man!"

"I'm a poor man."

"Should I consider a man with a weapon like yours, that makes clubs a joke, a poor man?"

A dead man does not cry over having lost his sight. How much worse could it get? This man was the magician, not him.

The overseer reveled in Arafa's desperation for a few moments before he spoke again. "One of my servants joined those who were chasing you, but he was at the back of the group, so he was not hurt by your weapon. He followed you alone, quietly. You did not notice him following you. He recognized you in al-Darasa, but didn't attack you—he was worried about your surprises. He hurried to me and told me everything."

"Might he have told anyone besides you?" asked Arafa unthinkingly.

"He is a faithful servant." The overseer smiled. He added, in a meaningful tone, "Now tell me about your weapon."

He began to see more clearly. *This man covets something more precious than my life,* he thought, but his despair was still complete. What was the way out?

"It's something much simpler than people think," he said softly.

The overseer's eyes narrowed and he scowled.

"It is within my power to search your house now, but I will avoid calling attention to you. Do you understand?" He paused. "You will not be destroyed as long as you obey me."

Menace shone in his eyes as he spoke. Arafa's heart was cold with despair. "I'll do whatever you want," he said.

"You've started to understand, my little magician. If I had wanted to kill you, the dogs would be digesting you now." He cleared his throat. "Enough of Gabalawi and Saadallah. Tell me about your weapon. What is it?"

"A magic bottle," he said slyly.

"Tell me more," said the overseer, staring at him mistrustfully.

For the first time, he felt a hint of safety. "Only magicians understand the language of magic."

"Can't you explain even if I promise you safety?"

Arafa was laughing inside, but spoke very seriously: "I was only telling the truth."

The man looked at the floor for a moment, then lifted his head. "Do you have much of it?"

"Right now, I don't have any."

"You son of snakes!" The overseer bit his lip.

"Search my house to see the truth with your own eyes," said Arafa simply.

"Can you make more?"

"Of course," he said confidently.

The overseer crossed his arms, agitated, and said, "I want a great deal of it."

"You can have as much as you want," said Arafa.

They exchanged a look of understanding for the first time.

"His excellency wishes to get rid of the accursed gangsters," observed Arafa boldly.

A strange look flashed in the man's eye, and he asked, "Tell me the truth. What made you attack the mansion?"

"Only curiosity," said Arafa innocently. "Killing that faithful servant hurt me, but it wasn't intentional."

"You helped cause the old man's death!" said Qadri, his eyes mistrustful.

"I have suffered terribly for that," said Arafa sadly.

The overseer shrugged. "We should all live so long."

You sinful old hypocrite! All you care about is the estate! thought Arafa, but he said only, "God give you long life."

"Only curiosity made you do it?" he asked again, suspiciously.

"Of course."

"Why did you kill Saadallah?"

"Because I'm like you. I want to get rid of all the gangsters."

The man smiled. "They are a deep-rooted evil!"

But the truth is that you detest them only because of what they take from the estate, not because they are evil.

"That is true, sir."

"You will be richer than you ever dreamed."

"That's all I want," Arafa said shrewdly.

"You won't be doing drudge work for next to nothing; you'll be free to work your magic under my protection, and you will have everything you ever wanted," said the overseer contentedly.

106

The three of them sat on the sofa, Arafa describing what had happened to him while Awatif and Hanash listened attentively, if nervously. They were afraid. Arafa concluded by saying, "We have no choice. Saadallah's funeral has not been held yet. Either we agree or we'll be destroyed."

"Or get out of here," said Awatif.

"There is no escape from his spies. They're all around us."

"We'll never be safe from him here."

He ignored her, the way he would have liked to ignore his own fears. He turned to Hanash. "What's with you? Not saying anything?"

"When we came back to this alley it was with a few limited expectations. You alone are responsible for the change since then, for these huge expectations. I was against your ambitions from the beginning, but I didn't hold back. I helped you, and bit by bit I started to be convinced, until all I hoped for was that our alley would be saved, that everything would be perfect here. Now you take us by surprise with a new plan, which will make us a kind of horrible instrument to terrify our alley. An instrument that can't be destroyed or even resisted, so that gangsters can be resisted, or killed."

"We'll never be safe after that," said Awatif. "He'll get what he wants from you, then get rid of you with a trick, the way he's doing now with the gangsters."

Deep inside, he was convinced by what they said, but he could not stop thinking about it. He spoke aloud, as if debating with himself. "I can make him dependent on my magic forever!"

"In the best case, you'll just be his new gangster," said Awatif.

"Yes," Hanash agreed. "A gangster with a bottle for a weapon, instead of a club. And if you want to know how he'll feel about you, remember the way he feels toward the gangsters."

"For God's sake," snapped Arafa angrily. "As if I'm the ambitious one, and you two don't want anything. I'm the faith that made believers out of the two of you. I spent nights in that back room, and almost got killed twice, only for the good of this alley. If you don't accept what we've been forced into, from no choice of our own, then tell me what we *should* do."

He challenged them with an angry look. Neither of them spoke. He felt squeezed by pain; the whole world seemed to him a suffocating nightmare. He was suddenly overtaken by the strange sensation that his suffering was revenge for his cruel attack on his ancestor, and this thought only heightened his pain and sorrow.

"Let's escape," pleaded Awatif in a whisper.

"Escape how?" he asked irritably.

"I don't know! But it won't be any harder for you than getting into Gabalawi's mansion!"

Arafa exhaled despairingly and spoke with the calm of a mourner. "The overseer is watching us now. His spies are all around us. How can we get out of here?"

Silence fell. What a silence! It was like the silence of the grave that held Gabalawi.

"You see," he gloated, "I don't want to take all the blame for our defeat."

"We have no choice," sighed Hanash, as if making an excuse. Then he added enthusiastically, "The future might bring a chance for us to escape."

"Who knows!" said Arafa distractedly. He went into the back room, and Hanash followed him. They began to fill some of the long-necked bottles with sand, pieces of glass, and other things.

"We should agree on symbols to show the steps of the magic processes, and write them down in a safe, secret notebook so that our work won't be lost, so that my death wouldn't be the end of our experiments. And I hope you're ready to learn magic. We have no idea what fate holds in store for us!"

They continued working very busily. Arafa happened to glance at his brother and saw him scowling. He pretended not to notice anything strange, but spoke genially. "These bottles will take care of the gangsters!"

"It won't help us, or the alley," said Hanash in a low voice.

"What did the poets teach you?" Arafa asked, his hands still working. "In the past there were men like Gabal, Rifaa and Qassem. What is there to prevent others like them in the future?"

"I used to think you were one of them, at times," sighed Hanash.

Arafa emitted a brief dry laugh. "Did my defeat change your mind?"

Hanash said nothing.

"I won't be like them in at least one way. They had followers in our alley. But no one understands me." He laughed. "Qassem could win supporters with a sweet word, but I need years and years to train one man to do what I do, and make a supporter out of him." He finished filling a bottle, corked it and held it admiringly up to the lamplight. "Today, these scare brave men and make their faces bloody. Tomorrow they might kill. I told you, there is no end to magic!"

107

WHO IS PROTECTOR FOR OUR ALLEY? *People began to wonder this* as soon as Saadallah was resting in his grave. Every side began to promote its man. The Al Gabal said that Yusuf was the strongest gangster in the alley and the most closely related to Gabalawi. The Al Rifaa said that they had produced the noblest man the history of the alley had ever know, the man Gabalawi had buried in his own mansion, with his own hands. The Al Qassem said it was they who had not used their own victory for their own good, but for the good of all; in their man's day, the alley had enjoyed undivided unity, and justice and brotherhood had prevailed. As usual, the disagreements began with whispers in the drug dens, then moved out into the air; the dust flew, and people prepared their hearts for the worst dangers. No gangster went out by himself, and if he spent the evening in a coffeehouse or den he was surrounded by followers armed with clubs. Every poet propagandized for his gangster. The shop owners and peddlers looked grim, their faces dark with pessimism. The people were so worried and fearful that they forgot the death of Gabalawi and the murder of Saadallah. Umm Nabawiya, the vegetable seller, was moved to observe, at the top of her lungs, "Life is hell! The dead people are the lucky ones!"

One night a loud voice was heard from a rooftop in Gabal. "Children of the alley, listen, and let's reason together. Gabal is the oldest neighborhood in the alley, and Gabal was its first great man. There is no shame in your taking Yusuf as the protector of your alley."

Loud, mocking responses came from the Al Rifaa and Al Qassem neighborhoods, along with curses and insults, and in no time children were crowding in front of the buildings and began to chant.

Yusuf, Yusuf, you little louse
Who told you to do what you did?

People's hearts grew blacker and angrier. The only thing that delayed the catastrophe was the fact that the bloodletting would involve three sides; either two neighborhoods would have to unite or a particular side would have to pull out. Things began to happen far from the alley itself. Two peddlers met at Bait al-Qadi, one from Gabal and the other from Qassem, and they got into a violent fistfight in which the Qassem man lost his teeth and the Gabal man lost an eye. At the Sultan Baths, another battle broke out between women from Gabal, Rifaa and Qassem while they were naked in the plunge bath. They sank their nails into each other's cheeks and their teeth into thighs and bellies; they pulled hair and hurled mugs, pumice stones, massage loofahs and cakes of soap. The battle left two women unconscious, a third having a miscarriage and countless bodies covered with blood. Early the same afternoon, after the combatants had gone home to the alley, the battle broke out again on the rooftops, only this time they used stones and the vilest obscenities. In no time the sky over the alley was filled with flying objects and screeches that echoed to the clouds. Then a messenger from the overseer secretly visited Yusuf, the gangster of Gabal, and invited him to have a meeting with the overseer. The gangster was careful to tell no one of his meeting. The overseer received him kindly, and asked him to do what he could to quiet people's fears in his neighborhood, especially as this neighborhood was next to his residence. When he saw Yusuf off, he said he hoped that when they next met he would be the gangster of the whole alley! Yusuf left the overseer's house intoxicated by this clear show of support, firmly believing that the top position was within his reach. It did not take him long to bring his territory into line. His people whispered about the status and prestige that tomorrow held for them. The news spread out of their neighborhood to the rest of the alley, and people's imaginations ran away with them. Only a few days later, Agag and Santuri met secretly and agreed between themselves to stop Yusuf now, and to draw lots to see which of them would be top gangster after their victory. At dawn the next day the men of Al Qassem and Al Rifaa attacked the Al Gabal. The battle was fierce, but Yusuf and most of his men were killed, and the survivors fled. Desperate, the Al Gabal gave in to the superior force. They set an afternoon for the lottery they had planned, and on that afternoon the men and women of Qassem and Rifaa hurried to the mansion at the head of the alley. Their throngs stretched as far south as the overseer's house and as far north as the gang headquarters that would belong to the lottery victor. Santuri and his band showed up, as did Agag and his band, and they all exchanged loyal and peaceful greetings.

Agag and Santuri embraced in front of everybody, and Agag spoke loudly enough for everyone to hear. "You and I are brothers, and we will always be brothers, no matter what."

"Forever—the toughest man anywhere!" Santuri agreed fervently.

The people of the two alleys stood opposite one another, separated by the open space in front of the mansion gate. Two men—one from Qassem and the other from Rifaa—came up with a basket filled with little cornets of folded paper. They placed it in the middle of the open space, then each man withdrew to his own side. It was announced to all that the hammer was Agag's symbol and the cleaver was Santuri's; miniatures of each filled the folded paper cornets, half and half. A boy was brought up and blindfolded; he would select one. The boy put his hand out in the tense silence, and drew it back with one cornet in his hand. He opened it, still blindfolded, took out what was inside and held it up.

"The cleaver! The cleaver!" shouted the Al Qassem.

Santuri offered Agag his hand, and Agag clasped it and smiled.

"Long live Santuri, protector of our alley!" everyone roared.

A man detached himself from the Al Rifaa crowd and approached Santuri with open arms. Santuri opened his arms to embrace the man, but in a flash of speed and strength the man produced a knife and drove it into Santuri's heart. Santuri fell over on his face, dead. For a moment there was only shock, but then screams, threats and rage exploded in a cruel and bloody battle between the two neighborhoods. None of the Al Qassem, however, could withstand Agag, and before long defeat crept into their hearts; some of them fell, others retreated, and before evening came the whole alley belonged to Agag. The Al Qassem neighborhood was loud with wailing, but Rifaa rang with delighted trilling and people danced in the street behind their protector—the protector of the whole alley—Agag.

A voice rose over all of the trilling. "Shhhh! Listen! Listen, you sheep!"

They looked in surprise at the source of the sound, and saw Yunis, the overseer's gatekeeper, walking in front of the overseer himself, who was surrounded by a halo of supporters. Agag moved toward this procession and said, "Your servant Agag, protector of the alley, and your servant!"

The overseer stared coolly at him. A terrible hush fell over the whole crowd.

"Agag," he said contemptuously, "I don't want gangsters or gang rule in this alley!"

Rifaa's people were stunned. Their smiles of victory and joy died on their lips.

"What does his excellency mean?" asked Agag, sounding very surprised.

The overseer spoke clearly and forcefully. "We do not want gang rule, or even one gangster. Let the alley live in peace."

"Peace!" sneered Agag.

The overseer threw him a cruel look, but Agag asked him menacingly, "Who will protect you?"

A hail of bottles, pitched by the servants, landed on Agag and his followers, and the explosions shook the walls. Sand and glass splinters wounded faces and bodies, and blood began to spout. Terror assaulted the people as a vulture attacks a chicken; they lost their minds, and their legs gave out under them. Agag and his men fell, and the servants finished them off. The shrieks from Rifaa grew louder, while Gabal and Qassem were loud with gloating cheers.

Yunis went down the middle of the alley, calling for quiet, until everyone fell silent, and then he addressed them in a shout. "People of the alley! Happiness and peace are now yours, thanks to his excellency the overseer, may God lengthen his life! From now on no gang will oppress you or take your money!"

The sounds of their cheers reached the heavens.

108

Arafa and his family moved, by night, from the basement in Rifaa to the gang headquarters to the right of the mansion. This was the overseer's order; he could not be disobeyed. They found themselves in a house that was more like a dream. They walked around the rich garden, the elegant halls and terrace, the bedrooms, sitting rooms and dining room on the second floor and the roof, whose every wall and corner was crowded with chicken coops, rabbit cages and dovecotes. For the first time they wore beautiful clothes and breathed sweet air, sniffing all the beautiful smells.

"It's a miniaturized mansion," said Arafa. "Only without secrets."

"What about your magic?" asked Hanash. "Doesn't that count as a secret?"

"No one even dreams of places like this," said Awatif, wide-eyed.

The three looked and smelled different—even their complexions were better. But no sooner had they settled in than a group of men and women visited them; the first said he was the gatekeeper, the second the cook, the third the gardener and the fourth the poultry manager. The rest were house servants.

Arafa was amazed. "Who told you to come here?"

"His excellency the overseer," said the gatekeeper, speaking for the rest.

Shortly afterward, Arafa was summoned to meet the overseer. Qadri spoke first, once they were seated side by side in an alcove off the reception hall. "We will meet often, Arafa. I hope I didn't trouble you by calling you here."

Actually, he was very troubled by the meeting, the place and the man, but he smiled. "I'm happy to see you," he said.

"Your magic has made us all happy. Do you like the house?"

"It's more than a dream," said Arafa shyly. "Especially the dreams of poor people like us. Today all kinds of servants reported to us!"

"They are my people," said the overseer, gazing steadily into his face. "I sent them to you, to serve and protect you."

"Protect me!"

Qadri laughed. "Yes. Don't you know that your moving here is the talk of the whole alley? They're saying among themselves, 'He's the one who made the magic bottles.' The gangsters' families want revenge, as you know, and everyone else is dying of envy. What with all that, you're surrounded by danger. My advice to you is not to trust anyone—or to go out alone, or too far from your house!"

Arafa frowned. What was he but a prisoner encircled by anger and hatred?

"Don't be afraid, though. My men will be all around you. Enjoy the life you want, in your house or here in mine. What do you have to lose except the desert and the slums? Don't forget that the people of our alley say that Saadallah was killed by the same weapon that killed Agag, and that the murderer who got into Saadallah's house used the same means to get into the mansion before that. That the same person killed Agag, Saadallah and Gabalawi, and that the person is Arafa the magician."

"This is a curse on my head!" cried Arafa convulsively.

"You don't have to worry, as long as you're under my protection, with my servants around you."

You bastard, you've thrown me into a prison. The only reason I wanted magic was to get rid of people like you, not to serve you. Now the people I loved and wanted to save detest me, and one of them might kill me.

"Distribute the gangsters' shares in the estate among the people, and they'll be happy with both of us!"

Qadri laughed scornfully. "So why get rid of the gangsters?" he asked. He fixed Arafa with a cold stare. "You're looking for a way to please them? Forget that. Get used to other people hating you, as I have, and don't forget that your real safety is my being pleased with you."

"I was and still am your servant," he said hopelessly.

The overseer looked up at the ceiling as if contemplating its embellishments, then looked down again. "I hope that enjoying your new life doesn't take you away from your magic."

Arafa nodded.

"And that you make as many magic bottles as you can!"

"You don't need more than we have now," said Arafa cautiously.

Qadri masked his irritation with a smile. "Wouldn't it be wisest to have plenty of them on hand?"

He did not reply. He was filled with despair. Had his turn come this quickly? he wondered. Suddenly he spoke. "Your excellency, if my staying here is a problem for you, let me go away and not come back."

"What did you say?" asked the man, looking confused.

Arafa stared at him candidly. "I know that my life is subject to your need for me."

"Don't think I take your intelligence lightly," said Qadri with a mirthless laugh. "And I admit that you're thinking soundly. But how can you think that my need for you ends with bottles? Isn't your magic capable of other things?"

But Arafa resumed his statement, somewhat sternly. "Your men are the ones who went around revealing the secret of the services I've done for you, I'm sure of that. But you also have to remember that you need me to live."

The overseer frowned menacingly, but Arafa went on uninterrupted. "You have no gangsters now. The only power you have is from those bottles, and you have too few of them to make any difference. If I died today, you'd follow me either tomorrow or the next day."

The overseer leaned toward him like a beast of prey, then suddenly snatched his neck in his hands, squeezing it until his body shook. Then he abruptly released his hold and sat back, with a smile of loathing. "Look what your impudent tongue made me do! We have no reason to quarrel. We can enjoy victory and live in peace."

Arafa was breathing heavily to recover from the shock, while the other man continued to speak. "Don't be afraid that I will take your life. I will protect it like my own. Enjoy the world, and don't forget your magic, whose blossoms we pick together. And know that if either of us betrays the other, he betrays himself."

Awatif and Hanash frowned as Arafa repeated the conversation for them in the new house. It seemed that all three of them lacked true safety in this new life. But they forgot the reasons for their unease at supper around a wonderful table covered with the most delicious foods and mellow old wine. For the first time Arafa's voice was raised in laughter, and Hanash's torso shook with mirth. They lived their lives as circumstances required. They worked together in a room behind the hall they had prepared for magic. Arafa diligently inscribed the symbols they had agreed upon in a notebook only the two of them knew about. Once, while they were working, Hanash told him, "What prisoners we are!"

"Lower your voice," Arafa cautioned him. "The walls have ears."

Hanash looked hatefully over at the door, and lowered his voice to a whisper. "Isn't it possible for you to make a new weapon, without his knowing, so that we could get rid of him?"

"We wouldn't be able to test it secretly, with all these servants," said Arafa crossly. "He knows everything that goes on with us. And if we get rid of him, the alley people who want our blood will get us before we could defend ourselves from them."

"So why are you so hard at work?"

"Because work is all I have," Arafa sighed.

Late in the afternoon, he would go to the house of the overseer, who sat him down and gave him drinks, and come home at night to find that Hanash had prepared a little hashish for him in the garden or the room with wooden screens, and they would smoke it together. Arafa had never been a hashish smoker, but he was carried along by the current, and he was worn down by boredom. Even Awatif began to learn these things. They all needed to forget their boredom, fear, desperation and depressed feelings of guilt, along with the high hopes of the past. Despite all this, the men had work, though Awatif had none. She ate until she felt sick, and slept until she was tired of lying down; she spent long hours in the garden, enjoying all its beauties, remembering that she was now pampered with the life Adham had longed for. It was boring! How could anyone want it badly enough to grieve over it? Perhaps it would be very nice if it were not a prison; not surrounded by enemies and hatred. But it would remain a prison, encircled by loathing, with no escape but the hashish pipe. Once, Arafa was late coming back from the overseer's house, and she decided to wait for him in the garden. Night advanced like a caravan led by its camel driver, the moon. She listened to the melody of the branches and the croaking of frogs. She heard the sound of the gate opening, and got up to greet him, but the rustle of clothing from the direction of the basement caught her ear. From where she stood, she saw the figure of a servant girl in the moonlight, heading toward the gate, unaware of Awatif. Arafa came staggering in. The servant turned to the wall leading out from the terrace, and he followed her, and Awatif saw them come together, hidden from the moonlight by the shadow of the wall.

109

Awatif exploded, as would any woman of Gabalawi Alley, and pounced like a lioness on the clinging twosome. She punched Arafa in the head, and he fell back, dazed, and staggered until he lost his balance and fell down. Then she sank her nails into the servant's neck and beat her on the head until her shrieks split the night's silence. Arafa struggled up, but did not dare go near the fight. Hanash came running, followed by several servants, but when he found out what had happened, he sent the servants away and got between the two women as decorously and skillfully as he could. He managed to get Awatif back to the house, though she was still hurling curses, insults and obscenities. Arafa reeled up to the room with the wooden screens that overlooked the desert, and dropped onto a cushion, alone in his hashish den. He stretched his legs out and rested his head against the wall, half conscious. It was not long before Hanash caught up with him, and sat across from him around the pipe, in silence. He glanced quickly at Arafa, but went back to looking at the floor until he broke the silence. "It was bound to happen."

Two eyes looked up at him, shamed but fugitive. "Light the fire!"

They stayed in the den until it was nearly morning. The servant left, and was replaced. It seemed to Awatif that the atmosphere around her provoked one slip after another. She began to assign some sinister motive to every movement her husband made, in line with her suspicions, until her life was hell. She had lost the one consolation she had enjoyed in this perilous prison. This was not her house, or her husband. It was a prison by day and a brothel by night. Where was the Arafa she had loved? The Arafa who had challenged Santuri by marrying her, who had more than once risked death for the alley, so that she even thought him the kind of man the poets sang of? Today he was nothing but a bastard like Qadri or

Saadallah. Life with him was a burning torment, an insomniac fear. One night Arafa came home from the overseer's house and found no trace of Awatif. The gatekeeper swore that he had seen her leave the house in the early evening, and that she had not been back.

"Where did she go?" asked Arafa. His breath reeked of wine.

"In the alley," said Hanash uneasily. "With her old neighbor, Umm Zanfil, the jam seller."

" 'No woman is won with gentleness,' as the people of the alley say. I won't do anything until she comes back humbled."

But she did not come back. Ten days passed, and then Arafa decided to go to Umm Zanfil's at night, intending that no one should know of his visit. At the appointed time, he slipped out of the house, followed by Hanash. They had gone only a few paces when they heard footsteps behind them. They turned around and saw two of the house servants.

"Go back to the house," Arafa told them.

"We are guarding you, on his excellency's orders," one of them replied.

He was enraged, but said nothing more. They walked toward an old building in the Al Qassem neighborhood and went up to the top floor, where Umm Zanfil's room was located. Arafa knocked at the door until it was opened by Awatif herself, her face sleepy. When she saw Arafa's face in the light of the little lamp in her hand, she made a face and pulled back, but he went after her and closed the door behind him. Umm Zanfil woke up, in a corner of the room, and stared bewilderedly at the guest.

"What are you doing here? What do you want? Go back to you wonderful house," Awatif said sharply.

"Arafa the magician!" whispered Umm Zanfil uneasily, staring at his face.

"Come to your senses. Come with me," Arafa told his wife, completely ignoring the bewildered woman.

"I won't go back to your prison," she said fiercely. "I'll never find the peace of mind I have in this room."

"But you're my wife."

"What's wrong with your other wives over there?" she said, raising her voice.

"Let her go back to sleep, and return in the morning," complained Umm Zanfil.

He gave her a harsh look, saying nothing, then turned to his wife. "Every man makes a mistake."

"You're nothing but one big mistake," she snapped.

He came a little closer to her, playing on every tender note in his voice. "Awatif. I cannot get along without you."

"But I've done without you!"

"You left me for one slip I made, when I was drunk?"

She twitched. "Don't give me the excuse you were drunk. Your life is one big mistake—you'd need dozens of excuses to justify it. There's nothing in it for me but trouble and pain."

"But at least it would be better than living in this room!"

She smiled bitterly. "Who knows? Tell me why your prison guards let you come to me."

"Awatif!"

"I will not go back to a house where I have nothing to do but yawn and socialize with my great magician husband's girlfriends!"

In vain he tried to dissuade her from her persistence. She met his gentleness with obstinacy, his anger with anger and his insults with insults. He left her in despair, then went home followed by his friend and the two servants.

"What will you do?" Hanash asked him.

"What we do every day," he said with listless resentment.

Qadri, the overseer, asked him, "Is there any news of your wife?"

"Stubborn as a mule, God preserve you," said Arafa, taking his seat by his side.

"Don't bother yourself with a woman when you have better than her," said the overseer disdainfully. He stared very hard at Arafa. "Does your wife know any of the secrets of your work?"

Arafa responded with a very suspicious look. "No one knows magic but the magician!"

"I'm afraid that—"

"Don't be afraid of something that hasn't a shadow of an existence." There was a long silence, which Arafa broke anxiously. "You'll never harm her as long as I'm alive!"

The overseer suppressed his anger, smiled and pointed invitingly to the two brimming glasses. "Who said anyone would harm her?"

110

When Qadri grew friendlier and more trusting toward Arafa, he began to invite him to his private soirees, which usually began at midnight. Arafa attended a strange party in the great hall, which abounded with all the most delicious foods and the finest wines; beautiful women danced naked, and Arafa almost lost his mind, with the liquor and the sights he saw. That night he saw the overseer's riotousness go beyond any limit, like a wild beast. The overseer invited him to a party in the garden, in a luxuriant bower encircled by a stream whose surface was bright with moonlight. They had wine and fruit, and two beautiful servant girls, one of them for the brazier and the other for the pipe. The tender night breeze was laden with the fragrance of the flowers, the lute melody and singers' voices.

> *Carnations as fresh as mint in the garden*
> *Soothe the manly men who smoke hashish.*

There was a full moon whose perfection could be seen whole when a verdant mulberry branch bent with the breeze, and its rays of light shone through the branches and leaves when the branch was still again.

The scent from the pipe in the girl's hand made Arafa as dizzy as a star in its orbit. "God rest Adham," he said.

"And God rest Idris," the overseer said, smiling. "What made you think of him?"

"Sitting here like this."

"Adham loved dreams, but the only ones he had were the ones Gabalawi put in his head." He laughed. "Gabalawi, whom you spared the trouble of old age!"

Arafa's heart contracted, and his happiness flickered out. He muttered sadly. "I never killed anyone in my life but one criminal gangster."

"What about Gabalawi's servant?"

"I was forced to kill him."

"Arafa," Qadri sneered, "you are a coward."

Arafa concentrated on the moon through the branches, leaving the drug party to the lute melodies, then stole a look at the beautiful servant's hand as she compressed the lump of hashish.

"Where are you?" cried the overseer.

Arafa turned to him with a smile. "Do you usually spend the evening alone?"

"No one here is worth spending the evening with."

"Even me, I have no one but Hanash."

"If you smoke enough, you don't mind being alone," said Qadri disdainfully.

Arafa hesitated a moment, then spoke. "Aren't we in a prison, Your Excellency?"

"What do you want?" said the man sharply. "We're surrounded by people who hate us!"

He remembered what Awatif had said, how she preferred Umm Zanfil's room to his house, and sighed. "What a curse."

"Be careful or you'll ruin our fun."

"May life be fun forever," said Arafa, reaching for the pipe.

"Forever?" Qadri laughed. "It would be enough if we could breathe one breath as young men in our whole lives, with your magic!" He filled his chest with the smell of the garden, sweetened by the moist late-night air. "Lucky thing Arafa is not without his uses," he said.

The overseer left the pipe in the beautiful girl's hand, and exhaled the thick smoke, silver in the moonlight. "Why do we get old?" he asked regretfully. "We eat the most wonderful food, drink the most delightful drinks and live the best life, but old age creeps up on us in its own time. Nothing can stop it. Like the sun or the moon."

"But Arafa's pills can make the cold of old age hot!"

"There is something you cannot do."

"What is it, sir?"

The overseer seemed mournful in the moonlight. "What is the most hateful thing to you?"

The prison he lived in, maybe; or the hatred all around him; or the goal he had failed to reach. "Losing my youth."

"No, you don't worry about that."

"Why not, when my wife is mad at me."

"She'll always find one reason or another to get mad."

The breeze grew brisker, the rustle of the branches grew louder, and the coals glowed in the brazier.

"Why do we die, Arafa?"

Arafa looked at him gloomily but said nothing.

"Even Gabalawi died," the overseer went on.

It was like a needle piercing his heart, but he managed to speak. "We're all dead, the children of the dead."

"You don't need me to remind you what you said," he said grumpily.

"Long may you live, sir."

"Long or short, the end of it is the grave that worms love."

"Don't let your thoughts ruin your fun," said Arafa.

"It never leaves me, death. Death, death, always death. It could come at any moment, and for the slightest reason, or without any reason at all. Where is Gabalawi? Where are the men the poets sang of? This was one death that shouldn't have been."

Arafa looked at his pale face and terror-stricken eyes. His mental state was the opposite of this place. "The important thing is that life is how it should be," he said gently.

Qadri made an angry gesture and spoke with a sharpness that killed their pleasure. "Life is how it should be, and better. Nothing is missing. Even youth can be restored with pills, but what good is that when death follows us like a shadow? How can I forget it, when death itself reminds me every hour?"

He enjoyed his discomfort, but quickly was disgusted by his own feelings. He watched the beautiful girl's hands with love and longing, asking inwardly, *Who can promise me I'll see another night's moon?*

"We probably need another drink," he said.

"We'll still wake up in the morning." Arafa despised this man, and sensed an opportunity he wanted to seize. "If it weren't for the resentment of the deprived people all around us, our life wouldn't leave a bad taste in our mouths."

The overseer laughed contemptuously. "You talk like an old woman. If we were able to make the alley people's lives better, up to our level, would death stop hunting us?"

Arafa nodded resignedly, until the man talked out his irritation, then said, "Death prospers in poverty, misery and bad conditions."

"And everyplace else, stupid."

"Yes." Arafa smiled. "Because it's contagious, like some diseases."

"That's a strange view to defend your ignorance." The overseer chuckled.

"We don't know anything about it," said Arafa, emboldened by his laughter. "It might be that way. As people live better, the pain lessens, life gets more valuable and every happy person wants to fight death to keep as much of his happy life as possible."

"None of that helps a dead man."

"But magicians will get together and dedicate themselves to resisting death. Everyone who's able will work magic. Death will be threatened with death."

The overseer emitted a peal of high-pitched laughter, then closed his eyes to dream. Arafa took up the pipe and sucked at it for one very long breath, until the coals glowed. The lute started playing again, after a silence, and the lovely voice began to sing, "Tarry, O night."

"You're a hash-head, Arafa, not a magician."

"This is how we kill death," said Arafa simply.

"Why don't you do your work alone?"

"I work every day, but he doesn't prevent me from working alone."

The overseer listened to the music for a while, without enthusiasm. "If only you succeeded, Arafa! What would you do if you succeeded?"

"I'd bring Gabalawi back to life," he said so quickly that the words seem to speak of their own accord.

The man curled his lip listlessly. "That's your own business, in your capacity as his killer."

Arafa frowned, pained, and murmured inaudibly. "If only you succeeded, Arafa!"

111

Arafa left the overseer's house at dawn. He had drugged himself into a magical world of cloudy sights and sounds, and his feet could hardly carry him. He moved toward his house in the sleeping alley that gleamed with moonlight. Halfway between the overseer's house and his own—in front of the mansion gate—a human figure appeared. He did not know where it had come from.

"Good morning, Arafa, sir!" it said in a near-whisper.

He was surprised by fear, perhaps triggered by the surprise, but his two bodyguards jumped on the figure and subdued it. He looked at it closely, and his unbelieving eyes told him that it was the figure of a black woman dressed in black from her neck to her feet. He ordered the servants to let her go, and they did.

"What is it, my lady?"

"I want to talk to you alone," she said in a voice that confirmed that she was black.

"Why?"

"A sad woman wants to tell you her troubles."

"God comfort you," he muttered irritably. This was said to beggars instead of giving them money. He was about to go.

"By your ancestor's dear life," she implored touchingly. "Please."

He stared at her angrily, but could not take his eyes from her. He wondered where and when he had seen that face before. Then his heart pounded so hard that it knocked the drunkenness out of his head. This was the face he had seen at the threshold of Gabalawi's room when he was hiding behind the chair on that doomed night! This was Gabalawi's servant, who shared his room! He was overcome with fear. His joints weakened as he stared at her in terror.

"Shall we chase her away?" one of his servants asked.

"Go to the gate of the house and wait there," he told them.

He waited until they had left, and they had the space in front of the mansion to themselves. He looked at her thin black face, high, narrow forehead and pointed chin, and the wrinkles that crowded her mouth and forehead. He said, to reassure himself, that she had not seen him that night, but where had she been since Gabalawi's death, and why was she here?

"Yes, ma'am?"

"I have no complaint," she said calmly. "But I wanted to tell you everything, to keep a promise."

"A promise?"

She moved her head close to his. "I was Gabalawi's servant. He died in my arms!"

"You!"

"Yes, me. Believe me."

He needed no proof. "How did our ancestor die?" he asked uneasily.

"He was terribly shaken after the discovery of a servant's corpse, and all of a sudden he died. I hurried to him to support his back. It was trembling! That giant, whom the desert itself obeyed!"

Arafa's sigh was so hot that it disturbed the night's silence, and he bowed his head sadly, as if to hide it from the moonlight.

The woman resumed her story. "I came to you to carry out his will."

He lifted his head to her, shaking. "What is it? Tell me."

Her voice was as calm as the moonlight. "He told me, before he passed away, 'Go to Arafa the magician, and tell him for me that his ancestor died pleased with him.' "

Arafa jumped as if he had been stung. "You liar! What are you trying to do?"

"What is wrong?"

"Tell me what kind of a game you're playing."

"Only what I said. God is my witness."

"What do you know about the killer?" he asked her suspiciously.

"I don't know anything, sir," she said innocently. "Since my master passed away, I've been bedridden. When I got better, the first thing I did was go to you."

"What did he tell you?"

" 'Go to Arafa the magician, and tell him for me that his ancestor died pleased with him.' "

"Liar!" said Arafa menacingly. "You think you're pretty smart. You know that I—" He changed his tone of voice. "How did you know where to find me?"

"I asked for you as soon as I came, and they told me that you were at the overseer's, so I waited."

"They didn't tell you that I killed Gabalawi?"

"No one killed Gabalawi!" She was very alarmed. "No one would have been able to kill him!"

"Whoever killed his servant killed him."

"That's a lie! The man died in my arms!" she shouted angrily.

Arafa wanted to cry, but could not produce one tear. He looked sideways at the woman.

"I will leave you, sir," she said simply.

"Do you swear you were telling the truth?" he asked her in a very hoarse and gruff voice, as if it were his tortured conscience speaking.

"I swear by the Lord, who is my witness," she said clearly.

She left as the hues of dawn were dyeing the horizon. He followed her with his eyes until she disappeared. In his bedroom, he fell in a faint. He came to a few minutes later, feeling exhausted to death, and fell asleep. His sleep lasted only two hours before he was awakened by inner anguish. He called Hanash, and the man came to him. He told him the woman's story.

Hanash stared at him in confusion, and laughed when the story was over. "What were you smoking last night?"

"I did not imagine what I saw last night. It was real, I'm sure of that."

"Sleep," said Hanash earnestly. "You need a good deep sleep."

"Don't you believe me?"

"Of course not. And if you sleep like I'm telling you to, and wake up later, you won't believe it either."

"Why don't you believe me?"

Hanash laughed. "I was at the window as you left the overseer's house. I saw you coming through the alley toward your house. You stood for a little while in front of the mansion, then kept going, with your servants behind you!"

Arafa jumped to his feet. "Get the servants!" he said triumphantly.

"No," said Hanash, cautioning him with a finger. "They'll only wonder about your sanity."

"I'll ask them to say what they saw, in front of you."

"The servants respect us little enough as it is. Don't throw that away."

A mad gleam came into Arafa's eye, and he spoke stuporously. "I'm not crazy. I didn't imagine it! Gabalawi died pleased with me."

"Maybe," said Hanash sympathetically. "But don't call any of the servants."

"If there's going to be trouble, it will land on you first."

"God forbid," said Hanash gently. "Let's let the woman speak for herself. Where did she go?"

Arafa frowned, trying to remember, then said worriedly, "I forgot to ask her where she lives."

"If what you saw was real, why did you let her go?"

"It was real!" Arafa insisted. "I'm not crazy. Gabalawi died pleased with me."

"Don't get excited," said Hanash patiently. "You need to rest."

He came close to him, ruffled his hair and gently pushed him toward the bed, staying there until he lay down. Arafa closed his eyes wearily, and fell into a deep sleep.

112

Arafa spoke calmly but resolutely. "I've decided to get out of here."
Hanash was so surprised that his hands stopped working. He looked around warily, and although the workroom was locked, he looked afraid.

Arafa ignored his surprise and went on, his hands working busily. "This prison just makes me think of death. I feel as though parties and drinking and dancers are the overtures of death. I smell the odor of graves in every garden of flowers."

"But *real* death is waiting for us in the alley," said Hanash uneasily.

"We'll go far away from the alley." He looked him straight in the eye. "And someday we'll come back victorious."

"If we can get out!"

"The bastards trust us. We can get out of here."

They worked on in silence for a while.

"Isn't that what you wanted?" Arafa asked.

"I had almost forgotten," Hanash murmured timidly. "But tell me. What made you decide that today?"

Arafa smiled. "My ancestor let it be known that he was pleased with me, even though I attacked his house and killed his servant."

The surprise came back into Hanash's face. "Will you risk your life for a vision you saw when you were on drugs?"

"Call it what you want, but I am positive that when he died he was pleased with me. Neither the attack nor the killing angered him, but if he saw the way I live now, the world couldn't hold all his anger." He lowered his voice. "That's why he reminded me that he used to be pleased with me!"

Hanash shook his head, marveling at this. "You never used to speak of him with respect."

"That was before, when I was so doubtful. Now that he's dead—the dead deserve respect."

"God rest his soul."

"God forbid I should forget that I was the cause of his death. That's why I must restore him to life if I can. If I'm able to succeed, we will never know death."

Hanash stared at him dejectedly. "All magic has given you so far are some stimulant pills and destructive bottles."

"We know where magic begins, but we cannot even imagine where it ends." He looked around the room. "We'll pack up everything but the notebook, Hanash—that's the treasure of our secrets, I'll carry it in my shirt. Getting out of here won't be as hard as you think."

Arafa went as usual to the overseer's house that evening, and came back to his house a little before dawn. He found Hanash awake and waiting for him. They stayed in the bedroom for an hour, until they were sure the servants were asleep, then slipped out to the terrace together, very lightly and cautiously. The snoring of the servant sleeping on the balcony over the terrace rose regularly, so they stole down the steps and headed for the gate. Hanash went to the gatekeeper's bed and lifted his arm that held a cane, and brought it down, but it struck only a lifeless cotton form and made a sound that disturbed the stillness of the night. So the gatekeeper was not in his bed. They were afraid that the sound might have woken someone, and stayed behind the door with pounding hearts. Arafa lifted the bolt and slowly opened the gate, then went out. Hanash followed him. They reclosed the gate and moved out through the silent darkness, toward Umm Zanfil's building, staying close to the walls. Halfway down the alley they met a recumbent dog that stood up curiously and ran toward them, sniffing. It followed them for a few steps, then stopped and yawned.

When they reached the entrance of the building, Arafa whispered,

"Wait for me here. If you hear anything, give a whistle and go to Muqattam Marketplace."

Arafa went into the building and crossed the hall to the stairway. He climbed up to Umm Zanfil's room, and knocked at the door until he heard his wife's voice asking who was there. He spoke rapidly, with feeling. "It's Arafa. Open up, Awatif."

She opened the door, and he saw her face, wan with sleep, in the light of the small lantern in her hand.

"Follow me. We're going to escape together," he said immediately.

As she stood looking at him dazedly, Umm Zanfil appeared behind her shoulder.

"We'll escape from the alley. We'll be the way we were before. Hurry."

She hesitated a little, then spoke with a hint of exasperation. "What made you think of me?"

"You can blame me later," he said with frantic longing. "Time is too precious now."

There was a whistle from Hanash, and confused sounds.

"The dogs!" he cried. "We've lost our chance, Awatif."

He jumped to the head of the stairs and saw, in the building's open hall, lights and human forms. He stepped back in despair.

"Come in," said Awatif.

"Don't come in," said Umm Zanfil roughly, in self-defense.

What was the point in going in? He gestured to a small window in the room and asked his wife quickly, "Where does it go?"

"The skylight."

He reached into his chest for the notebook, went for the window, pushing Umm Zanfil out of his way, and tossed it out. He hurried out of the room, closing the door behind him, and leaped up the few stairs that led to the roof. He looked over the front wall down to the alley. It was swarming with people and torches, and he heard the racket of people coming up toward him. He ran to the side wall abutting the next building on the Gamaliya side, but saw people getting there before him, led by someone carrying a torch. He went to the other wall, adjacent to one of the Rifaa buildings, only to see the lights of torches coming out of the door that opened onto that roof. He imagined that he could hear Umm Zanfil's cries. Had they attacked her place? Had they taken Awatif? He heard a voice coming from the door of the roof.

"Surrender, Arafa!"

He stood submissively, not uttering a word. No one came near him, but the voice spoke again.

"If you throw a bottle, we'll shower you with bottles."

"I have nothing on me."

They came at him and surrounded him. He saw among them Yunis, the overseer's gatekeeper, who now approached him, shouting, "You criminal! Bastard! Ingrate!"

In the alley he saw two men shoving Awatif along before them.

"Leave her alone," he begged passionately. "She has nothing to do with me."

But he was silenced by a blow to his temple.

113

Arafa and Awatif stood before the raging overseer, their hands bound behind their backs. The overseer punched him in the face until his fist ached.

"You visited me like a friend while you were plotting against me, you son of a whore!" he screeched.

"He only came to me to make peace with me," Awatif said, weeping.

The overseer spat in her face. "Shut up, you evil bitch!"

"She's innocent," said Arafa. "She has nothing to do with this."

"She was your partner in the murder of Gabalawi and all of your crimes." He roared, "You wanted to escape! I'll help you escape from the whole world!"

He called his men, and they came with two sacks. They pushed Awatif, and she fell on her face. They speedily bound her feet and pulled the sack over her despite her screams, then tied it shut with a tight knot.

Arafa began to scream with crazed agitation. "Kill us if you want, but tomorrow the people who hate you will kill you!"

The overseer cackled. "I have enough bottles to protect me forever."

"Hanash escaped, he escaped with all our secrets, and he'll come back someday too powerful for you to resist, and he'll rid the alley of your evil."

Qadri kicked him in the stomach, and he collapsed, writhing. The men jumped on him and did to him what they had done to his wife, then carried the two sacks outside and took them to the desert. It was not long before Awatif fainted, but he was still suffering terribly. Where were they taking them, and how would they kill them? Would they beat them to death with clubs? With rocks? Set fire to them? Throw them off the mountain? How terrible that the final minutes of his life had to be so horribly painful! Even magic could find no way out of this choking agony; his head, swollen from the overseer's blows, lay at the bottom of the sack, and he was almost smothered. He no longer had any hope of rest, except in death. He and his hopes would die, but that cackling man might live a long life. The people he had wanted to destroy would gloat over him. No one would even know what Hanash would do. The men carrying him to his death were silent. None of them spoke a word. There was only darkness, and nothing beyond the darkness but death. It was from fear of this death that he had hidden under the overseer's wing, and lost everything; now death had come. Death, which killed life with fear even before it came. If he could come back to life, he would shout at every man: *Don't be afraid! Fear doesn't keep death away, it keeps life away! People of the alley—you aren't alive, and life will never be possible for you as long as you fear death.*

"Here," said one of the killers.

"The ground is looser there," complained another.

His heart trembled, though he did not understand the meaning of their words—anyway, it was the language of death. He braced himself

for the expected torment, until he almost shouted at them, "Kill me!"
But he did not do it. Suddenly the sack was thrown to the ground, and
he groaned as his head hit the earth. Pain split his neck and spinal
column. He waited, moment after moment, for the onslaught of the
clubs, or something even worse. He cursed his whole life for the sake of
evil, the ally of death.

"Dig fast, so that we'll make it back before morning," he heard
Yunis say.

Why were they digging the grave before killing them? It seemed to
him that his chest was being crushed under Muqattam Mountain. He
heard a moan in which he immediately recognized Awatif's voice, and
his shackled body twitched violently. The sounds of digging reached his
ears. He marveled at how cruel men could be.

"You'll be thrown into the bottom of the hole," he heard Yunis say.
"Then you'll be covered with dirt. No one's going to hurt you!"

Awatif screamed despite her exhaustion, and deep inside he
screamed in a language no one knew. Rough hands lifted them up and
threw them into the bottom of the hole, the soil began to heap up, and
the dust rose in the twilight.

114

The news of Arafa spread through the alley. No one knew the real
reasons for his murder, but the people guessed that he had angered his
patron, which led to this inescapable fate. One day it was said that Arafa
had been killed with the same magic weapon with which he had killed
Saadallah and Gabalawi. Everyone rejoiced at his death, despite their
hatred for the overseer, and the gangsters' families and supporters
gloated most of all. They rejoiced at the death of the man who had killed
their blessed ancestor and given their tyrannical overseer a terrible

weapon with which to humble them forever. The future looked black, or at least blacker than it had looked before all the power had been concentrated in one cruel hand. They lost the hope that a quarrel might break out between two men, weakening both of them, so that one of them would seek the support of the people of the alley. Now it seemed that they had no choice but subjugation; to see the estate, its conditions and the words of Gabal, Rifaa and Qassem as wasted dreams, good only to accompany poets' melodies, not for anything else in this life.

One day a man stood in Umm Zanfil's way as she was on her way to al-Darasa, and greeted her, saying, "Good afternoon, Umm Zanfil."

She peered at him and almost instantly spoke in surprise. "Hanash!"

He came closer to her, smiling. "Did our late friend leave anything in your room the night they took him away?"

"He didn't leave one thing," she said in a tone meant to divert any suspicion from herself. "I saw him throw some papers out of the skylight. I had a look in there myself, the next day, and among the garbage I found a notebook, as worthless as it could be, so I left it there and came back."

A strange light came into Hanash's eyes, and he spoke urgently. "Take me there so I can find the notebook."

The old woman started, alarmed, and said, "Get away from me! It was only God's mercy that saved you the last time."

He put a coin into her hand to calm her fears, and they agreed to meet late that night when all eyes would be sleeping. At the appointed hour, guided by her, he stole down to the dump underneath the skylight. He lit a candle and squatted among the heaps of trash to search for Arafa's notebook. He went through the heaps, paper by paper, rag by rag, working his fingers through ashes, dirt, remnants of honeyed tobacco and scraps of rancid food, but without finding what he sought so eagerly.

He went back up to Umm Zanfil, angry and desperate. "I didn't find anything."

"I have nothing to do with all of you! You just come here, and trouble follows!"

"Please, just be patient."

"Days past have not left me any more patience or sanity. Tell me what you want from that notebook?"

He hesitated a little before saying, "It's Arafa's notebook."

"Arafa, God forgive him! He killed Gabalawi, then gave his magic to the overseer and left!"

"He was one of the good children of Gabalawi, but his luck turned on him. He wanted the same things for you that Gabal, Rifaa and Qassem wanted—even better things."

The woman gave him a skeptical look, and spoke to dismiss him. "Maybe the garbageman took away the garbage I left the notebook in. Look for it where they burn the trash in Salihiya."

And so Hanash went to the dump at Salihiya and asked for the Gabalawi Alley garbageman and asked him about the trash from the alley.

"You're looking for something lost! What is it?" the man asked him.

"A notebook."

A suspicious look appeared in the man's eyes, but he pointed to a corner in the room next to the bathroom.

"Good luck. Either you'll find it, or it's in the furnace."

Hanash began to look hopefully, patiently through the garbage. This notebook was the last hope he had left in life; it was his hope, and the alley's. Unlucky Arafa had died defeated, leaving only evil and a bad reputation behind him, but this notebook could redress his wrongs, finish off his enemies and spread hope throughout this infernal alley.

"Haven't you found what you're looking for?" the garbageman asked.

"I need more time. Bless you."

The man scratched his armpits. "What is it about the notebook?"

Hanash fought back his anxiety, and said, "It has my store's accounts in it. You'll see for yourself."

He kept searching in spite of his mounting fear, until he heard a familiar voice.

"Where's your bean pot, Mitwali?"

He quivered with fear at the voice of Shankal, the bean seller of the alley.

He did not turn around, but wondered uneasily: Had the man seen him? Would it be better to leave now? His hands searched more rapidly, until he looked like a rabbit digging its hole.

Shankal went back to the alley and told everyone he met that he had seen Hanash, Arafa's companion, at the Salihiya dump busily searching through the trash for a notebook, according to the garbageman. As soon as this news reached the overseer's house, a force of servants went to the dump, but found no sign of Hanash. When they questioned the garbageman, he told them that he had gone off on some business, and when he came back Hanash had gone. He did not know whether he had found what he was looking for or not. And no one knew why people began to whisper among themselves that the notebook Hanash had taken was the same magic book to which Arafa had entrusted the secrets of his arts and weapons. It was lost during his escape attempt, and ended up in the trash at the Salihiya dump, where Hanash found it. Word spread from drug den to drug den that Hanash would finish what Arafa had started, and then come back to the alley to take the most terrible revenge on the overseer. The prevailing view was that the overseer had promised a huge reward to whoever brought Hanash to him, alive or dead; his men said so, in all the coffeehouses and drug dens. No one doubted any longer the role that Hanash was expected to play in their lives. A wave of optimism and rejoicing rose up in their souls, washing away the scum of their despair and submission. Their hearts were filled with tenderness for Hanash in his unknown exile, a tenderness that now included Arafa too. The people wished they might cooperate with Hanash in standing against the overseer; perhaps in his triumph over the overseer they could score a triumph for themselves and their alley, securing a prosperous, just and peaceful life. They planned to cooperate in any way they found possible, as this was their only way to deliverance. It was incontestable that there was no defeating the magic powers the overseer possessed except by similar powers, which Hanash might be preparing. The overseer was informed what the people were whispering about, so he inspired the coffeehouse poets to sing the story of Gabalawi, especially his death at Arafa's hand, and how the overseer had been compelled to make a truce with him, and befriend him out of fear of his magic until he was able to kill him to avenge their great ancestor.

Amazingly, the people were lukewarm or mocking at the poets' lies, and had grown so stubborn that they said, "We have nothing to do with the past. Our only hope lies in Arafa's magic, and if we had to choose between Gabalawi and magic, we'd choose magic."

Day after day, the truth of Arafa was revealed to the people. Perhaps it had leaked from Umm Zanfil's building; she had learned a great deal about him from Awatif during the time she lived with her. Or perhaps it came from Hanash himself, from what he told people who met him in remote places. In any case, people came to know the man, and the wonderful, magic, dreamlike life he had been seeking for the alley, through his magic. They marveled at the truth and extolled his memory, and lifted up his name even above the names of Gabal, Rifaa and Qassem. People said that he could never have been Gabalawi's killer as they had thought, and others said he was the alley's greatest man, even if he had killed Gabalawi. They competed for him, until every neighborhood claimed him as its own.

And it so happened that some of the young men of our alley began to disappear, one by one, and it was said, to explain their disappearance, that they had found their way to Hanash's place, and joined him; he was teaching them magic, in anticipation of the day of their promised deliverance. Overpowered by fear, the overseer and his men sent their spies everywhere to search homes and shops and impose the cruelest punishments for the slightest offenses. They beat people with sticks for a look, a joke or a laugh, until the alley endured a nightmarish atmosphere of fear, hatred and terrorism. Yet the people bore the outrages steadfastly, taking refuge in patience. They held fast to hope, and whenever they were persecuted, they said, "Injustice must have an end, as day must follow night. We will see the death of tyranny, and the dawn of light and miracles."

About the Author

Naguib Mahfouz was born in Cairo in 1911 and began writing when he was seventeen. A student of philosophy and an avid reader, his works range from reimaginings of ancient myths to subtle commentaries on contemporary Egyptian politics and culture. Over a career that lasted more than five decades, he wrote 33 novels, 13 short story anthologies, numerous plays, and 30 screenplays. Of his many works, most famous is *The Cairo Trilogy*, consisting of *Palace Walk* (1956), *Palace of Desire* (1957), and *Sugar Street* (1957), which focuses on a Cairo family through three generations, from 1917 until 1952. In 1988, he was awarded the Nobel Prize in Literature, the first writer in Arabic to do so. He died in August 2006.

About the Translator

Peter Theroux is the author of *Sandstorms: Days and Nights in Arabia* (1990) and *Translating LA* (1994). He is the translator of several major Arabic novels. He lives in suburban Los Angeles.